MW00352977

INCANTATION

ALSO BY THE AUTHOR

Adam's Will

INCANTATION

STEVEN M. GREENBERG

THE STREAMSIDE COMPANY
Somers • New York

This is a work of fiction. Names, characters, places and
incidents are the product of the author's imagination
or are used fictionally. Any resemblance to actual events
or to persons, living or dead, is entirely coincidental.

First published in the United States of America in 2004 by
The Streamside Company
390A Heritage Hills
Somers, NY 10589
(914) 669-8588
streamsd@sover.net

Copyright © 2004 by Steven M. Greenberg

All rights reserved. No part of this publication may be reproduced or
transmitted in any form or by any means, electronic or mechanical,
including photocopy, recording, or any information storage and
retrieval system now known or to be invented without permission in
writing from the publisher, except by a reviewer who wishes to quote
brief passages in connection with a review written for
inclusion in a magazine, newspaper, or broadcast.

Library of Congress Control Number: 2003095720

Book design and type formatting by Bernard Schleifer
Manufactured in the United States of America
FIRST EDITION
1 3 5 7 9 8 6 4 2
ISBN 0-940185-04-0

ACKNOWLEDGMENTS

I AM INDEBTED TO Professor Vincenzo Gatto of Penn State University for his remedial Italian tutelage, and to Rosemary and Bob Reed of Detroit for giving me the 4-1-1 on contemporary urban usage.

Thanks also are due to Eugenie Gray for help with the editing, and thanks again to my wife Deena who gave up so many dinners out and weekends in the city so these pages could wend their way laboriously through my computer.

—STEVEN M. GREENBERG
July 14, 2003

CHICAGO

CHAPTER ONE

SEPARATION

HE MIGHT HAVE KNOWN.

Not all of it, of course. Not about the trip, and surely not about the incantation—no rational, scientific-minded person could have possibly envisioned that. But Cassie: yes, with her he might have anticipated something. Another man would have, certainly.

But Robert was the least intuitive of men—whether by inclination or training. Well, training obviously would have played a part. After all, a history professor of his stature, with such impeccable credentials, a brilliant mind, a lengthy and prestigious education—such a man is taught to set his sights upon the past, to study it, collate its facts, arrange them, question them, dissect, analyze, but never venture forward toward the future.

And Cassie herself could be—how might one put it?—unreadable at times. Misleading even, if she chose to be. She had that measure of control. Why, just the day before she'd been her old familiar self, sweet as candy; gliding around the sofa that evening to where he sat, dropping onto his lap in that patented feathery descent of hers, graceful and ethereal as a snowflake, then nestling there like a mother hen atop her two little eggs. She'd wrapped an arm about his shoulders, nuzzled the crook of his neck, then turned his face to hers with a pair of gentle fingers, locking him in inextricably with that black, magnetic gaze that was unique to her and her alone among the handful of women he had known with some familiarity in his thirty-seven rather placid years of life.

"So, Robert," she said in her chameleon voice, now sweet, now bitter—at this specific moment it was sweet—"tell me, are you getting a little tired of me yet?"

"Tired? What do you mean by 'tired'?" he asked.

"Well, *tired*; you know? Bored or sated, or whatever term you brilliant intellectuals use to describe it?"

"You're joking, right? I mean . . . how can you even *ask* me that?"

"I don't know. They say that people get tired of each other after a while."

"They do? After—what?—five years? . . . I thought it took . . . you know . . . like, seven."

"Seven?" She raised her eyebrows.

"Sure. Isn't that what they say? Like the seven year itch?"

"No, seriously. . . . I read somewhere it was only three. Three years for people to tire of each other. At least a little. . . . You know, for love to get a little . . . I don't know . . . stale, jaded—whatever the appropriate word."

"And where'd you get your facts from exactly? *Vogue*?"

"No, not *Vogue*, Robert. Don't make fun. . . . Look, I don't know where I read it. Somewhere, though."

"OK, well, anyway, why'd you ask me? Maybe *you're* getting tired of *me*."

"OK, look, never mind. Never mind. . . . So . . . are you gonna talk all night, or would you rather take me to bed?"

He chose the latter, naturally, as she must have known he would, and so they embraced with their usual abandon and slept with their usual exhaustion. And he awoke the following morning—their final one together as it seemed—feeling every bit as sated and complacent as he had ever felt with her in all their unnumbered hundreds of mutual awakenings to date.

He rose and showered and stepped from the bath to find—amazingly!—Cassandra out of bed as well. And when he spoke to her—something very basic, of course: "Good morning! What are *you* doing up?"—he found her actually cheerful, actually obliging. At six-forty-five in the morning! That, clearly, to a man who had cohabited five years with a woman like Cassandra, should have tripped off an alarm. But Robert being, if not exactly opaque then at least highly unimaginative, and Cassie being. . . . Ah, that impeccable control of hers! Which never let up until the very end, rather like a mouse trap, cocked, baited, and waiting unsprung for what might seem like all eternity to the tiny, unsuspecting creature that would happen to set it off at last.

That memorable day was Wednesday, April 12: just mid-way into the third week of the university's spring quarter, and the unexpected for Robert Martin was about to turn commonplace.

"What time is your class this morning?" she asked him over breakfast, pleasantly—actually *smiling* at seven-something in the morning, having brewed and poured his coffee into one of her designer cups for the first time in a year and several months.

"My class? Uh, eleven."

"Where do you have to be? Uh . . . is it far from your office?"

"No. Why?"

"Oh, no reason. I just wondered. Take an umbrella if you have to walk around campus much."

"What? . . . Uh, no. No, actually my class—the first one, I mean, the eleven o'clock—is right in Social Sciences, right downstairs from the office."

"Good. That's good. It's supposed to rain, I think. . . . I worry about you, you know?"

And so he left in absolute complacency—feeling a little guilty, perhaps, for causing her to worry so—and made it down to campus by half-past-eight, the customary time, the customary parking spot, getting to his office customarily early, shuffling through his usual mail, meeting with the Ph.D. candidate he'd been supervising in independent study, twice a week, every week, for the past nine months. He grabbed another coffee, black with lots of sugar, just like every other time, every other day, then made it to the lecture room ten minutes before class, ten-to-eleven. That was when Betty Jean Coughlin generally came in.

"Good morning!" he said, proclaiming his presence.

"Oh, hello, Dr. Martin." He watched as she felt her way to the left front row and eased into her usual place; whereupon he stood, walked over, and sat on the worn wooden chair to her left, scraping it on the floor a little to make certain she'd perceived his approach.

"I, uh . . . I made another tape for you," he announced.

"I've told you before, Dr. Martin, I don't want any special favors from anyone."

"It's not. . . . Look, Betty Jean, how many classes have you taken from me now?"

"Three. Uh, this is the third, I believe."

"OK, and every week of every class I've made you a couple of tapes, right?"

"Yes, but I don't ask you for them. I'm not a charity case, you know."

"Well, OK, I know that. I'm just trying to help. Look, you're, uh . . . I mean . . . I respect what you've done academically with your, uh, handicap. It's . . . it's really impressive. . . ."

"Hey, I didn't ask to be blind, you know. I do what I have to. It's no big thing, uh . . . sir, uh . . . Doctor."

"OK, I know." He touched her shoulder lightly with his fingers. "Look, I'm only trying to help. Just . . . here, I'll put the tape in your bag, OK? It's got some supplementary material for the next couple of lectures. It's in there, OK?"

"Yeah, all right. I'll . . . if you want me to use it, I guess I can. . . . Oh, Dr. Martin...?"

"Uh-huh?"

"Nothing. Never mind. . . . I don't need those tapes to pass the course, you know."

He stepped back over to his desk and sat down behind it. In a minute, the other students began to file in, singly or in pairs, then take their seats in turn. Miss Lipsky appeared before the rest, as usual, four minutes after Betty Jean. Then Jeffrey Carns, the class wit, bright but sarcastic; familiar, since he'd taken an introductory course from Robert a year before. Next those two pedantic Indian boys slid into their second row seats: Ravi Choudri and Jivan something—Pradhip or Pathip—aggressively competitive, the both of them. Then finally the remainder, the new ones, whose names Robert hadn't quite learned as yet, the silent majority, shy or unprepared, young men and women who seldom spoke and thus attracted little notice, Audrey something and Brett something else and Wong—last or first name; Robert didn't know for sure.

Last of all came Auntwon, invariably late or nearly late; just at eleven today. He was a strange kid, one of the few black students the faculty ever encountered in a European history course. Auntwon Miller, it was, or Milner—Robert wasn't exactly sure—sauntering back, as always, to the very last row of the classroom where he'd be least conspicuous. In the two and a half weeks that History 321 had run, Auntwon had never asked or answered a question—indeed, had never spoken at all—but instead sat stone silent, isolated; never interacting a single time with a single soul, neither professor nor fellow-student, exhibiting no clear sign of comprehension or interest, or even cognizance, as he drummed away on his desk with those agile fingers of his to some interminable metronome at play within his brain.

Then, as Auntwon's facile hands strummed out their silent rhythms, two rows in front of him, one seat to the right, the aforesaid Miss Lipsky—she of the invariably early arrival—a slightly plump, dark-haired woman maybe five years older than her fellow classmates, went about her own strange ritual, filling page after page with the most voluminous note-taking Robert had encountered in all his twenty years of academics, from freshman undergrad at seventeen to full professor now at thirty-seven. Like some obsessive courtroom stenographer, paid not by the hour but by the page, she sat there transcribing everything, every word her professor might have spoken and then some; enough material for a dozen textbooks, more verbiage than Robert himself and any number of his most loquacious colleagues might have spouted in a year. They were the most conspicuous of the group, she and Auntwon—Betty Jean aside. But even such as they were pretty much routine. Yes; for every course he had ever taught contained their like: characters and misfits, the good and the brilliant and the downright dull. Every single class for the full nine years of Robert Martin's tenure here at the University of Chicago.

So, everything considered, nothing all that remarkable really, today or yesterday or the day preceding that; nothing much, in fact, right up until the commencement that Wednesday morning of the eighth tri-weekly session of History 321, "The Renaissance in Italy." Yes, right up until then, eleven a.m. on Wednesday, April 12, 1999, Robert Martin, who—as he himself might have acknowledged—was singularly devoid of imaginative sense, was on solid and perfectly comfortable ground.

"Where did we leave off on Monday?" he asked the class.

"The Duke of Urbino," said Betty Jean, right on cue. Her last tape, he remembered, had ended with the appearance of the gallant Duke.

"Right. The Duke."

"You said he was into astrology . . . into the occult," said Jivan. "That's where we stopped.

"Right. Well? Any comments? I assume you've all read the chapter on Urbino."

"Everyone was into astrology then," Jeffrey interjected. "It was an age of mysticism. You told us that the first day. Didn't the psychic hotline originate in 1453?" Everyone but Auntwon laughed.

"Well, Mr. Carns, you've chosen your date well. OK, then, what event *did* occur in 1453 that might be relevant to our inquiry?"

"The fall of Byzantium?" Robert looked across the room, back in the third row. It was . . . ah, yes, the tall girl, Alice something. He glanced down at his list."

"Good. Excellent, Miss Cotterman. And why relevant?"

Now there was silence. Not a soul ventured a single, furtive look at him for an excruciating twenty seconds.

"All right, then, I'll tell you: because Byzantium itself was a fount of mysticism, a repository of ancient, unscientific thought. Paradoxically, though, its fall helped spur the Renaissance. How?"

"The migration of Greek teachers," said Jivan . . . Pradhip or Pathip, aggressively competitive as ever. He glanced down at his list: 'Prathip', it was.

"Right again. Excellent, Mr. Prathip. You guys are so smart, I feel like I'm getting some kind of charitable grant to come in here and pretend to teach you anything. . . . But let's get back to the Duke. . . ."

He did so, going on about Urbino and its ducal family for another forty minutes, entertaining a few of the students, boring the majority, he thought. "Any questions," he asked, after a digression on pre-modern economics that should have occasioned some. But no one spoke or raised a hand; no one even looked at him in a quizzical way, so he started up again. He'd finish Urbino by the end of the hour, he assumed, then get on to the Medici by Friday.

But then it was that he spotted her. Right in mid-sentence; something further he had added about the economy of Urbino: "...the profit of the condottieri," he had said, or words to that effect. What he saw, in truth, was just a shadow, back-lit through the open doorway, though he knew at once whose shadow it was, whose silhouette. How could he not have known? having sensed her presence in one room or another a thousand times, sensing it from the faintest sound she might have made or the merest flicker of such subtle movement as was uniquely hers. But here? Now? This was very odd, unanticipated, like her early awakening this morning or her placid humor despite it: Cassie? Here on campus? Now? What on earth could she be up to? She had never visited him at work before—well, just that one time to drop something off—and he had only left her . . . what? less than four hours ago?

Robert felt unnerved, anxious; his mind reconnoitering ahead. Had his mom been taken ill? His dad? Had there been some mishap with another relation? An unexpected tragedy involving a friend? Or . . . or might it be something with Cassie herself or with her parents? Could she be ill? Had she been to the doctor and...?

"We'll . . . uh, we'll pick up on that in a second," he told his stone-faced audience: Auntwon, Betty Jean, Jeffrey, and the rest of them, in reference to the incomparable Duke. Maybe a third of the students were actually listening. He could go out to Cassie and come back in again before the bulk of the class had ever fully realized he'd been gone.

He set his book down on the desk, on the very front angle where his buttocks had been propped, aware now that his hands were trembling, making the book shake visibly, too. No one seemed to notice it. Only Auntwon glanced up, then down again at the surface below, his fingers drumming casually, rhythmically, like five smooth pistons of a well-tuned engine—da-da-da-da-DA . . . da-da-da-da-DA.

Miss Lipsky wrote again into her notebook, convulsively. Hang on for a minute, he mumbled to them all, he'd be right back. Miss Lipsky took it down; scribbled something, anyway. There was vague murmuring behind him, like a crowd at intermission, as he reached the doorway, not looking back toward the murmuring, but dead ahead darkly through the opening, his heart heavy, as though it had been thrust downward to below his chest, down to some indefinable space below the rib cage, to his stomach, perhaps. He could disgorge it all, heart and lungs and arteries, given the proper stimulus. This, quite possibly, might be it.

"What's wrong?" he asked Cassandra. She wasn't smiling. Rather, she looked severe, though lovely to him and immaculate in her navy mid-calf skirt and suede jacket, black hair draped upon her shoulders and veiling her face in that sultry way she wore it: the hair and the slow curve of her cheek where the sweep of hair revealed it, and the wry and casual upcurve of her lips that made his mouth water when he glanced at her in the half-light at home or in the car.

"What is it?" he asked again, thinking, thinking. . . . She'd come to his lecture room just once before—when was it?—yes, yes, a couple of years ago. She'd brought him something then—the . . . the wallet he'd forgotten to gather up from their bedroom table. He reached behind him to his right hip pocket, feeling his wallet through the thin fabric. Her eyes followed his hand, though the motion had been most subtle. He saw the sweep of her pupils down to his hip then back again to his face. She was animated but expressionless, blank-faced, having read his thoughts, as she invariably had the ability to do.

"Robert . . . we need to talk," she said at last, looking . . . what? . . . different from this morning; very different. Not upset; no. Not grief-struck or angry, but . . . but . . . dispassionate maybe. Yes, dispassionate; entirely dispassionate like some wax or plastic mannequin of herself, faithfully copied though entirely insensate. Clearly something had happened, or . . . or was *about* to happen. He should have shut the door behind him for the students' sake; but it was too late now. Shutting it now would seem as though something had gone wrong between the two of them. But something really *had* gone wrong. Yes, indeed. He could read it in her eyes. He could hardly think, which precluded speech, so he just stood there silent, feeling just a little sick.

"We need to talk, Robert," she repeated, just on the impatient side of dispassion. He nodded. *We* meant *she*. It always did, always had. He knew that and loved her despite it, maybe loved her a little *because* of it—for into the crazy quilt of love are sewn the most discordant of fabrics. Cassie was intent on something. He could see it in her face, her posture. Nothing he had done, but Cassandra was like that, capable of picking a fight when it suited her purpose, to escape with the girls for a day or a weekend, say, or wheedle an expensive dress or piece of jewelry out of him, though he would have bought for her it gladly without the fight. Conflict put her in control, defined the interaction in her terms, her language. She had the skill, the ability, to provoke him into being the aggressor, making her the injured party. She would go away, do as she had planned, buy what she coveted. When she returned from the trip or the shop, he would be apologetic. What did it matter? Whatever made her happy, kept her bound to him, was acceptable, proper. Whatever rules she ordered, he obeyed them. And the fundamental rule was this: what he agreed to offer could never be offered as a gift, initiated by his own free will. To be acceptable to Cassandra, the prize must be extracted.

"Talk?" he asked. "What do you mean, 'talk'?" He'd left her just four hours earlier, with little talk—small talk, really, about his class, an umbrella—just two people chatting over newsprint, he with his cereal and freshly-brewed coffee, she with her yogurt and herb tea.

"What do you mean, 'talk'?" he asked again. He moved a little toward the wall, hoping to draw her there, away from where the students could see her, and him as well, as close as he needed to be to her, now, particularly, of all times. She yielded not an inch, though, tethering him there within the line of sight of at least the first two rows of paired eyes that stared meekly but attentively through the opening. Yes, he should have closed the goddamn door, should have closed it when the last of his students had entered the classroom forty minutes earlier. Then he never would have seen her in the corridor . . . though she would have found a way to fetch him if she had to. Somehow she would have found a way, for her will was strong, and whatever she desired, however far-removed or difficult of access, she invariably obtained.

"I'm leaving, Robert. I've taken my things, my clothes and . . . and the things I think you'd agree are mine."

"You WHAT? WHAT? What are you talking about? What the hell are you *talking* about!?"

"Look, Robert . . . I'm sorry but. . . ."

"Cassie, for God's sake! What the hell's going on?"

"'Cassandra', Robert. Not 'Cassie'. I've told you . . . I've told you a thousand times, 'Cassie''s a little girl's name. . . . I hate when you. . . . Oh, anyway, what difference does it make? Never mind!" She shook her head. "Look, I'm sorry. I Really am. We'll . . . we'll talk about it all some other time, OK?"

"Some other time! Some other *time*!"

"Yeah, I'll call you. . . . Look, I've got to go." She started to turn away but he caught her arm and held her back.

"Go *where*? Where do you think you're going?"

"That's *my* business, isn't it? . . . Look, all right . . . I'm truly sorry, but . . . this has been coming for a while. It doesn't help to over-dramatize it. . . . Anyway, I'll be in touch. We'll talk about it later. . . . There'll . . . there'll be a better time."

"A better time? *What* better time, huh? . . . OK, OK, go ahead and go then." He loosened his grip of her and took half a step backward. "Go! Jesus! You're acting like a . . . like some kind of stranger or something. Oh, hell, just go ahead and go."

She shrugged and shook her head casually, impassively, looking at him askance. He saw her hand move, up to waist level, as though to reach toward him. He put his own hand out to her and felt a set of keys thrust into it.

"Here are your keys," she said. "*Your* keys," were the words. *Yours*!

"Cassie, for God's sake! What are you doing!"

"Come on, Robert, don't be maudlin. It doesn't become you. Look, I'll be in touch." She turned full around this time and walked away, and he was powerless to follow, as she must have known he would be, precluded from following by the steadfast eyes of his students and the insurmountable wall of his propriety and the inertia of shock and depression that bore on him like lead within his veins and stones within his chest. He could not follow as she moved down the tiled corridor toward the exit where her car would be parked, so he turned back to his classroom, bearing an intolerable burden of anger, perplexity, and grief within him.

There were ten minutes of class time left; nine, now, when he looked at the clock. This was not something he could do, nauseated and faint as he felt. Not a minute more for the sake of all the students he had cosseted and tutored in his nine-year-long career. Federigo da Montefeltro, that hump-nosed Duke of Urbino, imperious and clever among his inlaid wooden chambers, failed him utterly.

"Uh, look, guys. . . . Look, something's come up. I'm, uh. . . . I'm

going to let you folks go a little early today. We'll start Wednesday with
. . . with where we left off."

"The economy of Urbino," said Miss Lipsky. Someone else raised a
hand: Jeffrey Carns, wearing a puckish grin.

"Yes? Uh, Mr. Carns?"

"*Today*'s Wednesday, Dr. Martin. You mean Friday."

"What?"

"Wednesday. You said we'd start on Wednesday where we left off."

"Did I? Yes . . . Friday, then. Friday." He turned from them toward
the mullioned windows, looking out at the somber day not yet bearing
the half-maturity of spring. The sounds of departing feet and wooden
desk legs on the tile floor came to his left ear, the scent of stirred dust
and post-pubescent bodies to his nose. She would be back in a day or
two—sure, she'd always come back, always. But what did she want this
time? And the keys, the keys. That was entirely new, unlike anything
she'd ever done before.

Tonight, without a doubt, he'd be alone, and the weight within him
and the sickness that he felt in the hollow beneath his chest were more
than he could bear.

The sounds ceased, Robert Martin turned from the window facing
what was not yet spring, and before him, at the exact end of the trajec-
tory through which his head and body turned, as though that trajecto-
ry had been calculated and plotted out to a tenth of a second of arc,
stood Auntwon Miller.

"You OK?" Auntwon asked, in so familiar and comradely a fashion that the two of them, professor and student, might have been fast
friends for a generation. It was the first time Robert Martin had heard
him speak. The first time ever, in the three weeks that History 321,
"The Renaissance in Italy," had run.

"Uh . . . yeah, I . . . I guess so. . . . Thanks for asking, though."
Auntwon nodded, rubbed one side of his nose with a finger, then the
opposite side with the back of his hand. When the hand dropped, he
cocked his head upward, lacking, as he did, a good six inches of height
to achieve eye-level parity with his professor.

"Thatcho lady? The one out in the hallway? One of the guys say
. . . *said* . . . it was."

"Yeah. . . . Yes, I guess so. We've been . . . I mean, she's been with
me for about five years now. Uh, we had a little disagreement, I guess.
Did . . . did everybody see us?."

"Yeah. They all could see it pretty good, I s'pose. Ditten look so little, though. You look bad, man . . . Doc . . . uh . . . Doctor. You sure
you OK?"

"Oh, I'll live. . . . Yeah. Yeah, I'll be all right. It's nice of you to ask,
though. . . . Nice of you to ask. . . . Uh, you know . . . this is the first time
I ever heard you talk . . . uh . . . 'Antwon', right?" Robert pronounced it
'*Ant*-won', as was the standard among the University of Chicago's pop-
ulation of nth generation African descent.

"Yeah. '*Aahnt*-won'—like wit'a 'u' in it so it come out right.
'*Aahnt*-won', you know?" Auntwon's rendering of his name sounded
nasally and authentically French.

"OK. Right, '*Aahnt*-won'—you never say much in class; how
come?"

"I don' know. Whey I went to school at—downtown, you know—
it wadn't so smart to talk too much. Show you know stuff and shit like
that. You don' want to, like, show off all 'at shit you been learnin', you
know what I'm sayin'?"

"Yeah, I think so."

"Anyways, jus' don't let no bitch mess wif yo' head, see? You the
Man. You too krunk to let some bogue-ass bitch do you like that. Jus'
like that guy Swann in Proust, him buyin' orchids for that bitch was
messin' him up, you know what I'm sayin'?" He pronounced Proust the
way Proust's mother must have: 'Proost', without, however, glottalizing
the 'r'; just right for accuracy without affectation.

"Proust? No. No, I haven't read Proust."

"Well, you gotta. Thackeray, too. Becky Sharp, man. Shit. Thass
what you got yo'se'f into, I bet. Look-a-here, Doc, you the *Man*.
Definitely the main man here, I mean, the bes' teacher I had here.
Anywhere, man, anywhere. I love this shit! I been readin' evvythang I
can get a-holt of on the Renaissance. I love it, man! You got me hooked.
. . . Look-a-here, though. You got ta watch out fo' them skinny bitches

—you know what I'm sayin'? They tough. You got to watch out fo' you own se'f, take ca' of business, you know what I'm sayin'?" Auntwon winked and slapped him on the arm with a gentle palm that lingered for an instant on the sleeve of his sport coat, squeezed faintly, almost indiscernibly affectionate, then turned away and walked out of the room, closing the door behind him.

The room was empty now. Beyond the gothic window, opening onto Fifty-Ninth Street and the renascent grass of its mall-like midway, the April sky darkened, promising rain; the driven rain of Chicago, propelled forever crosswise by such wind as seems too consistent to be fashioned by nature. Robert Martin felt like the sky, less April than December, as gray and leaden as the pendant clouds.

Full spring would come in days or weeks. Cassandra too: she would come back, as she had always come back; always, requiring something. And he would give it, unfailingly, just as he had always done. He thought that as he stood there facing the window. But something was clearly different this time: the keys, perhaps, or the narrow look in her eyes, or the fact that, for once, she hadn't really bothered to goad him into being the aggressor. He felt sick now, really sick in some inexpressible way, distraught enough that even Auntwon Miller had sensed it and felt a need to minister to his professor's obvious pain.

It was all very strange, and had he possessed a single spark of true imagination, Robert Martin would have grasped the whole of it right then; would have sensed that his life, midway into its thirty-seventh year, had passed a grand climacteric, whereafter the mundane would turn mystical, the rational surreal. Those keys thrust upon him by his beloved Cassandra would soon unlock the door to a boundless new future of things inconceivable, so that, in the fullness of time, his ability to dream and newborn sense of wonder would both expand to their maximum potentials. Though limited by all that he had learned and accepted, known and conceived, Robert's awakening capacity to see the invisible, to accept the surreal, would soon grow vast enough to usher him into a new kind of existence in a world of unenvisioned possibilities.

But that would be the future, past the Illinois spring and into a Tuscan summer. Now, in the present, he could see only what lay before his eyes, the grass, the clouds, the empty room. Had his foresight projected a trifle further outward, he might have guessed that two weeks hence, young Auntwon Miller would pass in, among a score of other less remarkable students' offerings, a mid-semester exam book filled to capacity with concise and crystalline verbiage worthy of a doctoral candidate's musings. He had seen Auntwon's eyes and heard his soft voice without quite comprehending that Proust and Thackeray were not the outer limits of his knowledge, but rather casual recollections close at hand; that Auntwon had forayed far from his classroom text to conquer Burkhardt and Pater, Ranke and two Medici historians, a dozen works on Renaissance art, histories of the Gonzaga and Este Families, and had begun analyses of Machiavelli, Guicciardini, and Colangio weeks before the class would reach the pungent prose of those three great early-modern, perceptive minds.

It would all be there in the crowded pages, fact and disputation and excruciatingly logical conclusion. And Robert might have been prepared for the whole of it a fortnight in advance, if he'd had a tenth part of the analytical foresight possessed by that teen-age ghetto mother who, in the wretchedness of a late and lonely pregnancy, found the prescriptive wherewithal to designate her offspring by the name 'Auntwon'. It was a label that made her baby somehow exceptional, distinct from all the other 'Antoines' and 'Antwons' in the city; a name that made him feel unique enough to challenge the peer interdict against learning and spend an eager, happy childhood consuming every book within a child's diminutive reach upward onto Chicago Public Library shelves.

Such was Auntwon Miller, though Robert could never have conceived it before all the facts had spread themselves out before him in orderly file. Had he possessed one small spark of imagination, the merest trace available for foresight, he might have been prepared for it all, from Cassandra to Auntwon to the Incantation, but he lacked even that, and, with vast stage set and curtain at the ready, as the grandest of our poets hath inimitably writ: Thereby hangs a tale.

~~~~~~~~~

CHAPTER TWO

EXPLANATION

EVERYTHING WAS GONE. EVERYTHING. HER CLOTHES, BOOKS, FABRIC samples, catalogues, exercise equipment: everything of hers remotely portable had been stripped from the place. It looked desolate. Everywhere he turned, every room he entered, showed conspicuous emptiness, vacuity of drawer and file and book shelf.

Even in the bathroom: her toiletries swept clean, as though she had never lived there. But in their bedroom, where they had slept and loved and tumbled out of bed just hours before—yes, there in the bedroom the scent of her perfume lingered indelibly, clinging to the bedclothes still rumpled from their prior night's embrace.

Ah, but now the place was so empty, so achingly empty! Robert had grown heartsick and was getting worse. Dazed, bewildered, he stumbled into the living room and sank into the sofa. There in front of him lay Cassie's keys splayed out on the coffee table, resting where he had dropped them fifteen minutes earlier. The keys—and even more the blatant desolation of the rooms around—presently began to make him frantic. He found he couldn't rest, couldn't concentrate. If he could only speak with her! If he could only hear her voice, tell her how he felt, find out what foolish little thing had set her off! Yes, if he could only find out *something*!

He sat bolt upright and reached for the cordless, dialing, first, the number of Cassie's cell phone again—this for the seventh time since she had left him in the corridor this morning.

"The number you have called is out of range or not in service at the moment . . ." it droned, as it had droned on maddeningly six times earlier when he had tried it: twice from his office, then three or four more times from the car. He shook his head, clearing it a little, and then dialed Cassie's place of work.

A secretary answered, a new one unfamiliar to him. Cassandra was forever losing secretaries and replacing them with others. "Ann Kensington Interiors," said the woman in a melodic voice, her tone entirely inappropriate to his mood.

"Yes . . . is Miss Fullerton in? Cassandra Fullerton?"

"No, sir, I'm sorry. She's not here at the moment."

"Well . . . do you know how I might reach her? Or where? . . . Where she might be now?"

"No, sir . . . she hasn't been in all day. If it's a business matter, sir, perhaps Mrs. Kensington can help."

He hadn't even thought of that in all his agitation, but yes, as a matter of fact, Annie might help a lot. An awful lot! "OK," he said, a little more brightly, "yes, please! Go ahead and put her on. That'd be great. Thanks!"

"Robert?" Annie answered twenty seconds later, sounding as ignorantly blissful as the receptionist, "what's going on?"

"Hi, Annie. Have you talked to Cassie—to Cassandra?"

"No. Why? What's wrong?"

"Uh, I don't know, Annie. I really don't know. . . . Did she say anything to you?"

"Say anything? About what?"

"Look, I don't even *know* what! . . . Uh . . . did she say anything about me? About being upset with me over something?"

"No, nothing. I mean, she hasn't said anything at all like that. . . . Lately, I mean—this week, last week, you know? And as for today, I haven't seen a thing of her. She didn't come in this morning. I was beginning to wonder. . . . So OK tell me, what's going on?"

"I have no *idea* what's going on. I don't even know what to *tell* you. We had a disagreement, I guess."

"You *guess*! When?"

"When? Today—a few hours ago. What time is it now?"

"Two-something. Maybe two-thirty."

"So maybe three hours ago, a little more."

"Where are you now? At work? On campus?"

"No. I, uh, I'm home. I came home. I canceled my afternoon class. . . . Look, I need to talk to her. Don't you have any idea where she might be?"

"Did you try her cell phone?"

"Yeah, yeah, sure. I've been calling it all day. It's not in service. Turned off, I guess."

"OK, OK, let me think. She'll have to show up here sometime this afternoon—you know, to get her list of clients for tomorrow. She's got a ton of work to do. . . . Uh, would you want me to tell her to call you or just call you back myself when she comes in?"

"I don't know. . . . Why don't you just call me back yourself, OK?"

"Sure. Listen, Robert, she'll be her old sweet self again in a day or two. That's how she always gets, isn't it?"

"I guess so, Annie. I don't know though this time; I'm not sure. This time is different. She gave me back her keys. The keys to the condo, you know? She put them in my hand. And . . . and the place is. . . . Her stuff is gone. Everything!"

"You're kidding! She. . . . Wow! OK, Robert, I see why you're upset then. All right, look, I'll call you as soon as I hear from her, OK? Is that all right?"

"Yeah, thanks, Annie. Thanks a million."

He set the phone down, but the depression—the agitation—was unrelieved. Or worse if anything. Yes, yes, a good deal worse. He couldn't relax, couldn't sit still. Standing, pacing, he did a circuit of the room, then another, then stepped into the remaining rooms one by one, *her* rooms, all of them, decorated by her, scaled by her, back in the days when money was as plentiful as the water in Lake Michigan, visible in all its cool, blue immensity from their east-faced windows.

"Look, Robert, look out here," she'd said, back—when was it?— three, four years ago? "You can see the lake. And this room—look, over here—it'll be perfect for my studio. We can have shelves made for the books and fabric samples, and you can take that third bedroom for your office. God, Robert, I'll be so happy here. *We'll* be."

So he had gone and bought it for her, bought everything for her— for *them*, as she had put it—spending half the royalties from *Colangio* in its first and most productive year. Then two hundred thousand more for the alterations and furnishings. . . .

What did all that matter, if it made her happy, kept her bound to him by comfort or pride or affluence . . . or whatever. . . . She was the only thing that really mattered to him, and had been since the day they'd met. . . .

Five years now. It seemed longer. He'd been an altogether different man back then, before Cassandra. Fundamentally different. Duller probably, less alive certainly, having lived the first thirty-two years of his life in monochrome, unremarkably, until that evening when she'd come up to him, spoken to him, touched his hand, and his world had turned Technicolor. Five years, mostly splendid, sometimes excruciating. But vivid, always vivid, so that he could remember every sound, scent, look, every gesture of hers from the first, as though he had lived it a hundred times. And perhaps he had; perhaps he had lived and relived those days and weeks a hundred times, and then a hundred thousand more, in his mind. Every word she spoke, every modulation of her features, from the beginning.

"Hi," she had said that indelible evening five years before, hardly looking up at him, smiling awkwardly like a chastised child. "Hi," she'd said, "my name's Cassandra . . . uh . . . Fullerton. . . . Gee, it's such an honor to meet you, Dr. Martin. *Gee!*" She offered her hand and he took it, temperate and dry, raising her gaze now, locking him in inextricably. She was a beautiful creature, dazzling, with her jet black hair and fathomless brown eyes. Not quite classically beautiful, no, but lovely in a fragile way, such that the radiance of her face was dependent on the incident light or the angle of view, flashing from ordinary to exquisite in a heartbeat.

"Gee," she said, "I won't wash my hand for a month," then gave him her patented mock-shy, sardonic smile. Sweet Cassandra. A thousand times he had fetched it back from memory: the words and then the way she'd gone and pressed her name and number into his palm, legibly printed on a napkin, then disappeared totally, unaccountably, though he searched the overflowing room for her through the tedious, interminable four remaining hours of the evening's festivities.

It was his party, for him and about him, and he was beleaguered, inundated, grasped and hugged and squeezed. Groups milled about his person, one succeeding another; thus he was unable to search for her properly, though he knew that she was no longer there. He felt her absence somehow, and thought of her obsessively as he smiled to friends and strangers, her name and number printed on the napkin in his pocket. Yes, there at the very apex of the seam, folded carefully and tucked down with his house keys, in his left front pocket where he could touch it from time to time, even while extending his fellow hand in salutation.

"Congratulations, Bob." "Well, so you're the famous Dr. Martin! And so young!" They slapped him on the back and clasped his fingers, giving their obligatory compliments. It was his moment of glory: one hardly wins the National Book Award every week. A *wunderkind* at thirty-two. He smiled and pressed and patted back: "Thanks . . . . Yes. . . . Nice to see you. . . ." Meaningless. All he could do was think of her—who can say how or why, what unimaginable chemistry or magic?—think and think only of her, through the chaos of the evening, as though she were the only reality of it, the only genuine substance. Technicolor. He made it home by half-past-twelve and dialed the number on the napkin. Sleep was out of the question.

"It's OK," she'd whispered. "I was up. . . . I was hoping you would call."

At 4:35, the phone rang, startling him the way an approaching siren would have, or the sound of shattering glass. Cassie! Yes, if it were only . . . if he could only speak to her—for a minute, an instant!—he'd know what to say: tell her, remind her: how they'd felt, what they'd meant to each other. And she would remember; yes, how could she not remember? Everything.

"Hello," he answered, tremulously. . . . But it was Shelly on the line; Sheldon. "Bobby? What's going on?" he asked.

"Huh? . . . Oh, *Shelly* . . . Shelly. . . . Oh, man, I don't even know."

"Annette said you were sick. That you canceled your afternoon class."

"She called you?"

"Yeah, she was worried. Shit, I wish I had someone to worry about *me* like that. Our goddamn secretary hardly knows my name."

"Huh? Oh, right. Well, Annette's been with the department a long time. . . ."

"So?" repeated Shelly, "What the hell's going on? Are you OK?"

"Yeah. . . . It's not me, Shelly. It's Cassie."

"*Cassie*! Hey, great! What else is new? What did she do to you this time—knife wound? Poison? Must be good!"

"God, Shel, she's gone. She left me. She came down to school this morning to tell me. I don't know what I'm gonna do. I just don't know, man . . . I just don't know."

"OK, OK. Look, she. . . . You've been through this a dozen times before with her, right? Maybe she wants a new car or something. She always comes back, Bobby. Always. You know that."

"No, no, it's different this time. I can tell. She gave me back her keys. Her *keys*, for God's sake! And . . . and the place is empty; all her things are gone. It . . . it's different this time. Final. I know it. I know *her*! Shit! She's really gone. She left me."

"Well, I hate to say it, but that would be the best thing that ever happened to you. Listen to you! She's sucked you dry. . . . Like a spider. . . . *Listen* to you, for Christ's sake."

Robert put his left hand to his brow, holding the phone with his right, but absently, as though the open line were dead. Shelly wouldn't understand. Couldn't. What did Sheldon know of love? He himself could never have imagined what genuine love was like until that evening five years ago, when she came into his life. Then the world had turned Technicolor, and every random enclosure that held Cassandra Fullerton within its favored walls filled instantly with butterflies and flowers. The uplift of her eyelids, the curve of her cheek, the way the soft darkness of her hair played over her neck and shoulders—that was what was meaningful, that and nothing more. Shelly wouldn't understand! . . . How could he?

"I don't know, Shelly. . . . I don't know what I'm gonna do."

"OK, OK. Look, what can *I* do? You want me to call her for you?"

"No . . . no, you can't. I tried to call. I tried a dozen times. She's got her cell phone off."

"So what happened?"

"I'm telling you I don't know. Honest to God, I don't know a thing."

"Well, were you arguing about something? Probably not. She puts that guilt trip on you whenever she wants something you can't afford. Look, I can't stand to hear you like this. It's getting worse instead of better. She's . . . she's a. . . ."

"OK, so tell me what to do. You're the psychologist. Tell me what you think I should do now."

"Come on, Bobby, I just teach psychology. I'm not in practice. It's not the same thing. But I know a manipulative woman when I see one. You want me to tell you what to do?"

"To get her back."

"Oh, to get her *back*. That's different. . . . Different from what I *ought* to tell you. Jesus, listen to yourself. You went from being a superstar academic to a drone. You're like a zombie half the time. Shit, if I had your looks and half your brains, I'd be out there tearing the world a new asshole. What the hell did she do to you to get you like this? That's what I can't understand, with all my psychological expertise."

"I know, I know. Look, I can't really explain it to you. I just . . . I just think about her all the time. You can't understand the way we were—*are*—together. It's like she's a part of me. I have no life without her. . . . I don't know what else to tell you; I can't really explain it. . . ."

"Look, Bobby, you don't have to explain obsessive love to me. What I don't understand is how a normal guy like you came to be so afflicted. I'm sure she struck some crazy kind of chord inside you, but man! Look at the shit she pulls. Can't you see it? Look what she's done to your life, for God's sake."

"I know, I know. . . ."

"Now listen, I'm gonna run home for a minute to check on Rochelle, then I'll be over, OK? I'll bring you something to eat."

"No, no, I'm not. . . ."

"Hungry. I know. I'll get you something anyway. Thai food, maybe. It slides down easy; all that MSG, I guess. It softens up your innards. I'll be there in a couple of hours OK?"

"Yeah, that would be great. I think I need the company more than anything else."

He set the phone down absently, but his pulse was racing, his mouth dry. It would be a full and endless hour until Shelly arrived. The sun was lowering in the southwest sky, sending ribbons of syrupy light onto the foil-papered wall of the room Cassie had used for her studio. But for a vacant desk, the room was empty now. There were depressions in the carpet where her stair-climber had stood and some scrolled-up papers in the waste basket.

Some fabric samples too, things she'd found no use for, having taken the time to sort through them before leaving. That was all; not a word, not a note, no trace of her at all but for the set of keys he'd dropped on the coffee table and the clear but evanescent scent of her perfume in the place.

Theirs was a corner unit, facing south and east, with views of the lake eastward and sunlight from the south nine months of the year. It was bright, cheerful; brilliant in the morning from reflection off the water, then magical in the evening, with the lake front-lit, pearly-gray or pastel: new and different every season, every hour of the day. Yes, Cassie had chosen well. "Look at the lake," she'd say, and he'd glance out, then back again at her. At this hour, the two of them had always been together. Always, these past five years, but for maybe a couple of dozen days; sitting beside each other on the sofa, facing the water, a book in his lap, a magazine in hers, he gazing across at her, light behind her hair like a corona, or slanting off her cheek from some chance reflection eastward. She would raise her eyes for a moment. "What are you looking at?" she would ask him, daily, invariably, almost as a ritual, knowing the answer, always the same: "You," he would say, and she'd smile, puckering, dimpling, then turn back to her magazine.

An hour more and Shelly would come. Things would be better then, more hopeful, less desolate. Robert stood and walked into the studio, then back to the bedroom, pacing again, wandering aimlessly. Five minutes passed. Ten. Then suddenly he stopped and turned, shaking his head. No. No, he thought, this was intolerable. Intolerable! He stepped back to the sofa and sat down by the phone. He had to know something. *Something*! Whatever it was, *whatever*, he simply had to know.

And so he pored through the sheaves of memory, his mind laboring manfully. Cassie had a friend—he thought for a minute. . . . Lenore, it was . . . yes, Lenore something. Cassie went through friends the way she went through secretaries, weekly, monthly. But this was an altogether current friend, as of March, April—last week, in fact, he thought. Yes, just about a week ago he'd heard her name again: Lenore . . . something. Cassie had mentioned her frequently, a dozen times or more in the past two months: "Lenore and I had lunch. . . . Lenore and I went shopping. . . ." He dialed Annie back, first at the office where there was no answer now, at five-fifteen, then at home, where he reached her at last.

"It's Bob again. Robert. Have you heard anything yet, Annie?"

"No, Robert. Not a word. She didn't call the office to cancel her appointments for tomorrow, so maybe we'll hear then. But it's just not like her not to check in at all. I don't know *what*'s going on."

"She has a friend. Lenore something. She's mentioned her a lot. Do you know who I mean?"

"Uh, yeah, sure. Lenore Barris. She works at Lewiston's in the Mart. She meets Cassandra for lunch sometimes. Barris, it is. She lives, uh, near you guys, I think. Somewhere on the North Side. I can get the number for you tomorrow. I'm sure we've got it in the office someplace."

"OK. . . . Or, no . . . no, look, I'll try to find it. . . . Barris, is it?"

"Yeah. She's single, I think, so it might be listed like that."

There were two of them in the phone book. Lenore A. and Lenore S. Lenore A. was the wrong one. "I get a lot of calls for her," Lenore A. told him. "She must be a popular girl."

Lenore S. was reticent at first. "Yes," she said, "I know Cassandra. What is this about?"

He told her, even to the part about the keys and the empty studio. "She's never done that before." His voice was breaking, sounding pathetic even to himself. Lenore S. relented.

"She went away. For a week, I think," she volunteered.

Where, he asked. With whom?

"Uh, I don't know if she wants me to. . . . Umm . . . didn't she tell you anything?"

"No . . . no."

"I don't know if I should. . . . "

"Look, Miss Barris—Lenore. I won't be able to sleep, eat. I can't function this way. Please, whatever it is . . . *whatever* . . . I've got to know. Please. Please! Look, I'll find out sooner or later. Just tell me what she said, what she's angry about. I . . . I can't change anything unless I know what it was that I did. Just . . . just tell me *something*."

"Oh, God!" she said, whereupon he knew that what was wrong was fundamentally wrong, not a new car she wanted or a fancy piece of jewelry. Not a bigger condo.

"His name is Howard Serkin. They went to Acapulco."

"They? Who the hell . . . ? She . . . she went with . . . a *man*? With another *man*?"

"She's been doing his place. Up in Winnetka. She didn't tell you anything?"

"Who is he? Who . . . who the hell is he? Serkin? Jesus! What the hell are you saying?"

"I'm sure she'll call you when she gets back. In a week, I think. That's all I know, though. Look, I'm sorry . . . I'm really sorry." Lenore S. Barris hung up.

He called Annie back.

"Do you know who this guy Serkin is?"

"You're kidding!" said Annie.

"Tell me! Did you know any of this?!"

"No, Robert! I hardly know what to say. We're doing his place. . . . My goodness! You've really got to hand it to that girl!"

"What? WHAT?"

"Sorry, Robert. I didn't mean it the way it came out. Look, I'm really sorry."

"Who is he?"

"You don't know?"

"No. How should I?"

"You never heard of Checkers Pizza?"

"Yes. Yes, sure, why?"

"He's the CEO—all five thousand outlets. He got a twelve million dollar bonus last year and built a new house in Winnetka, which we're decorating—Cassandra's decorating, that is. You've got to hand it to her, though. I'll say that. She's one of a kind, God bless her soul!"

The various odors of ethnic food were sickening to Robert Martin, though Sheldon ate ravenously, right out of the warm cartons and tins: larb, pad thai, spring rolls, some beige indistinguishable substance with lemon grass.

"Take some rice, at least," counseled Sheldon. "You need some food in your gut."

"I can't. I can't."

"You want something else? I'll go and pick it up. A hot dog, maybe? I never knew you to turn down a hot dog."

No. He shook his head. He felt sick, a lead weight inside him wanting out, though there was nothing much within his belly to come forth. Yet the heaviness grew suddenly irresistible. "I've got to. . . ." he began to say, then swallowed hard and rushed down the hallway to the bathroom. Reaching it, he flung himself onto the floor, thrust his face into the toilet's mouth and brought forth an amazing quantity of fiery froth that etched itself memorably into his nose and throat. *Acid*, he thought, *bile and acid: maybe I'll vomit all my guts out and die* . . . as his eyes filled, his throat closed off. He felt first feverish, then cold, then pulseless, weightless, faint . . . more faint, then more. . . . The lead within his chest had grown lighter now, and he felt burdenless, airborne, featherlight; so he dropped his cheek upon the cool, white rim and lost himself in sleep.

In a while—a second or a minute or an hour, precisely how long he couldn't quite say—Sheldon came upon him there, his face at rest on the toilet bowl, oblivious to contagion.

"Jesus, Bobby! You sick or something? You got the flu?" Shelly lifted his head and started wiping with a towel, first his mouth and then his back which was soaked clear through the cotton shirt.

"You sick?"

He shook his head.

"Jesus Christ!" Shelly got him to his feet, flushed the toilet, cleaned him up a little more, then led him out to the living room sofa. He took some sips of water from a cup that Shelly fetched from the sink while Shelly went and stowed the little tins of Thai in the refrigerator. Then they sat together on Cassie's designer furniture and talked.

"You OK now?"

"Yeah, I guess. I'll be all right."

"Jesus! So you had no idea?"

"No. Nothing."

"It was inevitable, you know. She's an ambitious girl."

"How am I gonna get through this, Shelly? How? Can you understand? Can you imagine what this is like for me?"

"Yeah, I guess I can."

"You don't know the way things were with us, between us. . . . Like in the movies. Like the kind of love they show in pictures. You know? Like that."

"Well, I certainly saw the way you felt about her. . . . "

"I *love* her. For five years, I've loved her. To the exclusion of everything else. You know that. You could see it. And she loves me too. I know she does. You can't be with someone like that and not know it. I know she loves me, no matter what happens or happened."

"OK. If she loves you, she'll be back. And if she doesn't come back, you've got to get on with your life. People get over these things. It happens every day, every minute."

"I could never get over that. *Never.*"

"Sure you could . . . you can. Look, she's treated you like shit. She's treated *everyone* like shit. Look at yourself, man! You look like hell! That goddamn. . . ."

"OK, OK, I know you never liked her, Shel. . . . I always wanted all of us to be closer."

"I never liked *her*? Come on, Bobby! Shit! Do you know some of the things she said to me? Do you? Cruel things. I don't need to be told I'm overweight. Those little comments of hers, though. She really knows how to put somebody down with a smile on her face, those goddamn left-handed little compliments. No wonder you never see anybody anymore! Do you ever see your parents?"

"Yeah. Sure."

"OK, when?"

"My folks? Maybe a month or two ago."

"Or maybe three. You can't get up to Evanston more than a couple of times a year to visit your family?"

"I don't know. . . . They don't get along all that well."

"Who? Your mother and Cassandra, right? They're not good enough for her. Like us. Rochelle and me. We're not good enough for her either. You remember that dinner Rochelle made for the two of you a couple of years ago?"

"Sure. Of course."

"Yeah, you should remember it. That's the last time you were at our house. Do you know why? Do you know what she said to Rochelle that night? I never told you, did I?"

He shook his head.

"She said she just *loved* the food, and she just *had* to have the recipes, in that sick little saccharine voice of hers. 'I bet your mother taught you to cook like this,' she said. 'I bet your mother taught you.' Let me ask you, Bobby, did you ever tell her about Rochelle's mother? Did she know about her when she said that?"

"You mean about. . . .?

"Yeah. Yeah, about Rochelle's mother running off and leaving her when she was twelve, and the ten years of counseling, and her father's breakdown. Did you ever tell her about that, I mean before that night? Did she know?"

"I don't know. Maybe she did. . . . Look, she didn't mean anything by it. It's just something you say at dinners. . . . "

"Is it? Did Cassandra ever to your knowledge say or do anything without intricate forethought? Did she?"

"I don't know, Shelly. I don't know anything anymore."

"Well I do. She alienated your friends and family because they saw through her, or didn't fit into her plans, or whatever the hell other reasons she might have had. Then she got you to spend all your royalties on her and this goddamn place so she could live like the society elite. And now she's apparently found another source of patronage with a little deeper pockets than yours, so she bails out without a word of explanation. Look, Bobby, we've been friends for, what? Twenty years? More? You were best man at my wedding, for God's sake. Shit, I love you like a brother. No, *better* than a brother—people don't get to pick their brothers. You're my best friend, and I'm yours, though maybe you forget from time to time. Listen to me. *Listen.* . . . Let her go. She's poison. There are a million pretty women out there who'd give anything for a man like you with your looks and your brains. Get on with your life; write, read, teach, love again, but pick somebody who's worth it, worthy of you. Forget Cassandra. Forget you ever knew her. Get your life together."

"Shelly, you don't understand. I love her. I'll always love her. Always. Always."

"Well you're a fool then, or a victim, or you see something I don't see, or know something I don't know. Whatever, you're in for the ride of your life emotionally. It's a long way down and a long, long way back up. I want you to know that I'll be here whenever you need me for anything. But it's going to take a miracle to get the both of us through it if you're half as bad as you seem."

Sheldon Rogovin was ultimately right about everything, Cassandra and the long ride and the miracle. Even the Thai food he perceptively selected was most appropriate. Robert got it down the very next evening into a vacuous gut that had lain as empty as the top half of an hourglass for an endless day and then some, a hollow innard that had not hitherto permitted the presence of food of any kind. But by the evening after, the rice and pad thai and unspecified substance in lemon grass found their way into the microwave. Their bulk and warmth then proved a modest comfort, though a good many days would pass before the actual scents and tastes of food would be to Robert Martin either discernible or enticing.

CHAPTER THREE

CONFRONTATION

"THATCHO BOOK?" ASKED AUNTWON.

Just as he had done two days earlier on that indelible morning of Cassie's rude departure, the kid had kept to his seat until the very last of the other students had stepped out the door, then sauntered forward to the front of the room. There he stood now, hands in his pockets, smiling in a sort of manufactured grin above the lecturer's desk as Robert slid the several scattered volumes and papers from the desk's abundant surface into the hollow of his briefcase.

The morning class had been a pitiable affair, haunted by such palpable distraction of their professor's thoughts that not a student among the twenty present had ventured a single question or volunteered a sole response through the fifty pained, interminable minutes from beginning to end. Only Auntwon Miller, alone now with Robert in the lecture room, seemed venturesome enough to approach him or engage him in conversation on this chilly, wet, and dismal Friday morning of Chicago's latent spring.

"My book?"

"Yeah, the one they sellin' at the Barnes and Noble. That book about Colangio, you know? Thatcho' book?"

"Yeah. . . . Yes, it's mine. I wrote it . . . almost six years ago now."

"It say on the cover you won a award, that right?"

"The National Book Award, yeah. It was a big deal when I got it, but that's a long time ago. A long, long time ago."

Auntwon cocked his head to one side and put a knuckle on the desk, leaning a little forward onto it. "Yeah, but the National Book

Award, man!—that's some serious shit, ain't it? . . . So, you write somefin' else since then?"

"No . . . well, just—you know—articles, reviews, that sort of thing. No more books, though. . . . Look, Auntwon, I . . . I'm not in the best shape to talk about this kind of stuff right now, OK?"

"Yeah, yeah, I figured that. So . . . yo' lady, right?"

"Yeah. Yes. Look, I. . . ."

"No, 'at's OK, man. I don' mean to jack you or nuffin', you know? I jus' figured it's, like, good fo' you to talk it out, you know what I'm sayin'?"

Robert let out a long, slow breath and shook his head. *Great!* he thought, *Just great! Just what I needed today, a therapist!* "Look, Auntwon. . . ." he managed to articulate, but the kid interrupted him again.

"OK, Doc, OK. Hey, look-a-here, man: I jus' wanna know you awright. You ain't yo'se'f, you know? I can tell. Look like you hurtin' bad, man. Real bad."

"Yeah, I guess it shows, huh? . . . Listen . . . was it that obvious? I mean . . . to everyone? To the other kids?"

"Man, nobody axed you nuffin', did they? All mornin' neither, man. Whatchu think?"

"Well, I'm sorry if I was. . . . Maybe I shouldn't have even come in today. Maybe you guys could've done better just reading the text yourselves or something."

"No, man. Hey, you sharp even when you out of it, Doc. I mean, you make, like, the subject come alive. Like I to'd you th' other day, man, I love this shit—mostly 'causa you, I mean. You make me wanna learn all of it. Evvythang, you know what I'm sayin'?"

"Yeah, well that's a true compliment, Auntwon. I appreciate it. Really. It's just that. . . ."

"OK, OK . . . so, anyways, look-a-here . . . I got to ax you somefin' 'bout that book you wrote."

"All right. Go ahead."

"Yeah, well . . . how come you don't, like, require us to read it if it so good? Fo' the class, I mean? It is, like, pertinent, right? Cain't get much more pertinent than Colangio to what we studyin'. So maybe you think it ain't so good a'ter all. Whatchu say to that, man?"

Despite the enormity of his grief, Robert smiled. For the first time since Wednesday, too; though the smile faded as quickly as it had appeared. "I don't know for sure how good it is, Auntwon," he answered. "It's hard for a writer to judge his own work. But, well, at the time it was published the critics said it was good—what with the award and all, I mean. And it got a lot of notoriety."

"So how come we ain't readin' it in class then?"

"I don't know—the appearance of self-interest maybe. There are better books for general use. . . . But it's been uniformly well-reviewed and it had a pretty successful run—amazing in fact for a historical biography."

"Made a lotta cheddar, too, I bet."

"What?"

"Money, man, money. Made a whole lot, I bet."

"Yeah, it did do that. Even now it still throws off some pretty decent royalties."

"How much it cost, you book?"

"Cost?"

"Yeah, to buy it, man—what it cost me to buy one?"

"Thirty dollars—something like that. You know, twenty-nine ninety-five sort of thing. Like that. It still sells enough copies that they haven't started to discount it to the wholesalers."

"How much you get f'om them thirty bucks?"

"Me? You mean royalties?"

"Yeah."

"Around fifteen percent, less my agent's cut. So maybe four dollars a book."

"So lessay I buy one; you gimme the four dollars back? It ain't right to make no money off one-a you students, right?"

Robert laughed aloud this time, forgetting his sorrow completely for just one fleeting moment. "Yeah, sure, Auntwon, I'm good for the four bucks. If I had an extra copy, I'd just give you the damn thing, but sure, I'll donate the four dollars. . . . Hey, you're a character, you know that? I didn't think a thing in the world could make me even come close to smiling today."

"Good, Doc, I was tryin' to cheer you up, man. You in serious need of some levity at this partic'lar moment."

"Well you've provided it—for that moment anyway. And don't think I don't appreciate it, either. . . . So, anyway, you want your four bucks now?"

"No, man, firs' I gotta go check out the book. If it ain't no good, shit, I'ma jus' take it back."

That weekend he drove. Purposelessly, to be sure; after all, Cassie was gone, still in Mazatlan or some other similarly fashionable venue—no point in looking for her here in Illinois. But he drove nonetheless. The car felt useful in some way, functional, the motion of it perhaps, the feel of going somewhere, doing something, moving, moving. Velocity made the time pass more quickly, less painfully. And the Oldsmobile's plush interior seemed a reliable constant: warmer or cooler, louder or absolutely silent with the push of a button, the flick of a switch.

On Sunday afternoon he drove north to Winnetka, past a hundred lakefront mansions, any one of which might have belonged to Cassie's pizza man, looking for a sign of her presence: the gray Mercedes, possibly, or she herself walking out along a brick-clad driveway or manicured lawn. She wouldn't be there, of course, for she was four thousand miles away to the southwest, but there was a vague kind of comfort in looking, in passing a place she had been, and would return to in a few short days.

Every morning brought her nearer. If he could just talk to her, he thought; if he could only reason with her. . . . Well, Wednesday she'd be home—not to *their* home, true, but capable of being reached, of being communicated with, of being—if need required—pled to.

On Sunday night he slept, finally, exhaustedly. Dreams came, sweet images and constructs of touch and scent that made him desperate when he awoke. But when he did awake, he recalled that it was Monday. Only two days now till Cassie's return. And besides, with the weekend now well past him there'd be the blessed distraction of work.

Which, thankfully, there was. Once on campus, he felt minutely but perceptibly better. He taught by rote, notelessly, spewing out that morning an endless stream of relevant facts about Florence, the Medici, the woolen trade, the treachery of old Pope Innocent VIII.

"You done better today, Doc," Auntwon told him after class. But the kid didn't linger very long. "I gotta go finish yo' book," he said, winking.

"You like it so far?"

"Cain't tell yet, man. I'ma letchu know."

"So?" asked Sheldon an hour later over lunch, "you hear anything?"

"No, she's gone till Wednesday, Annie said."

"Then what the hell good does it do for you to drive around looking for her?"

"You mean the weekend? I wasn't looking."

"No? What were you doing then?"

"Nothing. I just get in the car to do something; as a distraction, sort of. I don't know why, really. . . . It feels like I'm—I don't know—like I'm busy—like I'm. . . ." He shrugged and shook his head. "I can't explain it to you."

"You take the Xanax?"

"Yeah, a couple of them. It helps, I think. I'm sleeping a little more."

"Good. You'll get over it in time."

"Yeah? You think so? When might that be?"

"Oh, it'll get a little better from week to week, month to month."

"Year to year, I'm afraid. . . . If . . . just in case she . . . I mean, if she and I don't get back together again . . . how long can I expect this business to last, Shelly?"

"What business do you mean? Grief?—or love?"

"I don't know—well, let's say love. The kind of love. . . . *This* kind of love, I mean. How long does it last, do you know?"

"It varies—weeks, months. I can't tell you a definite time."

"You *can* tell me. You teach this sort of stuff, remember? How long?"

"I don't know; maybe three years. They say it takes three years for full recovery."

Robert smiled and dabbed the corner of one eye with a finger. "That's what *she* said."

"Who said, Cassie?"

"Yeah, the night before she left." He blotted the inside corner of the other eye with his napkin. "It was the last time we were—you know—together. Who could have ever imagined? . . . Three years, she said. Told me she read it somewhere. I said I thought it was seven—you know, like the seven year itch? But she said she read three someplace. . . . You know, Shelly, I could deal with three years or seven or any finite number if I thought I'd ever feel any better. Ever."

"Come on, Bobby. . . ."

"No. You don't know what it was like for me, do you? The way I felt—the way I still feel?"

"To be in love? Don't you think I love Rochelle?"

"Of course you do. I know you do. Maybe you even love her in the same way I'm talking about but less demonstratively; I don't know. All I can say is that I thought I knew what love was like before I met Cassie, too. But I didn't . . . I didn't. . . . With Cassie everything was—how can I explain it? Different. Qualitatively different, I mean. It was like . . . like something from a movie, you know?—the kind of love they show in movies. . . . How can I even put it into words? . . . I don't know, it was like . . . like finding the exact counterpart of yourself, the exact pattern you have somehow fixed in your mind of the perfect person you want to be with—*need* to be with—and then having her love you in the same way you love her. Looking into her eyes, touching her, and feeling—I don't know—a kind of electricity. I never felt that kind of thing before with anyone else. I don't think I ever will again, that I ever *can* again. That's the saddest part—you know?—thinking you'll never feel the same way again. That's the worst God damned part of it."

"OK, OK, look . . . all that goes away in time. It's a kind of dependency, like a chemical addiction. . . . It *is* a chemical addiction, actually."

"How? I don't understand what you mean."

"Well, love is chemical, you know? We've isolated the pathways, the mediators."

"Mediators? What the hell does *that* mean?"

"OK, there are these two substances—chemicals—that the body produces. In the brain, you know? And when they're released they engender the feeling of love. Got it? So that means there are two kinds of love, in other words. There's a kind of low-grade love, like maternal love or the love of a spouse of many years. Cuddly love, I guess you'd call it. Arm-around-the-shoulders sort of thing. That's what most people feel when they're with their loved ones. It's mediated—produced—by a chemical called oxytocin. The person we love elicits the release of oxytocin and we get a kind of feeling of well-being. It's like a mild narcotic, I guess. When we lose the person, whether by death or, well, whatever, the chemical isn't released and a kind of withdrawal sets in. That's the grief reaction. It's nothing but a drug withdrawal in effect."

"So that's what I feel now? The lack of—what is it?"

"Oxytocin. . . . Probably you feel that in part. But I didn't get to the other thing yet, the other mediator. There's a second chemical called norepinephrine that gets released in passionate love—you know like a powerful physical attraction? That's the strong one—like heroin, I guess. Anyway, the way you're talking I'd guess you're probably in withdrawal from both chemicals at the same time."

"That sounds like it. Yeah, that sounds *just* like it. So do you understand how awful that is for me? What I'm going through?"

"Thank God, I don't . . . exactly."

"You haven't felt that kind of thing, have you? You can't relate to it from direct experience, right?"

"No, thank God I can't. I haven't. Maybe I don't have that much norepinephrine in my neurons. Oxytocin, though, I think I've got a pretty good supply of."

"You know, Shelly, I would have said the same thing as you five years ago. The exact same thing. Cassandra changed my whole life; I don't know whether ultimately for better or worse, though. Maybe it's better never to know what that feeling is like—that kind of love. . . . I mean, if you'd never known it, you wouldn't ever miss it."

"Like me, I guess. Maybe I'm the lucky one in the long run."

"Who knows? I mean—don't get me wrong here—Rochelle is a wonderful person, and I know how close the two of you are. But if you haven't felt the way I have for someone—just the way I have—you just can't imagine how the—what is it—norepinephrine? You can't imagine what that's like."

"Yeah maybe you're right. Maybe it's the most wonderful experience in the world. . . . But I'm not the one on Xanax."

"OK, OK, point well taken, but. . . . All right, maybe you think I'm a fool to have gotten myself into all of this, but you work with lots of fools clinically, don't you? Or crazies, maybe. . . . You teach about them anyway. Look, you must have studied patients that . . . well, people like me with too much norepinephrine or whatever. You must have seen cases, read about cases?"

"Yeah, sure, every day."

"And what usually happens to them? To the patients?"

"They get better, like I told you."

"All of them?"

"No, not all, but many do. . . . A lot of them do."

"What about the rest?"

"The rest?"

"Yeah, the worst ones, the ones who've had the biggest doses of both chemicals—norepinephrine and the other one—and suddenly lose their chemicals without preparation and without any prospect of getting them back. What happens to them?"

"Different things. I don't know the outcome of every case. Everybody's different."

"Come on, Shelly, what happens in the worst cases like mine. People in love as much as this? I'm sure you know the statistics."

"The statistics?"

"Yeah. Don't tell me you've never seen a complicated case. What happens to them? What happens to the worst of them?"

"What happens to the worst ones, Bobby, is suicide or murder. So take your fucking Xanax!"

On Thursday, driving home from campus by way of his by-now-inevitable detour around the Merchandise Mart, Robert saw her car.

Oh there were a hundred gray Mercedes roadsters in Metropolitan Chicago superficially like hers, but the specific car that Cassie drove was somehow distinctive to him, perceived more than seen, like the timbre of her voice amid a thousand other voices or the flicker of her shadow in a darkened room. So, yes, he knew at once that it was her vehicle and no other, parked as usual in the street-level lot she always parked in, half a block east of the Mart's east entrance. He pulled in along the street, got out of the Olds, and stood waiting on foot just across from the lot. From there, the Mercedes' shiny gray trunk was visible, though deep in shadow, and beyond it in unobstructed view the building's nearest exit door.

He waited on foot scarcely moving for an hour, his heart in his throat. Then, at five-fifteen he saw her emerge from an east-faced doorway: Cassie, his Cassie, distinctive in form and manner from every other being in the world. She was wearing her beige suede jacket, carrying a carton, walking that walk of facile elegance that had always seemed innate in her. Still too far away to see . . . but in a minute she drew near enough, and he saw her face, her features. . . .

There was anger in his heart and sorrow, too. They welled up for a moment, crested, then were gone. My God! he thought, how beautiful she was! How perfect! The one thing in all the world so perfect; the one person capable of . . . of what exactly? . . . Oh, sure, he remembered, as she turned her steps now into the parking lot: those chemicals, those lovely compounds Shelly had talked about. Compounds potent enough to displace anger, narcotic enough to assuage pain. How sweet they were . . . that feeling . . . that ineffable feeling. If he could only get it back somehow for good; get *her* back, his beloved Cassie . . . what more on earth could he wish for, ever. . . . Well, here and now were the place and time; there'd never be better. Never. All that was required of him was the right set of words, the *specific* set of words, and she'd be back in his arms, beside him in their bed tonight.

And so he rushed across the street, fending off a braking car, coming up behind her unseen as she approached the Mercedes' trunk.

"Cassie—Cassandra!"

She turned. He saw her dark eyes widen, then narrow again, as black and impenetrable as a moonless night. The carton she held sat against her chest and belly, projecting outward as a kind of barricade, a bumper, separating them. Otherwise he might have made a move to get in closer; made a move, perhaps, to touch her, to hold her. But the carton, bumper-like, kept him away.

"Why Robert!" she said with a synthetic smile, her tone neither warm nor cool, but as tepid and robotic as her expression; assertively nonplused. "What in the world are *you* doing here?"

"What . . . what am I *doing*! My God! I had to *see* you, to *talk* to you."

"Oh? What about?" She shrugged the carton up higher onto her little-girl breasts, adjusting the weight, though it didn't look particularly heavy.

"What about! My *God*, Cassie!"

"Now let's not make a fuss, Robert. Look, I'm sorry about everything—the way things worked out. Can't we just leave it at that?"

"No. No we can't! . . . God, don't you know how much I've been hurt by this? How much. . . ."

"I'm sorry, Robert. I really am."

"Sorry! What do you mean 'sorry'? Sorry about what? Look, I don't even know. . . . What is it exactly that you're sorry about?"

"Well, everything. . . . *You* know. . . ."

"No, I *don't* know. I don't know anything. . . . How *would* I know? How could you just leave me like that? Walk away like that, as though . . . ? Don't you think you owe me a little more than just walking out the way you did."

She turned away for a moment, cool as an iceberg, and popped open the Mercedes' trunk with her remote. In one graceful, seamless motion, she set the carton inside, closed the trunk lid, then turned back around to face him, impassive still, but now slit-eyed and with her arms crossed defensively below her breasts where the angle of the missing carton had lain.

"All right, Robert, what exactly is it that you think I owe you?"

"Well, an explanation for one thing—or a little more of an explanation than I got, at least. . . . I mean . . . what did I *do*? What the hell did I *do* to deserve that kind of treatment from you? From you of all people? . . . Of . . . of all the people in the world."

"Look, Robert, it isn't about you, all right? This isn't about you at all."

"No? What's it about then? They said you went away with someone—with a guy."

"Who said that?"

"Annie told me. And that other friend of yours . . . Lenore."

"Well they both ought to mind their own damn business! Both of them!"

"So, is it true, then? Tell me."

"Why? I don't have to account to you."

"You. . . . How can you . . . ? I mean . . . the way we were together . . . how can you talk to me like that? How can you . . . ? Look, are you gonna just throw everything away? Is that . . .?"

"I'm sorry, Robert," she interrupted, "you've got—we've both got to be strong now."

"Strong! How the. . . . How the hell can I be strong? OK, look . . . look. . . . Do you love him? Just tell me that and I'll leave you alone— if that's what you really want me to do. Just tell me that one thing. Tell me to my face."

"I've said everything I'm going to say: I don't have to account to you or anyone. I don't owe anything to anyone. . . . What? The car? You want your little car back? I don't really need it now. Take it. Here, take the keys; I'll get a cab." She put the car keys out toward him with precisely the same motion she had used a week earlier in handing him the keys to their condo, but this time, grasping her firmly by the wrist, he pushed her hand away.

"No. No, Cassie, you keep your goddamn car. I want you to have it. I want you to keep it as a memento; it'll be my humble contribution to your new multi-million dollar life-style."

Robert's face felt strange, flushed from the anger that arose in him, yet at the same time perfectly bloodless, drained totally of life. His heartbeat ticked in his ears, his fists clenched purposelessly, involuntarily, as he turned away and began to walk toward the Oldsmobile, away from this woman—this woman, Cassandra Fullerton, whom he had loved so long that it seemed to him forever . . . forever. But before he had taken more than half a dozen steps toward his car, he began to feel the sudden fury ebb. Instantly the old leaden weight came again to his chest, the selfsame sensation that had come upon him a week before on that terrible day Cassandra had first thrust her set of condominium keys into his hand.

And instantly the enormous sheaf of memories sprang open, then spilled forth in copious flood: Cassie's dimpled smile, her pout, the delicacy of her hand upon his chest, the perfumed scent of her body in his bed. "God, Dr. Martin!" she had said so sweetly that indelible evening five years before, "I won't wash my hand for a month!"

He spun back around toward the place where he had left her, but it was only to hear the Mercedes' engine cough, then click, then whirr. He saw the car lurch back, start forward, then speed out past him onto the street. It turned left, tires screeching, then ran on quickly through the stop sign at the corner and westward past the north face of the Mart. In fifteen seconds more, it was out beyond his line of sight.

"Man, you done great today! You back to you old se'f, Doc. You back to you own se'f." Auntwon, as always, had waited for the classroom to empty, then stepped up to the front of the room. "See? They even axed you some questions today. You notice that?"

"Yeah, Auntwon, I did. I feel a whole lot better."

"You back wif you lady then?"

"No, not exactly, but I had a kind of closure. Just the other day, in fact. I'm not a hundred-percent recovered yet, but I'm on the way."

"Yeah, thass great, man! Thass really great. . . . Hey, look-a-here, man, I finished yo' book."

"Did you? What did you think of it?"

"Iss good, man, *real* good. Expecially the way you, like, integrate the, you know, contemporary events wif the life of Colangio. It give, like, a journalistic kind of feel to the biography, you know what I'm sayin'? Like a multi-disciplinary type of approach."

"Yeah, actually that's just what I was trying to do with the book— not that many critics picked up on it, though. Did you come across that nice *Sun-Times* review or something?"

"Review? Naw, man, I jus' read the book. Reviews ain't worf shit. They somebody else's opinion of a conclusion you s'posed to come up wif you own se'f."

"So they are, Auntwon, so they are. That's pretty insightful of you. . . . So—you want your four bucks now?"

"Naw, man, the book be truly worf thirty bucks, and I got all that scholarship money and shit anyways. I'm gonna bring it in fo' you to autograph fo' me, OK?"

"Sure, I'd be honored to."

"I got some questions, though, man—I mean Doc."

"OK, sure. Go ahead."

"Well, whatchu think happened wif Colangio in the end?"

"Which end do you mean?"

"The 1503 end, man, of course. 1503."

"You mean when he stopped writing?"

"Yeah, when he stopped evvythang. I mean, he ditten produce nuffin' fo' the last—what?—twenty-fo' years of his life, right? No books, no letters, not even a, like, quote or nuffin'. It be like he went from writin' five books a year to gettin' caught in the event horizon of a black hole, you know what I'm sayin'?"

"Yeah, I think so. No one has satisfactorily explained that—his withdrawal, I mean. All we know is that he wrote prolifically and, as I said in the book, very profoundly until 1503, then just stopped. Nobody knows why."

"Well you read all that stuff by him, right? Evvythang he wrote, I mean. You ain't theorized about it—to yo' own se'f?"

"No. A historian's duty is to report the extant facts, analyze them, relate them to other extant facts, but never to speculate. Speculation is anathema to history, you understand what I mean by that term?"

"By 'anafema'? Yeah, that from the Greek, right? The Greek be like 'somefin devoted to somefin', but the Orthodox Church used it to mean 'devoted to evil', so it got to, like, signify a kind of preface to excommunication. I don't think you mean that ezackly, though, in this particular context, since you talkin' 'bout more like a intellectual misdeed than a genuine evil, right? But I know whatchu mean: dude writin' history jus' s'posed to tell what he know fo' sure."

"Yeah . . . yeah, that's just what I meant. . . . Listen, Auntwon . . . where did you learn all that stuff about the word 'anathema'?"

"Man, I don' know. I musta read it someplace. But, look-a-here, man, all that shit about Colangio—the way you relate it in the book, it just don't make no sense."

"What doesn't make sense? His not writing?"

"No, man—Doc—it's more'n that. He jus'—you know— drop outta sight, like. Poof! You know? And . . . and where he get all that money f'om? He jus', like, suddenly become rich? Man, how you gonna explain that?"

"I can't. It's a mystery like all the rest of his later life. . . . Listen, what got you so worked up about Colangio anyway? I mean, he's been dead for almost five hundred years now."

"Yeah. I don' truly know, man. What got *you* interested in the dude? I mean, like, *you* the one wrote the book, aintchu?"

"Yeah, well he and I share a basic philosophy: we're both objectivists—you know, opponents of the illogical."

"Yeah, OK. Well, I can relate to him too in a diff'ent way. I guess I kinda like, identify wif him somehow."

"You *identify* with him? How's that?"

"I don' know; him learnin' all that shit so easy and . . . and not bein' really interested in studyin' law like his daddy wanted him to do. Diff'ent ways, in ovver words. . . . But if you so interested you gotta wonder about it too, man, don'tcha? I mean, it weird: he go out and purchase this big palace, right? Live like a millionaire and all like 'at? Don't publish nuffin' no mo'? Man, that gotta come f'om someplace, all 'at cheddar—you know what I'm sayin'? You cain't tell me you ditten get curious about it."

"Well, sure; I wondered about it—just like everyone else. Everybody's wondered about his dropping out of society since the day it happened—even Machiavelli wrote about it in a letter—you know, it's quoted in the book. But, as I said, historians don't speculate. Maybe some day more facts will emerge and we'll get an explanation. Things like that surface all the time—newly-discovered letters and so on. Just last year, in fact, they found a box of papers in Siena that are supposedly in Colangio's hand. They could be forgeries, of course, but who knows? Maybe they'll turn out to be genuine and there'll be something in them—you never can tell—though I doubt it. But those kinds of things come to light all the time. So maybe in a decade or two someone will unravel the whole mystery. Maybe *you* will if you turn out to be a research historian."

"Yeah, man, you never know. . . . So, what they find in them papers you talkin' 'bout? In that box like you said? You know?"

"Not really. They asked me to work them up, but I declined."

"*Declined*! Man! Who axed you?"

"Oh some guy there—in Siena, I mean. An archivist or something."

"So how come you ditten do it?"

"Well, you know: my ex-lady friend and all. . . . She wasn't much into travel."

"So maybe you could do it now. You know, since you gettin' better and all and she no longer a impediment, right? Ain'tchu curious?"

"I don't know. A little maybe. Most of those so-called discoveries turn out to be garbage in the end—you know, either forgeries or copies of things that are already published. Anyway, they probably found some other researcher to work them up by now. I'm not the world's only authority on Colangio."

"No, but you the main one, right?"

"Yeah, I suppose so. I really did read everything he wrote. Every letter and paper. Everything."

"Well, there gotta be a explanation fo' what happened wif him. Somefin' absolutely crazy I betchu. No dude gonna change that much wifout some explanation fo' it."

"No? Maybe you're right—who can say? Maybe he got abducted by aliens or something."

"Yeah, Doc. You jus' jivin' 'bout that shit, I know. But I betchu if the actual truf ever emerge, it gonna be a whole lot stranger than that."

CHAPTER FOUR

~~~~~~~~~

DISTRACTION

"WHAT IS IT?"

"I don't know," said Sheldon. "Something Rochelle made. . . . Cookies, I think. They smell like chocolate chip."

"God, Shelly, if I ate half the junk you dragged in here the last two weeks, I'd weigh a ton. Look, enough's enough. Tell her to stop!"

"Hey, my wife worries about you. What can I say? . . . Look, I worry too, Bobby. How you doin' today? How do you feel?"

"Fine. I'm fine now. I told you that. Look, Monday was an aberration, all right? It's normal to have good days and bad days, isn't it?"

Sheldon nodded.

"Well, today's a good one; I'm perfectly fine. . . . Anyway I'm a whole lot better than I was a week ago; *that's* for sure."

It *was* for sure. These last couple of days he'd been really pretty good. Terrific, in fact, compared to how he'd felt in the beginning. Back then he'd been a ghost, a cipher, purposeless. But when last Wednesday afternoon he'd seen her, *heard* her, then slept on the experience, letting that sleep salve his mind in whatever way sleep's mystery salves hurt minds, why, the very next morning he'd awakened to find his unbearable burden of grief lifted like a summer cloud. On Thursday he'd been responsive, by Friday fully functional, then finally, beginning Monday afternoon, practically back to the old Bobby Martin of pre-Cassie days. These past few mornings he'd talk, laugh, socialize. . . .

Unless he'd had a dream of her the night before. Twice it had happened since his recovery began. The first was last Wednesday night; but she'd been cruel in that dream, as cold and distant as on the afternoon preceding. He'd awakened angry, determined to get going with his life.

Then the bad dream had come. Sunday night it was, or Monday morning early; more vivid and convincing than life itself, bringing sensations that were at once exquisite and intolerable. "I love you, baby," she'd murmured to him with that sweet look in her eyes. "It's never been like this before. Never, never. . . ." And he could somehow see her through the darkness, smell her, feel her body close to his. Exquisite and intolerable, it broke him again. Half of Monday he'd been a drone, frightening Shelly, silencing his students once more.

But these past two nights had been dreamless—at least as far as he could remember. So today, and yesterday too, were pretty good indeed. So pretty good that he had gone and arranged something special.

It was Wednesday; the last Wednesday in April. Two long weeks had come and gone since Cassie's departure—two weeks exactly, almost to the minute in fact; for Sheldon had stepped into the room today just seconds after twelve, and Cassie had said her curt good-bye precisely two Wednesdays before at eleven-thirty-five or so. Fourteen days, then, almost to the minute, and every working day among them Shelly had been there, just at noon or a minute after, leaving his eleven o'clock seminar in Fisher, diagonally across the quadrangle, ten minutes early to make it. Every day; letting his six students leave when he left, or giving them some busy work to do when he'd gone. Then he'd drag himself the eight- or ten-minute walk across to Social Sciences, getting to Robert's door at very nearly twelve, not knocking, but barging right in, as though the office were his own and Robert himself some loitering intruder.

Every day for two weeks past. And nearly every day he'd carried something with him in his hands or tucked up underneath an arm, some book or sweet or magazine he thought Robert might like: a consolatory offering in tangible form to cheer the most inconsolable of friends. Not that anything had helped very much: cookies were a miserable substitute for the thing that Robert most craved. But Sheldon was kind and loyal, and did the best a kind and loyal friend could do. So on this Wednesday noon, the fourteenth day now of Robert's first pained then rather more rapid recovery, he was back again, bringing along that flat metal pan topped with aluminum foil, which now resided on Robert's desk awaiting some indeterminate final disposition.

"So? You ready?" asked Sheldon. "I'm hungry. You can eat the cookies later. . . . Let's go."

"Yeah, OK, in a minute. Look, Shelly, just hang on for a minute, OK? I asked one of my students to join us. I said I'd buy him lunch today. . . . I . . . I'd kind of like you to meet him anyway."

Sheldon shrugged. "Yeah, yeah, sure, if it'll make you happy. . . . So . . . OK, what's the story with this kid you want to introduce me to? What's so special about him?"

"OK, he's. . . . You know I give a mid-quarter exam. . . ."

Shelly nodded. "I know you used to."

"OK, well, I still do. Look, I know it's not required, but I give a mid-term anyway—not really for credit but more or less to see which kids need extra help or encouragement. You know what I mean?"

"So this kid's a flunky, right? Is that it?"

"No, no. That's not it at all. Just the opposite in fact. Look, he's a black kid. Talks like a gangster rapper. Maybe I've had five, maybe six black kids take a non-intro history course in the nine years I've been here. Anyway, this kid hands in an essay written like a Ph.D. candidate's paper."

"So he's cheating? Plagiarizing?"

"No. No way he could have done that. They write out their essays right there in front of me. No, he wrote it, all right. I've never seen anything like it since I've been here, not even from grad students."

"So you want my professional opinion? Hey, lots of black kids are smart too. It's not all affirmative action."

"Come on, Shelly, you know I don't mean that. It's just . . . look, you'll have to meet him, OK? Then tell me what you think."

"OK, sure. . . . Hey, you really *are* getting better, Bobby. You really are. I think maybe you're starting to get back to your old self again, huh?"

"I hope so, Shel. After I saw her last week. . . . Well, *you* know; I told you how it went. . . . She was like a stranger. . . . Like . . . well, like that was *it*, you know? *Done*. No point in beating a dead horse. . . . Anyway, it gave me that sense of closure I must have needed. After that I was—I don't know—resigned, I guess you'd say. The worst of it is over now; I'm sure of that. But . . . God, Shelly, sometimes it still gets pretty bad . . . really pretty bad. Like Sunday night with that goddamn dream. Or sometimes when I'm alone and I've got time to think. . . .

You know, at home with all the familiar things and memories. . . . It was our place, you know? Just the two of us. She was always there with me. . . . And the scent of her. It's still around, in the bathroom, the bedroom. . . . But . . . I guess I don't think of her every minute now. Not every minute. Every two minutes maybe or every five, so I get a little bit of comfort in-between. And today's a good day too. Lots of other things to do. Distractions, I suppose. All that stuff helps. I still love to teach. I've got that anyway. . . . At least I've got that."

"Jesus, Bobby . . . look . . . OK, OK, I'm sorry I brought it up. . . . All right, anyway, when's this kid coming? I'm getting hungry."

"Yeah, OK. . . . So have a cookie."

Sheldon started to say something, some clever rejoinder if he could think of one. But before he got a word out—funny or wise or consolatory—he was interrupted by a knock at the door.

Now there are quite as many types of knocks on academic doors as there are varieties of academically oriented knockers. First you have your shy student: unprepared, summoned against his will to a critique. He will tap lightly, backhand, on the lower part of the wood with a single knuckle, reticently, hoping not to be heard. "I came but no one answered," he will say the next morning. If you pop the door open, confronting him, he will look surprised, abashed, wishing he were somewhere else.

Then, clear at the opposite pole, you will find your confident scholar: exquisitely primed, jubilant at the thought of any interaction that might validate his skills. He will rap smartly forehand, in-your-face at eye level, twice usually. Tap-tap. Just so. Open the door on him and you will get a remarkably confident grin.

Then comes the secretary: deferential, reluctant to disturb, though needful that her presence be noted. She will knock once, with medium force, wait a moment or two, then tap a second time once or twice. She will greet you with a slight smile, polite but not excessively familiar.

And your colleague—not Shelly, of course, who will simply barge in, but another: Aaron Gold, for example, or Henry Josephson. They just bang away and bellow at the same time: "Hey Bobby, you in there? It's me, Aaron. . . ." or Henry . . . or whoever.

Bump-barrump-bump-bump came the knock, a drummy, boisterous, musical sound, multi-fingered, administered with skill and rhythmicity and some bravado. Sheldon's eyebrows raised, corrugating his pink, hitherto unwrinkled forehead. Robert smiled.

"Come in," he said. The door swung open and Auntwon Miller was in the room.

He was altogether different today, not subtly different but quite another person indeed. Robert remarked it at once, in the boy's posture, his bearing, half-way through the introduction:

"Shelly, this is Auntwon; Auntwon, Dr. Rogovin."

"It's a real pleasure to meet you, sir." Auntwon put out his hand with just the proper mixture of deference and civility. It was extraordinary! He seemed straighter, taller, his face more expressive, dignified in a way. And his voice! That was totally different, too, the accent, the language. He sounded . . . how? The rounded vowels, the clipped consonants; it was a newscaster's voice, black, perhaps, but professionally articulate. Robert was justifiably astounded.

"Look, Auntwon . . . Sheldon—um, Dr. Rogovin here—is a friend of mine. I asked him to join us for lunch, if that's OK with you. I thought the two of you might like to meet each other."

"Yes, sir," Auntwon answered, "it's an honor to meet one of your . . ."—he turned to Sheldon—". . . one of Dr. Martin's colleagues. His class is . . . and he himself, really, he himself is the finest teacher I've ever had. It's been a . . . a revelation, I'd say, to study with him."

Jesus! thought Robert. But for the tattered orange jacket and penetrating eyes, this was a different kid entirely, a watershed change from the Auntwon Miller he'd come to know and relate to over the past two weeks. Robert couldn't quite figure what to make of it. But as the seconds passed, Auntwon's newfound speech and manner began to strike him as more and more discordant, more and more pretentious. Robert felt like the butt of a terribly unfunny joke, and the longer he considered it, the more vexatious it became.

He followed the two of them silently as they passed out of the building abreast, keeping a couple of yards behind, picking up a word or two here and there. "How do you like the university." "Fine, sir, just fine . . . challenging, though . . . some real scholars here. . . ." The day was cool and blustery. A brisk wind drove at them, coming off the lake, spattering their faces with an invisible mist of rain, droplets so minute and massless that they didn't fall, but rather blew horizontal with the wind, then flew like dust up nostrils and around spectacle lenses into places where rain is generally debarred from entering by the physical laws of fluidics and gravitation. Chilled and soggy, they made it to Medici on 57th Street, a four-block walk, getting in right away, thankfully, into a booth by the windows with a modicum of privacy. Auntwon was able to maintain his untoward eloquence, but got caught up on the menu, what with its choices of grilled vegetables, chicken marsala, and sun-dried tomatoes in varying combinations. A cheeseburger was all he could manage, though he ordered it articulately and with aplomb.

"Dr. Martin tells me you wrote a hell of a paper for him the other day."

"Well, thank you, sir, and you too, Dr. Martin, for the compliment. I haven't received a grade yet, but I'm glad to hear the answers were acceptable."

Acceptable! Yes, they were acceptable all right, thought Robert. Just odd from a kid who spoke intermittent ghetto English. It was surrealistic, other-worldly; devoid of a comprehensible explanation. OK, a put-on, certainly, but how? In what way? Which was the genuine Auntwon and which the fraud?—The scholar? the rapper? the withdrawn kid who never spoke? And anyway, what difference did it make? No matter how you looked at it, fraud today or fraud the past two weeks or fraud a month before, it was a palpable affront. Robert felt hurt, betrayed. Again. Twice in two weeks now. Someone else playing on his trust, his naiveté. Like Cassie: hadn't owed him a thing, she'd said. After five full years, not even a simple explanation. Five years! Christ! And now Auntwon too! How could you even *imagine* things like this? People you thought you knew, people you cared about, and they about you, who turned out to be strangers; simply strangers after all!

". . . So what do you think, Bobby?" It was Sheldon, asking him something. Auntwon looked on, poised and military.

"What's that, Shelly? I was daydreaming, I guess."

"Yeah, I can figure what you were thinking about without too much trouble—or *who* I should say. . . . *Whom*, I mean. Whom. . . . Look, you're making me illiterate, for God's sake." Sheldon laughed. "What I asked was if you thought maybe Auntwon here should apply for an assistantship. What do you think about that?"

"Yeah, sure. Why not?"

He could think of *one* objection: which of the two Auntwons would apply? Would it be this dignified kid or the other one, the one he'd come to know—or *thought* he'd known—over the past two weeks? All that solicitous talk about worrying how he'd felt, asking about his book. . . . The kid was just making fun of him. That was the pathetic truth of it. Just making goddamn fun of him after all!

Shelly didn't talk much once the food came. He never did. Food was serious business to him, to be taken unalloyed. But having eaten his meal in silence, ordered dessert, and finally scraped the last of his hot peach cobbler *a la Medici* from its subjacent bowl, his natural loquacity returned in full.

"So Auntwon," he asked, "what do you plan to do with this great fund of historical knowledge you're acquiring. Would you like to teach?"

"Well, I've been thinkin' about it."

"Is that your major, then? History?"

Turned out that it wasn't. Auntwon explained, more or less grammatically, but with a lapse now and then into street phraseology, that he was actually in pre-med.

"*Pre-med*!" the repetition popped right out of Robert's mouth with scarce the delay between input and output of a reverberation unit. "You're in *pre-med*?" Pre-med? Whatever guise Auntwon had assumed, whether rapper or news-man or even total mute, he was nonetheless easily the most promising history student Robert had yet encountered in his nine years in residence at the university. But . . . in *pre-med*?

"Yeah, technically."

As he related it, his "auntie" had arranged everything—'aahntee' was the boy's pronunciation—sending in the application for his scholarship, picking his courses, paying what she could for his books and transportation. "You see," he explained, "she . . . she sorta decided on medicine for me. She say . . . uh, *says* I'm the one who's gotta provide for the family . . . that . . . that I'm the only one they got . . . uh, *have* to do it, being good in school and all. The only boy, anyway—she don't . . . *doesn't* . . . put much stock in girls. My auntie is a strong woman. I mean, not the type of person you can convince of something contrary to what she has her mind set on, you know? She's a . . . a good person, though, a fine person."

"Your aunt, you mean," said Sheldon. "What about your mother?"

"Yeah. Well, Auntie raised me. My mamma . . . uh . . . she wasn't around too much of the time when I was growin' up. I see her . . . um . . . not a lot; once in a while, you know? She lived with my auntie too for a while. All of us have. She got a house full, I'll tell you. . . . Anyway, medicine's been the thing. When Auntie says it, it generally gets done. That's the way things have always been with us. Once she seen . . . uh, *saw* that I was good in school, well, everything was pretty much decided on . . . 'predetermined', I guess you'd say."

"You listening to this, Bobby?"

"Yeah. Sure."

"I think you need to, you know? Your friend Auntwon here is trying to tell us something—if you're not too preoccupied, I mean. See, other people have their problems too, sometimes almost as bad as yours; and not always of their own making." He turned to the boy. "Your professor's had a lot on his mind lately. Maybe that's why he didn't ask you about this stuff before, or maybe didn't listen if you tried to tell him."

"That's not fair, Shelly. I know I've. . . ."

Auntwon put his hands up, one hand palm out toward either man, interrupting them. "Hey, hey, wait, guys! Come on! Look, I'm fine. I didn't mean to talk so much about myself. Doc . . . uh, Dr. Martin's the one who's had the real problems lately. I've been tryin' to help out as much as I can . . . um, you know, whatever I could do."

"He knows about Cassandra?" asked Sheldon in something between a hiss and a whisper. He looked incredulous.

"Yeah," said Robert, "she was just outside the lecture room the day she—you know—came to talk to me. They all saw some of it, I guess."

"So this is your therapist, then? . . . Auntwon?"

"Come on, Shelly. It's not like I went to him for counseling or anything."

"No?" Sheldon was really wound up now. Once he got like that, you couldn't hope to stop him. He turned to Auntwon. "Well let me get your clinical opinion then, *Doctor* Auntwon. What do you think about a brilliant guy like Bob Martin here getting involved with a sadistic, control-freak-type woman like Cassandra Fullerton to the neglect of everything important in his life? How does a guy with everything: looks, brains, even money—if she left him any, that is—how does someone like that with a thousand pretty women after him go for the meanest bitch in Chicago, then, when she dumps him, mourn her the way you'd mourn a kind, devoted spouse you'd lost? I don't get it at all. You seem to be the therapist in charge. Maybe you can explain it to me."

Auntwon leaned forward, both hands on the table, and shook his head. "OK, guys, chill, OK? Look, Dr. Rogovin, sir, nobody came to me for counseling, OK? Look, I was just tryin' to help. Like . . . as Dr. Martin said, I was just *there* that day, you know? That's all. And as for explainin' how anybody feel . . . uh, *feels* about anything or anyone else, my theory is, it's like particle physics, you know what I'm . . . what I mean?"

"No," said Sheldon. "I don't know what you mean at all. What the hell does particle physics have to do with it?"

"Well, there's like this principle. Heisenberg's Principle. You know what that is?"

"No," said Sheldon. Robert shook his head.

"OK, well, it says that you can't know both the momentum and the absolute position of a point particle, that the attempt to measure one perturbs the other and makes it uncertain. What it really means is that everything that happens in the universe is only a matter of probability, that *nothing* is absolutely certain. Like, for example, there's a chance that I could walk through the wall over there. Not a good chance, but maybe one in ten to the hundredth power. You see?"

"No," said Sheldon.

"Not exactly," said Robert, who wasn't quite sure of anything just then.

"Well, it means that *everything* could be possible, you know? Ghosts, unicorns, time warps, headless horsemen, people falling in love with bitches or caterpillars, even; all like that. Maybe not likely all the time, but possible. It means that, you know, science, physics, biology, medicine, all those . . . uh, um . . . disciplines. . . . They just give us, like, approximations, probabilities. History's more absolute, though, because it deals with what's already done, what's already happened. The past can't change, you know? Of course it's meaningless in terms of, uh, like cosmological truth, you know. Then there's string theory, now. They say that might give some . . . uh, definitive answers."

Sheldon stood up. "String theory, eh? Well, guys, that's all I can assimilate right now. Look, Bobby, I think you've got the perfect therapist here. And you know what? I'd encourage him to stay in medicine. He can't do too much damage there. Maybe kill a few hundred people is all."

That struck Auntwon funny. He shook his head and laughed, then slid out of the booth to say good-bye to Sheldon and shake his hand. "Next time we'll do string theory, OK?" Sheldon said. Auntwon laughed again and slid back into the booth, directly across from Robert. Sheldon grabbed the check and headed for the door.

"Hey, wait," said Robert, "it's my turn." Shelly waved him off and disappeared downstairs.

The kid had a sort of sheepish grin on his face, a mischievous sort of look with pinched-off eyes, crinkled at the corners.

"Man, he *awright*!" he said. That did it.

"OK, Auntwon, what the hell's the story? What's going on?"

Auntwon grinned a little wider now, the angles of his eyes crinkling more, then still more. In a second or two, he broke into an unrestrained, lip-retracted, crescentic, full-toothed smile.

"So what the hell's going on?" Robert asked again, practically hissing it. He was furiously angry now, though striving desperately toward restraint. This kid, unquestionably, was mocking him.

"Whatchu *mean*, Doc?"

"Come on, you know *exactly* what I mean. So . . . so, what is it now? You're back to Auntwon the rapper, is that the story? Come on, this is bullshit! Look, after what I've been through in the last couple of weeks, I just don't get the joke, you know? Maybe my sense of humor is a little frayed. So how about explaining it to me, huh? What's the story with this sudden personality change you seem to be experiencing?"

"You mean like how I talk? You noticed that, huh?"

"Noticed it! Come on, Auntwon! Nobody likes to be made a fool of."

"OK, OK, chill, Doc, chill. Look, I don't mean nuffin' by it. . . . Nuffin' disrespectful, I mean."

"Well, I deserve some explanation, don't you think?"

"OK, Doc, OK. . . . Look, you know that joke about the dude goes into the bar?"

"The guy in the bar? Sure, that narrows it down to maybe ten, twelve thousand jokes I've probably heard. Hey, come on, Auntwon. . . ."

"OK, OK, ho'd on a second. So this guy go in this bar and sit down and talk in this, like, little squeaky voice. I cain't do it too good, but like a squeaky little girl's voice: like 'Gimme a beer, man.' Like that, OK?"

Robert nodded.

"And then the bartender, he answer the same way, in that same little squeaky voice: 'Sure thing, man. Here you go.'... OK?"

"Yeah...?"

"And then another dude come in. Big guy, wif a deep voice, real low: 'Hey, bartender, gimme a whiskey.' Like that. Got it?"

Robert nodded again.

"And then the bartender go over to him and talk to him in like a real low voice now: 'Here you go, man. Here's you' whiskey.' Like that, OK? Then he get up and leave, the big guy, I mean, and the guy wit' the squeaky voice call the bartender over and say 'Hey, man, you been makin' fun of me?' So then the bartender say in the squeaky voice again 'Naw, man, I was makin' fun of that other dude jus' left.' . . . You get it?"

"Not exactly. I mean, I get the joke, but not the relevance . . . exactly."

"OK. Say you best friends wif . . . uh, say the Cardinal of Chicago, right? And you and him talk jus' like all them white dudes in Chicago talk. You know, like 'da Bears and da Bulls.' You know what I'm sayin'?"

"OK."

"And say he ax you out to dinner wif the Pope."

"OK."

"Well, you all three gonna speak Latin, prob'bly, right?"

"Maybe. . . . Yeah."

"Yeah, but when he leave, you gonna go back to 'da Bears and da Bulls,' right?"

"OK, I get it, but who am I supposed to be, the Cardinal or the Pope?"

"You bof, Doc. You the Cardinal 'cause I talk to you like a friend, like the way I talk to people close to me, my auntie, my sister—you know? If I talk white to you, it mean that ain't me talkin'. It's, like, phony—you know what I'm sayin'? I cain't be phony like that witchu. I don't wanna be, you get it?"

"I think so. . . ."

"OK, good. So you the Cardinal, like the friend, you know? But you the Pope too. That's 'cause I respec' you like the Pope. You the *Man*. The best. I learn from you. More than from anybody, man. Hey, look-a-here, I made up my mind jus' these last couple-a days. I'm gonna give up that pre-med shit. Jus' like Colangio did wif that law stuff, you know? I don't want that; that science shit, you know? It ain't no thang—I mean, it ain't hard and all—but it ain't worf learnin' neither. Man, what I love is this history stuff, the way you teach it. That's what I wanna do. Nuffin' else. You done sold me on it, man. My auntie gon' be pissed, but you the one gonna have to deal wif her."

"Me! What do you mean by that? I don't even *know* your aunt. I don't even know who she *is*."

"Oh, you will, Doc. You sho-*nuff* will."

※※※※※※※

CHAPTER FIVE

COMMUNICATION

"ROBERT?" SHE SAID, AND HE RECOGNIZED THE TIMBRE OF HER VOICE before the first syllable of his name had fully sounded.

"Cassie? Cassandra?"

"How are you? How have you been?" she asked.

"Jesus! Cassie! Cassie!"

"Cassandra, Robert. Remember? It's Cassandra. . . . Oh, never mind! Look, I suppose you're pretty upset with me."

"God! Cass . . . I . . . I don't even know what to say. What, uh . . . God! . . . God, I thought . . . I mean, the way you talked to me last week. . . ."

"Yes, I'm sorry about that. I guess I was a little cruel to you, wasn't I? . . . So? How've you been? . . . OK?"

"OK? Have I been OK, you asked me?. . . . Look, Cass. . . . I just . . . I don't understand it. What did I do? What the hell did I *do*? How could you just leave like that without an explanation? And then . . . and then to talk that way to me. . . . To me of all people. . . ."

"I know. OK, look . . . I'm sorry about everything, OK? Really. I didn't mean to hurt you. What can I say to make you feel better?"

"What can you say?"

"Yeah. I don't. . . . This isn't something I enjoy, you know."

"Well how do you think *I* feel? I just don't understand it. I'll *never* understand it, as close as we were. I'm . . . I don't know . . . look, I'm barely starting to function now. A couple of weeks ago I couldn't . . . couldn't eat or sleep. Don't you know what I've been through? Don't you know how I feel? God, Cassie, I'll never understand this. Never . . . I . . . the way I felt about you. . . ."

"OK, Robert. You're only making this harder for me. I never wanted to hurt you. It just happened."

"All right, all right. Look, maybe we can talk, you know? Just sit down and talk. Maybe there's something I did unconsciously to hurt you. . . . Why don't you meet me somewhere, or . . . or maybe come over here. Yeah, we can. . . ."

"No, Robert, listen . . . I . . . I can't do that right now. I'm sorry. It's not possible."

"Not possible! But, then . . . why did you call? What the hell are you calling me for if not. . . .?"

"Um, look. Robert . . . the joint account we had . . . our . . . my accountant wanted to be sure that the taxes were paid on the interest. You know, to see if I had any obligation."

"Obligation? That's what you called for? To see if you had an obligation?"

"Uh, mostly . . . but I wanted to make sure you're OK, too."

"And now that you know I am?" he asked.

"I feel better."

"You do."

"Sure I do. But . . . the taxes . . . were they. . . .?"

"Yeah, yeah sure. Everything got paid."

"I knew it had been. I told them. You're an angel. I . . . I'll always remember you, you know."

"God, Cassie. . . . "

"Look, I've gotta go. I'll be in touch, OK?"

"Cassie, wait."

"Goodbye, Robert. Stay well."

That was Sunday evening, a little under three weeks from the day she'd left. For an hour after, he'd been angry, bitter, but the hostility abated as quickly as it came. By Monday morning, sleepless, haggard, Robert Martin was inarticulate with grief, frozen to his desk chair like a porcelain effigy of lassitude. He made it through his lecture at eleven, barely audible, so that even Auntwon knew to stay away from him when class was through. Then, back in his office, at their habitual meeting time for lunch, Sheldon tried to cheer him, but without effect. "Go home," Shelly said at last. "There's no point in your staying here like this."

He should have listened: Annamae Harper came a little after noon.

Annette pried the door ajar a crack. "Bob," she called, in a minuscule voice, "there's a woman here to see you."

"Who is it? A student?"

"No. Family, I think. . . . She wouldn't say who she is exactly."

"I can't, Annette. I really can't today."

"She's pretty insistent. I think she'll wait here anyway . . . wait for you to come out, I mean."

Great! he thought: *just great! Picked just the perfect day!*

He cupped his forehead in his palms. OK, OK, he told Annette, show her in; show the woman in. He'd force himself through it somehow, get rid of her quick, cut her short, whoever the hell she was, whatever the hell she wanted.

So Annette went back across the hall and ushered in a massive woman, tall and thick-boned, with sufficient gray-beige-surfaced flesh to inundate a lounge chair. He offered her a seat, most reluctantly on his part, and she took the one without arms, unrestrictive, sturdy. The metal gasped a little when she sank onto it, but then recoiled a fraction of an inch to evidence, to its undoubted credit, a sort of defiant and assertive resiliency.

She was Auntwon's 'aahnt,' she informed him: "I come to see you about Auntwon . . . Auntwon Miller, I mean to say." Annamae Harper was her name. She wore a navy dress so dark that it looked black at first, until the windowed daylight, gathering in intensity with the departure of a cloud, grew brilliant enough to catch a fringe of bluish luminescence in the fabric, defining for certain the actual hue. Her hands, which she kept in front of her, folding them delicately over her abdominal hump, were very large and emphatically clean. Not just unsoiled, mind you, but bleached in a way, looking somehow formerly dirty but since then scrubbed and laundered so exhaustively that the minutest adherence had been removed from them and they stood now, sanitized as surgeons' hands, awaiting further duty.

"You know who I mean by Auntwon Miller?" the woman asked, stirring minutely in her chair.

"Yes, of course," answered Robert, forgetting his grief for just a moment in the formidable presence of Annamae. "Of course I know him. Auntwon's a remarkable young man. Really remarkable."

"Remarkable?" she repeated, looking by now potentially combative. "Is that what you say? Oh, he *remarkable* all right. I don't need you to tell me that. Look, Mister . . . Martin, right?"

"Yes, that's right. Robert Martin."

"OK, Mister Martin, look, Auntwon is a fine boy, a special boy. He's . . . he's. . . . God sent him to us. That I know. He sent him for a purpose. You understand?"

He did understand; about Auntwon's uniqueness, anyway. But this was not a good day to discuss it, not a good time. For the brief remission of grief had remitted. Cassie came back into his mind—her coldness, her icy distance on the phone—came back like some re-occurring dream. It was a stranger's voice he'd heard. The one woman he had loved in all his life, the only one, ever, sounding like a person he'd scarcely met. "What can I say to make you feel better?" she had asked, having called about the taxes, nothing more. . . .

"Look, Mrs. Harper, this isn't a very good day for me. I'm . . . I'm just not feeling well today. Maybe we could talk another time. . . . "

"No Sir, no Sir! I come all the way down here to talk and you jus' gonna have to listen to what I gotta say."

He was beyond disputation, beyond defense, empty, drained, voiceless. So he listened, intermittently, Annamae Harper's words in one ear and Cassie's in the other.

Annamae was Auntwon's great aunt, she explained, his maternal grandmother's sister. She and her husband—"Harper" she called him—had raised Auntwon from an infant. First the grandmother had died of "sugar;" legless, blind, decrepit. Then Auntwon's mother "run off," returning two years later to bequeath to the Harpers another fatherless child. "She's a good girl," Annamae said, "a decent girl . . . only, she got herse'f in with a bad crowd."

The story sparked Robert's interest again, displacing Cassie for the moment. Auntwon had been a prodigy, teaching himself to read before he was three with the sole aid of Sesame Street and some magazines left lying around the house. By seven or eight he was devouring books wholesale; by ten he'd become a whiz at math, then science, then everything else he'd put his mind to. Annamae had done what she could with her limited learning and income: she could hardly teach him herself or pay for private school. But, working as a domestic, she had borrowed books from employers, begged for others, bought what she could afford, then plodded with Auntwon to the library when her personal resources ran dry. His schoolmates were merciless. "Uncle Tom," they called him. "White Boy." He'd learned to keep to himself, masquerade his brilliance. When the University of Chicago called, offering him a scholarship, it was a joyous liberation.

The narrative took only a minute or two, flowing from Annamae like a fountain. It was arresting, addictive, and, for the brief time that it lasted, Robert's attention was maintained. But when the words slowed, then halted, and the tale was fully told, Cassie came back into his mind like the reawakening of a dull, incessant pain once one's narcotic dose is spent. Cassie, his Cassie, who would never be with him again; never again in all the years of his life that were to come. . . .

"Did you hear what I said?" asked Annamae.

"Yes, Ma'am. Go ahead." *Never, no matter what he said or did, never again. . . .*

"Well, what did you say to him?"

"Say to him?" *Auntwon, she meant. Auntwon. She was asking. . . .*

"Yes. I axed you what you tolt him to make him wanna just drop right outta his medicine class like that."

It was a numb day, a vacant day; mindless. Shelly'd been right; he should have gone home an hour ago. What purpose was he serving here? What beneficial function?

"Look, Mrs. Harper, I can assure you that I told him nothing of the kind. Nothing to persuade him one way or the other. He's a good student, a remarkable student. That's all."

"Well, if you ditt'nt tell him, then who did?"

How did *he* know? Ask Auntwon, he said to her—not very nicely, either. But then he looked up again and she had tears in her eyes, so that he realized he had hurt this poor, suffering woman, though he hadn't meant to; hadn't meant to at all, but had only spoken so out of his own pain and sorrow. For Cassie, that was, who had been so sweet back at the beginning—that first evening, slipping a napkin in his hand with her number. And sweet lately, too, three weeks ago or thereabouts, sitting by him on the sofa, the onyx hair fringing her cheek. . . .

"He's all I got . . . all *we* got." said the woman, Annamae. "The Lord sent him to us, but He know best, and whatever He do is for the best. I know that. But, look, we had such hope for the boy, and I did everything I could, and Harper, too . . . my husband. . . . "

It was all too much, what with Cassie first, and now this grieving woman, so that he felt his own eyes fill and start to spill over. He would have turned his face away, hidden it, but where was there to turn except away from the woman? And that would have wounded her even more deeply, from her not understanding why. So he kept very still, but the sorrow and the hopelessness which couldn't be suppressed welled over and poured forth, as he dropped his face upon the surface of the desk beneath him, onto his shirt sleeves, wetting them now, unashamedly, and his shoulders shook with sobs.

It was very quiet in the room, but he felt a hand upon his shoulder, rubbing gently, as lightly as his mother's touch upon his skin when he was young and sick in bed.

"Don't cry, now. Don't cry. Iss awright. Itta be awright." It was the woman's voice. Annamae. The hand moved to the back of his head, then another on his brow, lifting it, and an arm against his temple, pulling leftward. And he was against her, his neck to her body, his cheek to the soft abdomen with her breast like a pillow atop his head. "Don't cry now. I'm sorry. I'm so sorry. Itta be awright."

Then he went and told her everything, as though she were some personal analyst or wizened older sister. It was inappropriate, yes, but what was he to do? Could he dam a raging stream? The words poured from him like his tears. He would have told them to a milkman if he had to, a short-order waitress. They sat together in the chairs facing his desk and talked a long while. Annette, out in her office or wandering in the corridor, somehow found the unexpected insight to leave the two of them undisturbedly alone.

"She be back," said Annamae. "Any woman be crazy let a man go like you: any man love a woman way you do. She be crazy." In some unaccountable way, it comforted him.

So when he was done, his own grief fully spent, he let her talk too and listened now without a second's inattention. Auntwon, she related, was their fondest hope, their 'salvation'. A gift from God, he'd been set apart from all the other members of the Harper household, becoming their lone direction, their sole purpose. They'd sacrificed everything for him: she, 'Harper', the other children—her two and Auntwon's sister. They—all of them—had gone without all but the essentials, sharing in their fixed determination to nurture Auntwon's genius.

For the cost of a movie, the boy could have a needed book; for the expense of a vacation, he might take a summer seminar. Libraries, thankfully, were free; museums too on certain days. As for Auntwon, his force-fed education was an established fact. In some uncertain time—five years, ten perhaps—he'd be a doctor, return the family's benefactions tenfold, providing for everyone, everything: aunt, uncle, mother, cousins, sister. Auntwon knew and accepted it, never having questioned the decision—Annamae's decision solely—reading the books she had bought him with her pennies, absorbing their contents effortlessly, obediently.

But when he'd finished with the program and set out, a graduate in medicine, to ply his trade, to prescribe and treat and operate, would he himself be fulfilled? This Annamae had not considered. Kind as she'd been, selfless as she'd always acted, she'd never really known the child, only what she'd wanted him to be.

"You've got to let him follow his heart," Robert told her. "Maybe he's just not cut out to be a doctor . . . a medical doctor, I mean."

"No. No, he is. He gotta be. It's God's will, Mister Martin. It's God's will. What else he gonna do? Jus' teach like you?"

"Well, why not?"

"So he gonna be poor like us, then? With all his brains? No, that ain't what God got planned for him. Not Auntwon, smart as he always been. I won't have it, Mister Martin, him havin' to struggle the way we do! Auntwon just ain't gon' be poor like we been. He ain't! I won't have it! Not with all them brains, you hear?"

"Well, *I'm* not poor," said Robert. "I'm a different kind of doctor, but I do all right."

"On a teacher's salary?" asked Annamae, shaking her head.

"Yeah. A teacher at the university here gets paid pretty well. . . . And then there's extra income from publications. . . ."

"What that mean?"

"Books you write, articles. . . . "

"You writ a book?"

"Yeah, I did. A big seller, too. Auntwon could. . . . "

"They pay you fo' it, that book?"

"Sure did. A lot, too."

"No foolin'! How much?"

She'd asked, so he told her. It must have been a revelation of some kind, too, for Annamae's face changed, grew—how might one describe it?—contemplative, perhaps. Like the face of Columbus when he first caught sight of land, or Washington at Trenton with the Hessians in their bunks, or Sutter at his mill when the very first piece of gold rattled glittering in his trough. She didn't say another thing, just stood and shook his hand and left, and he never heard a doubting word from her again.

Miss Lipsky, of all people! Who would have dreamed it? Yet here she was with Auntwon, lingering in her place one row in front of him, one diagonal seat away, sitting there inert, with her overstuffed notebook stowed silent on the desk top. As the students filed out, singly or in pairs, tall, befreckled Jeffrey Carns came up to ask a question, some old, familiar, standard issue raised at least once by someone in the course, once at least without fail, every quarter History 321 had been offered. Robert answered it by rote, succinctly: Well, actually Lorenzo de' Medici *may* have known about the Pazzi conspiracy of 1478, just not the specific time and place. OK? Jeffrey seemed satisfied. He stepped out through the doorway, and Auntwon came at once to do his customary obeisance, ambling toward the lecturer's desk up front, as always, but today, amazingly, with Miss Sandra Lipsky in tow.

"Man, whatchu *say* to her th' other day, Doc?" Auntwon asked, standing by the corner of the desk, Miss Lipsky's hairline just visible over his right shoulder.

It was Friday, May 5, six weeks into the academic quarter, a little over three since Cassie'd left. And then her phone call five days before, debilitating for a while, but finally resulting in a second act of closure, a more conclusive one for him, so that he'd healed a little further afterward. This last recovery, painful at first, had advanced materially with Annamae's visit. So Robert's talk with Auntwon's 'aahntie' had been useful in some peculiar way; maybe putting trouble in perspective, hers and his, played out each to each, like strangers mutually commiserating on a plane. Not that Cassie was forgotten—far from it—but Robert had scarred over from his anguish quite enough by now to leave him relatively sociable. Thus dialogue with Auntwon—and even Miss Lipsky, if it came to that—was truly welcome in a way that it could not have been before for three weeks past.

"You musta told her somepin' extra special." The kid was beaming, his face all teeth and lines. "C'mon, Doc, whadju say to her? I gotta know."

"Your Aunt?" asked Robert, teasing a little, holding back a smile.

"Yeah. Yeah. C'mon, man. It musta been, like, *real* good." He was glowing, radiant: yet another Auntwon, ghettoesque in diction, as before, but ebullient in manner, joyful. He looked like a worker who had lost his job, won the lottery, then bought the very company that had fired him. Miss Lipsky, her mouth now visible beside Auntwon's shoulder, smiled mutely.

"Doc here saved my ass th' other day," Auntwon said, half-turning backward. Miss Lipsky smiled a bit more eagerly and nodded. She'd moved a couple of inches to her right, Auntwon having shifted as much to his left, so that the whole of her face was now in view and maybe a third of the light blue sweater she had on. She was ten pounds overweight, twelve perhaps, but pleasant-looking, with a cream complexion and dark brown eyes like Cassie's. Auntwon, though an inch or two her inferior in height, had a fine, intelligent face, and, with his intellect and dynamism, was no less attractive than she, no less interesting. By campus standards, they made a tolerable couple. And Auntwon seemed happy, glowing, so maybe in the throes of incipient infatuation. Ah, Robert remembered that sensation well, as though he'd lived it a week before; a day! So sweet and delicious a feeling that he might have felt a twinge of resentment—of veritable envy—had the couple been other than the two familiar kids before him now.

"So whadju say?" asked Auntwon for the fourth time.

"I told her you were gonna make a lot of money writing books."

"Like you, you mean?"

"Yep."

"What, like a million bucks?"

"Yep. . . . Well . . . more like seven hundred and forty thousand."

"*Damn*, Doc, you the *Man*! God *damn*!" He turned to Miss Lipsky. "Ain't he, though? Ain't he? God *damn*!"

Robert smiled. It was nice to smile; nice, too, to see somebody else smiling, happy. Particularly Auntwon.

"Hey, you better today. I can tell." Auntwon turned to Miss Lipsky again. "Don't he seem better to you?"

Miss Lipsky, smiling mutely, nodded yes.

Now this was odd, singular. Even Robert sensed it, though he clearly lacked the wherewithal to imagine the reason for the oddness, let alone foresee its fruitful and dramatic outcome.

Yet here was Auntwon Miller, heard speaking to another student. That was a remarkable first, so clearly, therefore, odd. And this other student to whom Auntwon spoke: well, she wasn't just anyone, but Miss Sandra Lipsky, with whom no one had much been noted to converse. Thus far, then, odd and odd doubly. But in conclusion, to top them both off, triply and climactically peculiar, the said Miss Lipsky, that furious stenographer, writing much but speaking little and appearing to take interest in her surroundings only for the purpose of encapsulating them in notes; this same Miss Lipsky seemed somehow to be aware of the nature and possibly the cause of her professor's late mental lassitude. This was strange indeed, but since Robert lacked the requisite foresight to decode it, he simply leaned back in his desk chair and watched events unfold.

"Sandy here read your book," said Auntwon.

Robert nodded. "*Colangio*?"

"Yeah, sure. You got another one?"

"No. . . . No, silly question." He turned to the girl. "Well, what did you think?"

"It's good, Dr. Martin. *Really* good."

"Well thanks. I guess I. . . . "

"She don't understand somefin', though," interjected Auntwon. "Same thing as I axed you."

"About Colangio becoming a hermit?"

"Yes," said the girl, "exactly." She stepped all the way around Auntwon to a place at the front of the desk. There was a sheepish sort of grin on her face now, silly and self-conscious. She didn't look at Robert directly, but, rather, glanced over at Auntwon, then back at the surface of the desk, seeming, if anything, a little more silly or shy than before. . . . In love, thought Robert. Indisputably. These kids invariably had some amazing surprise in store for you.

"Sandy got a theory, fo' you." Auntwon poked at the girl with a finger. "OK, tell him. Go on."

"Well," she began, dimpled and reddening, "I think it was the woman . . . his wife, you know?"

"Ginevra," Robert offered.

"Yes, that's right, Ginevra. . . . I think . . . I think he . . . that he loved her so much that nothing else was important to him after he got back together with her. After she left that convent and all."

"Yes, there may be some validity to that. You know when I wrote the book I had never understood exactly . . . well . . . I had never known anyone as romantically involved as that, you know?"

"And you do now?" she asked.

"Yes, a few. . . . uh, friends of mine and . . . well, other people."

"So . . . then . . . do you think I'm right? That that's the explanation?"

"I don't know. As I told Auntwon the other day, a good historian never speculates. But, all right, if I had to guess, I'd say there had to be another reason for it, a different one."

"Why?"

"Well, mostly because of the chronology. He—Adalberto, that is—wrote his last extant letter on November 6, 1503. The one to Machiavelli about his unemployment. You may have noticed it; it's quoted in the book."

"Yes, near the end, right?"

"Right. Anyway, he didn't get together with Ginevra for another seven weeks. He stopped his journal at the same time too, six or seven weeks before she even left the convent she was living in."

"But maybe he—*they*—were planning it."

"Maybe. But it still doesn't explain all the money he acquired—I mean, he bought that huge palace and everything. And the journal . . . it just stops at the same time—November 14, I think it is—with no mention of Ginevra at all. No, I think there's some other factor we know nothing about. Not that I'm speculating what that might be, though."

"I guess that makes sense," said the girl, hugging the thick notebook to her chest and swaying a little from side to side on one foot.

"Well it does and it doesn't. We still don't have a reasonable explanation. But what you say is worth considering and—who knows?—maybe it'll be proven right in the end."

"Yeah," Auntwon added, "Doc said they found some more papers of Colangio's just, like, a year ago."

"Really?" The girl looked up now with manifest interest. "What kind of papers?"

"Oh, they're probably nothing. Such things usually are. . . . Anyway, I'm glad you took the time to read the book and that it spurred your interest. It was thoughtful of Auntwon to have given it to you to read."

"No, Doc," said the boy, "she got it at the Barnes and Noble jus' like me. . . . Hey, man," Auntwon chuckled, "now you owe us eight dollars, right? Fo' apiece?"

"Absolutely. I'm flattered that you both made the effort. . . . So, you want your eight bucks now?"

"Naw, man. Look, you can keep the cash, OK? We gonna let you off the hook this time—right Sandy?" The girl smiled again. "But you gotta do us kinda like a favor. In exchange, you know?"

"A favor?"

"Yeah, like that."

"Well, what is it?"

"Naw, firs' you gotta say you gon' do it, and then I'm'on tell you what it is."

"Now how can I promise you if I. . . . "

"Man! It ain't nuffin' bad. You think I ax you to do somefin' bad?"

"No, but still, I. . . . "

"C'mon, Doc, you got to trus' me now, you know? C'mon, man—promise!"

Well, what the hell, Robert thought: "OK, OK, I promise. . . . So what's the favor?"

"OK, listen up: you gotta come wif us to a party. Over to Sandy's place. She havin' some folks over to . . . to, like, he'p me celebrate."

"Celebrate?"

"Yeah. You know, gettin' outta that science shit and all like that."

"So it's OK?. . . . With your aunt, I mean—your changing majors?"

"Yeah, sure. I jus' gotta write that book now is all. That ain't no thang. . . . So what? You gon' come? You awready promised, man."

"Sure, Auntwon. What else I got to do?"

"Great! Hey, Doc, you startin' to talk intelligibly now. . . . And listen up, man, one mo' thang: I totally disagree wif Sandy-here's postulate."

"About Colangio? You mean with Ginevra?"

"Yeah, like that bein' the sole cause and all. You know I can relate to that Colangio dude like a brother ('brovver', he said). That book be like my own sad tale—all but fo' that love part; you know what I'm sayin?"

"Yeah, come to think of it, I can really see that, Auntwon. There are a lot of parallels that I wouldn't have imagined until I talked with your aunt. She told me. . . ."

"Yeah, yeah, don' pay no attention to nuffin' she say. She be, like, biased and shit, you know? Anyways, like I said, I can relate to the dude; whatchu got is a man that jus' outta noplace give up evvythang he up till then devote his whole life to achievin', right?"

"Sure, in a way," said Robert. "I guess that's true."

"Well, I don' know nuffin 'bout his girl friend, but love ain't no more'n, like, a chemical reaction, you know what I'm sayin'?"

"Yeah, right, I had that lecture a week ago."

"Say what, man? Whatchu mean?"

"Nothing. Never mind. Somebody already explained to me about oxytocin and all that chemistry of love business."

"OK, cool, man. You up on thangs then, Doc; I shoulda knowed. OK, so then you realize that shit don't last too long. It only work fo' a while and then it be like totally gone, right?"

"I've heard tell."

"OK, so then anybody change that much fo' that long, it gotta be like more fundamental, right? Diff'ent chemistry, you know what I'm sayin'? You know fo' a dude like Colangio to give up evvythang he believe in and, like, aspire to—that gotta be like a change in his—you know—*weltanschauung* and shit, right? Like a . . . like a . . . a *epiphany* sort of thang. You know, like Moses and Saul of Tarsus wif them burnin' bushes or Jean Jacques Rousseau an' that, like, spiritual conversion? You know what I'm sayin?"

"Yeah, maybe. I see what you mean, but we'll probably never know for sure."

"Yeah, you prob'ly right. Anyway Sandy be wrong wif that love theory. But I wanted you to hear it anyway."

"Oh? Why?" The girl had by now drifted over to the window and stood looking out at the intermittent sunlight. Some object on the mall must have caught her eye, for she seemed oblivious to the conversation behind her, even with the periodic mention of her name.

"Man, 'at be like a classic example of how women think—you know, always wif that love and shit as a cause fo' evvythang they don't ezackly understand. Too mucha that oxytocin and all them other vasoactive amines jammin' on they brains."

Robert laughed. The kid was smart. No doubt about that. He'd make a fine historian, once disabused of his speculative tendencies and rapper prose. An evening in his company would be a delight, not to be blunted by the likes of Miss Lipsky or whoever else happened to turn up. Besides, the university encouraged fraternization between faculty and students, so long as the proper decorum was maintained. It was something he had largely foregone for the sake of Cassie these past five years. . . . Well, that was over now; time for him to get out of the doldrums and back into society again. And if these kids were amenable, their impromptu little party wouldn't be the least appropriate place to start. What the hell, it might even be fun!

CHAPTER SIX

ASSIGNATION

AUNTWON HAD SAID SEVEN, SO HE FIGURED QUARTER-AFTER WOULD BE good. It was at the woman's place, Miss Lipsky's, just north of the university on forty-seventh. A yellow brick apartment building, they told him. Park out in front. He took along a bottle of *pinot noir*, Cassie's favorite wine. She'd left behind a case of it the day she walked out with all the other things she'd laid claim to as hers. Probably not worth carting away with her, now that she could have Chateau Rothschild or whatever the hell else it was your profligate millionaires consumed. Shelly had a couple of bottles of the *pinot* now, offerings that Robert dragged along to meals Rochelle had cooked for him. "Oh, *wine!*" she'd said, invariably, then set it on the counter top unopened. Shelly drank Scotch and Dr. Pepper, alone or in combination. Maybe the *pinot* reminded them both too much of Cassie to be potable. So the Rogovins had gone and stuck each proffered bottle on a shelf, then opened something else: Burgundy or riesling or a nice sauterne. One day they'd drag the *pinot* over to someone else's place for dinner: relatives, maybe, or fellow faculty—folks who'd never even *heard* the name of Cassie Fullerton, and thus could drink the goddamn stuff in peace.

Like these kids here, his students. All they knew of Cassie was that day outside the lecture room. "Don't be maudlin, Robert," she had told him, then turned her back and vanished down the corridor. Hell, let the students drink her wine—Miss Lipsky anyway; she was of age. Fermented grapes in whatever form would be pretty much the same to her.

It was twenty-after-seven when he pulled up. Lots of places on the street to park: the habitat of student residents who didn't need a car, so left their Mustangs and Camaros back in Duluth or Springfield with Mom and Dad. It was a mixed neighborhood, but safe-looking, clean; some younger children lingering on the sidewalks, exulting in the final play of daylight before their ultimate incarceration at dusk.

He stopped in front of the building's entrance. It was an older structure, pre-war, late '30's, early '40's, six or seven stories of dirty-amber brick with grated casement windows. Robert tucked the wine beneath his arm and pressed the button alongside number 212. "S. Lipsky," read the narrow strip of characters beside it, in elegant hand-lettering that looked as nicely and professionally done as the engraved text of a wedding invitation.

"That you, Doc?" said Auntwon's voice. "Ho'd on. I'm gettin' it."

The buzzer sounded and he stepped into an entryway, antiquated, with worn carpeting and plastered cracks in the ceiling. It was dustless, though, and clean, well-maintained; the paint uniform and fresh; the carpet worn evenly from wall to wall, out beyond the normal flow of traffic—worn, that is, more by a vacuum's constant ministrations than from countless years of footsteps. There was an elevator to his right, but he took the stairway opposite. One flight up, number 212 faced him directly as he came up from the stairwell.

Miss Lipsky opened the door, smiling in a self-conscious sort of way. She had on tight jeans and a loose beige sweater that made her look slimmer than she'd looked in class, not unattractive. Auntwon was standing two feet behind her, clad trendily in baggy khaki pants and an oversize sweatshirt, the top of his head defined by a blue baseball cap turned backward so that an arc of forehead skin showed errantly through the space above its elastic rim.

"See? What I tell you, Sandy? See? I to'd you he'd come!"

The girl turned her head back toward Auntwon, who on his part made a sort of knowing face. Complicit; conspiratorial. There was something up between them, clearly, Robert thought. God, this might turn out to be . . . what? . . . Oh, hell, their engagement party, maybe, for all one knew. Sure: stranger things had happened in the past nine years than that, from gay student orgies to the shy little co-ed in History

103 who turned out to be a porn star. Yes, one really couldn't tell: maybe this evening these two nice kids would hit him with a real surprise!

Miss Lipsky smiled again wanly, made a sort of subtle bow, then backed off toward the kitchen. As she moved away, Auntwon stepped around her, put out his hand, grasped Robert high up on the arm—squeezing affectionately, as was his custom—and led him past a kind of low half-wall with plants atop it into the center of the living room.

It was exactly the sort of interior he'd visualized. L-shaped front room-dining room combination, kitchen off the latter; hallway running back to whatever else the place contained: two bedrooms, most likely; single bath. A lot of students had lived in such apartments when he was in grad school. Some of the faculty too; many still did. Everything looked . . . what? Not brand new; nor very old either. The sofa, the lounge chairs, the dining room set: they went with the apartment somehow, fit in; neither new nor old, neither elegant nor tacky. They were . . . they were . . . what? He thought about it while Auntwon led him to a big gray sofa and all but tucked him into it. . . . Now seated, amid the accumulated scents emitted by the furniture, in contact with the fabric minutely worn in only one specific way, he saw its history, felt its past. Yes: parents' things, these were; typical. Bought new, cared for, then replaced and given to the college kid when Ken or Natalie or Jessica—or Sandra Lipsky, here—departed the family home.

"Hey, Doc . . . *man*! Thass cool, man; I mean, you showin' up and all. Man, I ditten know for sure you was gonna make it till I heard you voice downstairs, you know what I'm sayin'?"

"Why? I promised you I'd come, didn't I?"

"Yeah, yeah, sure. That don't mean nuffin mos' t' time wif mos' folks. You a hon'able man, Doc. Trus'worvvy, you know?" Auntwon arched an eyebrow and looked over his shoulder toward the kitchen whence an acrid odor had arisen which was now wafting in thick and palpable as fog to where they sat. There was a sound, as of water splashing in a sink, then another like the dull thud of a pan being dropped on porcelain: clunk! Then water began to splash again.

"Hey, whatchu wann' drink, man? You want somma this here wine you brought? I go get a corkscrew."

"No, no, that's OK, Auntwon. Look, I don't really feel like any wine right now. I just brought it. . . . "

"What, to get rid of it, I bet. . . . Somebody prob'bly give it to you, and then you take it over here, and then Sandy prob'bly take it over to some ovver dude's house one day. Damn bottle prob'bly been circulatin' fo' ten years like that, like one-a them Susan B. Anthony dollars nobody ever use. Ain't nobody ever gonna finally drink it, I bet."

He set the bottle on the coffee table in front of the sofa, disengaging his fingers from its neck the way a poulterer might let loose a dead chicken. "OK, OK, how 'bout some Coke or Seven Up or somefin' like that? Or maybe tea? What? Sandy makin' dinner; you could smell it." The boy leaned over, down close to Robert's ear, and in a voice marginally louder than a whisper added: "I ain't sure we gonna be able to eat any of this shit, though; you know what I"m sayin?"

"Well, that's all right. It's fine with me if we all go out for something; or order in from somewhere—on me, I mean. . . . So how many more people do you think are coming—do you have any idea?"

"Huh? Oh yeah. . . . I don' know fo' sure. . . . I mean, not e'zackly. We see, OK?"

"Sure. That's fine with me."

Auntwon nodded, pursed his lips, then pointed with a thumb toward the wine. "Man, you smart not to drink that shit." He bent down, pushed the *pinot* over to the far side of the coffee table, then sat down next to Robert on the couch.

"What, *pinot noir?*"

"Yeah. Yeah, that . . . whatever, *pinot* shit and . . . like, all that ovver shit they drink. Beer and shit like that, you know what I'm sayin'? It's the alcohol, man. You know, evvy time dude be like takin' in, like, one glass-a wine or, like, one bottle-a beer. . . . Any alcohol, I mean—you know what I'm sayin?—it, like, kill a hundred brain cells, you know? Like, neurons. That's what they say. . . . Me, I ain't got no hundred neurons to give up jus' like that. I mean, like, poof! there go the Battle of Fornovo or, like . . . the League of Cambrai or . . . or . . . Pico della Mirandola, you know what I'm sayin'?" Robert nodded. "Me, I want to retain that shit; *all* that shit, man. Evvythang, you know? Like you, Doc. I want me a mind like you. Man, you oughtn't to drink that alcohol shit neither. We ain't got but, like, a billion neurons to begin wif, and—you and me, man—we jus' cain't risk losin' a single one. You know what I'm sayin'?"

"Yeah, I guess. . . . So . . . where did you learn all this stuff, anyway? . . . I mean, about the alcohol and all."

"Man, I don' know. Some science class or ovver I guess. Or maybe I read it someplace. I don' know."

"You've got a lot of knowledge in that head of yours, but. . . ."

". . . .what? But what, man?"

"Well, you won't get offended...?"

"Naw, man . . . Doc. You could say 'bout anythang wifout offendin' me. . . . I mean, like, excep' fo' a . . . well, like a racial slur or somefin'. . . . Shit, even that be OK f'om you, 'cause I know you woot'n mean nuffin by it, you know what I'm sayin'?"

"Yeah. Thanks. That's nice. . . . Anyway, what I wanted to say. . . . You know, it doesn't bother me the way you talk. I mean, I'm kind of getting used to it by now. I guess it kind of sounds natural to me—you understand?"

"Yeah, sure. I, like, explained that whole thang to you, right?"

"Right. You did. And it was a nice explanation, too. Flattering, I mean—to me. . . . But . . . look . . . you're thinking of teaching some day, aren't you? I mean, you said that was what you had in mind if you switched your major to history, right?"

"Yeah, sure. Like you, man—Doc. Jus' like you."

"Well that's fine, but—now don't take this wrong, OK? . . . Look, Auntwon, you won't be able to teach the kind of stuff I do in . . . well, whatever dialect you call it: Ebonics or whatever. You understand?"

"Yeah, sure. Man, I awready showed you I can talk however . . . OK, that I can converse in whatever type of language I find requisite to the duties I have to perform. OK? How's that? That better?"

"Yes. Well, maybe something in-between the two. . . . Look, I'm not saying this for *my* sake, you know. You're going to have a lot of colleagues to deal with wherever you work—whatever institution you wind up teaching at, you understand?"

Auntwon nodded.

"Well, they're going to be friends of yours too, like me. It's just that they'll expect a certain . . . I don't know, maybe professional demeanor, I guess. Do you understand what I'm saying?"

"Sure, Doc. Sure I do."

"Unless you want to teach African-American history in a high school or something. . . ."

"Shit, man, you kiddin'?"

"I didn't think so."

"No, I don't mean it like that, Doc. I mean, well, evvy black kid got to know about his . . . uh, forbears . . . progenitors, you know? Like I read 'bout evvythang there is to read about Dr. King and Malcolm and . . . you know, DuBois and Marcus Garvey and all like that, but . . . well, that jus' a *part* of history, you know what I'm sayin'? Look-a-here, you like jazz?"

"Yeah, sure."

"Well, jazz is black music pure and simple, you know? Like Charlie Parker, Mingus, Coltrane? But if I was gonna teach, like . . . well, let's say music history or music theory, OK? Well you got to start with the basics; like way befo' they was a thang called jazz. I mean, what? you gonna skip, like, Bach and Mozart? Like, Beethoven, fo' 'xample; you gonna skip all that shit he done? I mean like the chamber music and evvythang. And . . . and . . . like Poulenc and Corelli and Hindemit'— uh, Hinde*mith*—you know what I'm sayin'? How you gonna understand music that way, man? Shit, you cain't even understand what jazz *is* wifout knowin' what came befo' it. . . . Like OK, OK, let's say the black man invented blues, OK? I mean, that's, like, a accomplishment, right? Nobody gonna argue wif that. But, shit, somebody a long time befo' that come up wif musical notation, and . . . uh, like polyphony and then chords and shit . . . and . . . and what about the saxophone and the fuckin' *piano*, man?—oh, sorry Doc, I ditten mean to cuss like that in front of you. But you understand what I'm sayin', though: jus' 'cause I'm black don' mean I got to deny all the greatness of non-black cultural achievement. I mean, maybe one percent of my DNA say I'm black; all the rest is just plain human. . . . Hey I'm sorry 'bout the cussin', though. I guess I got, like, carried away and shit."

"Yeah, that's OK. It's OK. . . . God, Auntwon, you're really something, you know? . . . Look, you *do* know what I mean, though—about the language thing—don't you?"

"Sure, man. And you got to understand what I said; you know, about history bein' history period and not jus', like, one little part of somefin' to the exclusion of evvythang else right? . . . But you know, you right about whatchu say. I'm gonna. . . . Hey, look-a-here; I'll make a deal witchu, OK? You be nice to Sandy tonight and I . . . I'll try to talk . . . uh, like in a more polished manner. . . . I mean wif—*with*—you too, OK?"

"Sure. OK. That would be nice. But with, uh . . . Sandy. . . . Why *wouldn't* I be nice to her?"

"No, but you gotta . . . I'd like you to be extra specially nice tonight, OK?"

"Why? Is it her birthday or something?"

"Yeah, somethin' like that. You promise?"

"Sure. Why not? . . . Um, by the way, Auntwon, do you really know as much as all that about classical music? I mean not just the composers' names and dates, but...?"

"Sure, Doc. Don't . . . uh, *doesn't* everybody?"

The food was inedible. If Sandra Lipsky had any talent whatever in her stenographic soul, it was assuredly not culinary. Nor conversational, either, for the three of them sat in utter silence through the meal. No one else showed up, so there were only Robert, Auntwon, and the putative chef, scraping the seared flesh from their chicken, crackling with their teeth on the uncooked rice. Mercifully, the girl had bought a loaf of fresh-baked bread that morning, a crisp but doughy deli rye; and that, sliced thick by hand and spread with soft, salted butter from a stick, served acceptably, in lieu of an entree, for the substance of their dinner.

"I'm afraid I'm not much of a substitute for your other friends," Robert said when they had finished. "Weren't the others. . . . Uh, couldn't they come?"

"No. That's right, Doc. They must've all had other . . . uh, activities tonight. Isn't that right, Sandy?"

"We didn't. . . ." the girl began to say. "... I mean . . . there wasn't anybody else. . . . Uh, nobody else was invited but you."

"I don't understand. I thought. . . ."

Just then Auntwon stood up and pushed his chair back. "Look, Doc," he said, "... uh, Sandy. . . . I gotta split, OK?"

Robert looked at his watch, which said 8:37. Not much of a party after all, he thought. He hoped mightily that it wasn't *really* the poor girl's birthday, but rather some less significant event: a celebration for a successful paper of hers, say, or the offer of a summer job. . . . Well, whatever the occasion, whatever the circumstances, it had been nice of the two young kids to try and get him out for an evening, to treat him so considerately in the very worst season of his life. Yes, it had been thoughtful and considerate and kind.

He nodded to himself, set his napkin on the table, smiled across its cluttered surface at the seated Sandra, smiled over his right shoulder at the now standing Auntwon, then slid his chair back and started to get up.

"I guess you guys have work to do anyway. . . . For your classes I mean. . . . Look, Auntwon, I'll head out with you . . . uh, Miss Lipsky, thanks for the fine meal. I . . . I really have enjoyed the evening."

"No, Doc," said Auntwon, "you don't have to leave just yet. Why don't you hang out here for a while . . . I mean, uh, stay around here for a while with Sandy? You two can talk a little, OK?"

"No, no, hold on. I'm gonna go ahead and take off too. I'll head out with you, Auntwon." The girl, who had gotten up and was now standing at eye level across the table from him with a soiled dish in her hand, set the dish back down, turned on her heels, and walked away down the unilluminated hallway without another word.

"See what you done!" said Auntwon in a loud whisper, looking amazingly distressed. "A deal's a deal, man."

"What? What did I do?"

"She—Sandy, I mean—she wanna spend some time witchu. Don'tchu get it?"

"What do you mean? Isn't she...? I mean, I thought she was your. . . . "

"Mine! Shit! White woman like that? My auntie kill me. . . . OK, OK, come on out here wit' me. Sh-e-e-e-it!" Auntwon pulled him to the door of the apartment, opened it, then turned and hollered down the hallway the girl had just traversed: "Hey, Sandy, we goin' out fo' a minute. Be right back, hear?" There was no response.

Auntwon led him out and closed the door—not latched, but just touching the jamb—then dragged him by an elbow over to the stairwell, maybe ten feet away from the apartment's entrance.

"Look, Doc, you cain't jus' split like that. I mean, like, now; so quick. . . . Sandy was countin' on you stayin' fo' a while, you know what I'm sayin'?"

"No, Auntwon, I *don't* know what you're saying. Suppose you explain it to me."

"Look, man . . . Doc . . . Sandy really dig you, you know? She jus', you know, wanna spend a little time witchu . . . uh, quality time, you know what I'm sayin'? Cain't hurt nuffin'."

"Jesus, Auntwon! What the hell are you talking about ? You mean you. . . . you set this whole thing up, the two of you? That's why you asked me over? For some party that wasn't really a party, but instead some kind of . . . of . . . what . . . a date?"

"Yeah, yeah, she always be talkin' how you so cute and shit. How crazy you' girl friend got to be. So I figure, look, she want some company; you got to ha' some company jus' about now. That's what I come to the conclusion you need, Doc. . . . 'Bout time to clean out them tubes, you know what I'm sayin'?"

It wasn't funny . . . but then it was, sort of, in a mistaken kind of way, so he bit his lip, to some effect. "OK, so—what?—you're trying to get me laid too? That's just what Sheldon said the other day. Same thing exactly. God, the two of you!"

"Dr. Rogovin, you mean? He tol' you too, huh? See, Doc? Then this be like a second opinion; like a complimentary consultation, OK? Hey, man, you got to go fo' it, you know what I'm sayin'?"

How could he even suggest that? What the hell had they been thinking of, the two of them? "God, Auntwon, what's the matter with you? You know I can't do anything like that! Come on! You must know that I can't and won't and . . . and wouldn't under any circumstances. You're smart enough to know that. You of all people! . . . Look . . . look, I'm leaving. You explain it to her. That's the *least* you can do."

"No, ho'd on, Doc. Ho'd on." Auntwon took his arm, but gently, the way he'd grasped it before, with just a hint of pressure on the sleeve. It was the way he'd always touched him: every day of every class, three days a week, for the past four weeks of the quarter since Cassie'd vanished down the gray-tiled corridor. . . .

"You leave now, how she gonna feel? Walk right out, not even say goodbye, thanks for the meal. . . . "

"No, I *did*. I thanked her. . . . "

"Not proper, though. *Damn*, you got up and like to run out wif me 'fore she even got the table clear. That ain't right, man. OK, maybe she cook like shit but that don't mean you got to do her like that. Man, you ought to understand better 'n anybody what that feel like. After what you been through. . . . I was there, too. I seen it. You wanna treat somebody else the same way you got treated? Man, I don' get that. That jus' don' make no sense."

"So what do you expect me to do? How would you suggest I handle it now?"

"OK, listen up, man: Jus' go back in and talk to her fo' a while, show the lady some respec'. Half a hour, maybe. Tell her you sad, you know? Melancholy, right? Despondent, disconsolate. In the throes of a severe depression. Like white folks talk, you know? Say she a sweet kid, that if you was ready to go out wif some woman, it might be her. You ain't gotta fuck some lady to be nice—sorry, Doc, but I got to say it. Thass what I'd do, and I ain't even got shit done to me like you did. If I had, I'd be even nicer'n what I awready to'd you."

Antwon started smiling again, and it was infectious. Robert couldn't bite his lip this time, for it had been retracted laterally, top and bottom, up and down, pulled out of reach of even the most prescient of incisors by the merriment muscles of his face. Grinning almost as broadly as Auntwon had when he'd first appeared in the doorway a couple of hours earlier, Robert gave a hesitant consent:

"Auntwon, you missed your profession, you know? You should've been a salesman."

"Me? Shit, man . . . Doc . . . salesman be almost as bad as goin' to medical school."

She was sitting in an armchair facing the sofa when he stepped back through the door, the side of her face illumined starkly by a floor lamp.

"I . . . I thought you'd left," she said.

"Uh, no. . . . Look, I'll keep you company for a while. I've got a couple of minutes before I have to go."

"Why? . . . I mean, where do you have to be so early? It isn't even nine yet."

He stepped back over to the couch and sat down, across the coffee table from her. The tangential light made her look older. And sad, very sad, like an innocent child suddenly betrayed in its trust. He guessed she was twenty-five, or maybe a year or two more.

"It's not that," he explained. "Not a time thing. Just that . . . I don't know . . . I've been kind of down lately. This is really my first time out in a while . . . I mean . . . out anywhere."

"I understand," she said. "I know what you've been through."

"You know? . . . What? You mean from Auntwon? Did he tell you about my . . . about what happened?"

"Auntwon? No, Auntwon didn't say anything—about you, I mean. . . . I think *I* was the one who told *him*."

"Wait a minute. I don't understand. . . . If it was you who said something to Auntwon, how did *you* know? How much could you guys . . . uh . . . what exactly did you hear that day?"

"Hear? . . . Oh! . . . no, it wasn't like that at all. I know what you mean. . . . When that woman came to see you, right? . . . No, I . . . it wasn't that I *heard* anything; I just kind of *know* things. I *read* them. Here, wait, I'll show you." She got up and went back down the hall. A light flashed on through an open doorway, then blinked out again as she stepped back into view. She came out toward him with a kind of notebook in her hand, moved around the coffee table, and sat down directly beside him on the sofa.

It wasn't exactly a notebook that she brought, but something larger: an artist's drawing pad, oversize, maybe twelve-by-fifteen. She shuffled through it, then spread it open on the table's surface in front of him. The right-hand page showed a diagram, a double circle sectored pie-like by intersecting diametric lines. Within each sector lay a little clump of neatly-printed text, done nicely in flowing italic, just like the name downstairs in the narrow plasticized strip beside the doorbell.

"What is it?" he asked.

"It's your chart."

"My chart? . . . Of what?"

"Your horoscope."

"What, like astrology?"

"Yep. It's for a Virgo. You're a Virgo, right? August 20, 1962."

"Yeah, that's right. Where'd you...?"

"Oh, there's lots of places. The faculty directory, the Internet. . . . Hey, you're in *Who's Who*, didn't you know?"

"Yeah, I did. But . . . look, this astrology stuff . . . you're not serious about it, are you? I mean, this diagram, you really took the trouble to plot something like that out?"

"Sure. It works. . . . Hey, I knew about your problem, didn't I? I know you're sad, you've been hurt by someone close to you. Betrayed, it says here. See this line? It's Jupiter."

"Come on!"

"No, really, you can tell things. . . . Here, let me see your palm."

"My palm?"

"Yeah, I took a course. I can get more information for you. . . . You know, I wouldn't just do this for anyone, but you're so . . . so *nice*."

"Look, Miss Lipsky. . . . "

"Sandy."

"OK, Sandra—Sandy. This is all very interesting, but now I really *do* have to go. I . . . I'll talk to you about it tomorrow after class."

"OK, I understand. Just let me see your palm first. Then I won't argue with you. I'll show you to the door if you like."

He opened both hands, and she took the right one, pulling it gently toward a table lamp beside her. It wound up in her lap, whereupon she started tracing the creases on it with a fingertip, then rubbing his palm the way a lover would, delicately and rhythmically in a two-inch circle. In another situation, at another time, it would have been powerfully and unmistakably erotic.

"Look, Sandra, this just isn't something I feel comfortable with. I. . . ."

"What? I'm just doing a reading for you. I mean, I'm not, like, holding your hand or anything. . . . OK, wait, just let me finish. . . . Here. . . ." She slid her finger down the center of his palm. "This is your life line, see?" She, Miss Lipsky, had a half-smile on her face, coquettish, in a perfectly overt way.

"OK, that's. . . . "

"Wait. Look. See how it kind of branches off right here in the middle?" She used her fingertip again. Seductive or crazy, he wasn't precisely sure which, but it was time to go. Definitely time to go.

"That supports what the planets say, Jupiter especially. See? It's a major change in your life, right here. . . . You're thirty-seven, right? I know you are. See how the angulation comes a little before halfway? That means a major change in your life right about now. . . . I could tell you a lot more if I knew some other things: the exact time of day you were born, the place, the birth information of . . . of the woman you were seeing."

The woman he was seeing! He pulled his hand away and stood up, looking down at her. "OK, look, I'm sorry. I've got to go. I . . . I'll talk to you tomorrow in class."

"No, no," she said, clearly agitated now, "you sit back down here! I'm not done yet. . . . Listen, Dr. Martin, I went to a lot of trouble to run this chart for you. The least you could do is wait till I'm finished. You might learn something, you know? Maybe . . . maybe if you'd paid more attention to your astral projections in the first place, you wouldn't have even *had* your . . . you know . . . problem."

He turned to face her and she stood to meet his gaze, angry, confrontational. "*My* problem?" he told her. "This isn't *my* problem, this pseudoscientific crap you came up with. Your . . . your charts and palm readings. This stuff is ridiculous. I can't understand how anybody, any intelligent person, would believe such total nonsense. You . . . you must be crazy to think I would. . . . "

Her eyes were filling, brimming, her mouth trembling. It cut him short. He hadn't meant to say what he had, or maybe he *had* meant it, all of it, but would have said it in a different tone, a different manner.

"Get out!" she said, quietly, then again louder: "Get out! Go! Get out of my apartment! I don't want you here. Leave! Leave!"

"I. . . . Look, I'm sorry. I didn't mean. . . . I didn't mean what I said to come out that way. I'm sorry. Really, I am."

"Please go," she said, quietly again. "Just please, please go."

For the first time in a year, he was late, missing a departmental meeting, then an appointment with Alan Hirschman, another of his doctoral candidates. By the time he finally made it to the Social Science Building, grabbed the books from his office, and ran down the steps to the classroom, it was five minutes after eleven, the students in a state of anticipatory disarray.

She was there; Auntwon too. But their aspects were reversed, Auntwon's eyes on him, glaring; hers reddened, downcast, on her enormous notebook. She never looked up, never met his gaze in the forty-five minutes of class time remaining. At twenty to twelve, with just ten minutes to go before the end of their hour, having concluded in haste and confusion the pontificate of Alexander VI, he made a brief request.

"I'd appreciate it if Miss Lipsky and Mr. Miller would meet me after class for just a few minutes. Thanks."

He talked a little more, halting, jumbled: Julius II, the warrior-pope, nephew of old Sixtus. . . . But his mind was elsewhere. What he had said last night was sickening. No . . . no, indefensible. He was amazed even to see her there, amazed that she'd seen fit to sit in the same room with him, follow his lecture, take her indefatigable notes in the same obsessive way she had these several weeks past. After a moment or two, the thought crossed his mind that the girl might not stay after class as he'd asked but, rather, walk out with the others, angry, defiant. But when the hour was done and he nodded to the students, dismissing them; when the chairs had finished scraping, the feet shuffling; when the chamberful of raw, aspiring scholars had fully disassembled and drifted out the door, he looked up and saw her, standing in front of his desk in pretty much the same position as Friday; identical, really, in pose and posture, but for a little slouch this Monday morning and the absence of her awkward Friday grin. She looked beaten, emotionless, gazing downward at the lecturer's desk like a sacrificial victim at the altar, hugging that fist-thick notebook to her belly with crossed, defensive arms. Auntwon, wide-eyed but no more animate than she, gazed on mutely by her side.

"Listen, Miss Lip- . . . uh, Sandy. You too, Auntwon, you too. I want you to hear this, too. . . . What I said last night . . . the way I talked, I mean. . . . Look, I'm sorry. I feel terrible. I . . . I didn't sleep more than an hour or two thinking about it. . . . I have no excuse. Maybe . . . I don't know, maybe I've been depressed, distracted, but to take it out on you was wrong. It . . . it makes me sick to think about it. . . . I've got to talk to you, to make it up to you in some way. Take you to lunch maybe. Both of you, right now. Or noon. Noon. How about it?"

She looked surprised, then vacant, blank; wondering, perhaps, how to respond. Maybe a little gun-shy too, the way he had humiliated her, like some tortured prisoner asked forgiveness by a sadistic guard.

"I can't right now," she said. "I mean . . . noon, either. I've got a . . . a meeting. I . . . I'm sorry." Auntwon watched the two of them impassively, shifting his eyes from one to the other like a spectator at a tennis match.

"All right, tonight, then. Why don't you guys meet me tonight for dinner. We can go to Medici, if you like, after your classes . . . or some-place else if you want. Anywhere."

"Hey, c'mon, Sandy," Auntwon offered, speaking at last, "won't hurt nuffin' to go."

"I don't know. . . . Well, maybe," she muttered. "What time would you want us there?"

"Anytime. Look, after you guys are done with classes. Say, five-thirty? Six?"

"Yeah," she answered, after a moment. "I guess that would be all right." Auntwon nodded silently, wide-eyed but expressionless.

"Good. Excellent. See you both at Medici. Five-thirty, then."

A little after three he sent Annette out to get some little thing to give to her. "How close a friend," she smiled. "Purely platonic," he answered, unsmiling. She came back with a little gift-wrapped box.

"What is it?"

"Perfume. Same as always, *Quelques Fleurs*."

"Not the stuff we used to get for Cassie!"

Sure, she said, the only kind she knew to ask for. By that time it was four-fifteen; much, much too late to take it back. "Is that OK?" she asked him, wrinkling her brow.

"Sure, Annette. . . . Yeah, sure. . . . Thanks."

He got there early and waited by the door. Miss Lipsky came exactly on the half-hour.

"Thanks for coming," he said

"That's OK," she answered, distantly.

"Have you seen Auntwon?" She hadn't. Not since class. They wait-ed ten minutes more in pained silence, then took a booth on the ground floor in the back. The waitress brought them water and menus. When she walked away, he began:

"Look, uh, Miss . . . Sandy, I'm really sorry for what I said . . . the way I talked to you."

"No, it's all right. Forget it. I mean, I've kind of gotten used to it. A lot of the kids think it's crazy too, only . . . only I just didn't expect it from you. Anyone but you, you know? It made me feel . . . I don't know . . . humiliated, I guess. That's a terrible feeling, humiliation. Terrible. . . . I didn't sleep much myself."

He went on with his apology, his explanation: how he hadn't been himself, the sorrow that he'd felt in his life, the loneliness. It wasn't her or what she'd said; no, not at all, but him, just him. He, of all people, who should have sensed the pain he might inflict, having felt so recently its pangs.

"It's OK," she said. "You don't really have to explain."

"Yeah, well. . . . Here. Look, I got you something. . . . A peace offering, I guess." He took the little box from his pocket and set it on the table, sliding it gently over to her.

Her mouth relaxed, her eyes moistened, looking up at him, then down again at the foil-wrapped box. She pulled the ribbon and peeled the paper away carefully, folding and setting them aside on the table. "What . . . what . . . perfume? Oh, you didn't have to . . . to get me anything like that. It wasn't. . . ." She stopped and started crying, sobbing.

"God! Look, I'm . . . I've been a jerk lately. Just forget everything I said. . . . "

"I've . . . I've gotta get out of here. I'm sorry. I've got to go." She scrambled out of the booth, and he followed, throwing a ten on the table to cover the soft drinks they had ordered. Once outside, she started walking back toward campus. He followed quickly, keeping at her side.

"Look, Sandy . . . wait." She stopped abruptly and faced him, passive and limp, her eye-liner matted into a little raccoon's mask.

"Do you. . . . Have you got a way to get home?"

"No . . . just the bus."

"OK, let me drive you."

"I need to talk," she said outside, sitting in his car. "I can't be alone right now."

She led him up the steps, the box of perfume in her hand, unlocked the door, and put him back onto the sofa they'd both occupied the night before.

"I've got to wash my face, OK? Stay there, OK?" She turned and vanished down the hall. A light went on in a doorway, then a door closed with a little click, blocking out the light. Water ran.

He felt enormously better, absolved, in a way. He had sinned and been forgiven, once and for the very last time. Whatever travesty of reason Sandra Lipsky might summon from the recess of her hallway, whatever charts or diagrams she might display, whatever hand caresses she might apply in the form of metaphysical inquiry, he would sit there attentive, unjudgmental. Whatever it was she said or did, he would keep his God damned mouth impenetrably shut.

She came down the hall chartless, maskless, turned right into the kitchen and emerged with the *pinot noir*, two glasses, and a corkscrew. "Will you open it," she asked. He nodded and scraped away the foil.

She sat across from him on the armchair, and he poured the wine. They each drank a glass, silently, without eye-contact. "Auntwon warned me about this," smiled Robert when his glass was empty. "It kills your brain cells."

"Yeah, he told me that too. . . . He—Auntwon, I mean—talks differently to you, or . . . when you're around, you know? Like a . . . I don't know: Ghetto talk, kind of. When he's with me, alone or with some other people there, he sounds more normal, more like standard English, I guess. Have you ever noticed that?"

"Yes. It's, uh, it's kind of an inside joke between the two of us."

"He's a character, all right. I knew he wouldn't come to dinner tonight. I had a feeling, didn't you?" She stood and picked up the bottle of *pinot*. "How about a little more? I'm gonna have some." She came around and sat beside him on the sofa, pouring enough to fill their glasses again. "It's good wine."

"Yes, it was. . . . "

"Your girl friend's?"

"Uh, yeah. How did you know that?"

"I know lots of stuff. . . . I *told* you."

"You're not angry with me anymore?"

"Well, just a little bit still." She smiled, though. He was feeling the wine and guessed that she was too. "One more thing and I'll forgive you completely."

"What's that."

"I want to kiss you just once. Then you can go if you want to . . . or whatever you want."

"I. . . ." He shook his head, but that just added to its lightness. He was floating, misty, comfortable, absolved now from foolishness and unpardonable sin.

"Please," she whispered, staring into his eyes, looking like an orphaned child which was, however, not particularly unhappy about its abandoned status. She put her hand up to the back of his neck and pulled him to her, pulling his mouth into hers gently but with surprising assertiveness. She tasted like Cassie, like *pinot noir* and Colgate and Scope, minty and grape-like, sweet and clean and wet, and the roll of her cheek, where his nose came to rest, bore the unmistakable scent of *Quelques Fleurs*. It was Cassie, Cassie! and her tongue touched the inside of his lips the way it always had and he opened to it, unresisting, breathing in the wine-scented air of her exhalations—Cassie's exhalations—grasping and being grasped the way a cold, exhausted swimmer would grasp at a life-line, the way the life-line would be clung to, unrelentingly. Then, after a long and lingering moment, misty with wine and twice-used breath and the taste of another's soul, they both came up for air.

"I want you," she said. "I've wanted you since the first day of class."

She shouldn't have spoken. It broke the spell. It was the wrong voice, the wrong verbiage, not Cassandra by a long shot, no, but a stranger, an impostor, some mannequin dressed in a loved-one's scented garb. He backed his head away, then his body, pushing back to arm's length, looking at her in the angular lamp-light, shaking off the wine. There, in tight jeans, blue sweater, ten pounds over her optimum weight, five years older than her classmates, sat Sandra Lipsky—Miss Lipsky—the young girl-woman who had glanced at him daily from the third row, Mondays, Wednesdays, and Fridays, just into the seventh week now; scribing furiously in her thick notebook, handing in her mid-term exam. A young girl, a student. No. *Worse* than that: his ward, for God's sake; his protegee, a child given unto his care by parents, peers . . . the University of Chicago itself. How could he have *allowed* himself...? How could he even have *presumed* . . . ?

"I . . . I shouldn't have let. . . . I shouldn't have done that. . . . Look, uh, Sandra, this . . . this just can't happen."

"No. It *is* happening. No one has to know."

"I'll know . . . *I'll* know. Look, I can't. It isn't right. I just . . . just can't." He stood up. "I'm gonna go now. Let's just forget about every-thing. This isn't . . . it just isn't right." He shook his head again to clear away the wine's effect, which was indeed now starting to dissipate from sheer anxiety and shock.

"No," she said. "Yes it is. It is right. You sit back down, uh, Dr. Martin! Don't you *dare* leave now. I've put a lot of effort into this, and I won't have you ruin everything."

"I'm sorry." He started for the door.

"If you leave now—listen to me—if you leave now, I'll . . . I'll. . . ."

"I'm really sorry, Sandra. It was all my fault. I should have known better. I'm truly sorry."

"Sorry! You're sorry! After leading me on like that! You just . . . I saw how you looked at me in class. . . . I could see. . . ."

He shut the door, muffling her voice. Then, in a moment, whatever continued sounds she might have uttered in his lengthening absence were rendered totally indistinguishable by his footsteps on the stairs.

CHAPTER SEVEN

TRANSLOCATION

THEY'D FOUND IT A YEAR BEFORE, BEHIND SOME WOODWORK OF THE PALAZZO Lungobardi in Siena. Robert was apprised of the discovery shortly after it was made, and had since been furnished fully with the details, though he'd had throughout that twelve months' time neither the will nor the opportunity to participate in a study of the little box's contents.

A wall of the Palazzo's paneling had been in need of restoration. Behind it, buried in the masonry, conservators had come upon a wooden casket, which, when opened, was seen to contain a quantity of papers, indisputably aged but fresh and well-preserved. Brought to the city archives of Siena and there briefly examined, they were readily adjudged to be hitherto unknown and, indeed, unreferenced manuscript pages in the hand and style of one Adalberto Colangio. Within a week, a fax had been sent to Professor Robert Martin at the University of Chicago:

Dr. Robert Martin,
I would wish to inform you that a box of not published manuscripted papers which appear to be of Adalberto Colangio have been found in the Palazzo Lungobardi. This was the residencia of the Sgr. Antonio Lungobardi, and known priorly as the Casa Tornabuoni, in which dwelled Sgr. Colangio during the final decades of his life. There are many questions in regarding the authentic qualities of such documents. The Archivi Municipali and Dpto of the Historia, Univ. di Siena will welcome you most cordially if you will wish to study these papers and provide with some opinion on the authentic qualities thereof.

> Sincerely,
> Taddeo Fabbri
> Archivista Principale
> Municipalita di Siena

Now this, remember, was a full year before his beloved Cassie was even to *meet* the distinguished Mr. Serkin of franchised pizza fame. Robert thus had been immobilized, enraptured, ensnared most blissfully in the designer-worthy apron strings of the Woman of his Dreams. No, he told Sgr. Fabbri; he could not come. For his Cassandra, it could be taken on faith, would never have subjected her estimable self to unluxurious travel devoid of profit, and Robert, at that time, was utterly functionless without her by his side—not to mention in his bed. He wrote to Sgr. Fabbri that his duties at the university precluded any absence. "*Mi dispiace*," he faxed, in answer to the unsyntactic summons, "*non posso venire.*" Sorry, just can't make it.

So the Archivist had faxed again, then written repeatedly at monthly intervals, coaxing, dropping tantalizing hints of the papers' uniqueness, of their undoubted authenticity. The box had been wax-sealed with Colangio's signet, the papers within showed signs of being of the proper antiquity, and, more to the point, displayed writing in a hand and style very much like those of the great Colangio's known manuscript works.

It was all very intriguing, to be sure, and Robert grew more than a little curious as the months passed and additional facts came in. After all, Colangio had become something of a friend to him these past six years, as familiar in a way as one's college roommate—as familiar as one's brother, practically, but for the sounds and scents of proximate physical contact. Hearing from him again—new words, perhaps, never before heard by another living soul—would be a revelation. A revelation, moreover that could be the shape, form, and substance of another profitable book.

Success, wealth, notoriety might be Robert's lot a second time. All that was required was a sojourn in Siena, a few months' cushy research, then half a year of casual effort with the pen. The university would back him; his publisher too. Nothing all that burdensome required . . . but still he could not go: for Cassie—the way his love for her had taken root these past five years—had grown more valuable than a dozen Colangios. More than a thousand. She'd become the solitary focus of his life these days, relegating Colangio and all his historical ilk to the status of amusing afterthoughts. There were other suitable scholars, he faxed the *Archivista*. Why not give one of them a call?

Then at last back in January, just three months before Cassandra's unenvisioned exit, the dogged Sgr. Fabbri had played his last trump card. In an oversize envelope sent express mail from Siena, Robert found a half-dozen copies of the papers themselves. To his utter amazement—for false leads are the rule in Renaissance research—the writing style and hand were as familiar as the Archivist had suggested they might be, and—much more to the point—the text was not. What Robert saw before him on his desk in reasonable quality reproduction was part of a hitherto unknown manuscript of Adalberto Colangio, a commentary on, or biography of, St. Francis of Assisi. Adalberto having been celebrated for his rationalism, and St. Francis having been equally renowned for his spiritualism, the subject and author seemed entirely at odds.

So it was seductive indeed. . . . But still he could not go, for Cassie wouldn't hear of it. She had work to do, she said, five or six projects balanced one upon the other, with a single particularly important new commission—some fast food chief executive with a home, as she described it, half the size of the Field Museum. Work on something like that, of course, would have to take precedence. As for another one of those boring research projects Robert might get stuck working on in Italy: "If it's so important," she suggested, "go yourself." There was as much chance of that as of him paddling solo to Siena across the ocean. So "*Mi dispiace*," he wound up faxing Sgr. Fabbri for the fifth and final time.

He heard nothing more. The three months passed in a succession of passion, anxiety, and grief. And so forgotten was the project now—even after Cassandra had departed with her CEO and could no longer be an impediment to the journey—that Robert would likely even yet not have departed for Siena. If not, that is, for the added stimulus of Auntwon Miller and Sandra Lipsky. . . . Oh, and Aaron Gold, too, who would inevitably though unwittingly play his essential role in the drama with no whit less skill and not an iota more of prescience.

Robert found the envelope on Wednesday morning, taped to the knob of his big walnut door. "Meet me in my office at one," said the handwritten paper inside. Aaron's name was signed below.

"Sit down, Bobby," Aaron told him when he got there. He took a metal chair, university-issue, identical to the one in front of his own desk that Annamae had grappled with a couple of weeks before. Aaron's chair didn't flex as much for him as had his for Annamae. She was not a woman to be trifled with, Auntwon's formidable aunt, thus the boy's legitimate plight. Still, things had worked out well enough for Auntwon in the long run. One thing at least, it occurred to Robert, he had managed to get right.

"You know why I asked you here today, Bobby?"

"Uh, no, Aaron, not really. You want me to do a summer seminar or something?"

"No, it's not about a seminar. . . . Look, I got a call."

"A call?"

"Yeah. A student's family. . . . A girl's mother called me yesterday morning."

"A girl? OK, well?"

"It's one of yours, I'm afraid. One of your students."

"Oh? Who?"

"Last name's Lipsky."

"Lipsky! . . . Sandra? Did you say her *mother* called you?"

"Yep."

"What on earth about? Not about *me*, for God's sake."

Aaron nodded.

"About me?"

Aaron shrugged. "Yeah, about you. She made some accusations. . . ."

"Accusations! Come on, Aaron! . . . OK, about what? What the hell did she accuse me of? This I've *got* to hear!"

"OK, Bobby, OK. I never considered it to be all that credible in the first place. But. . . . Look, do you want to tell me anything first? . . . Not that you really have to, you understand."

"Yeah. Yeah, *sure* I'll tell you. Sure. Big deal! I kissed her, OK? Once. In her apartment. I . . . we both had a little wine, you know? . . . I mean, I'm not excusing it. I realize that what I did was wrong, but God! this is a little excessive, don't you think? I mean . . . God!"

Aaron, actually, didn't look all that upset. He seemed, to judge from his expression, more bemused than irritated; more sympathetic, in fact, than anything else. He was a longtime friend, a mentor, and would clearly do everything in his power to defuse whatever situation obtained. Robert knew that perfectly well. Still, there was no denying that this was something of a transgression, a breach of trust on any teacher's part, no matter which participant was the aggressor, which the wronged. An instructor and his student? Whatever the specifics, it was the former who would be adjudged the guilty one, assumed by his very position to own superior judgment, higher ethics. Had Robert a daughter in school, of whatever age or temperament, touched even as minutely and consensually as young Miss Lipsky had been by her professor—no matter what the rhyme or reason, what the offer or enticement—he would have been angered, would have asked for an inquiry, an explanation; demanded a public apology if the facts required. Sure . . . but even so, even *so*, how could the girl have *betrayed* him that way?

He shook his head in disbelief. "Look, Aaron, what did she. . . . Is there a specific complaint?"

"No, Bobby. We've got that much in our favor. It's just sort of an inquiry now. . . . How about you fill me in?"

So he did, telling Aaron what he could about those strange two days: his invitation to a "party"; that astrologic nonsense the girl had dropped on him; his reaction to it—a little harsh, perhaps, but reasoned and appropriate; then the argument they'd had; his apology; the wine, the perfume. . . . He didn't mention Auntwon, though. Better for the kid's sake to leave him entirely out of it. Hopefully the vindictive Miss Lipsky would have had at least the common decency to have done the same.

"That's it?" asked Aaron.

"Yeah, that's all there is—or was. . . . Why? What did she say?"

"Well, as to her specifically—the girl, I mean—I really don't know. But her mother seemed to think there was a little more to it than that."

"Well, there isn't. . . . Or wasn't. That's the truth."

"OK, look, I believe you. Hey, I mean . . . the girl's had her problems before. Whatever she's said, whatever the mother says, I'm sure it's readily containable. There are . . . uh, kind of extenuating circumstances that let you off the hook, or at least put you in a sort of protected confraternity—a kind of union, if you like." Aaron chuckled mischievously, evincing a cheerfulness that Robert found a little odd given the gravity of the supposed allegations made. "I don't think Miss Lipsky—or *Mrs.* Lipsky, for that matter—is in any position to do you a whole lot of harm."

"I don't understand, Aaron. What do you mean by that?"

"This girl, Bobby—I did some research. Well, I mean, it's all right there in her records, for God's sake, if anybody'd bothered to look closely enough. Which I took it upon myself to do, by the way, on your behalf. . . . Anyway, Miss Lipsky's got quite a fascinating history."

"Such as? . . . What kind of history, Aaron?"

"What kind? The same kind as you . . . uh, managed to observe—well, you apparently didn't observe quite as much as some of the other fellows did." Aaron leaned back and chuckled again.

"OK, Aaron, how about telling me what the hell this is all about!"

"It's about her sleeping with faculty, Bobby. Look, I made some calls, asked some questions. . . . Your inamorata—or prospective inamorata, as you describe her—she's screwed half the English department; and three or four of the guys from Psych, too, before she switched majors. She's quite an academic groupie, I understand."

"You gotta be kidding, Aaron! You gotta be. . . . I mean . . . I can't believe. . . . "

"No, no, it's quite true, all of it. And we may only know the tip of the penile iceberg, so to speak, so you might want to get checked out for hoof and mouth disease or something. . . ." Aaron laughed out loud now, as merrily as a prankster, then, with the subtlest of transitions, turned gravely solemn. "Seriously, though, I'd like you to lay low for a while; take off maybe, for a month or two. We need to get Miss Lipsky—Sandra, right?" Robert nodded. "Yes, OK. Well, we need to get little Sandra safely and definitively out of the university, and I think it would be wise—judicious, that is—for you to absent yourself from the Chicago area during the process."

"Yeah, but . . . I can't just take off like that. I've got stuff going on, you know? And anyway, I didn't do anything . . . well, nothing all that terrible, I mean. . . . "

"Hold on, Bobby, hold on. Look, I'm on your side here, remember? It's just that . . . well, OK, if I have a question on Renaissance history I come to you, right? Well, this administrative business is my specialty. You're just going to have to let me make the call here. . . . Look, it's for the girl's sake as well as yours. She's gonna get in big trouble this way sooner or later, get shot by a jealous spouse or get someone else shot. . . . Bobby, I'm going to give you a direct order here. You know I have your best interests at heart. You've just got to trust me on this. Let me do what has to be done."

"I don't know, Aaron. . . . "

"Bobby!"

"All right . . . let's say I agree, just for argument's sake. . . . When would you want me to leave?"

"Now. Within a week or two."

"Before the quarter's over?"

"Preferably. We want to act before the quarter is over. The trustees, you know?"

"But . . . where? Where do you suggest I go?"

"Where? Where else? They've been pestering us for a year, for God's sake."

"Siena?"

"Yeah, Siena. We'll call it a sabbatical. You get your salary, expenses, and six months off, more if you need it. The university gets publication rights to the research. OK?"

"I don't care, Aaron. This has really been a tough time for me, you know?"

"Yeah, Bobby, I know. I've heard what's been going on with you and Cassandra. . . . Look, I'm sorry, really, but you're better off without her. . . . That's an even *better* reason to get your ass out of here."

Robert shook his head. "Everybody seems to feel that way. I mean, Shelly, for example. He never liked her, for whatever reason. But the way things were with us . . . well, *you* know; you saw us together. . . . I mean, I'm better now—more angry than anything else—but still, some days. . . ."

"OK . . . look . . . Shelly was right, whatever he told you. She, Cassandra, was—*is*—a really awful person." Aaron sat forward and put his elbows on the desk, pausing for half a minute, looking as though he were searching for the perfect word or phrase to convey a particular shade of meaning. Looking, that is, the way a man might look at a funeral in the dismal hope of providing consolation without exacerbating grief. "All right," he said at last, "you remember Greta?"

"Greta! Greta Ziegler? Sure. Why? Did you hear from her?"

"No. Nobody's heard from her since she left. . . . She was with you for—how long was it, a year?"

"Something like that; a little more maybe."

"What did you think of her?" Aaron raised his eyebrows. He was up to something, clearly.

"Of Greta? Well, you know. She was special. Smart. The best we ever had in the department, by far—the best teaching assistant, I ever worked with, anyway. . . . She must have her Ph.D. by now. . . . God, it's got to be—what? two years or more since she left?"

"Pretty girl, wasn't she?"

"Yeah, she was. Exceptional."

"Cassandra must have thought so too. They were friends, weren't they?"

"I don't know. . . . No, not really friends, I guess. They went out to lunch a couple of times."

"I never did tell you what happened with Greta, did I? Why she took off the way she did, I mean."

"No. . . . No, I never heard a thing about it from you or anybody else. I just figured she met a guy or something . . . you know, something like that."

"Yeah, well, it wasn't like that at all. Actually, she'd had some problems in the past, emotional problems, I suppose. She'd been hospitalized back when she was in high school. Then she'd been all right for a long time. . . . She was an innocent kid, trusting. She confided in your girl friend, told her the whole story: I guess she'd had shock treatments, medication, that kind of thing. Whatever . . . she picked the absolute worst person to tell. Cassandra can be ingratiating that way—you know, get people's confidence. Anyway, Greta came to me before she left. She was a wreck. Cassandra had told her she was too sick to be around young people—teaching, I mean. She came to me and asked me if I thought that was true. She was just about hysterical by then, shaking . . . her head was even shaking, she was so agitated. That's the last time I saw her. She didn't even listen to what I told her, just took off. I wrote a recommendation for her later to McGill in Montreal. She's still there, I imagine."

"And you think Cassie was to blame for it? That she precipitated it?"

"Did I give you that impression, Bobby? That I *thought* Cassandra was to blame?" Aaron took off his glasses, rubbed his eyes, sat back in his chair, then leaned forward again, elbows on desk, arms crossed in front of him, in exactly the same position he'd been in before. Just one thing had changed: a long, blue vein had arisen in the center of his fore-head, looking like some dirt-gorged earthworm caught in an ephemer-al moment of repose. The vein first bulged a little, then deturgesced into a band-like, gray-blue stripe, before Aaron finally resumed: "I didn't say I *thought* anything, Bobby: what I meant to convey to you was that I was *sure* Cassandra manipulated that poor girl into leaving here. I *know* it happened just the way I told you; maybe even worse if any-thing. I *know* it, Bobby. Probably I should have told you back then—not that it would have made much difference anyway."

"But why would Cassie have done something like that, Aaron? Why?"

"Why? Because she didn't want a girl as pretty as Greta around you. Whatever else she dragged around in that malevolent little head of hers, I'm sure she cared enough for you to feel jealousy, or at least to protect what she considered proprietarily hers. She was a bitch to every-body else long before she started being a bitch to you."

"God, Aaron, you should have told me all of this when it happened."

"Yeah, Bobby? What difference would it have made? Would you have left her because of it? Consider, now, would you?"

"I'm . . . I'm not sure. . . . Maybe not."

"That's exactly what I thought. Now get your ass on that plane to Italy!"

He was dreadful at good-byes and always had been, never knowing quite what to say, how to shake hands or embrace with just the right emo-tion; not showing everything in his heart lest he seem a sentimental fool, yet still opening up enough to give a glimmer of his true affection, the fondness that he truly felt for a lifelong friend like Shelly, and even for Auntwon now, his protegé and guardian both in some peculiar way these past few weeks.

Annette had booked him on a flight the following Wednesday evening, not leaving much time for preparation, or even thought. Aaron had want-ed it that way, and had so arranged the arrangements. First, on Thursday morning, Taddeo Fabbri was faxed in Siena, and got back to them the very next day, manifestly surprised and delighted. Everything would be prepared on the receiving end, from retrieval at the airport to a work place in the Sienese Archives building. On Sunday, Robert drove up to Evanston to see his folks, supportive as they'd never ceased to be. He'd missed their subtle kindness, which went so far this solemn day of leave-taking as to omit the merest mention of Cassandra, the least question as to the abruptness of his trip. They might have *said* things, *asked* things that were uncomfortable to answer. Somehow, they seemed to know enough not to, keeping silent but for benedictions and affectionate farewells. He'd thanked them for everything with his eyes, a solemn smile, and then a warm, sincere embrace.

So Monday morning came, and, with it, his parting lecture to the students of History 321. None of them spoke much or asked any questions, not even Jeffrey Carns, who seemed to have misplaced all his clever witticisms, his wry observations. Miss Lipsky—for she'd been given a reprieve to finish the quarter—took the last of her notes, looking up periodically from those fleeting hands of hers with a sort of vacant gaze, masklike, expressionless. As for the rest—Ravi, Jivan, Melissa—they all seemed a little puzzled, not quite knowing what to think, how to react. After all, a tenured professor departing in the eighth week of the quarter: it was amazing, unprecedented. . . .

Especially without a reasonable explanation. For all they had been told was that Dr. Martin had found it essential to take a leave of absence for personal reasons. Well, what else could he say? "My girl friend left me and I came within an ace of sleeping with your classmate Miss Lipsky over there in the third row?" Hardly. There were aspects of history that were much better kept suppressed.

So he went on with his Grand Summation: the Renaissance, ladies and gentlemen, boils down to this. . . . Crystalline verbiage, sententious thoughts. And the kids? They all pretty much stared wide-eyed at him through the whole fifty minutes—well, not Auntwon or Sandra; or Betty Jean, of course, who was incapable of staring—but all the others, hoping, maybe, for some little hint, a shard of bone he might toss them: a "mother is sick" or "book being published" or where or why or "see you next semester."

But there was none. He had nothing more to give. Thus, the long, painful fifty minutes of pithy recitation passed, continuous, unquestioned; and finally, the hour spent, Robert introduced his score of bewildered-looking kids to the associate who'd been assigned the class for its last two weeks of lecture and the final exam. It was David Kasner, a post-doc fellow Robert had supervised the year before. David knew the

Renaissance period well and would do a creditable job. At the end of the hour, he stood up next to Robert and said a word or two. Then the students all filed down to the front of the room—all but Auntwon, that is— and crowded around the two of them, Dr. Martin and Dr. Kasner, now enclosed in a tight circle. "Hello," the various voices said to one, "goodbye" to the other. Miss Lipsky closed her ponderous notebook, rose, came forward, swerved a bit, passed the gathering quickly in a wide parabolic arc, and instantly was out the door.

"She feel bad, Doc, you know?" Auntwon shifted from one foot to the other, glancing up at Robert with his head half nodded to his chest, so that he looked both penitent and vulnerable, like the faithfullest of dogs that has just soiled a priceless Persian rug. "Sandy really feel bad," he repeated. "I guess I do too."

"No, Auntwon, you shouldn't. You for sure shouldn't. It's as much my fault as anyone's. I never should have talked to her the way I did. That's what started it all. I realize it. That was the problem, the fundamental cause. It's just that. . . ."

"Whassat, man?"

"I just. . . . I just can't imagine why she said the things she did. You know, lies; things that never happened. She made stuff up. I . . . I don't know, I just can't understand why she'd *do* that to me—not that I didn't deserve it in a way. . . . I mean, what I did was wrong: going there— you know, going back there after—but . . . but how could it have helped her to embellish it, to try to hurt me gratuitously? That's the thing I can't understand."

"Well, maybe she ditten."

"How can you say that? She . . . look, she had to tell her mother that stuff—whatever exactly it was she *did* say. She must have said something. Otherwise. . . ."

"Yeah, well, jus' keep a open mind about that, OK? Maybe you oughtta talk to her about it 'fo' you decide. You got to get the fo'-one-one, you know?"

"The what?"

"The fo'-one-one, man. You know, like, information."

"Oh. Yeah. Well, I'm not gonna get the four-one-one from *her*, that's for sure. We're not likely to be communicating any time soon, you know."

"Yeah, well, anyway, she feel bad, like I say, man. . . . Hey, you leavin' Sunday, right? Maybe you two could talk befo' you go."

"Well, I'm sure as hell not gonna call *her*."

"No, I s'pose not. If she wanna tell you somepin', maybe she call you. I don' know. Maybe she call you in Italy a'ter. Where you gon' be?"

"Siena."

"Where Colangio come f'om, huh?"

"Yeah. Look, I'll e-mail you when I get settled."

"So whatchu gon' do there, man? Work on them papers you talked about?"

"Yeah. . . . Hey, by the way, what about our bargain? You know, I was nice to your friend Sandra, wasn't I? Just the way you asked me to be. You said. . . ."

"Yeah, I know. My diction, right? OK, you . . . you're right about that. I . . . I'm gonna try, I promise. It'll be a challenge, but I'll try. . . . So, OK, anyway, what about, uh, your apartment? You . . . uh, do you need me to, like, water the plants for you or somethin'? I mean if nobody, uh, you know, has me arrested before I get across the lobby to the elevator?"

"No." Robert laughed. "No, uh . . . Shelly—Dr. Rogovin—is gonna take care of everything for me—sell it all, as a matter of fact. . . . Hey, you're a character, you know that? I guess I told you that already, huh?"

"Yes, I believe you did, Doc. In an antecedent conversation."

"OK, OK, look, maybe you can change your diction like fifty per-cent. You know, somewhere in between Puff Daddy and John Dryden. How's that?"

"Yeah, that'd prob'ly feel better anyway, man. . . . Hey, you say you're gonna sell all-a your stuff?"

"Yep, all but the books. It's just a lot of bad memories to me now. . . . That is, unless you need something. Some furniture for an apartment when you get one or . . . or how about for Annamae? If she can use anything . . . a couch or table, maybe? . . . The stuff won't bring much at auction anyway. Not half of what I paid."

"Naw, Doc. We got . . . *have* pretty much all we need at home.

Auntie wouldn't take, uh, anything like that anyway. And me, I'm gonna stay right at home and save up for a trip to Europe if I can afford it next year. I got me . . . uh, I mean, I got a job lined up too. And Auntie say, uh, *says* that if she wins the lottery she's gonna split it wif me for the trip, you know? Harper, he goes out and buys two tickets evvy week, then puts 'em in the cookie jar till they give out the numbers. Be like a ritual wif . . . uh, *with* him."

"OK, well I'll be hoping they win. It'd be great if you could come to Siena this summer. I'll really miss you, you know? You've been a real friend, a sincere friend. Between you and Shelly, the two of you helped me get through the absolute worst time of my life."

"Yeah, well, look at what *you* done for me. I mean, taught me all that, uh, stuff, you know, and . . . and . . . look, I prob'bly be stickin' tubes up peoples' behinds till I was too old to find the right hole it s'posed to go in if you hadn't-a got me outta that medical bullshit the way you did. *Man!* That was slick!"

"OK, OK. Well, anyway, I *am* grateful. Sincerely. I'll be thinking about you a lot."

"Yeah, yeah, me too. . . . Hey, by the way, what about them . . . uh, those papers? You say you're gonna be workin' on the ones they found? The ones we talked about?"

"That's the plan."

"Wow, man! Well, you got to promise me somethin'."

"Sure."

"You got to let me know right away if you, like, figure somethin' out. I mean, like what happened to Colangio in those last twenty years. You think the papers might have some information on that?"

"I don't know, Auntwon. I doubt it, but . . . who can say? There might be something in there. There's a good chance they're from the right time period, anyway. After he'd stopped writing—well, the works we know about, at any rate."

"Yeah? So how you tell that?"

"How can I tell?"

"Yeah, like when they were written? How can you tell that?"

"You can figure it out from the handwriting style. Colangio's writing changed over the years in a pretty consistent way. It becomes—I don't know—sort of smaller and more crowded as he gets older. Some of the last things he wrote by hand are almost totally illegible; it took me literally hours to get through each page of his last few manuscripts until I learned how to distinguish the letters. . . . Anyway, the guy in Siena—the chief Archivist, I guess he is—sent me a few photocopies, and they're indisputably late, sometime in 1502 or after—and actually, they look like they were written later than anything I've seen of Colangio's so far. But it's going to really take a trained eye. It's no wonder the guy kept pestering me to go there and do the work-up. I doubt that many other people could make much sense of it without three or four months of preparation."

"Yeah, Doc, like I said, you the *man*. . . . Well, anyhow, you gonna find some really crazy shit in there, I bet. Like I to'd you, you know?"

"Yeah, the aliens, right?"

"No, man. *You* the one who said aliens, remember? What I said was that it's gonna be a whole lot *stranger* than fuckin' *aliens*—'scuse me, Doc—and I truly believe you gonna find out in the end I'm right!"

Everything was packed, two huge cases of Cassie's filled with clothing and books—things he absolutely couldn't do without. Then there was that other box of supplemental materials he'd probably need: Sheldon could mail it out if his work required, if the Siena manuscript really did turn out to be *bona fide* Colangio; and, more important, writings of sufficient value and originality to justify a scholar's time and effort. He'd filled the sturdy carton to its top: the remaining volumes of the *Cambridge Histories*, works on philology, paper analysis—things he might not find in Siena, even at the university. Robert slid it over next to Cassie's custom sofa and sat down on the spot where he had always sat at sundown, watching her as she read her magazine, a strand of hair across her cheek. Then the evening light would sweep behind her, like a corona setting off the onyx of her hair, and she would glance up every day, predictably, as in some required ritual, and ask what he was looking at. And he would answer, as always: "You. At you." Then she would shake her head, and smile, and go back to her reading.

He sat there on the sofa she had selected and ordered and shared with him these past few mesmerizing years and looked around the apartment for the very last time—not in sorrow, but in remembrance;

no longer in anger, but in resignation. Tomorrow he would leave this place forever, and as he strove to fix that understanding firmly in his mind, the telephone rang.

"Uh, Dr. Martin?"

"Yes?"

"It's Sandy. Sandra Lipsky."

"Well!"

"Look, I wanted to talk to you. To tell you something. . . . Uh, Auntwon said it would be all right."

"Yes, he thought that you might call. Well, go ahead. What was it you wanted to say?"

"I . . . I wanted to apologize. . . . You know, for the way I acted . . . uh, at my place. . . . What I said and all . . . and the rest of it. . . ."

"Oh, yes, well, as to that, it was as much my fault as yours. I mean, I . . . I behaved improperly myself. I'm just as much to blame. . . . No, *more*, as far as that goes; I should have never. . . . Well, you know what I mean."

"Uh-huh, I think. Anyway, they told me it was you who had arranged for me to finish out the quarter, and I wanted to thank you for that."

"It's OK. I thought that would only be fair."

"So you must know about the other, uh, problems I've had, then."

"A little, maybe. Listen. . . ."

"No, no. That's OK. That's not why I called."

"OK, then, why did you?"

"I wanted to make sure you knew what happened."

"You mean the rest of it? The phone call to my department head?"

"Yes. I . . . I didn't mean for that to happen. Intend it, you know? Uh, I mean, them getting the wrong idea about us. People . . . the other professors thinking . . . you know . . . I didn't know that talking to her would lead to that. Really I didn't."

"You didn't know!... Well, you must have said *something* to make her think. . . . She wouldn't have any way of making all that up, you know."

"Oh but she *had* to. It wasn't from anything *I* said."

"No? Well, what exactly *did* you say, then?"

"I . . . I told her I was concerned about you. That you were unhappy and I wanted to help you if I could."

"That you were concerned about me? How would she know...? All right, anyway, you must have said more than that."

"Well, no, not really. I mean, she asked me how I knew about . . . you know, how sad you were and everything, and I told her."

"What? What did you tell her?"

"Uh, about you coming over and all."

"Oh, my coming over! And how did she react to that little piece of information?"

"Uh, she didn't seem upset or anything. She asked if there'd been any physical—you know—stuff . . . between us."

"Uh-huh? And what did you say to that?"

"Nothing. Just that you kissed me."

"That *I* kissed *you*?"

"Well, I guess I exaggerated that a little."

"Yeah. What else did you exaggerate? What else did you manage to say?"

"Nothing."

"No? Well, where would she get the rest of it, then? Are you saying she just made the whole thing up out of thin air?"

"Yes, she must have. She had to."

"All right, all right, look, this is going nowhere. It . . . not that it matters all that much anyway, but why would you call her about me in the first place? Why would you even have to *talk* to her about what happened between us?"

"Well, I was just calling her to tell her what the chart said. You know, to explain to her that your life was changing, taking on a new direction. That you needed someone else in your life to make you happy."

"You mean like you, right?"

"No, no, Dr. Martin. Not like me at all. Someone else. Somebody you don't even know yet. I called her to tell her that. And also to get her exact time of birth, you know, to get the chart as close to accurate as possible."

"Her time of birth! You called your mother to get her time of birth?"

"No, Dr. Martin. For heaven's sake, what do you think I'm talking about? Didn't they tell you anything? I called your lady friend Cassandra Fullerton. *She's* the one who told all that stuff to my mother!"

SIENA

CHAPTER EIGHT

INITIATION

"COSA SUCCEDE!" SHRIEKED THE WOMAN ON HIS RIGHT, GRABBING HIS elbow, jerking it sharply toward the armrest.

"*Niente, niente. E la ruota . . . uh . . . il carrello d'atterragio. Non La preoccuparsi.*" Every time the plane had jerked, bumped, accelerated, slowed, or made the faintest unfamiliar sound, the young signora had practically pulled him into her seat. Twenty times—thirty, maybe—in the last hour and fifteen minutes. Now they were approaching Florence, and the landing gear's deployment had set her off again.

Robert patted the goose-fleshed forearm that had been interlinked with his for the past seventy minutes. It was cold, trembling. "*Ci stiamo preparando per l'atterragio in Firenze. . . .*" came the flight attendant's voice from the speaker above his head. He looked out the window, seeing land now, the Arno, straight as an Oklahoma highway, muddy as the Mississippi, carrying half the Tuscan highlands with it out toward Pisa and the sea.

"*Il fiume,*" he told the woman. "*Tutto bene. Atterremo subito.*" There were structures visible now from the diminishing height. Little boxes with off-white stucco walls and orange-tiled roofs lay strewn along the river. Beyond them, beside them, rolled hectares of low-slung hills, with spring-green crops or clumps of shrubby trees: olive, poplar, fig, a periodic pine. Then lower still as the wing flaps braked their speed and the woman pulled once more upon his arm—"*Precipita! Lo sapevo!*" "*No, no, signora, tutto bene, tutto bene!*"—some vehicles came into view, a narrow road, a man standing in his garden, a tethered horse. The Tuscan countryside, thought Robert: it was much like the face of an old friend, as sweetly familiar to him after all these frantic years as Lakeshore Drive in summer or that beige brick house in Evanston, the commodious abode of his childhood. Yes, yes, he realized with a smile, Tuscany revisited, even after all the torment he'd been through, felt an awful lot like coming home.

"*L'ora locale é le dieciventitre*. . . ." said the flight attendant's piped-in voice, professional, metallic, and comforting. Ten-thirty, nearly. He had slept maybe an hour or two on the trans-Atlantic flight to Frankfurt, then grabbed a roll and coffee, making it to the gate of his connecting leg to Florence with half an hour to spare. Strange, he wasn't very tired now. It would catch up with him later; this evening or tomorrow—the inevitable jet lag. But in a week that too would be gone, like all the rest. He'd have his work to keep him busy; a great discovery perhaps. Yes, surely that: it was his friend Colangio, mentor, teacher, about to speak to him again after all these many years: some unexampled masterpiece, possibly, or a clue to those last two impenetrable decades. . . . Well, unless the whole thing was a clever hoax or knowledgeable forgery. . . . At any rate, it felt good to be here this morning, good to be back in Tuscany, exciting to return to his adoptive home.

"*Ah, Gesú Maria, c'é qualcosa che non va! Lo so, lo sapevo!*"

"*No, no.*" He patted the woman's arm, comforting. "*Tutto bene. Atterremo.*"

He felt the lurch of wheels touching tarmac. "*Ah, tutto bene, tutto bene. Siamo qui.*" Her arm relaxed at last and she was still.

Benvenuti a Firenze, proclaimed an overhead banner at the arrival gate. Fabbri was standing directly beneath it, a man unlikely to be missed, what with the identifying placard in his hands and the singular appearance of his person. He was tall, six-foot-eight or more; slightly stooped; thin, bordering on gaunt, with hollow cheeks and eyes, a small but slightly beaked nose, straight, nondescript hair, and olive skin, darkly shaded by shaven heavy bearding. In his hands, held at chest level, was a computer-generated sign that read: "DOTT. ROBERT MARTIN, PHD," precisely done in one-inch characters within an ornate but entirely gratuitous baroque-style border. The elegance of the placard and the extreme inelegance of the man who bore it made the most remarkable contrast imaginable.

Robert waited for some passengers to clear a path, stepped over to a point where his eyes were level with the center of the sign, dropped his carry-on and lap-top directly in front of a pair of enormous and heavily scuffed shoes, and craned his neck upward.

"*Buon giorno,*" he said to the enormous man.

"Dohc-tohr Mar-*teen?*"

"*Si, sono io. E Lei? Signor Fabbri, suppongo?*"—(Signor Fabbri, I suppose?) Robert stuck out a hand, then adjusted it a foot and a half upward to reach a set of thin, cold, spidery fingers. Fabbri's left hand, immobile, clung resolutely to the sign.

"*Ah, Signore . . . mi scusi . . . Dottor Martin! Bene, bene! Benvenuto!*"

"*Spero che non abbia aspettato molto tempo.*"

"*Ah, no. Grazie. Solo.* . . . Only one half hour I am wait-een. We speak Een-gleesh, OK, *dottore?* For the prac-tees, OK?"

"Sure, if you like. *Certo.*"

Fabbri bent down, picked up Robert's carry-on bag, and lurched away from the departure lounge, looking, with his long legs, jerky gait, projecting shoulder bones, and anterograde posture, like a long stalk of celery on stilts, tottering, broad end up, about to topple forward onto the flat of a vegetable tray.

"It was nice of you to take the trouble to pick me up," said Robert, shouting a little from half a stride behind.

"*Come, signore?* 'Peeck'?"

"Uh, '*venire a prendere*'."

"*Ah, si.* 'Peeck.' I shall remember. . . . *E´ un piacere.* . . . Peecking you. A pleasure, signore. . . . *Quanto tempo* . . . eh . . . how long you stay weeth us, eh?" Fabbri spoke loudly too, turning his head back toward at Robert in his wake.

"Um, I'm not quite sure. I guess a few months, anyway. Three months, four maybe; maybe longer. *Forse tre o quattro mesi.*" Fabbri was two full strides ahead now. He glanced around again and slowed his pace a bit, letting Robert draw practically abreast of him.

"*Ah, bene, bene. Dove.* . . . Eh, where do you stay for thees time?"

"The Garibaldi. You know it?"

"Of course, the Garibaldi. This is verr dear, though, no? Verr dear I theenk."

"Uh, expensive? I guess it probably is a little. It wasn't too bad when I stayed there before."

"Yes? Ah, you must at that time stay to the city then, for the book, no?"

"What?"

"When you come to Siena before, you come for the book? On Colangio."

"Oh. Yes, that's right. It was for research. Just about six years ago, I think. . . . I think I stayed for ten or twelve weeks in all. The hotel was about five hundred dollars a week then, but I guess it must be more now."

"*Ah, si, si, molto, molto.* Well, we shall find you a better place, no so espensive, eh? I ask Caterina to . . . *eh, come si dice 'indagare'?*"

"'Investigate.' We say 'check' usually. 'Check'."

"Ah, good. 'Check'. I shall remember. I ask her to check; Caterina, you know, my *segretaria*, eh, eh, 'segretary', I think, eh? . . . *Eccolo!* Here is the baggage place. We must to find your theens."

They took the highway out of Florence forty minutes south to Siena. It was clear and bright. May 18, but hot and dusty as July. Windows cranked open, dry air, soot, and diesel fumes in their faces, Fabbri's seat slid back as far as it would go, but still so little room for those formidable legs that his knees abutted the wheel. Two southbound lanes with the sporadic traffic of a Thursday afternoon: the little Fiat, surcharged with baggage to its very ceiling, labored up the inclines and coasted down declivities until, abruptly, after a gentle curve, a hill rolled by and there directly in front of them loomed the uplands of Siena. There was an exit ramp, then a busy two-lane road which very soon began to climb. It was lazy at first, a gentle slope, then steeper, curling upward. They followed the bus route he had taken from Florence six years before. He remembered that. A day much like this one, he recalled, bright, sticky, late August, just a week or so after *palio.* . . .

A Sunday, it was, that day he'd arrived. There was a bus stop near the stadium, with the church of San Domenico conspicuous on the right. He'd climbed down the bus's precipitous steps into a congested square, full of kids queueing up for McDonald's. Duffel bag in one hand, jacket in the other, he'd passed out the far end of the square heading downhill through the narrow, cluttered streets. Then the path had led him up again, exhaustingly. It was hot, thick, in the afternoon sun, so he'd consciously bypassed the ancient monuments temporarily for the devilish heat and the ballast of a dozen books wearying his shoulder. He'd brought along a map, so located the Via Roma readily enough, exiting through the Porta Romana in the city's southeast wall; out at last to his hotel.

Six years ago, yet he remembered the place as if it had been yesterday. The Albergo Garibaldi: elegant, cool and spacious, with a room made up awaiting him, so he'd gone straight up and collapsed there in the solace of that soft, down, double bed. There he'd lain inert for an hour or more, rising around three for a quick shower and change of clothes. At last, refreshed enough to venture forth, he'd gone exploring in that specific window of time between late afternoon and early evening; that crystalline moment of a summer day when the fire of the sun has diminished, and the heat of noon-time, baked into brick walls and stone pavements, wells up to warm the evening breeze. It was just at that particular juncture that he'd set out on his walk, and what he had seen in the process had seemed a miracle.

Back along the Via Roma, through the Pantaneto, down a covered alleyway into the Campo, he had raised his eyes, and springing up before him, like a genie from a bottle, was a perfect city perfectly frozen in time. Monumental and intricate, it was a construction of the fourteenth century where not one particle of matter, not one reflecting ray of light seemed to have been altered in the past six hundred years. Like some classic automobile, an Auburn or Stutz or Marmon, say, whose owner had gone off to war the day he had driven it home; and it had sat there, untouched, unopened, a buried monument to a buried soldier, sealed up airtight in the family garage. And all the while sons and grandsons had been born, grew old, and died; and here was the old Marmon, finally discovered by some fourth-generation descendent. It was no doubt caked with dust. It was flat-tired. Its tank of fuel had long ago evaporated. But its leather still smelled fresh from the tannery, its wood still reeked of recent varnish, its steel and brass and plate-work gleamed and dazzled with reflected light, and not so much as a fingerprint marred the regularity of its glossy paint.

Such a thing had seemed Siena, a relict of frozen antiquity, a capsule of buried time, as though the entire municipality had been somehow laminated, Scotch-garded, and rustproofed against the centuries, then stored on a mountaintop for most of a millenium awaiting Robert Martin's visit, or anyone's. Half a dozen years had passed since that unique experience, and still he remembered his singular impression of it.

"You must rest now," said Fabbri in the lobby, while a bellman put the luggage on a cart.

"No . . . uh, I think I'll drive over with you, if that's OK. I'd just like to get washed up a little first. Can you wait a few minutes?"

Sure, Fabbri said, and plopped down on a couch. So Robert went up to his room, brushed his teeth, washed his face, changed his shirt and pants, and then, with no more than ten minutes having elapsed, he was down and in the little Fiat and on his way to town.

'Town' is to say the old town of Siena, within its city walls. Vehicles are limited there to certain routes, both by the narrowness of the streets themselves and by municipal ordinance. Even taxis and delivery trucks face restrictions. But officials like Fabbri, Principal Archivist of the City, would have not only unlimited capacity to navigate the town, but an invaluable place to park in it as well. That is the greatest perquisite of all, and, with such precious dispensation, and a little sticker in his window to proclaim it, he headed toward his designated spot.

"You are no tired?' Fabbri asked as they passed through the Porta Romana, the cobbled streets deserted but for the *Archivista*'s car.

Sure he was, said Robert. But it was better not to sleep now. Weary though he felt, ashen-eyed, sleep this early in the day would only make the jet-lag worse. Get some sunlight on your face, the pundits wrote, try to acclimate your body to the new local time. It was a lesson he'd learned well from prior trips.

It was a lovely day, clear and bright, though hot. And he was back in Siena, the prettiest town in the prettiest country on earth. That alone seemed enough to stay awake for.

But then there was his curiosity too. That strange new manuscript in a hand like Colangio's—perhaps actually *written* by Colangio himself—by now it had become to Robert a subject of considerable interest. After all, he had traveled all this way, past two part-continents, an ocean, and half a millenium to see it. Adalberto—*his* Adalberto—was almost like an old friend now, a man he had communed with, felt a kinship for: a kinship quite as intimate as any scholar might feel for his subject across five long centuries of intervening time. Those newfound papers, if they turned out genuine, might yield some revelations, some clues as to the historian's last two dozen years on earth—years that were a mystery even to contemporaries: "*Dove e andato Colangio?*" Machiavelli had written in 1505 to a mutual friend. "Where has Colangio gone? Riches must have silenced his pen."

But what if, contrary to Machiavelli's best information, the riches hadn't silenced it completely? Yes, what if Colangio, despite his long-awaited bride, despite his sudden and amazing wealth—or maybe just before their acquisition—had written just this one more thing; just this one more undiscovered work? Then walled it up forever. When? Why? What extraordinary secrets might it hold?

"Has anybody been through the papers?" he asked the *Archivista* abruptly, breaking a long interval of silence.

"'Been through', signore?"

"*Controllato. I documenti sono stati controllati?*"

"*Ah, controllati.* . . . The papers of Colangio? No, dottore. You weel be the first."

Amazing! he thought. After five hundred years, and then another dozen months of his own neglect . . . well, assuming, of course, that they were genuine—but if they were . . . !

They parked near the Piccolomini Palace, just half a mile from his hotel, and as they walked toward the entrance, Robert looked up at the building. Three-storied, rigidly symmetrical, faced in rough-cut, monumental stone block, the impeccably Renaissance palazzo was Fabbri's workplace and would be Robert's too for the next few months. The Sienese state archives had been housed there for a century and more. So, too, were the new-found papers, residing in a third-floor storage room since their discovery the year before, lying dormant, fallow, awaiting this visit like some sealed-up pharaonic tomb filled with—what? Fabbri led him through a monumental doorway and into the courtyard of the building.

"You know the Palazzo?" the *Archivista* asked him as they started up its granite steps together.

"Yes, sure. I worked here for a while—six years ago, you know?"

"Ah, for the book, for *ricerca*, no?"

"Yes, that's right, for *ricerca*—research. I got a lot of information here: Colangio's birth, death, taxes, his parents' records, the marriage registration—that sort of thing. I must have spent a couple of weeks here all told. . . . I don't remember seeing you back then."

"*Si*, I was . . . eh, *assistente—come si dice?*"

"'Assistant'. It's about the same."

"Ah, *si. Beh*, I have been assistant to the *Archivista* then. I become *Archivista* for myself . . . eh, *quattro anni fa.*"

"Four years ago. I see. Well, maybe we passed each other in the corridor back then." Robert looked up at the man, thinking: no, probably not; he would most likely have remembered.

Fabbri shrugged, then pointed from the stairway. "You have seen the *museo* then?" They stepped onto the landing of the second floor, where a sign for the *Museo delle Tavolette della Biccherna* pointed to the rooms containing it.

"Sure. I took a ton of pictures there—a lot, I mean." Ten rolls, he recalled, slides of the *tavolette*, which were the painted covers for Siena's annual municipal account books. A new one had been commissioned for every year of Siena's history, clear through Colangio's lifetime and then for a good century before and after. Robert had studied all of them six years before, photographing each one in the series from 1460 through 1527, from Colangio's birth, that is, until his death. Viewed together, in chronologic sequence, they gave an extraordinary picture of the city during the Renaissance. In half a millenium, amazingly little of its physical form had changed.

"You use these for the book?"

"What's that?"

"The peec-tures. From the *museo*. You use these?"

"Well, not the pictures themselves—I mean I didn't put them in as illustrations, but rather studied them myself to get an idea of the time and place Colangio lived, you understand?"

"Ah, *si, lo spirito dell'epoca*, no? How you say?"

"'Spirit of the age'. Yes, that's right. The *tavolette* give a terrific sense of that, I think. And I read a lot of contemporary documents too—*documenti contemporanei, ha capito?*"

Fabbri nodded and led him up the final flight of steps to the third and topmost floor.

"Here," said the *Archivista*. "Your room to work is here." He pointed down a long, gray corridor with five identical doorways opening into it from the left. "My *ufficio* . . . eh, office, eh? the one-two-three door down there." Fabbri pointed backward down the intersecting passage with his other arm. "I am there if you need some-theen. . . . Here, come, come, I show you to your room."

They stepped through the second doorway in the left-hand corridor into a spacious chamber with two arched windows on the outer wall, a worn plank floor, and a frescoed ceiling. The fresco showed a mythological scene, but it was cracked and faded, done by a minor painter in the decorative Sienese style, but third-rate and of little artistic value. Still, it was old and indisputably historic, and would have held an honored place in any American gallery.

Art not excluded, the room showed a pretty typical interior for a Renaissance palace like the Piccolomini, built about 1470 for two nephews of the Sienese Pope Pius II. Robert knew the history as intimately as he knew his own. Pius was a humanist, classicist, and literary raconteur. Born Aeneas Sylvius Piccolomini, he had occupied the papal chair at the time of Colangio's birth. Though he himself had died a few years before the palace was begun, his family had lived here, dining, sleeping, working in these very chambers. Colangio had no doubt visited often. Having known the Piccolomini as generous patrons of his father, he might well have been ushered up the same stone flights Robert had climbed to enter this very room. Perhaps he had once stood on this very spot, trod these very floorboards, gazed up at the identical fresco, and out through the big, arched windows at a near-identical scene to the one below them on the street today.

Yes, Siena looked much the same now as it had in those *tavolette* from five hundred years ago. This room too, no doubt. It had probably changed little since the Renaissance, but for the cracks and pits of time. Robert glanced about it, finding it familiar in a generic sort of way. It wasn't the exact same room he had worked in six years earlier, but similar, remarkably similar. The lighting seemed brighter than before; perhaps it had been improved throughout the building. There were dropped fluorescents now, looking very recent, supported by some struts and wires entering along the ceiling moldings. On the wall opposite the windows were metal shelves, brightly lit, half-filled with boxes and cartons of various size and construction; then, over at the far end of the room, three more banks of shelving, crowded, less well illuminated. Finally, closer to the door, adjacent to the near window, stood a large library-type desk, drawerless, with a visored lamp atop its bare, worn surface and a couple of straight-back chairs pulled up snug against its edge. Fabbri led Robert to the desk, put him into one of the chairs, snapped on the lamp, walked over to the shelving on the wall opposite the windows, picked up a small wooden box, brought it over to the desk, and set it on the surface.

"You know you must use the gloves, dottore."

"Yes, of course." A pair lay on the right side of the desk: white cotton gloves used by conservators to protect their precious documents from the toxicity of human skin. Robert slipped one on. He set his yellow legal pad off to the right and placed a pen and pencil from his pocket beside it.

"If you require anytheen else, my *segretaria* can be of *assistenza . . . aiuto . . . la parola, dottore. . . .* "

"Help?"

"*Si*, hailp. Hailp! *Maledizione!* She will be of *hailp*. I will send her soon in leetle time, OK?"

"*Grazie tante, signor Fabbri, ma non avró piu bisogno di niente oggi.*"

"*Ee*nglish, signore! *Ee*nglish! I must *prac*-tees!" admonished Fabbri, shaking his head gravely.

"OK, sorry. . . . Uh, I won't need another thing today—unless, well, maybe some coffee might be all. But thanks."

"OK, signore . . . dottore. We weel check on you lah-ee-tayr. I send Caterina to find the coffee now?"

"No, no, it's all right. I'll go myself in an hour or two.. . . . I . . . I'll need to get out into the daylight anyway. You know, for the jet lag."

Fabbri shrugged and stepped out, leaving him alone in the room. It was one-fifteen and the sun had moved a little past its zenith, sending some shafts of yellow light in through the big, arched windows to his left. The place was cool and quiet, the desk well-lit, what with the lamp and overhead fluorescents. The little box of carved and polished walnut in front of him looked clean and new, despite its certified antiquity.

He slid it nearer to him, adjusting the lamp shade upward, then glanced at his watch. One-seventeen: the palace would be staffed until six or so, thus lots of time to get a general idea what the box contained. It was exciting, electric. Here, right in front of him, after five hundred years of slumber, sat the Colangio manuscript he had traveled half a world from home to see. He pulled the second cotton glove up onto his right hand, like a fighter readying for his bout, opened the lid, and reached inside.

Whew! There was a musty smell; not particularly unpleasant, but potent. The scent of long interment, perhaps, though somehow voluntary interment. Of hibernation, say—an earthy sort of walled-up smell, redolent of safekeeping rather than decay, an odor, perhaps, of purposeful and restorative rest.

It was the papers themselves that were scented thus, a thick sheaf of them, dusty, yellowed, but—from first inspection at least—structurally sound, neither mildewed nor desiccated; unspotted, unfissured. Miraculously, that secret space the box had been immured in must have kept the right humidity, the proper temperature, for preservation. Good quality paper too: that must have helped a lot. Stuff made back in an age when paper was a semi-luxury product, produced from fine and costly fibers, neither acid nor alkaline in excess or they would have been largely dust by now, even in the best environment.

Robert lifted the thick stack clear of the wooden chest and set it on the desk's surface, pushing the box back out of the way. The assembled manuscript was an inch and a half in thickness—what with the paper's weight, maybe two hundred folio pages of twelve inches by fifteen. He ran a gloved finger along the edge, estimating. . . . Two months or three of intensive labor to transcribe and translate. Then collation and analysis. . . . The end of summer, possibly. He'd set to work today.

The pages were tied loosely with an ancient string, now ragged, frayed, and thoroughly discolored. Decayed so, it was clearly of poorer quality material than the paper itself. The acidity of the string had eaten not only at its own fibers, but at the outermost surface of the paper as well, leaving a narrow cross of brown discoloration on the pages at front and back, then a russet stripe midway along the outer edges of the stack, top, bottom, and sides. Fortunately, both frontmost and hindmost pages were, except for the cruciform discoloration, entirely blank.

Robert undid the tattered string; Fabbri must have replaced it after he had made his photocopies, tying it again in a gentle bow. He tossed the string into the box and lifted the empty face sheet from the pile. Directly underneath was a crowded hand-printed page, its ill-formed lettering squeezed tightly together in the manner of all such Renaissance manuscripts. A working copy most likely, it bore marginal notations—mostly numbers and figures—and several of its letters had been circled and underlined.

It seemed interesting, of course, as to antiquity—it was indisputably old—but mere antiquity meant little by itself. Most such writings of the premodern age looked pretty much that way. Authors of the time, hoping to conserve their precious paper, would pack as many words as possible onto a single page. This one was virtually covered with ink, and made more so by the underlining and encircling. He set it beneath him and adjusted the light, moving the lamp closer and pushing its shade down and back. There was a magnifier on the right-hand side of the desk, over where the gloves had been, and he reached for it, examining the text carefully, looking for specific characteristics: a certain crude compactness, a particular way the cursive letters scrolled. . . .

Yes! he thought, then said it to himself out loud: "*Yes! Damn!*" It was Colangio's hand! Absolutely, certainly. He hadn't been able to tell for sure from the photocopies—not a hundred percent for sure, anyway. But now, here, there could be no mistaking it: the curvilinear 'f's and 's's with their oval finials; the horizontal extension of the letter 'g', the sheer indecipherability of half the text. Colangio, his old friend, speaking to him again after all these years! And with brand new words, unfamiliar thoughts! How could he not have traveled here a year ago? . . . But then Cassie had been with him a year ago, and what manuscript page, what revelation, what intellectual accomplishment could even have compared to the ecstasy he'd known with her? . . .

A minute passed, and then another, as he started to think, to drift . . . but finally the strange, familiar writing lured him back, slowly, magnetically. What was that? There. . . . An 'n'? Yes, 'n' for sure; and here a 'c'. Then—what? Ah, 'q'-'u', unmistakably joined. With magnification and study a full word emerged, then another, first doubtful, then certain. "*Nacque nell' anno 1181, Francesco. . . .*" the first line started off, when he had pried its meaning from the jumble. 1181. That was the birth year of Francis of Assisi—St. Francis, as Fabbri's faxed descriptions and copied pages had implied. So it *was* about St. Francis, after all. St. Francis, of all people! An uncongenial subject if ever there was one for Adalberto Colangio: Francesco d'Assisi: the mystic who preached sermons to birds and beasts, tamed wolves, presided over miracles; the steadfast ascetic who lived a spiritual life, renouncing all things material in the process; the mystical divine who miraculously received the stigmata, the wounds of Jesus' body, on his own. Yes, all those things and then a hundred more: examples of the irrational, the medieval, the downright bizarre, in Francis' life and works. What a subject for Colangio, that primordial voice of reason and scientific thought in a premodern world! It scarcely seemed possible!

Robert lifted off a dozen pages, looking at the thirteenth, then a dozen more, looking at the twenty-sixth or thereabouts, scanning the cramped text for definite words, meaningful content. Strange. Yes, indeed, this was—all of it, in fact, from start to finish—a biography of St. Francis of Assisi. 'Francesco this', 'Francesco that'; then St. Claire, Francis' female counterpart; here a reference to Perugia, there to Assisi, both habitual haunts of the celebrated saint. Robert shuffled to the last pages, finding the narrative continuous into the 1220's, thus very near the proper story's end, since Francis died in 1226. Remarkable, and well worthy of analysis: an older, unknown, unexpected Colangio writing the type of work that would have been anathema in his earlier years. St. Francis of Assisi, of all subjects! Utterly remarkable!

Robert moved down to the very last paragraph on the very last page of text, and to its final words, ending abruptly in the middle of a thought: "*e quest' incontro con Clara . . .* and this meeting with Claire took place at a location between the two holy houses (*Case Santissime*), wherein Francis gave his blessing to his sister in God." Inexplicably, the 'qu' in 'quest', the 'l' in Clara, and the 'ell' in 'sorella'—'sister'— were circled, and there were two long black trails of underlining linking them to the right hand margin, where the number '174' had been inked in—visibly in Colangio's hand. Beneath the last line of text appeared the word "Completa!"—complete!— accented and underlined. And there the writing stopped abruptly, half-way down the page.

Two more folio sheets followed, entirely blank. Then finally, at the very bottom of the stack, just above the vacant, string-stained endpiece, Robert came upon a folded, unsevered double-folio page with another single sheet of paper pressed between its halves. The single sheet looked peculiar, even in such bizarre company; even to Robert Martin, who wasn't much attuned to the peculiar, never had been, but would become so presently.

At the top of the strange single sheet was an arrow, as of a compass, directed on a slight diagonal toward the page's upper edge. The rest of the surface was blank—entirely blank like the endpapers and the double sheet enclosing it, but for the arrow at the top and one thing more: a single line of text at the very bottom of the page. "*Solus ad bonum,*" it read, in the only Latin verbiage Robert had noted thus far in his brief examination of the papers. "Only for good," the inscription said, mysteriously.

Strange, thought Robert. *What on earth could it mean?*

COLLECTION

ROBERT SLEPT FROM SUNSET UNTIL FIVE, WHEN HIS BLADDER WOKE HIM, clamant, full to bursting. He struggled up, found the bathroom in the dark, felt his way back to bed again, snuggled in, pulled up the covers, but then slowly, gradually came around, half-awakening into a sort of muddled, jet-lagged stupor. He turned on the lights, rinsed his face, read propped-up in bed for an hour or so, thoroughly uncomprehending, then, at seven, got up for good, shaved, showered, ate an enormous breakfast at the hotel buffet and, finally, made it to the Piccolomini by opening time at nine.

The place was quiet, cool and comfortable; distraction-free. And he was sufficiently awake now, having shaken off his long, inebriated sleep. He set to work at once and within an hour had finished the page he'd just begun the day before. It was the manuscript's third, running now to six full pages printed out longhand on the legal pad to his right. Three pages of manuscript text, in—what, six hours now? But that was pretty much routine. This sort of business went slowly at first, always, until one got into the rhythm of it. In a week or so, he'd be right back up to speed: a full page an hour, maybe more. Two months or three, then, to finish the work, then a lengthy collation and analysis of what he'd found.

He leaned back in his chair and pulled off the gloves, scratching his head, rubbing his eyes. Tedious, yes, but fun too in a way—you never quite knew what amazing thing you might encounter next. It was like a hunt for buried treasure half the time.

Not that he'd found a single thing of value as yet; but with only three pages done, and considering that he hadn't so much *read* them as just *copied* the material. . . . Still, what he *had* seen had looked pretty strange. Nothing at all like Colangio's other works, but, on the contrary, amazingly simplistic and primitive.

He put the glove back on his left hand, picked up the next page of manuscript and set it back on the protective mylar sheet in front of him. "*L-a-g-u-e-r-r-a-t-e-r-m- i-n-a-t-a-f-r-a-. . . .*" Robert transcribed each letter to the pad at his right, decoding them, arranging them into comprehensible words, lingering here and there, with or without illuminated magnification, over a cursive stroke or ink smudge to determine whether the character it meant to form was an L or T or F. Such was Colangio's penmanship. "*La guerra terminata fra Assisi e Perugia. . . .*" was the passage. Francis was now a prisoner of war in a dungeon in Perugia, about to discover his religious bent. . . . Three full pages of this stuff—six in transcription—with not a particle of value in the lot, not a statement of interest, not a single critical judgment, just the first three pages of a Legend of St. Francis that might have been taken verbatim from some medieval hagiography. Drearily routine, it just wasn't Colangio.

Oh, the subject of course, which was uncongenial at best. Still, Adalberto had written of saints before, St. Catherine of Siena, for instance, and Thomas of Canterbury. But he'd told their stories with historical accuracy, analytically, with a questioning eye and a discerning pen. What, though, was one to make of this?

Robert flipped back through his legal pad to page one. There, at the beginning of the second paragraph, lay the first of the narrative's remarkable lapses into medievalism. "*Quando nacque* . . . When he was born, his mother had a vision. . . ." A *vision*! Now in every other work of Colangio's—every one, without exception—the great historian had *mocked* those kinds of things: revelations, omens, astrologic signs directing day-to-day events. And then, finally, in his *Discorsi* he'd been downright scathing toward the men who had included such frivolities in their works. "*Qual'uomini non devono scrivere,*" he'd admonished: "Such persons shouldn't write." Yet here it was, right on the very first page: "a *vision,*" for God's sake! This could hardly be the same Colangio who'd concluded in his *Discorsi*: "*Non vi é nessun destino. . . .* There is no fate, no metaphysical power that governs a man's life beyond the vagaries of chance, the doings of fellow individuals, and the sole and sovereign exercise of his own indomitable will."

That was Colangio, that and not some mystic story of a vision! Yet here sat the legend unquestioned, put down in autograph text as fact. And there were more such, many such, right here in the first three pages; three manuscript pages filled with allusions to divine influence, descriptions of miracles, astrologic projections. It was bizarre, inexplicable, as though it had been copied out in pen and ink by the renowned Colangio from a lesser author, a less reputable source. But why? Why in the age of printed books, would an internationally famous scholar take the time to copy something so insipid, so unenlightening? . . . And from whom?

It made no sense at all. But then the whole last part of Colangio's life made no sense either, so this was just a lesser mystery superimposed on a greater one. . . . Well, there was plenty of time, thought Robert. Today was just his second day of research, just the third page of a manuscript completed with a couple of hundred more to go. He'd find an answer in the end if there was an answer in there to be found.

First he'd struggle through the text—copy, translate— then wrestle with those annotations—whatever on earth they happened to signify— then, finally, figure out that crazy blank page.

That strange and fascinating page with its mysterious arrow and enigmatic line of print! There was something odd about it, something magnetic. It lay there in its folded cover within an arm's reach on the desk top. Its peculiarity lured him, but he left it alone a while, for the sake of his work.

Fabbri's secretary appeared in the doorway at eleven. She was an attractive woman of forty-five or thereabouts, nicely dressed, coifed, and cosmetically adorned, as Italian women are wont to be, with raven black hair like Cassie's—longer, though, and pulled back in a sort of loose bouffant. Her face was a trifle lined and incipiently flaccid, but otherwise she looked impeccable, with delicate, classic features, and flawless skin.

"Doctor Martin?" she greeted him, in practically unaccented American English.

"Yes, and you must be. . . ."

"Caterina Paschiale. I am Signor Fabbri's secretary. Is there something you require, something that I can help you with? Signor Fabbri asked me to check on you today."

"No, not really. I'm just getting started, really. Thanks, though. I'll let you know if I need anything."

"All right, I'm just down the hallway. The third door down to the left, you know?"

"OK, yes, Signor Fabbri showed me."

"Is your lighting all right? Do you need another lamp?"

"No, no, uh . . . Caterina; the one here on the desk is enough. But thanks anyway. And thanks for your offer of help too, but I'm getting along just fine right now. Other than the musty smell of these papers and the lack of a coffee machine in the building, this place feels pretty much like my office back at home."

"And where is home for you, Dr. Martin?" She stepped into the room and halfway over to the desk, holding a file folder to her chest like some forty-something schoolgirl.

"Chicago. Are you familiar with it?"

"Yes, of course. The Bulls. Everyone knows about Michael Jordan, even in Siena." She smiled. "Well, dottore, may I get you some coffee then, since we have no machine here? I can run over to the Campo. . . ."

"No, thanks, not right now. I'm fine for the time being, really."

"Well, then, is there something I can type for you, or copies I can make? We have a color copier. An American Xerox."

He smiled at her persistence. "No, Caterina. Thanks, though. This stuff. . . . It just takes time. I've got to sift through it letter by letter to make out the words, then word by word to get a sense of the meaning. No one can really help me do it. Colangio wrote like . . . like a four-year-old kid on hallucinogens, you know what I mean?"

She laughed. "What a funny thing to say! But you exaggerate. His writing can't really be as bad as all that, can it? May I see what you are working on?"

He motioned with his head, beckoning her over. "Yes, of course. Here, take a look." She stepped to the desk and bent down above the page he was transcribing. "All right, see this?" he said, pointing with a finger. "It's the word '*mercante*'. Can you make it out?"

"Where?"

"Here, these letters. See the 'm'?"

"With the circle around it?"

"No, below that. On the next line down. Here."

"Not really. How can you see that that is an 'm'?"

"This little squiggle. Hey, 'm's are Colangio's easiest letters to make out!"

"*Mio Dio!* This will take a year for you to complete, no?"

"Well, not quite that long, I hope. I finished two pages of it yesterday and another one this morning, but I'm just getting started. I should be able to get through about a page an hour once I get in the groove."

"'In the groove', signore . . . uh, dottore?"

"Yeah, once I get up to speed, I mean; get going, you know?"

"Yes, I understand. So what is it—this manuscript? Is it a diary? A journal?"

"No. Actually, it's a biography. The life of Francis of Assisi—San Francesco, you call him. Adalberto Colangio wrote the damn thing—which is really strange."

"Yes, I knew it was written by Colangio. I remember when it was discovered. . . . But why do you say it is so strange?"

"Have you ever read Colangio?"

"I suppose so, in school. I wasn't really a very good student of history, though."

"Well, anyway, he was a rationalist. He spent his whole life debunking superstition. . . . Uh, showing how irrational beliefs—superstition, and even religion in a way—couldn't be relied upon in history, or indeed in any other human affairs. A lot of people consider him the first really modern man."

"And it is strange, I suppose, that he wrote about a saint?"

"Yes. Well, depending on how he presents the facts of St. Francis' sainthood. . . . So far it's very strange. . . . And then there's this—this crazy sheet of paper." Robert reached over for the blank page, slipping it out of its folded cover. "What do you make of it?"

"What can I *make*?"

"Uh, what do you think it might be? . . . Mean, that is."

"Well, nothing. It is empty, isn't it? Except for those words. . . . They seem more legible than the others you showed me."

"Yes, I guess they are. *'Solus ad bonum'*, it says. I have no idea what that signifies."

"Perhaps it is a scrap of paper—incomplete, I mean. Perhaps it has no significance at all."

"Yes, probably you're right. Who knows? Maybe the whole manuscript is meaningless, really. Maybe they just sent me here to get me away for a while."

"To get you away? Yes, well the weather is fine now in Siena, and. . . . Well, at any rate, you shall figure everything out in time, I'm sure. . . . Uh, dottore, Signor Fabbri tells me that you are staying at the Garibaldi and that it is very expensive. He asked me to find you another place to stay. You will save a lot of expense to stay in a lodging."

"A lodging?"

"*Sì*. Many people have lodgings in their homes. For the students, you understand. I myself know of a woman who has very fine lodgings at very reasonable cost. She lives within the city as well, very near to the Piccolomini."

"Yes, well, maybe I'll look into it."

"I have called her for you—at Signor Fabbri's request, of course—and she has a room available. They—she and her daughter, I mean—are very fine people."

"All right, great. I'll get back to you on it. . . . I'll let you know."

"Yes, well . . . I have already arranged a time for you to see the room. It will be on Monday afternoon at two o'clock. I shall give you the directions Monday morning before you go."

Robert shook his head. "Uh, look, Caterina, I'm not particularly unhappy with the room I've got for the present. I'm not sure. . . ."

"No, dottore, please. It is all arranged. You will like the woman very much, I assure you."

"Yes, I'm sure you're right, but. . . . Look, Caterina, I just barely got settled into the hotel. . . ."

"Please, dottore. I have already told her that you would see the room."

"All right, all right. Look, this woman. . . . What is she—a relative of yours or something?"

"No, dottore, no relative. I used to tutor her daughter. In English, as a matter of fact."

"I see. Well, that's understandable; your English is very good. . . . So do you still?"

"Still?"

"Uh, tutor her. Are you still tutoring her?"

"No. *Dio mio*! She is in the university now, the girl. She speaks far better English than I ever have done. They are very fine people, the Dall'Olmos. You shall see. I shall bring you the directions on Monday."

"All right, all right. I suppose I can have a look at the place if it'll make you happy."

"Ah, not me, dottore, not me in the least! It is Signor *Fabbri* that you will make happy by going. And yourself as well. It was not in the least for *my* sake that I made the arrangements, signore. . . . But . . . ah, *dimenticavo*! I almost forgot to tell you why I came in here in the first place: Signor Fabbri has invited you to join him for supper."

"Today? . . . Tonight?"

"Yes, of course; this evening."

"I don't know, Caterina. I wouldn't be very good company today; you know, with the time change and all. I've been up this morning since five. . . . Look, maybe I'll take a rain check. Can you tell him that?"

"A rain check?"

"Yes. You know, go some other time—a different day."

"No, dottore, that wouldn't suit Signor Fabbri at all. I shall tell him you'll be ready at six o'clock when the palazzo closes."

It was strange, bizarre. Robert pushed his chair back, got up, and stepped over to the window, holding the blank page in his gloved left hand. Surely there was something he'd missed, a thin spot in the paper from erasure; a residue of ink somewhere. He held the sheet up to the light, up against the pane, squinting into it, and the whole thing came alive with transmitted sunlight, revealing . . . nothing.

Oh, there was the nap of the paper yellowed with antiquity, minute filaments of warp and woof, delicately made. He saw a little structured pattern here and there, too, a couple of part-circles in the paper's fabric—a watermark probably, for watermarks were common in paper from the Renaissance era. But that was all; the center of the sheet was perfectly blank, pristine, with no evidence of thinning, no sign that text had been removed, no trace of markings of any kind, pen or pencil, past or present, ever. Robert shook his head, turned around, and held the sheet upward, leftward, away from his shadow, letting the sunlight fall upon its surface unobstructed. No, there was nothing there. Absolutely nothing. Just that arrow at the top and the single line of text below, at the very bottom margin of the page: "*Solus ad bonum.*"

He stepped back to the table, sat down, pulled his chair in again, and pored over the page with the illuminated magnifier, now for the twentieth time. The little arrow at the top of the page had an inverted v-shaped tip and a hollow circular tail. It wasn't precisely vertical, but angled maybe ten degrees to the right, north-north-east on the compass. Why? And then that writing at the bottom, "*Solus ad bonum.*" It stood out in a way. Robert had remarked the singularity of it without quite realizing what it was that made it singular. Oh, it was in Colangio's hand, all right, but somehow Adalberto had drafted it clearly, distinctly, which was extraordinary for him. Well, not just extraordinary, but practically *unique*.

That was it! Just the thing that Caterina had remarked. The line—the only writing on the page—was legible, graceful; not like Colangio's usual calligraphy, with letters blending into indistinguishability and words jammed together like colliding trains. No, this one particular inscription was effortless to read, print-like, done in careful, purposeful penmanship with luxuriant spacing. Robert closed his eyes in thought, pondering. He'd seen that kind of writing someplace else in Colangio's works, deliberate script, precisely drawn. Where had it been, though? . . . Where? . . .

He pulled off the cotton glove and ran his fingers through his hair, ruffling it upward in back, by the neck line, trying to visualize the thousands of Colangio's manuscript pages he'd read through over the years, trying to remember. . . . Legible writing in . . . in. . . . The journal! Yes! That was it! Colangio's journal! Interspersed throughout it were passages written just like this line, deliberately, in a clear hand. They were . . . they were. . . . Of course! Copies of Ginevra's letters, every one of them, printed out carefully just like this. Something vitally important to him, obviously. But what had these words in common with those letters? And what in the world could the three words mean?

Robert slipped the sheet back into its folded cover, set the magnifier down, shook his head in frustration, and glanced at his watch. One-twenty already! Four hours gone now; two full hours since Caterina had left. And what had he accomplished? He looked at the legal pad to his right on the table, a large numeral nine within a circle at its top. So eight long pages of transcription done, representing—what was it now?—just four pages of manuscript text? And this after, what? Eight hours' work? No, nine. He'd started yesterday, Thursday, going from one-fifteen to closing time at six; and then the four more hours so far today, so nearly nine total. Two hours per page, just for transcription and rough translation! God! It would take all of four full months at that rate just to get through the basic work of organizing the material, and then the collation and analysis. . . . No, no, he'd have to do better, go faster, not get so damned distracted. It was just that crazy page, though, the peculiarity of it, the mystery. Well, he thought, whatever the mystery was, whatever the meaning, he certainly wasn't going to figure it out today.

He picked up the next page of manuscript. St. Francis had come upon the Bible now. "*Bibbia*," it said, in Adalberto's illegible print. The first 'i' and final 'a' were circled and conjoined to the numeral '23' in the right-hand margin. *Wonderful!* thought Robert, shaking his head in frustraton. *Here comes that old time religion! Now things will be really getting good!*

Fabbri took him to L'Agrigento on the Via Antonioni, getting a place in the back by the kitchen. It was six-thirty by now, a little early for peak dinner hour, so most of the tables were empty, their white cloth surfaces standing ready, awaiting imminent occupancy. Officious servers shuttled about expectantly, carrying food to the occasional early diners, removing refuse, trying to look busy. The effluvia of various Sicilian dishes were pungent, palpable, overpowering.

"It's my treat," said Robert. "*Paghero io, va bene?*"

"No, no. We share, at least, dottore."

But Robert insisted and waved off the *Archivista*'s protests. He ordered some wine, then each of them picked a pasta dish and entree, a substantial final meal of the day, as is the custom in Italy.

"So," said Fabbri, when the waiter stepped away, "Caterina has found for you a place to live?"

"Yes, I'm afraid so. She's rather—how should I put it?—*forceful*, isn't she? *Caparbio?*"

"Ah, yes, she control—this is *corretto?*—*controllare?*"

"Yes, 'control' is the perfect word."

"*Si*, she control everytheen. Everytheen I do. She make the time for me to peeck you at the *aeroporto*. She peeck my car for me. Everytheen."

"And you like that?"

"No! Like? No, of course no—well sometimes is good, but. . . . But . . . *beh*, is Caterina *natura* . . . eh, 'nature', no?"

"Nature. Right. . . . Well, so why do you put up with it, then? You know, *accetare? Perché?*"

"*Perché! Perché!* She do everytheen so long, so good, nobody else know how to do it, or even where to find lot of theens. Ten years she is here. Ten years. More than me, eh? More time, you know? *E, e,* nobody speak Eenglish like Caterina too. Is *imperativo*, Eenglish. For the *Archivista. Imperativo.*"

"Yes, I suppose so. She really does know the language. . . . You know, I was wondering about that: she hardly has an accent—uh, *accente*, you know? *Come?* . . . How did she learn to speak English so well?"

"*Ah, si.* She live many years there. In America."

"Oh! Well, that explains it, I guess. . . . What was she doing there?"

"*Come?*"

"*Cosa ha fatto in America?*"

"*Ah, si. Niente, niente.* Her father work for Olivetti. In California. You know thees?"

"Olivetti? Sure. They used to make typewriters, didn't they? *Macchine da scrivere?*"

Fabbri nodded and began to answer, but just then the waiter returned with their wine. The two men sipped in silence for a while, savoring the dry *brunello*, nibbling on the bread, dipping it in olive oil. Fabbri dropped his napkin, then bumped his head on the table in the act of retrieving it.

"*Ah, scusi*," he said, rubbing his temple. "These theens I do all the time. *Sempre ineleganza.* Eh, never mind, never mind. . . . *Beh*, how you are proceeding with the *manoscritto?*"

"The manuscript? Uh, it's a little slow. *É noioso*. I explained it to Caterina this morning."

"*Noioso, eh?* How you say in Eenglish? You say 'slow'?"

"Tedious."

"Ah, 'tedious'. I shall remember."

"Yes, it's . . . it's different, the manuscript. Not like the other things I've worked on by Colangio, you know?"

"No? How does it deef-ferent?"

"How? It's, uh, simplistic. '*Semplice*'. . . . The text is a biography of St. Francis, as both of us thought, but it's written in a naive way—*ingenuo*—that takes miracles and omens at face value—uh, *valore nominale*—not at all like Colangio's other works. He's known as a rationalist, you know? A skeptic. *Un scettico*."

"*Scettico, si, si, capisco. Ma* . . . but, if it so much is deefferent . . . eh . . . could it no be sometheen like a early writing? *Una giovinezza, no?*"

"No," Robert answered. "*Nessuna giovinezza*. I've read everything Colangio wrote—in the original manuscript form, I mean: *originale, scritto a mano*. The writing—the handwriting—uh, it's definitely later: later in his life, middle-age or after. Almost certainly during the years we thought he hadn't written anything, *ha capito?* Sometime around or after 1503, I'd guess."

"*Beh*, so maybe he was getting *senile* (seh-NEE-lay, he said, in Italian, the spelling in both languages being the same). *Come si dice in Inglese, dottore: seh-NEE-le*."

"*Lo stesso, ma pronunciato 'see-nael' in Inglese*."

"*Ah, ho capito*. I shall remember: 'see-NILE', eh?"

"Yeah. Right. Senile. Uh, I thought of that." Robert shook his head. "The senility I mean, but it doesn't really apply. *Non spiega*. I mean, the manuscript's grammar is OK, and the spelling seems pretty standard for the time. No, I'd say he was perfectly sane when he wrote it, and in posession of all his faculties, uh, *sano di mente e ragionevole, lo sa?* . . . But . . . there's something else. . . . Something strange I found: a sort of blank sheet of paper. . . ." Robert described the peculiar page with its inscrutable little arrow and mysterious line of print. "I must have spent three hours just staring at the damn thing these past two days."

"Yes," said Fabbri, "I have notice thees page too when I look through, but I have no pay much attention. You find it below the other pages, no? Weeth sometheen like a cover around, eh?"

"Yes, exactly. That's it. A folded folio cover. The page was slipped inside."

"Ok, yes, I see thees too. I see thees page, *ma . . . ma non ho pensato che importa niente. . . .* Have you hold it up to the light?"

"You mean to look for transparencies—*trasparenze?*"

Fabbri nodded.

"Yeah, I did. There's something . . . a faint watermark, maybe—I don't know the word for 'watermark' in Italian. *Non so la parola. . . .* OK, well, anyway, there's a faint pattern—uh, *figura*—in the paper. That's all. Some indistinct circles or something—*circoli*. But no erasure. . . . Uh, I don't know the word for 'erasure' either. When you rub something off a page, like pencil marks."

"Rub off? *'Cancellatura'*, maybe?"

"Yes, 'cancellatura', then. That's right."

"But you can see a *figura*, no?" asked Fabbri. "A seer-cle? A *filigrana*—how you call it? 'Waterprint'? *'Filigrana' in italiano?*"

"'Watermark' you mean? That's 'filigrana'?"

"Ah, *si,* 'watermark'. I shall remember. You must check weeth fluid, you know?"

"Fluid?" asked Robert. "What kind of fluid?"

"Special fluid. You know stamps, dottore? *Francobolli?*"

"Postage stamps?"

"*Si*. Postage stamps. *Francobolli*. You know? I have a *collezione*. Deef-ferent stamps have deef-ferent *filigrane*. To see the *filigrana*, you must dip in the fluid the paper. . . . I show you, though. Later I show you. When we finish to eat, I take you to my home and show you how to see the *filigrane*.

They ate heartily, the both of them, and headed out in Fabbri's car. It was a ten minute ride out past the Medicean fortress along Via Ricasoli to the *Archivista*'s place, a modern apartment building—'modern' meaning twentieth century, Mussolini era perhaps, thus a wholly different concept of modern than, say, a contemporary structure in Chicago, or even

Rome. The unit was up one flight of steps, on the second floor, down a long corridor that smelled of olive oil and worn carpeting. Stopping at a door on the left a good forty feet from the stairwell, Fabbri fumbled with his keys, dropping them once on the wooden floor, then bumping his head on the doorknob when he went to pick them up. Finally, rubbing his scalp, he managed to get the door unlocked and Robert found himself a moment later inside a modest-sized apartment, sparsely decorated with furniture looking old but not antique, purchased new, perhaps, but aging with its owner to a sort of awkward pre-senility.

"Sit. Please, sit, sit, dottore. Make yourself at the house."

"'At home' we say. 'Make yourself at home.'"

"*Ah, si.* 'At home.' I shall remember. I am learning much, now that I have the opportunity to speak with so intelligent of a teacher." He motioned Robert onto a sofa and disappeared into the kitchen, returning three minutes later with a freshly opened bottle of blood red *Carmignano*.

"Please to take some wine weeth me, dottore."

"'Bob.' Why don't you call me 'Bob'? Or 'Robert'. Either one, OK?"

"'Bobbert'? It is unusual name. I have no hear before thees name 'Bobbert'."

"No, 'Bob'. That is the nickname for Robert—Roberto. The *nomignolo*, you understand? *Ha capito?*"

"*Ah, nomignolo, si.* Dottor Bob. Or Roberto. Roberto, I like verr much. And you call me 'Taddeo', OK?"

"Sure. Good. Taddeo it is."

"Bob . . . *Roberto* . . . I have not many visitors here in my home. This is *piacevole* time for me. *Come si dice?*"

"'Pleasant,' we say. 'Pleasant occasion'." Fabbri poured two glasses of wine, setting the bottle on the table. It was a good dry *Carmignano*, a premium wine, costing much more than the commonplace Italian table wines universally available for a few dollars a liter.

"*Si, si.* 'Pleasant occasion.' I shall remember. . . . I have few visitors."

"Why is that? No women in your life?"

"Women? No. No women. I mean, I like women, you know. But I have bad luck weeth them. *Sfortuna.* Really bad. And you? You have better luck, I guess."

"Well, not lately. . . . It's a long story."

"Long story? *Beh*, we have lot of time to say it."

"Uh, no, we say 'long story' when we don't want to talk about something. *Un soggetto spiacevole, capisce?*"

"*Si, si. Capisco, capisco.* We weel talk some other theens then, OK?"

"Yes. Sure. Good. . . . Uh, what about you? No family here? Uh, *genitori?*"

"*Si, si. Mia mamma e due sorelle* . . . two see-sters, eh?"

"Here? In Siena?"

"Yes, of course. We are born here."

"But no girl friends?"

"No, Dottor Bob, I become, weeth a woman . . . *troppo imbarazzato.* How you say?"

"Flustered."

"*Si*, flustered. I shall remember. . . . I become very flustered and then I do like a fool, you know?"

"Some women find that charming in a man. I think I was like that a little when I met my . . . the woman I was with the last few years. She liked me better for it, I think . . . for a while, anyway"

"Yes? And what happened? *Ma, no*, this is the beeg story."

"'Long story'."

"*Ah, si, si. Scusi.* 'Long story'. I shall remember. *Mi scusi.*"

"No, it's all right. She left me, but I'm starting to get over it. Slowly, though. I just have to wait a little while longer to be my old jolly self again."

"Well, thees is better news, then. *Prego*, take leettle more wine." Fabbri poured until both their glasses were full again, and they sat back quiet for a moment, sipping. Then the *Archivista* set his glass down on the coffee table in front of the sofa, got up, went across the room, then disappeared down a hallway to the left. In a minute or two, he returned carrying a thick book in his arms with a flat box stacked atop it. He set the book and box on the coffee table beside his wine glass. The box held various accessories to the *Archivista's* stamp collection: tweezers, packets, a little bottle of something. The book turned out to be an album, stamped in gilt lettering on its front cover and spine with the words "*Italia Repubblica.*"

"You must examine your strange paper weeth fluid."

"But . . . you mean a watermark, right? Even if there *is* a watermark, it had to have been put there when the paper was made. Like the stamps. An image in the paper itself can't have any information of significance, except maybe where and when the stuff was manufactured. You understand what I'm saying? For Colangio to have left any information in a watermark, he would have had to have produced the paper himself. *Capische?*"

"*Si, si, ho capito. Ma,* thees is for a true *filigrana,* yes, but they have a trick in the days of the *Rinascimento* to write in *acido.* How do you say?"

"Acid. Ah, like lemon juice? The way kids do? They did that then too, in the Renaissance—*nel Rinascimento?*"

"*Si, con limone, o . . . o con aceto.* How you say?"

"Uh, 'vinegar'. They used that to...?"

"Yes, yes. Mix sometimes of the both. And other acid too. I have no see myself, but there are peec-tures of such documents in books. Very secret writing. If it is present, the fluid weel bring it out. Here, I weel show you *filigrane* on the *francobolli.*"

He turned to the middle of the album and lifted a little blue postage stamp from its transparent holder, then took a small black tray from the box, set the stamp on its flat bottom surface, printed side down, picked up the bottle of fluid, dribbled a few drops into the tray, and handed it to Robert. The volatile liquid, its pungent fumes scented of naphtha or benzene, had conjured up a miniature image on the gummed side of the stamp, a distinct cluster of five-point stars, showing slate gray against the paler color of the uninked surface. In a few seconds the fluid evaporated, and, as it did, the image faded. In a moment it had disappeared completely, vanishing without a trace like some magician's dove, stowed away in limbo until the illusionist's sleight of hand should fetch it back to life again.

"You see the *filigrana?*"

"Yes. Yes, I do! I did! That's . . . it's amazing!"

"Yes, OK. Here, I weel show you another one."

Fabbri went through five more demonstrations, conjuring from the tiny gummed surfaces alternately bold or delicate watermarks; here miniature stars, there little winged wheels, once an intricate honeycomb. They were extraordinary images, entirely absent without the fluid, yet, in its presence, clear and unmistakable. An arresting display, no doubt, but Robert's mind had already raced ahead beyond the little stamps with their formalistic patterns to that enigmatic page! That vast blank surface with its meaningless line of print and queer, directional arrow: what wonders might this magic fluid summon from its fabric? What mysteries might accompany those faint, translucent circles he had discerned eight hours earlier in the palace window's sunlight? Some acid-etched inscription written by the great Colangio himself in guarded and meticulous secrecy five centuries ago? Robert could hardly restrain his impatience to find out.

"*Eccole*," said Fabbri. "Those are all the types of *filigrane* in the *francobolli*—eh, stamps—of Italia, in the *Repubblica* time. You see?"

"Yes, yes. It's fascinating. The stamps are fascinating. Really. You have a wonderful collection."

"Ah, *grazie mille*. It is . . . eh, *completa*. . . ."

"Complete."

"*Si*, 'complete'. I shall remember. It is complete except for one single stamp."

"Yes? One stamp only? Why don't you get it?"

"Ah, Dottor Bob, thees is verr rare."

"And expensive, too, I guess?"

"*Si*, the *mille lire pacchi postale*—*come si dice* . . . for to mail packages?"

"Uh, parcel post?"

"Maybe. There is one such stamp with *filigrana ruota alata*, the wheel weeth a wing, like I show you on the deef-ferent stamp. Very espensive in the *pacchi postale*, costing maybe, one thousand five hundreds of dollars. But then there is another one with *filigrana stelle*, the stars. You know. I show you that one too. On the first stamp, the blue one. The *filigrana stelle* on the *mille lire pacchi postale* cost maybe one thousand lire only, less than one dollar. Otherwise same. Same stamp *nella facciata*."

"On the front."

"*Si*, front."

"And that's the only difference between them? The watermark?"

"*Filigrana, si*."

"Well, if we discover some really valuable information with that fluid you showed me, and it helps me write another book half as profitable as the last one, I'll buy it for you."

"You weel buy me your book, Dottor Bob? It would be a great honor."

"That's a deal, Taddeo. I'll buy you the book and mail it to you parcel post, with the *mille lire filigrana ruota alata* on the package."

∽∽∽∽∽∽∽

CHAPTER TEN

INSCRIPTION

ALL RIGHT, HE'D NEED A PAN, SOMETHING FLAT AND OBLONG; A LITTLE like Fabbri's postage stamp tray, but bigger, much bigger, so that a manuscript page of folio size would fit inside. Eleven by fifteen, maybe, or slightly more, yet not so huge as to waste a lot of fluid. And it would have to be dark enough to show up the watermark, and shallow enough for light to reach its bottom unobstructed. A baking pan, say, but of such exact dimensions and qualities that a thing of that specific type might be difficult to find.

Robert stopped at a crosswalk, waiting for the light to change, thinking. . . . Yes, a baking pan would do just fine; a cookie pan, even, if he could get one in black or navy. He'd try a housewares store first. Then, if he couldn't locate anything suitable there, maybe a photography shop might have something close enough to suit his purpose just as well.

The rest of it would be a snap. He ran through the little list of requirements in his head, walking down Via di Pantaneto enroute to the Piccolomini: a well-ventilated place to work, overhead lighting, a sheet of glass to set atop the pan—just in case he'd need a surface to copy anything—if, in fact, there turned out to be anything there to copy, after all!

And the fluid: yes, of course. Archival quality fluid—Fabbri had emphasized that—a pure, non-caustic chemical solvent that would be absolutely safe to use with rare and costly things of paper—like a delicate sheet of manuscript from the Renaissance era, or that parcel post stamp the *Archivista* coveted to fill the last empty space in his album. Get a couple of eight ounce bottles at Filatelia Crespi, Fabbri had told him, a little stamp shop over on Via dei Montanini, just a five minute walk from the Piccolomini. They'd be open, at last, today, this Monday. He'd stop there after lunch.

He made it to the palazzo by nine-fifteen, feeling finally awake, invigorated. Nine long hours he had slept; nine delicious, restorative hours—finally adjusting to the time change—from eleven last night until eight this morning, awakening today as relaxed and comfortable as he had ever been those lazy Saturday mornings at home, lounging in his jeans and tee-shirt, putting up water for Cassie's tea. Then the twenty-minute walk to the palazzo, thinking all the while about the useless manuscript, the mysterious blank page, and now, suddenly, the prospect of some long-hidden watermark that might unlock the secrets of both! All that pondering had sparked his wakefulness, his excitement, so that now, this Monday morning, on entering Fabbri's office, he was half beside himself with curiosity. What amazing revelations might that strange blank page yield in Fabbri's magic fluid? He could scarcely restrain his eagerness to find out.

"Good morning!" he greeted Caterina, who was sitting at her desk in the *Archivista*'s outer office, typing into a computer.

"Ah, good morning, dottore. How was your dinner with Sgr. Fabbri last Friday?"

"*Bene, bene*. He showed me his collection. Have you seen it?"

"His collection?" She nodded. "The stamps? No, not actually. I have no need to see them. I keep a list."

"You keep a list? . . . Of his stamps you mean?"

"Yes. I look for items that he needs. On the Internet, for example. And in shops occasionally."

"You. . . . He asked you to manage his stamp collection for him?"

"Yes—well, not directly: I had occasion to see his correspondence from a number of stamp dealers and asked him for a list of items he was looking for. We have managed to find all except two stamps of the *Repubblica* period."

"Oh, well I think he's down to just one now."

"Yes, the *mille lire pacchi postali*. But he doesn't count the magenta airplane error that was printed with the wrong design. It is a secondary number in the catalogue, and there is no space for it in his album."

"I see. . . . Well, that's impressive! You do quite a lot of things for him, don't you?"

"Do things? What do you mean?"

"Well, *you* know, uh . . . take care of things, anticipate his needs. . . ."

"Yes, of course. Isn't that my duty? . . . Uh, dottore, by the way, remember you have an appointment today. . . ."

"What? Oh, right; the room, you mean. The lady you called on my behalf, right?"

"Yes, may I give you the directions now?"

"No, I can get them later I guess. You'll be here?"

"Of course."

"OK. . . . Look, is the boss in?"

"Of course. He is expecting you."

"Should I . . . ?"

"Yes, of course. Just walk right in."

"*Buon giorno, buon giorno!*" said Fabbri. The *Archivista* sat propped at his desk, looking awkward, neglected, and rather pleased at the prospect of a visitor. There was a sort of latent expectation about him, a look of awaiting something—a stimulus to get him going, maybe, or a change of batteries. He seemed lost, dispossessed, discharged from urgent duties like some bewildered ship's captain confined to his quarters by victorious mutineers. An unkempt captain, though, dressed tattily in a worn brown suit that looked a bit too small, bought straight off the shelf, or tailored ineptly, or picked up secondhand from a man not quite as lanky or with arms a little less long. There was a cut on his chin—got shaving, no doubt, rather than mutinously—and a shard of tissue paper adhered to it, like a dab of cherry ice cream that had dribbled downward from his lips and settled on the next protruding surface. Looking pensive, though smiling affably, he raised a hand and beckoned Robert in.

"*Viene*, Dottor Bob. You have slept well, I hope?"

"Yes, very well, thanks. From eleven last night on. I feel terrific. . . . Just, you know, antsy—uh, *ansioso, capisce?*—about that page. . . . The watermark, that is. The *filigrana*."

"Ah, yes. Of course. You will go today for the fluid?"

"Yes. Uh, the Filatelia Crespi, right?"

"Yes, yes, Crespi, *si*. And a black . . . uh, *teglia*—pan, I theenk, in Eenglish. You must no forget. . . . Do you want to take the *pagina* today?"

"To take it?"

"Yes, of course. You must take it from the palazzo to examine. One must not use the . . . *sostanza incendiabile* in the palazzo. How do you say?"

"Uh, 'flammable substance.' Or 'inflammable,' either one."

"OK, I shall remember. 'Flammable' and 'inflammable' mean the same? They are of the same meaning? It does not seem correct."

"I think it is, though."

"OK. . . . *In ogni caso*, one cannot use such *sostanze* in the palazzo. How you say again?"

"'Substance'. Or 'fluid', you can say. Either one. . . . All right, I understand. So am I allowed to take it out, then, the page? Carry it out with me, just like that?"

"No. No *you*, of *course*, no, but I can take for you, in my hand case, eh? Nobody check me. I geeve you thees afternoon when we are fee-neesh for the day."

"Are you sure? . . . You can't get in trouble for that?"

"*Trouble? Me? Fabbri?* I am the *Archivista Principale*! Who weel give trouble to me? Nobody!... But you must remember, Dottor Bob, you must use weeth lot of air, *ventilazione*, you know? How you say?"

"'Ventilation'. It's about the same. . . . OK, I know. I'll, uh . . . I'll keep a window open or something. . . . What is the stuff, anyway, the substance? Do you know what kind of fluid it is? The chemicals?"

"Chemicals? Ah, *chimichi, si*. In the fluid?"

"Yes."

"*Beh,* like fluid for . . . uh, *pulitura a secco*, you know? But leetle deefferent. More safe, eh?"

"Like dry-cleaning fluids, you mean?"

"Yes. Yes. 'Dry cleaning'. Good. I shall remember."

He worked on the manuscript for an hour or so, but he was much too distracted to get very far. At last, at ten-fifteen, he dropped his pen, pulled off the gloves, and plodded down the palazzo's steps to do his errands. Caterina caught up with him as he was just stepping through the exit door.

"Dottor Martin!"

"Yes, Caterina. . . . I was just going out for a little while."

"Yes, as I can see, but . . . you remember your appointment?"

"The appointment? Yes, of course. What time was it for?"

"Two."

"All right, Caterina, but. . . ."

"No 'buts', dottore, please. I have made specific arrangements, you understand, and you must go. Here, I have the location marked on this map." She reached into her purse, took out a street map, and opened it. "You see? It is very near, on Via San Martino, number 127, where the 'x' is. Here. You see it?"

"Yes."

"Then be there just at two. The woman's name is Dall'Olmo, Teresa Dall'Olmo. It is written here beside the address. The woman I know, whose daughter I have tutored, you remember? I spoke to her again this morning. She will be expecting you."

"All right, Caterina. Thanks. I do appreciate your efforts."

"Well, it is nothing. . . . Anyway, you will find it much less costly than the place where you are presently staying."

"Yes?"

"Seven hundred thousand lire a month. That is. . . ."

"Four hundred dollars, right?"

"Yes, about."

"Well, thanks for your trouble; really. *Grazie dell'aiuto, Caterina.*"

"*Ma figurati*! It is my job, signore . . . dottore. Noon, promptly. Remember."

"OK, Caterina, I promise I'll be there."

He grabbed a cup of coffee in the Campo, then headed to the *filatelia*. First things first. The fluid, the pan: once he had them secured, he'd be able to relax a little. There'd be plenty of time from now until two; then he'd get the damned inspection over with. After all, he'd promised. And Caterina would be in to check on things; that was for sure.

Well, all right, he'd have done what she'd asked. The room's too small, he'd tell her, or too dirty, or too loud. What could you expect for four hundred bucks a month? She might run the *Archivista*'s life, but not his! No, he had no list of stamps for her to find him, no letters to translate into English, no automobiles to buy. The hotel was just fine for him right now. A little pricey, yes, but he could afford it. After all, he wouldn't need a new Mercedes this year, or walnut cabinets, or goddamn diamond tennis bracelets, either! No, those days were well behind him. For lack of anyone else to spend money on, he might just as well pamper himself!

He found the woman's place five blocks from the palace, just where Caterina had marked it on the map. There was nothing near the door that looked remotely like a bell, no button or lever or pull of any kind. But a brass knocker on the paneled wood practically screamed out to him for use, so he clapped it a few times with clattering effect, then waited, warily attentive to the environment around him.

It was an impressive structure that he stood before, built, from all appearances, in the eighteenth century. There was the ubiquitous off-white stucco facing on its second and third level, then stone cladding on the ground floor. Far overhead, the gently sloping roof, though largely invisible from his angle of view, showed projections of the same curved orange tile that covers ninety-five percent of the gently sloping roofs in Siena. All things considered, then, a fine and relatively modern dwelling for a downtown Sienese family. Caterina had gotten her facts perfectly straight about that.

A minute passed before the latch clicked and the mammoth door swung inward. One expects a giant to move such a portal, but the figure Robert saw daylit in the doorway was a slender woman of medium height, well past middle age, with a kindly, smiling face. Her skin looked sweetly wrinkled—lined, that is, by laugh lines, smile lines, stellate around the eyes, circumflex about the mouth, thus benevolently aged. She wore an apron, stained ruddy with what appeared to be tomato juice of varying hue and provenance, beneath it a dark skirt, black or the deepest shade of blue, and, protruding through the apron's top, a beige blouse, clean but slightly frayed at its wrist-length cuffs.

"*Signore,*" she said in articulate Tuscan, "*come posso aiutarLa?*"

"*Buon giorno, signora. Sono venuto per vedere l'alloggio.*" He'd come about the lodging, he explained.

"*Ah! Prego, signore, entri, entri!*" She led him through the doorway into a vestibule with polished stone floor and walls, then up a steep flight of steps to the second level. Through an entrance to the left of the landing was a sort of sitting room, furnished in English Victorian style, all curved, tufted, and velvet-trimmed, looking very out of date and very out of place, but immaculately clean and inviting.

"*Si sieda, signore. Lá, sul divano.*" She motioned him onto a sofa, one of two in the abundant room, both colored an identical dark blue which blended tastefully with a cream, blue and brown Turkish carpet neatly filling the center of the floor. Everything smacked of well-maintained but faded elegance, the woman not excepted. "*Prego, signore, si accommodi. Desidera qualcosa da bere?*"

"*No, grazie, signora,*" said Robert, with a waggle of his hand. He wasn't thirsty. He set his packages on the sofa beside him: the baking pan in its gaping plastic sack and the little paper bag from the Filatelia Crespi containing two eight-ounce bottles of *Archivista*-recommended SuperSafe Watermark Fluid.

"*Lei parla bene l'italiano. Da dove viene?*"

"*Dagli Stati Uniti,* the U.S.A. *Da* Chicago."

"*Ah,* Chicago. Al Capone." 'Ahl Cah-*POH*-nay', she said, smiling gently, whimsically.

"*Si, signora. Sfortunatamente, é morto molti anni fa.* Mr. Capone, alas, was dead these many years. The woman smiled more broadly, evincing an engaging sense of humor. That, thought Robert, would be a happy omen for whatever lucky person *did* wind up renting her reasonable room at some point in the future. The nice little lady seemed just as sweet and pleasant as Caterina Paschiale had promised she would be.

"*Ma, l'alloggio?*" he asked: the lodgings? He'd have a look at them, then leave. After all, what was the point in wasting her time, his time, and the whole damned afternoon in useless repartee? Now that he had his two bottles of fluid and an appropriate pan secured, he could relax—maybe even get through another dismal page or two of St. Francis' Strange Adventures. The prospect didn't sound so awful right now. To tell the truth, it might make the time pass a little quicker until six, when Fabbri would smuggle out that mysterious blank page for him in his briefcase.

"*Ah, Caterina ha telefonata. . . . Scusi, signore, ma qui non c'é la cucina per gli ospiti.*" The little lady was staring at the baking pan's rim, which had found a portal of egress between the tank-top straps of the plastic bag. No kitchen for guests, she had admonished. Robert laughed. The pan, he explained sheepishly, was for something else. Not cooking, in fact, but a scientific experiment. At work.

"*Si, capisco, capisco. Va bene. Allora, vuole vedere la camera? Scusi, signore, ma non parlo l'inglese, neanche una parola. Ma mia figlia lo parla bene. Studia l'inglese all' universitá.*" Her daughter studied English at the university, but, sorry, she herself couldn't speak a word. Fine, he thought. It was all the same to him—English or Italian, daughter, son or pet python: show him the room, and let him be on his way. She led him up another flight of steps to the third floor, then through another doorway to the left, and into the quarters in question.

My God! he thought, looking around the room. *Unbelievable*! The place was huge! A veritable suite! Twin beds pushed together into a sort of king-size arrangement, just like his bed at home—or the one he'd *had* at home, with Cassie, for Sheldon would arrange for its disposition soon. Then a sofa, a desk and wooden chair, lots of closet space, another lounge chair in the far corner, and, best of all, a big tiled bath, attached and private, with tub, shower, bidet. . . . It was bigger, better, and more comfortable than his room at the hotel, at a tenth the price—if Caterina had heard the woman right. Damn! he thought, that Caterina was amazing! Maybe he'd be better off letting *her* translate the manuscript and write his second book.

"*E l'affitto?*"

Seven hundred thousand lire, she said, just as Caterina had reported. Four hundred dollars a month!

When was it available? he asked her. What was the very soonest he could move in?

"*Subito*," she told him. Immediately. "*Puo attendere. . . .*" Could he wait a bit? Her daughter would be home soon from her classes at the university. She'd speak English with him—good English too, *perfetto*—arrange things, see to any of his particular needs. No, he explained; he had something important to do. He'd call back later. She nodded obligingly and smiled. The pan in its plastic sack in one hand, the fluid in the other, he followed the signora down to the big front door. "*Mille grazie, signora, per tutto*," he said: thanks a lot for everything. He'd be back toward the end of the week with his things.

"*Eccola*," said Fabbri, handing him the page in its folio cover. "Remember, Dottor Bob, you must do the *ventilazione* for the *vapori*, eh?"

They had walked around the corner from the palace to the Piazza del Campo, which was alive now with pedestrian traffic and pigeons. Around the circuit of its scallop-shell slope, outdoor restaurants were seating their early diners, mostly tourists eating at an hour in Siena when only tourists ate. Couples passed by distractedly, undisturbed by groups of youngsters at play. Older men and women, mostly workers heading home or retirees out for an evening stroll, moved diagonally up- or downslope through the enormous brick-paved piazza, unmindful of its ancient historicity and unattentive to the fine gothic buildings towering above.

"Hey, this is terrific, Taddeo! I don't know how to thank you." Robert, gazing up at Fabbri's face, patted the *Archivista* affectionately on the arm.

"*Ma figurati*! We are friends, dottore. And it is no-theen, no-theen . . . *niente*."

"Well, can I return the favor in some way? Is there anything I can do for you in exchange? Something I can get you from the States? Some American stamps, maybe?"

"No, no. *Grazie*. It is not in the leastest bit necessary. Just be sure to make the ween-dow open. You can do thees at the hotel?"

"Yes, yes, I always leave a window open at night. I'll follow your instructions to the letter. . . . Maybe tomorrow I'll have a some amazing revelation to tell you—*una rivelazione, capisce*?"

"*Si, si, ho capito*. Well, I look to hear some-theen . Maybe some buried treasure or some-theen good like thees."

"Yeah, sure. Who knows?—Oh, by the way, I'll be moving out of the Garibaldi this weekend."

"Moveen out?"

"Yes, Caterina found another place for me to stay. To live."

"*Ah, si! Una pensione*?"

"No, no. It's some woman she recommended. Caterina used to tutor her daughter. Dall'Olmo is the name, Teresa Dall'Olmo. Do you know her?"

"Yes, of course. Her husband was a . . . *era in politica*, you know?"

"A politician—*un politico?*"

"No, *ma dietro le quinte*, you understand?"

"Behind the scenes. Yes. Like a party boss?"

"*Si, un famoso avvocato*—lawyer, you say, but verr' big. He die about ten years . . . eh before now. *Dieci anni fa.*"

"Ten years ago."

"*Si*. Ten years ago. 'Ago': I shall remember. . . . *Un gran' scandalo*, thees was. He holp his brother with money from the *appaltatori.*"

"Contractors."

"Yes. Contractors. I shall remember thees also. 'Contractors'. Is verr' good word I theen, 'contractors.'"

"Yes. Well, that explains the house. I thought they looked pretty well off . . . uh *ricci.*"

"No, no *ricci*. He lose-ed all the money with the brother business, the *scandalo*. I think he kill himself, but they say his heart. I think some other theen though, some pills maybe. Maybe use a gun. I can no say for sure. Nobody talk about it after."

"So *that's* why she rents the room! I see! It's sad, isn't it? She seems like such a nice lady."

"*Si, si*, verr' nice. People say so. I have no meet her myself, but people say. And Caterina teach her daughter, eh? I never hear thees before."

"Well, I'll ask Caterina for some more details tomorrow. She really does take care of everything, that secretary of yours—I was laughing about it to myself this afternoon. She could probably finish translating the manuscript for me if I gave her half a chance."

"*Ah, si*, and write another book for you too, and maybe win another prize," said Fabbri. He spoke the words which in any other context would have been droll, sarcastic in a bitter sort of way. But he wasn't smiling. Instead, he looked solemn, grave; as serious as a convict on death row.

It was an awning window and when he pushed the bottom of the sash outward, the evening warmth of Siena wafted in. Comingling with it, flavoring the still air, came the omnipresent scents of diesel, dust, and heated pavement. Seven stories up, his room looked out on a little courtyard with two grizzled trees and an empty fountain at its far end. Some children were playing with a stick and soccer ball across the fountain's desiccated basin, and their piping sounds of youthful energy slipped into the room with the agile dust and stale, oppressive air.

He looked at the clock on the nightstand. Its carmine numerals, appropriate to the temperature outside, read 6:39. It was early evening now, but the sun was still sufficiently high to drench the room in a warm saffron tint, almost liquid in its substantiality. Robert slid the room's computer desk a little closer to the open window and snapped on a lamp atop it, flooding the hollow of the pan with a clinical sort of light, intense and colorless. Yes, he thought, touching the pan's black surface with a finger, that should do just fine.

He took one of the bottles of fluid from the paper bag, unscrewed its top, and sniffed. No, the fumes weren't particularly strong or, for that matter, particularly objectionable. Still, it seemed only prudent to follow Fabbri's admonition that that the place be ventilated well. He set the top back on the bottle and reached for the blank page, slipping it from its folio cover and placing it, face downward, on the bottom of the pan.

Opening the bottle again, he dabbed a little fluid on one corner of the sheet, testing its effect. That too the *Archivista* had insisted on, and it would be best to do exactly as he said. Moistened by a drop or two, the corner of the page darkened, clarified, and then began to dry. In fifteen seconds the area had returned to its original appearance—exactly—looking just as bright and virginal as it had looked before. He touched the area and it felt normal, had a normal texture. So! Just as Fabbri had said, the stuff was safe enough, simple enough to use.

All right, then. Robert wiped his brow, moist from the window's heat and his own anticipation, then took a deep breath. It was time at last. He'd waited all weekend for this! If Colangio—his dear, old, familiar friend Colangio—had some long-buried secret to reveal, it was about to come to light.

There was a hot but active breeze wafting through the window now, facilitating the ventilation. Robert took another lungful of air, instinctively, half in excitement, half in preparation for the fumes, then poured out an ounce or so of fluid, sloshing it around the pan, wetting the document fully. . . .

And the paper came alive!

Six perfect circles, arranged hexagonally, with writing inside each and below each, then more writing in the page's center—though the words were at first entirely illegible, so jumbled were they and so diaphanous. This was no watermark! No, no, it was just as Fabbri had guessed! an inscription, drawn purposefully, etched in pen and acid ink on ancient paper. Something written five centuries before by the greatest genius of the Renaissance, then stowed away in secret like some priceless pilfered gem. A cryptic message from the great Colangio suddenly unearthed after half a millennium! It was . . . well, not just amazing, but . . . but . . . *breathtaking*!

Robert, trembling now palpably, adjusted the light, shifting it to a spot directly above the pan, then set his head against the lampshade and peered directly downward. . . . But it was too late: the last faint evidence of writing had vanished to invisibility, the breeze having absorbed the volatile liquid like a sponge, effacing the evanescent imagery. He mopped his brow again, turned to the window, drew in another hot but uncontaminated breath, then wetted the paper a second time, his hand so tremulous from excitement that a bit more fluid escaped than he'd intended, maybe two or more ounces this time.

The page literally swam in it, floating for an instant, then settling quickly to the bottom of the pan. Now he felt the vapors in his nose and throat, tasted them, and turned his head instinctively away. . . . But in a little while the paper lured him back. Taking the shallowest of breaths he set his head against the lamp again, peered downward into the pan, and gazed upon the image once more, etched in gray on antique white.

It was a diagram, clearly, with its six circles arranged into a larger pattern—a hexagram, maybe, but with its connecting edges missing. Each circle was perfectly drawn, by handheld compass or traced around a coin, each was about an inch in diameter, and each held writing within or directly underneath its outline. Then there was more writing, a large block of it, in the center of the hexagram.

Robert stared into the pan, trying to make out some of the lettering, but was unable to . . . because . . . because it was . . . it was . . . ah! *backward*. Which meant the sheet was upside-down—that is, the lettering had been done on the *front* side, according to the ink inscription at its bottom edge. He wasn't at all certain that so ancient a page in such an inundated state ought to be handled, so he waited a minute or two longer until the last trace of fluid had evaporated once again, then flipped the redried paper right side up.

The room smelled powerfully of solvent now. Now, without question, it *had* grown offensive; so better, Robert thought, to let the fumes dissipate a bit. He stuck his head out through the window's narrow opening and caught some fresher, though hot and dusty, breaths. Below, in the courtyard behind the hotel, the shadows had lengthened and the children had gone. Their soccer ball lay abandoned in the fountain's empty well.

Robert stepped over to the *frigo-bar*, took out a beer, went back to the window, sat down, and drank the contents of the bottle thirstily. Five minutes had passed, or ten, since he had begun his experiment. It was 6:52 now, and the air within the room smelled weakly again of dust and diesel but scarcely at all of solvent. He took the last draught of beer, set the bottle down, lifted the paper—crisply dry now—and held it up against the light. No, there were no adverse effects whatever. None. Fabbri had been absolutely right. You couldn't make out the slightest trace of the watermark now—well, maybe those two part-circles he had seen originally; but nothing else. Nothing. It was incredible! Like . . . well, like magic almost. Something he never would have dreamed of had it not been for Fabbri. Thank heaven for the *Archivista* and his blessed little stamps!

He set the sheet of paper back into the pan, right side up this time, poured in another ounce or two of fluid, adjusted the light, and bent downward to read. The pattern simply leapt from the page now with the proper lighting and immersion. Each of the six circles had printing inside and beneath it. The lettering was clearly in Colangio's hand, though purposefully done—in the same style, that is, as the *"Solus ad bonum"* inked in at the bottom of the page. Then there was that additional block of text in the very center of the hexagram. Robert began reading the words in the two-o'clock circle, but had only deciphered a few of them before the paper dried once more and the images vanished. *"Torlo per lo frate sole,"* they said: "An egg yolk for brother sun."

What? he thought. What in the *world*...?

This time he wetted the page selectively, dripping fluid only over the area of the adjacent circle, at four o'clock. He adjusted the lamp, then angled the pan slightly, tilting it a little upward, so that the light penetrated diagonally, providing an optimal view of the four o'clock circle and the lettering within and beneath it.

Following the letters carefully with an overhanging finger, he read—quite clearly now, for his eyes had grown accustomed to the translucent script—viewing, after five hundred years of silence, Colangio's long-buried, secretly encoded, and carefully printed words. Which turned out to be:

"*Per sora luna, una conchiglia d'ostrica*—For sister moon, an oyster shell."

~~~~~~~~~~

CHAPTER ELEVEN

INVESTIGATION

"BOBBY?" HE SAID. "JESUS! WHERE THE HELL HAVE YOU BEEN? I HAVEN'T heard a thing from you since you left last week."

"I know, Shel, I know. Look, I couldn't call before now. Everything was really up in the air. Anyway, I'm finally getting situated. . . ."

"Yeah, but you could have gotten word to me, though. OK, OK, look, I'm glad to hear you're all right. Where are you? Give me a number, for God's sake. What if I had to get hold of you for something? Like the condo, for instance. What if I had a question? It's a lot of money to . . . to just delegate to somebody, you know."

"Yeah, I know. I'm sorry. It was a lot to ask of you."

"Come on, that's not what I meant at all, Bobby; you know that. Look, I'm happy to do it for you. . . ."

"So what's happening with the damn thing, anyway? You get anywhere?"

"The condo? Shit, yeah. There's twenty people want it. The realtor said you'll get four-seventy-five for it."

"Really? That's more than we paid."

"Sure. The area's hot with the *nouveau riche*. Lincoln Park, you know? And the furniture. . . . You got any idea what's in there? Some of those antiques? . . . I had a woman come in and look at it for an appraisal. Just to get an idea, you know, so we don't get ripped off. Anyway, she said like over a hundred and fifty grand for what you got in the place. Jesus! That girlfriend of yours sure knew how to spend your money."

"Did . . . did you call to see...?"

"Cassie you mean? Yeah, I called her. She didn't want any of it.

Shit, she hardly needs your trinkets now. That guy she latched onto, you got any idea what he's worth?"

"A pretty good idea."

"She doesn't need your nickel-dime furnishings; that's for sure."

"Is she...?"

"Who the hell knows how she is or what she's up to? She dismissed me in a couple of seconds on the phone. Of course, there's no love lost between the two of us, Cassie and me. 'Say hello to Robert for me,' she says. 'Tell him I think of him often.' Shit, there's your message for you, but it was in that disgusting saccharine voice of hers. I can't do it the way she does."

The words brought all his sorrow back, so that Robert couldn't speak for a moment. Sheldon must have detected something in his silence on the phone.

"Are you OK, Bobby? I shouldn't have told you. . . . I shouldn't have said anything."

"No, no, that's all right. I'm fine." But he wasn't. His voice was weak and halting and utterly betrayed him.

"Look . . . look, are you really doing OK?" asked Shelly. "Are you. . . .? Is everything working out all right there?"

Robert took a moment to collect himself. "Uh . . . yeah. I'm . . . I'm, uh, kind of settled now." There was a drop of moisture at the inner angle of each eye, which he wiped with a knuckle, first one, then the other, then dried the knuckle on his shirt. "We . . . uh . . . I, that is, I found a place—a room—with a nice family . . . uh, a nice lady and her daughter. . . . Anyway, I'll be moving there . . . in a few days, I guess. . . . I'll have a separate phone line, so maybe I can email after that."

"Good, good, I'll expect to hear from you more often then. . . . So how's the work going?"

"What?"

"The work. Your papers. Manuscript. Whatever the goddam shit you're supposed to be doing there."

"I don't know, Shelly. Look, what difference does it make?"

"OK, OK, don't get so huffy. I just asked about your work. . . . Hey, you're upset about Cassie, right? I know you. I'm sorry I even told you, but you might as well hear all this stuff now. And from me. Better to hear it from me, you know? You're gonna have to close the book on her sooner or later, Bobby; and better sooner than later."

"Yeah, I know that, Shel. I know that. . . . Look, I *am* doing better, though. I *have* been. . . . It's not just her; it's the research too. The whole damn thing's been pretty frustrating. I feel like I'm wasting my time here. . . . Like it's a kind of exile, you know?"

"So come home. Drive over to the pizza guy's place and sit outside in your car to catch a glimpse of her. Follow her to work. Call her up to hear her voice on the phone and then hang up like some teen-age schoolboy."

"Come on, Shelly. . . . Look, I'll be fine. I was in a good mood when I called you."

"Why?"

"Why what?"

"Why were you in such a good mood?"

"I don't know—because of the room I found, maybe. . . . And I do enjoy getting back to research again, even a project as futile as this one seems to be."

"So what's so futile about it?"

"Lots of stuff. . . . Look, it's too involved to talk about on the phone."

"What—you're worried about the nickel? Hey, I'll call you back if you can't afford the bill."

"No, it isn't that. . . ."

"So what is it then?"

"I don't know. . . . This thing is turning out to be more like a . . . a puzzle than anything else. It's really out of my field."

"How? What do you mean by a puzzle?"

"Look, it's complicated, but. . . . All right, well I came across something crazy in the manuscript I've been working on."

"Crazy? Like what?"

"I don't know. . . . I found this bizarre watermarked page in the box the manuscript was in."

"Watermarked? Like something in the paper?"

"Yeah, like that, but not originally *formed* into the paper—I mean, it's like a kind of secret mark done purposefully after the fact, like with acid ink."

"So that sounds pretty interesting, doesn't it? What does it say?"

"I don't know. Crazy stuff. Meaningless, basically. Like a magic diagram kind of thing."

"A diagram? To do what?"

"That I don't know yet. Maybe it predicts the future or something—Look, I just found the damn thing last night."

"You found it?"

"Yeah, there's a kind of fluid that shows up watermarks—it's a long story. . . . Anyway, I'm going to show it to the archivist this morning. He seems pretty knowledgeable about these sorts of things. I'm hoping that he'll have some suggestions as to what it all might mean."

"Well, that sounds pretty interesting to me—hey, a hell of a lot more interesting than that erudite crap you usually get stuck working on."

"Yeah, maybe. But I'd prefer the erudite crap right now. At least I'd have aome idea what I'm supposed to do with it."

"So what do you plan to do with *this* stuff?"

"I don't know. I'm not really sure—probably just keep looking."

"Looking? For what?"

"Oh . . . yeah . . . well, there's a part of it missing."

"Missing?"

"Yeah. There's a block of writing in the center of the diagram that refers to something called a '*carmen*'—an incantation. I'll have to figure out where *that* is."

"Well where *could* it be?"

"I don't know; it's got to be in the manuscript someplace, maybe in the text or in another watermark. . . . I'll just have to look."

"So what are you gonna do with it once you find it?"

"Good question! . . . I'm not a hundred percent sure of that either. I guess—well, I'm hoping—that it might provide some clue as to what the diagram itself represents. And if I can figure *that* out, I might have some information as to what crazy stuff Colangio got himself into during the last part of his life."

"Yeah, he dropped out or something, didn't he?"

"For twenty-three years."

"And you think this might explain it?"

"It might help . . . if I get lucky."

"Wow! That would be something! You'd make a million bucks on *that* book."

"It'd be a real sensation, all right. But . . . I don't know, this whole business seems really nuts to me. It's not the kind of research I was ever trained to do. . . . Listen, Shelly, anyway . . . let me ask you something—from a psychologist's point of view. . . ."

"Sure, go ahead, ask."

"About Colangio: this . . . this stuff is uncharacteristic of him. . . . No, that's the wrong word—it's more than that; if what I found is what it looks like, it represents a total watershed change in his mind set; in his world view, I mean. Up until November 1503 he was a confirmed rationalist—well, *you* know; you read the book—then suddenly all this lunacy shows up a couple of months later. . . . Listen, is it possible for somebody to change that much in such a short time?"

"Of course it is."

"OK, how?"

"How? Some kind of incredible mental shock is how. Something that must have turned his universe completely upside-down."

"Well, like what?"

"Hey, that's what *you're* getting paid to figure out, Bobby. Why don't you call Auntwon? He'll probably come up with an answer for you in twenty seconds on the phone."

"The boss get here yet?"

"Yes, dottore. He arrived some moments ago. Go right in."

Fabbri was seated in his customary place, propped behind his desk, his arms folded on its surface, looking entirely inert. He smiled, though, and came to life a bit when Robert stepped into the room.

"Dottor Bob! *Ah, benvenuto*! Sit down, sit down."

"Good morning, Taddeo. How are you this morning?"

"Ah, fine, fine. And you?"

"Great, just great. . . . Listen . . . I'd like you to have a look at something for me."

"Sometheen?"

"Yes, there was something in that page you gave me—a watermark, just as you said."

"Ah, *si*, in the *pagina*. What is it you find?"

"I don't know—a kind of diagram, I guess."

"Ah, good; thees is interesting, no? What is it you find? A diorama, you say?"

"No. A diagram—*diagramma*—like a chart, you know? It's a. . . . Well, here, let me show you. I made a copy."

Robert dropped the legal pad on Fabbri's desk, pulled up a chair beside the *Archivista*, sat down, and turned the pad to its very last page. There on the yellow, green-lined surface lay a faithful rendering of the image he had found the night before. It was finely drawn, detailed, the proportions exactly to scale, the arrangement of the circles and text a virtual replica of the image he had coaxed out with his fluid twelve hours earlier. Better, indeed, than the diagram itself, as to it's clarity— after all, this was Robert's *metier*: he had learned the scientific tech- niques of document reproduction well and fully from many years of practice: precise angles, proper arrangement of text, accurate form of lettering; the use of flattened calligraphic pencils, millimeter rules, the compass, the caliper. He had become in essence a Renaissance copyist with contemporary tools. So the chart he set beneath Fabbri's view was as exact a copy of the original as though its pattern had been traced— from a fluid-borne image that was effectively untraceable—with a fine- point pencil on a light-box.

Fabbri shifted the pad to where the light was better, tilting it a little on the desk. And what the two men beheld on the surface beneath them was:

Six perfect circles arranged in the form of a hexagram, six circles geometrically placed but with their edges unconnected, like so many transparent poker chips arrayed with radial symmetry about a central point. The yellow page, with its even, green lines, looked like the rec- tangular face of some novelty clock made for a lawyer from his note pad, fractionally off-kilter, with inch-wide circles at each even hour— six hours only, from the two o'clock position clockwise around to twelve. Within the diagram, at its geometric center, was a block of text, compressed and minuscule, running on to twenty lines or so; then more writing within and beneath each circle.

Robert had copied out the writing verbatim, following the exact format and calligraphic style that Colangio had used, forming the circles with a compass, lining up each segment of the diagram with a ruler—and inhaling a toxic brew of fluid in the process. As a final step, when the paper had thoroughly dried and his transcription of the watermark had been complete, he'd held both sheets of paper over a lighted TV screen and, for the first time, traced: that little tilted arrow at the top of the page and the Latin inscription below. "*Solus ad bonum*," the latter read, enigmatically.

"*Che cos'e!*—what is it!?" exclaimed the *Archivista*. "*Non ho visto*. . . . Eh, I have no seen anytheen ezackly like thees before now."

"OK. Well, that's unfortunate. I was hoping that you had." Robert peered around Fabbri's shoulder. Yes, the damn thing *was* strange; well pre-Renaissance in its verbiage and syntax. And then that diagram. . . . Nothing *he* had ever seen before, either; still he'd thought that maybe, with all the documents the *Archivista* had been through. . . .

"What do the writeen say?" asked Fabbri. "I can no read thees verr' good."

"No, it's hard to make out. . . . Here, let's see. I'll read it to you. Hopefully something in the words might ring a bell—uh, *far ricordare qualcosa*."

Robert slid the pad over in front of him and examined it again. The inscription in the center of the diagram was in Latin. It had struck him from the first as likely the most important part of the whole business, a sort of operator's manual for whatever task the chart was supposed to perform. So he read it out first. The words were repetitious, formulaic; he condensed them for Fabbri, giving just the essence of their meaning, reading the edited Latin, then translating, interlinearly, as he went along: "Arrange objects (*res denotatas*)"—the words said paraphrastically—"each in its circle; read incantation (*carmen inscriptum*) twice, precisely one hour after sunset (*solis occasus*); specify the wished-for thing (*rem cupitam*);" then blow out the candle—"let breath extinguish fire (*fac extinguere ventus ignem*)." The exhaled breath, like the arrow at the top of the page, must be directed precisely toward the sun at its point of disappearance, the Latin text instructed.

"What can thees mean?" asked Fabbri.

"I haven't a clue. . . . I was hoping *you*'d be able to tell *me*."

"*I*. No, no. . . . *Beh*. . . . Well what it is suppose to do?"

Robert shrugged. "No idea. . . . Some kind of magic spell I guess—*un incantesimo*. Maybe for astrology—*astrologia*; or witchcraft—*stregoneria* . . . or to predict the future—*previsione*, you know?"

"*Ah, si*, verr' strange, verr' strange. . . . *E i circoli...?*"

"The circles?"

"*Si*, 'seer-cles'. The *oggetti*—'objects', eh? These are the names for the objects—here below the seer-cles, no? Like thees one—what it says? *la conchilia d'ostrica?*"

"*Si, una conchilia d'ostrica e cinque cose piu.*" An oyster shell and five more things. A different object for each circle, specified by name within or beneath each one: something apparently to be placed in or on each circle for the diagram to 'work', though what it might 'work' to accomplish was entirely beyond Robert's utmost reach of speculation . . . for the present.

He read the words of all six circles for the *Archivista*. They were in Italian, not Latin like the instructions. Archaic Italian, true, but close enough to the modern idiom to be comprehensible to a modern-day Sienese as written. Robert started at the bottom, with the six-ten circle, which contained the words "*per frate vento, vento di polmone*": for Brother Wind, air from the lungs. Air was the bottom circle's object—breath, actually—easy enough to come by, though who 'brother wind' might be was anybody's guess. Diagonally across from 'air', the topmost circle read: "*per frate focu, accendi una candela di cera d'api*"—light a candle of beeswax for 'Brother Fire'. He ran through the rest quickly, for they were just as bizarre as the first two: the oyster shell (*conchiglia d'ostrica*), holy water (*acqua santa*), soil from an olive grove (*suolo d'oliveto*), and an egg yolk (*torlo d'uovo*). The remaining brothers, sisters, and other associated kinfolk were: Sister Moon—the oyster shell was for her—Brother Sun (the egg yolk), Sister Water (holy water, naturally), and Mother Earth (soil, as one might expect). Gather up the six named objects and your game board was complete, except—oh yes, that one last thing was missing—the incantation, those specific words one was supposed to read twice through before the iteration of the "desired thing." It was certainly not on the page, and if it was, in fact, hidden somewhere in the manuscript—well, discovering it might take a bit of time.

"So what does thees mean about the *rem cupitam?*" asked Fabbri.

"The 'desired thing'? I'd guess it's what the diagram's supposed to do—the task you'd want it to perform. . . . Like—I don't know—an answer to a question, maybe, or a voodoo curse you'd want to place on somebody. Maybe if I had that incantation I'd know a little more, but as it is. . . .

"Ah, *si, si, ho capito.* . . . *Ascolta,* Dottor Bob, listen. . . . I recommend you no look any more to find thees—'incantation' you say, eh?"

"Right, 'incantation'."

"*Bene.* I recommend you no. Such theens can be . . . eh . . . eh, *pericoloso.*"

"*Pericoloso!* Come on, Taddeo! This crazy stuff dangerous? It's all a bunch of nonsense as far as I'm concerned, fairy tales—*fiabe, lo sa?*"

"*Si, si, fiabe, fiabe;* most probably you are right. But still you must be careful with such theens. You must be verr' careful."

"OK, I'll be extremely careful. Vigilant. I promise you that." Robert shook his head.

"Yes, thees is like . . . eh, *stregoneria—Come si dice 'stregoneria'?*"

"'Witchcraft', we say. Or 'sorcery'."

"Ah, si. 'Weetchcraft'. I shall remember. *Beh* . . . is verr' dangerous. . . . Tell me, my friend: are you no a religious man?"

"No, Taddeo, not really. Most metaphysical things are pretty much lost on me, religion included. *Non sono superstizioso, neanche religioso* . . . uh, *particolarmente.* Why?"

"*Eh, non importa.* It does not disturb you then that thees is . . . eh, *sacrilego?*"

"Sacrilegious? How?"

"*Eh! Stregoneria?* Witchery? Is verr' *sacrilego,* no?"

"Well if the damn thing had any possible validity I guess it might be. As far as I'm concerned, though, it's just a means of getting inside Colangio's head during those last twenty-odd years of his life. *Per comprendere il suo motivazione, eh?* The more I can find out about what he was doing after 1503, the more I'll know about the man himself toward the end of his life. If he was into witchcraft, I need to know why; and if I have to study witchcraft to learn why, I'll just have to do that too."

"Ah, but maybe there are reasons why you no must learn such theens."

"Maybe. But the job of an academic is to find out every fact possible. . . . Hey, if I were studying Churchill, I'd have to learn about cigars and World War Two."

"Ah, *si*, but you would not wish to start a deadly fire or bring back Signor Hitler in the process, eh? . . . Please, Dottor Bob, be verr' careful."

He pulled out the papers and set them on the mylar sheet. "*Pericoloso,* the man had said! It was amazing how naive Italians could be, educated people too. . . . Robert smiled to himself and set about his work.

Through the rest of the day—Tuesday it was—he pored through the text, not trying to read it in detail, no, but rather scanning for Latin passages, for formulaic repetitions of words that might signify the presence of the incantation he sought. A hundred pages done by Tuesday night, the remaining ninety-odd on Wednesday. But there was nothing. Nothing at all.

On Thursday he began his search for a second watermark, holding each page up against the light, pulling the lamp shade off for better illumination. He knew what to look for this time: just the faintest trace of a pattern, like those spectral circles he had seen in the blank page that first day at work. He scanned each sheet in succession, backlit by the naked bulb, finding . . . absolutely nothing once again.

On Friday he scanned the text a second time, hoping to discover some hidden passage he had missed—something marked perhaps by the strange annotations on each page. He checked each one, each circled letter, each corresponding line, each numeral in the margin. . . . But there was nothing yet again. Finally, midway through the afternoon, he just gave up and went back to St. Francis' useless and pathetic tale.

Doc!" said Auntwon two hours after midnight Siena time—it was early evening in Chicago. "Man! Whassup? How you *doin'*?"

"OK. Good."

"Man, it got to be like one in the mornin' there!"

"Two, actually."

"Wow! Iss good to hear f'om you, man."

"I just called to find out if you passed the course."

"Ha, ha. You a riot. You a real comedian, man."

"Everything OK with you? Annamae sounded good when she answered."

"Yeah, she ain't won the lottery yet, though, so I don' guess I be seein' you anytime soon."

"Hey, there's a lottery every day, isn't there?"

"Yeah, you never know, Doc. . . . Hey, so whadju find out f'om them papers? Strange stuff, like I to'd you?"

"There *is* some strange stuff, as a matter of fact. *Really* strange."

"Yeah? Like what, man? Give it up!"

"Hey, there's not much to give. The manuscript itself is . . . well, it's a biography of St. Francis, as I thought, but it's more like a hagiography—you know what that is?"

"Sure, like the *Golden Legend*, right? Like Voragine?"

"Don't tell me you read Voragine!"

"Not all of it, man. That religious shit get pretty dull, you know what I'm sayin'?"

"Yeah, yeah. . . . Jesus, Auntwon! You're amazing!"

"Hey, Doc, that ain't no thang. . . . So OK, what else you find in there that so weird?"

"Well that's the really crazy part. There's this strange blank page with a kind of watermark. . . ." Robert explained about the diagram and how he'd found it, then came to the business of the missing incantation. "It's got to be in there somewhere," he concluded in exasperation.

"So you look fo' it?"

"Did I look! Are you kidding? I looked everywhere."

"Well, like where, man?"

"Everywhere. I mean . . . in the text, in the pages themselves—you know, for another watermark. . . ."

"You use that fluid on 'em?"

"No, I can't take them all out of the building to check with fluid, but I held each sheet up to a light—you know, a light bulb. I went over them for hours. If there'd been a watermark, anything, I would have seen it—some sign of it, anyway. I made out a little of the pattern on that blank sheet before I ever even *heard* about the fluid, and I know just what to look for now. . . . Believe me, I checked and rechecked. If there'd been anything there, any kind of watermark, I would have seen it. But there's nothing. Absolutely nothing. I'm positive."

"Well, it got to be in them papers *some*place."

"That's what I thought."

"You sho' they ain't nuffin' else?"

"Like what?"

"They ain't nuffin' weird? Nuffin' else even a little bit out of the ordinary?"

"No, not really. . . . Just the annotations. . . ."

"What annotations, man? Whatchu mean by that?"

"Well, the pages of the text are annotated, sort of. Some of the letters are circled and—I don't know—numbered in a way."

"Numbered like how?"

"I don't know, the circled letters—maybe there are four or five of them on each page—are connected by lines to the margin, and each line has a number written at its end."

"Like diff'ent numbers?"

"Different?"

"Yeah, they repeat or they all diff'ent?"

"Different, I think. I haven't noticed any repetitions."

"So that it, man. It got to be like a cryptogram."

"A cryptogram?"

"Yeah, like them puzzles in the funny papers. You know, you gotta unscramble some words, then some of the letters in each word be circled and you put 'em togevver and unscramble those. Like a cryptogram, man. Hey, *you* know what I'm talkin' 'bout."

"Yeah! Yeah, I do! That's great, Auntwon. I hadn't even thought of that. Damn! I bet that's just what it is—a cryptogram! That crazy thing—that incantation or whatever the hell it's supposed to be—might be right there in those letters! That's terrific! Damn! I'll get to work on it first thing Monday morning."

"Yeah, man, call me and let me know."

"Sure. . . . Oh, by the way, I should have Internet access in a day or two. I'll be able to email."

"What, they just puttin' phone lines in you hotel?"

"No, no, very funny. I'm moving to a different place—a real nice room. With a nice Italian family—at least the mother is nice; I haven't met her daughter yet. I'll have my own phone."

"So when you movin'?"

"Day after tomorrow—well, tomorrow, I guess, now that it's Saturday morning. I'm moving Sunday."

"And then Monday you gonna check out that cryptogram thang, right?"

"Yeah."

"OK, Doc, I expect to hear f'om you then. Man! this is some wild shit you got goin' there!"

CHAPTER TWELVE

HABITATION

TWO THICK VOLUMES FIT INSIDE THE BAKING PAN, AND THAT SLIPPED SNUGLY into the suitcase, taking not much more room than the books alone had done. He had to kneel on the second bag to get it closed, but, in the end, there was room enough for everything, clothes and books. . . . And at last even his jogging shoes slid in, and the last little bottle of watermark fluid, too, though he wasn't likely to need *that* again for anything. . . . Well, thought Robert, on the other hand, one never knew for sure. . . .

He shrugged, smiled contentedly to himself, and pushed the heavy suitcase down over the edge of the mattress, letting it slide smoothly to the floor. Whew! Well, that was it! Finally. And with a good half-hour to go until he'd planned to leave. Excellent, excellent! He could rest a little now, and that was precisely what he did, settling into the arm chair at the far end of the room, putting his legs up on the bed, surveying the products of his labor. . . .

Which were two enormous cases resting upright on the carpet. Cassie's cases—or ones she'd bought, at any rate, with his money; oversize Louis Vuittons to take their finery on trips—well, *her* finery mostly: hair dryers, cosmetics kits, a surgical-precision manicure set, since she never *had* quite trusted her various manicurists' likely contaminated equipment. For the past year or so, the big bags had even hauled her weights, for God's sake: three and five pound dumbbells, so she could have her workouts anywhere, even that memorable night last December on the auto-train to Florida.

"Get it down," she'd ordered.

"What, the suitcase?"

"Yes, I want my weights."

"Here? On the train? Tonight?"

But he'd done it, digging through some fifty pounds of clothing to find what she'd asked for. My God, but those bags had gotten stuffed with a lot of things: designer gowns and pants suits and custom-fitted jeans—her things alone, for he'd carried nothing but a garment bag on most of their trips: one suit, a couple of jackets, shirts, slacks, a book or two. Well, that would hardly have sufficed for the present multi-month extravaganza— what with all the research stuff and extra clothes he'd had to bring. . . .

So Cassandra's capacious luggage had been just the thing—the *only* thing she'd left him, really, that he had found some practical use for. Well, true, there was the unpalatable *pinot noir*, and those antique pieces Shelly was peddling at sixty cents on the dollar. But the Louis Vuittons had actually proven helpful. Why she had left them behind had been a mystery at first, until he'd looked more closely—hauling them down from a counter in her dressing room and finding, on doing so, some gouges in the leather.

At first he'd been reluctant to fill them with his books and clothing. Not, of course, because of the gouges, but rather for the same reason her *pinot* had seemed undrinkable. Then finally, on due deliberation and with the passage of a few days' time, he'd come to the conclusion that, yes, perhaps those big, stylish bags might come in handy after all. And indeed they had. Considering all the necessities he'd had to drag along, and then the precipitancy of his departure, there was no denying that.

But the size! the weight! That would be the problem now—a major problem too—what with him having to navigate those two long flights of steps alone. After all, there'd be no bellmen at the Dall'Olmos'; no cart; nor elevator, either; just an old woman and a younger one. They might point the way, or give encouragement, or hold a door for him if need be, but he would be the one who'd have to haul the cases up to his room, one at a time, step by painful step, looking like the perfect fool. Still, it was Sunday. And early enough—what was the time now, 12:45? What else did he have to do today? What did it matter how clumsy he might look to the Dall'Olmos? His check wouldn't bounce.

A bellman came within minutes of his call. He was a small man, fiftyish, who wrestled the handsome cases onto a cart, then wheeled them downstairs to a little Fiat taxicab at the entrance. "*Dio mio!*" said the driver, but he managed, artfully, to stow the luggage in his vehicle; which conveyance, grossly overburdened, Robert now directed to Via San Martino, *numero centoventisette* (127), scarcely a kilometer and a half from the Garibaldi's fashionable entrance.

The door was open when he arrived—not just unlocked but wide open—looking, for all its gaping patency, remarkably uninviting. Looking desolate almost, like some grand abandoned mansion standing doorless in a ghost town. In such a way, the place seemed vacant, deserted, and a little surreal. Robert leaned in and tapped at the wood of the open door with his knuckle, producing a hollow sound that echoed softly down the gray stone vestibule.

In a moment some other sounds reached his ears: sounds of voices, they were, discernible though not quite decipherable, coming from somewhere past the staircase. Then another noise followed: a door opening, then closing with a dull thud—that too out beyond the stair-case—then footseps, ringing hollow, like his knock on the open door; and an instant later a young woman appeared at the end of the hallway, stepping around the foot of the stairs. From where he stood, out in the blatant sunlight, his eyes adjusted to its glare, Robert saw her dimly at first, then ever more distinctly as she approached him at the door.

"Ah, signore," she said with a smile, her hand touching the big door's weathered wood, "you are the new tenant?" She was slender, of medium height, dark-haired, hazel-eyed, wearing fashionably distressed jeans and a white pull-over top, a twenty-something girl, neither very beautiful nor very plain, but somewhere in-between. She looked nice, though, pleasant, with wide, expressive eyes that spoke of intelligence and candor.

"Yes, and you must be . . . ?" Robert gave her back a smile of reciprocity.

"I am Filomena Dall'Olmo. My mother told me you would be arriving today." She tilted her head a little, crinkling her eyelids in the incident sunlight, then finally putting a hand up to her brow to form a kind of makeshift visor. Beneath it, though the top half of her face was now in shadow, Robert could see her eyes directed up at him, straight into his own. It didn't seem a confrontational sort of look at all—or didn't have that feel to him at any rate—but rather seemed a look of innocence and trust, the wide-eyed visage of a friendly child, one might call it. Yet at the same time, decidedly un-childlike, this young Miss Dall'Olmo showed in her stature and bearing a confidence, a self-possession, an assertiveness, as striking as those of the most socially adept of his female colleagues at the university. It was an attitude he found immensely impressive.

"I . . . *we* . . . have just come home—from church in fact—and I was about to go out again for a few minutes to pick up something. Some bread, actually. Uh, but let me help you with your things first. Please." She stepped out through the doorway and grabbed one of the two huge cases by its handle, lifting it two or three inches off the ground and carrying it inside before Robert could summon a simple word of protest. "Wait, uh. . . ." was all the verbiage he got out, and that reflexly. But she was gone by then, half-way down the vestibule. Leaning left to counterbalance the formidable weight, she half-carried, half-dragged the slightly larger and visibly heavier of the two bags across the stone floor over to the foot of the stairs. Robert, lifting the other bag gamely, just inches off the ground, followed.

"Look, I'll carry that, miss. Leave it," he told her when he had reached her, but she waved him off, then turned toward a closed door just beside the bottom step.

"*Mamma*," she called out, in a little girlish voice, diminutively disproportionate to the formidable strength she had just displayed, "*l'ospite e´ arrivato*." This last phrase, as spoken Italian is wont to be, was less iterated than sung.

"I'll get it, miss . . . uh, signorina. You don't have to. . . ."

"No, no. You will need additional help with this, signore. You cannot possibly carry everything alone." She hoisted the suitcase again, using both hands to get it airborne, then started up the steps forthwith.

"Wait," said Robert. "Please. Leave it. I'll. . . ." But she was well on her way by then, up another riser to the fourth step, then the fifth.

"Come on, signore. . . . I'll just help to get you—whooh!—into . . . your room . . . and—whooh! . . . and . . . then be off on my . . . my errand." The girl was breathing hard now, halting on each platform for a millisecond, dumping the bag upon it with a thump, then lurching on, the bag alternately slapping against her calf like the clapper of a bell, then striking the next level with another thump Tap-thump-tap-thump. . . . Too exhausted himself to protest, too breathless to mouth the words, Robert followed her laboriously up the steps, the enormous case in hand, half a flight behind.

They were all-but-apoplectic by the time they reached his third floor chamber, dropping their burdens beside the double bed, one after the other, panting, staggering, drenched in sweat. *Cielo*!" said the girl—Filomena—after she had taken the time to get a dozen good, full breaths into her lungs. "Whew! Signore! . . . What do you have in the suitcase, signore, rocks? I must sit for a minute. Do you mind?"

She dropped into the desk chair facing him, her brow soaked with perspiration—smiling, though, looking up into his eyes, making him feel a little self-conscious. At the limits of exhaustion, then, her manner hadn't changed. She still maintained that strikingly candid attitude he had remarked downstairs, the almost-but-not-quite-offensive presumptuousness that had so impressed him when he'd met her at the door.

But her bearing seemed now somehow more defined, re-amplified into a sort of frank familiarity. This was hardly appropriate for a first encounter between two such people, hostess and tenant, junior and senior—particularly in Europe, and more particularly in a conservative small Catholic city in Europe. No, hardly appropriate. Yet somehow she managed to carry it off—the familiarity and the friendliness—so that it passed as perfectly matter-of-fact, perfectly proper in some peculiar way. Perhaps it was the plainness of her, Robert thought: the comradely boyishness in her friendly, guileless face. She fit as comfortably into the room and into the moment as Auntwon might have, or Sheldon.

Robert sat down on the edge of the bed across from her, at eye-level with her. "My God, those steps!" he muttered, after another pause, then more distinctly: "How in the world did you make it up the staircase with that bag? I . . . I told you I'd. . . ." He wiped his brow, wetting his forearm with the perspiration. "You should have let me. . . ."

"Oh, no, signore." The girl was breathing hard, pausing between pairs of words to articulate them audibly. "No, you . . . are . . . the guest. . . . It is . . . our duty to . . . to . . . provide . . . assistance." She sat facing the daylight of a window at the far end of the room opposite the door, a big double window with open shutters, over past the bed, so behind him and a little to his left. Her features, being front-lit, were more visible to him now, more legible than they had been before, downstairs. And the window light was harsh, so that the girl averted her eyes from his direction to escape its glare. Thus unobserved, he took the opportunity to study her a little more intently and with genuine interest.

She was—how might one phrase it?—decent-looking, really; kindly-looking. A little like her mother, perhaps, but vigorous, athletic. Hers was not at all the kind of athleticism that Cassie wore so assertively on her sleeve—not that sculpted, fat-free look of in-your-face perfection—but, rather, a much softer variety of lean. A leanness that was undesigned; owing more to activity, that is, than to exercise.

Robert's general impression was that of a woman casually glamorless—not really as flat-out plain as he had thought her at first, down in the unforgiving sunlight. No, for she had a kind of youthful radiance interjected into the equation. But clearly there was nothing here of the true exoticism possessed by extraordinary females: by Cassie, for notable example, with her immaculate hair and perfect nails and sensually-artful make-up. This Filomena, by contrast, looked rather interesting but ordinary, with her narrow face; trusting, childlike eyes; little nasal hump; nondescript black hair; and straight, linear mouth.

He had known such women in his college days: girls neither masculine nor feminine, or, rather, those to whom the ascription of gender simply didn't apply. One sat beside them in class or at a party and gazed distractedly at someone else. They were friends but never lovers, confidantes but never intimates. Poor Filomena Dall'Olmo was precisely of that species. She would make a fine young woman to live next to; an undistracting female to be around; a companionable and uncomplicated friend; and, one day, to the appropriate but undiscerning man, a faithful and unintimidating spouse. In his present state of mind, Robert concluded, he couldn't have found a more suitable host.

"Books," he answered finally, in response to her previously posed question. He was breathing more comfortably now, though his shirt was soaked through and his hair matted down to the neckline.

"What?" asked Filomena. "I'm sorry?"

"You asked me what was in the bags—why they were so heavy. They're full of books . . . not rocks. . . . You asked if they were full of rocks, remember?"

She chuckled. "Ah, yes, of course. Oh, well that's quite all right, then. Books are well worth carrying."

"Oh? Yes? You like books? You like to read?"

"Of course. I like them ever so much better than rocks, which are so little informative. Books are what I do with my time, mostly." Her English was exceptional; flawless almost, though decidedly British in syntax and intonation. Caterina and whatever subsequent teachers she had studied with had taught her well.

"Yes, your mother said you're at the university."

"I am. In what you would call graduate school." Yes, that seemed right, he thought. She looked to be in her early twenties, maybe as old as twenty-five, though it was hard to tell for certain.

"Oh? In what?"

"In what? . . . I don't understand, signore."

"What field of study? *Cosa studia Lei?*"

"Ah, *Parla italiano, si. L'ho sentito. . . . Beh, studio letteratura inglese.* I am studying English literature, actually."

"Really!"

"Yes. I shall finish next year, then teach. There are a great many positions for teachers of English here. Everyone needs to speak your language these days. All through Europe, in fact."

"Well, you'll make a fine teacher. You speak very well. . . . Uh, I met your former tutor. Miss Paschiale, you know? Actually, she was the one who recommended the place—uh, your house."

"Ah, yes, Caterina. *Mamma* said so. How is it that you happen to know her?"

"I'm, uh . . . I'm working on a project at the Piccolomini. A research project."

"Yes, my mother said you are a professor, uh, from . . . New York?"

"Chicago."

"Ah, yes, Chicago. The Bulls."

He laughed. "That's right. That's what we're known for, apparently, that and Al Capone."

"No," she said, "I am only teasing. Hemingway was from near Chicago, and Sandburg, and . . . uh, Saul Bellow. I've read all of his novels."

"I know him, actually—Bellow, that is—from scholarly functions and things."

"Really? That is very impressive. Do you teach at the university?"

"Yes. Nine years. I'm on sabbatical. Do you know what that is?"

"Of course!... So you are a Ph.D.?"

"Yes, in history."

"Ah, dottore . . . uh, I'm sorry; I don't even know your name."

"Oh, that's right. It's Robert. Robert Martin. Roberto, I guess you'd call me."

"Roberto! Yes! As in *For Whom the Bell Tolls.* . . . Roberto is a perfect name for you. I shall call you that, if it is all right. Do you know the story?"

"Story? Um, no, not really. The only Hemingway I read in college was *The Old Man and the Sea.* I picked it because it was his shortest book. Twentieth century American literature is not exactly my strong suit."

"Well, I shall teach you to like it, Roberto. And you can teach me all about history. I think we are going to be good friends."

"Yes, Filomena," he answered, smiling, "I suspect you might be right."

Having slept incomparably well in his commodious new quarters, Robert was waiting impatiently at the Piccolomini's front door when the place opened the following morning. He nodded to the porter, took the granite steps two at a time, grabbed the walnut box from its shelf, put on his gloves, pulled out the papers, drew in his chair, and immediately got to work.

Setting the cover sheet aside, he picked up the first page of text and placed it on the mylar pad in front of him. Seven of its letters were circled and connected by lines to three different numbers in the right-hand margin. Robert tore a fresh sheet of paper from the legal pad and copied down the letters, jotting their corresponding numbers alongside: f-s-t—67, u-s—106, o-r—28. He moved to page two, which showed six circled letters and two corresponding numbers, then to page three, which had no letters circled at all. In thirty minutes more, he had gone through forty-two pages of the manuscript, filling a five-inch-long vertical column with the copied letters and associated numbers he'd written down.

Some of the entries were numbered in sequence, so he tore out another sheet of paper and arranged the copied letters in numerical order when he found a complete or fairly complete run. The series went from sixteen to twenty, then from twenty-three to twenty-six consecutively. But they

were hopelessly jumbled as written: l-l-o-m-c-h-q-u-n-f-f-a-u-p-i-r-a-a-r. .
. . and so on for nearly two full five-inch lines. He arranged them vertically in two columns, then alternately across, then arranged vowels and
consonants in parallel rows, cross-checking for intelligible words, Latin
or Italian. But it was useless, futile. It would take an expert—a gifted
cryptographer—to extract some meaning from the mess. Robert sat back,
pulled off his gloves and threw them down on the table in disgust.

It was hopeless, maddening, like the entire project! Magic figures!
Incantations! Secret codes! Had this been the final outcome of
Colangio's life? The greatest mind of the Renaissance reduced to utter
lunacy! How? Why? What could be the meaning of it all?—If, indeed,
there was a meaning.—And if there was—if there had ever been one—
where might one begin to look for it? In an oyster shell? an olive grove?
In a beeswax candle? . . . Or more logically in that box somewhere—
an answer to everything? But where? Where?

Well, wherever it was, he wasn't going to get at it today, that was
for sure. Not this way. Robert stacked the manuscript back in a pile and
reached for the box to toss it in. . . .

And just then, *just* then, thankfully, he heard some voices in the corridor. Two different people there were, Caterina and another woman she was
speaking with, out beyond the doorway to his right. Turning toward the
entrance to the room, angling his chair in that direction, he saw their forms
appear in the opening—first Caterina's, whose sound he had distinguished;
then the girl's, Filomena Dall'Olmo, facing Caterina but glancing over
toward him with her eyebrows arched in a sort of unarticulated greeting.

He had seen her again last evening, after he had gotten his things
put away. It was a little after nine, when she'd come up to his room with
a couple of books for him to read—novels by Hemingway and Joseph
Conrad; things he hadn't the slightest intention of ever opening, though
he'd been too polite to tell her so. Instead, he'd thanked her and patted
her on the shoulder with a hint of dismissal, but she'd stayed on, talking interminably about her teachers and courses until he'd yawned and
stretched his neck and finally excused himself to get some sleep.

"We have a visitor, you see," said Caterina. "Such a pleasant surprise! My best student—Yes, yes, you were!—I hardly see her any more,
dottore."

"Yes. Good! Hello, Filomena. Come in. Come on in, both of you. I was just about to take a break." It was a truth but an incomplete one: '*short* break,' he might have said. He looked down at his watch in the act of rising to greet them. 4:12, it said; so less than two short hours remaining in his workday. His guests were no less welcome, but it would be better if they didn't stay too awfully long.

"All these years and she has never come to visit!" said Caterina with a sort of pouting pseudo-petulance. "Can you imagine? And only right across the street!" What she meant by that allusion was that the University of Siena, which Filomena had attended on a daily basis for several years, stood directly across the Via di Pantaneto facing the Piccolomini's front door.

"I . . . that is," said Filomena, "I thought that with the two of you here, I could, sort of, uh, kill two birds with a single stone, you see."

"Yes, well, come over and sit down, both of you." Robert pulled two more chairs around to the business side of the desk, but Caterina excused herself, patted Filomena on the shoulder, and left. Whereupon the girl, alone with him now in the cavernous room, stepped over and dropped into the chair he had placed beside his own. Once seated, she leaned forward and looked up at him in that friendly, confident manner she had evidenced from the moment that they met.

"Well! What a nice surprise!" he told her, not a hundred percent in earnest. "Done with classes for the day?"

"Uh, no. . . . That is—I still have a bit of research to do this afternoon, but. . . . Ah, are those your papers? On the desk there?"

"The manuscript, you mean? Yes. Would you like to see it?"

"Yes," the girl answered, leaning forward in her chair, "very much, indeed."

"Here, have a look." He motioned with an elbow, then opened the papers to a random page. "As you can see, it's very old. They found it last year right here in Siena. It's by Adalberto Colangio. You know who he was?"

"Yes, of course. We were required to read a number of his writings in school, Colangio and Machiavelli and Guicciardini as well. In the *liceo*, you know?"

"The *liceo*? I think so. That's sort of a pre-university prep school, isn't it?"

"Yes, well, it's before the university, that's right. For classical education, and. . . . um, anyway, that's where I read it."

"OK, good. Well, this happens to be a newly discovered work of his—something nobody had any idea even existed. Until last year, I mean. It's sort of a biography of St. Francis. I got about a tenth of the way through it before I kind of changed direction."

"Changed direction? What do you mean?"

"Well, it's a long story. Here: you see these annotations? The circles and lines?"

"Yes."

"Well, I've come to the conclusion that they might be the important part of the manuscript and the text itself practically useless. It's a long story, but Colangio seems to have gotten sidetracked in his work near the end."

"Sidetracked?"

"Yes. Crazy, maybe. Or impaired in some other way. . . . I don't suppose they used hallucinogens in those days...?"

"Hallucinogens! No, I don't think so. But . . . well, that sounds like rather intriguing work. You may make a great discovery from it. Something very significant. Colangio was a very important man to Siena."

"He was indeed. To all the world, in fact."

"Yes, I suppose so. . . . I should very much like to see what you have done up to now with your research."

"You mean the text? The transcription? It isn't very exciting. It's really awful, in fact. Colangio might actually have copied it from another source. . . . It's the annotations he made that seem to be original, and I've barely started on them as yet. . . . But if you'd like to see what I've done so far—the St. Francis stuff, for what it's worth—I'll be happy to show it to you. It's all on this legal pad here."

"Ah, I see. Well, perhaps later. May I? At the house?"

"Sure, of course, if you like. Come upstairs this evening.

"Oh . . . oh I was forgetting . . . I mean, I had forgotten: I shall be back at home rather late tonight." We shall be driving to Firenze this afternoon. *Mamma* has a bit of shopping to do. Perhaps we shall be back by nine o'clock, if that is not too late. . . . Is . . . is there anything that you require? I mean . . . that I can get for you in Firenze? We go to a big shopping center there."

"No, thanks. There's nothing that I really need."

"All right, then, I'll be off." She stood up, smiled again, headed for the door . . . and then turned back. "If it is not too late this evening when we get home, may I still come up to see the transcriptioning?"

"The transcription? Yes, of course."

"Well, *ciao*, then. Are you sure there is nothing we can get for you in Firenze?"

"No. I mean, yes, I'm quite sure."

Filomena smiled again and turned to leave.

"Oh, Filomena!" he called out within a second of her disappearance from the doorway.

Her head popped back instantly into view, as though she had been waiting there just beyond the jamb in certain expectation of his call. "Yes, signore . . . uh, Roberto." She was smiling rather shyly now, looking a little over-eager, he thought, like a child awaiting a cake-and-ice-cream treat.

"Do you know if anyone still makes candles out of beeswax?"

"Yes, I believe they do, Roberto. When *Mamma* and I get to Florence, I shall try to find you some."

There were footsteps in the corridor outside his room. People were leaving. Robert looked at his watch, which read five minutes to six. Already! He shook his head in disgust and closed up the pad, stuffing two wrinkled yellow sheets between its pages, then taking a third, filled with columns of numbers and letters, crumpling it into a ball, and tossing it dejectedly into a waste basket. Stacking the pages in a little pile, he set the pile back inside the box, pulled off his gloves, put the box back into its place atop the middle shelf, gathered up his pad, pens, and pencils from the desk, and headed out the door. Caterina came up to him at the stairhead and they started down the steps together.

"Well, how are things going, dottore?"

"Things? Oh, good and bad. A little frustrating at the moment."

"Ah you shall surmount all of your difficulties, I am sure. . . . How is everything at the Dall'Olmos'?"

"Oh, *that*. That's just fine. The room is absolutely perfect. . . . I really have to thank you for finding it for me."

"No, not at all, not at all. . . . Well, what about the girl?"

"Filomena?"

"Yes, of course Filomena. . . . I'm afraid she likes you.".

"Likes me?"

"Yes, indeed. Can't you tell?"

"No. I mean, I'm not exactly sure. She seems very nice. A little persistent, though. I . . . I don't want to hurt her feelings, but. . . ."

"Oh, you won't, I assure you. She's a very determined girl."

"Determined? How so?" he asked her. "What do you mean by 'determined'?"

"She's um . . . very. . . . She usually gets her way, I mean. But . . . but . . . well, I mean that in a good sense, though. Do you understand?"

"No, not exactly. . . . Look, I've just recently been through a big emotional crisis. I'm just not particularly good company now; I mean as a friend or confidant or . . . whatever else she has in mind."

"Dottore!" Caterina stopped at the bottom of the steps facing him. "Filomena is a normal twenty-five-year-old woman. What do you *think* she has in mind?"

"Well, I'm. . . . Look, I don't want to offend her or anything, but. . . . How do you suggest I handle it? Doesn't she have a boy friend or something?"

Caterina shrugged and raised her eyebrows, meaning nothing in particular that Robert could discern. In a moment, they had reached the outer door of the palazzo and stepped out together. He followed her the twenty-odd steps to the corner of Via di Pantaneto and Via Rinaldina, from which the broad expanse of the Campo could be seen in all its pink medieval splendor on this incandescent evening at the very end of May.

"Well? Tell me. How do you think I should handle it?"

"Have you heard her story?"

"Story? . . . No, I don't think so. . . . Unless you mean about the courses she's taking. And the books she's read. . . ."

"No, dottore." Caterina smiled and shook her head sadly. "This has nothing at all to do with any books or courses she has taken. . . . All right, then, buy me a cappuccino and I'll tell you some things about the Dall'Olmo family that it would be best for you to know."

CHAPTER THIRTEEN

COMPASSION

FILOMENA CAME ALONE TODAY. "*CIAO, ROBERTO!*" SHE CALLED FROM THE doorway, speaking in such a diminutive voice that it sounded strange when used to utter words that, in Italian, evidenced such frank familiarity.

He had thought about her much since his talk with Caterina the night before: what she'd been through, how hard these last ten years must have been for her, her courage, her determination. Caterina had told him everything, and it had affected him deeply. But now, this morning, all thoughts of her had been entirely displaced by his obsessive need to find that missing incantation. It was nearly two p.m. when she stepped into the room, thus almost five long hours clearer that Colangio's annotations would take nothing less than a mainframe computer and half a year of labor to decode. Thus, the better part of the day wasted, with nothing to show for it but a pair of reddened eyes and a mood vexed with frustration.

He turned in his chair, resolved on being friendly. He was going to be nice, kind; that he'd decided yesterday. Yes, after what the poor kid had lived through, after he'd heard it all from Caterina, he had quite made up his mind: if anyone needed a friend to talk to, a confidant, it was this young Signorina Dall'Olmo. What, after all, had the girl been crying out for since she'd first spoken to him? Not love; not romance, no—but simple friendship. That was it, for sure. Why, if she'd come upstairs last night, at midnight even, when his eyes were all but closed in sleep, he'd have listened to her with rapt attention, spoken to her with paternal concern, as much as she'd wanted, as long as she'd felt the need.

If only he had known some of it before—yesterday morning, say; for he'd been unfeeling—a little sarcastic even—when he'd seen her yesterday. . . . Yes, if only he had known! The poor kid, finding her father like that! What does that do to a child? Jesus! The old man must have had some idea what was going to happen to his little girl when she come home and walked into that room. . . . What kind of man . . . what kind of person . . . ? Well, it was far better, thought Robert, that he knew about it now. Far better. Caterina had been absolutely right in telling him. From now on he'd be gentler, kinder, more understanding. . . . In one all-encompassing word, a friend.

She took the chair beside him that she had taken the day before. "Well, Filomena! *Come stai?*" he asked her—now in the Italian familiar too, parroting her own usage: "How art thou?" They'd become real comrades, linguistically, at least: 'thee', 'thou'. . . . Whatever her interpretation, her 'take', the girl didn't seem to react to it, or else just took the words in stride, changing neither her expression nor her manner. Her smile was just as warm, but no warmer, just as open, but no more manifestly open, than it had been the afternoon before.

"*Benone, Roberto. Mamma* said that you speak Italian very well, and I see that she is right. But I would prefer that we talk in English mostly, if that is all right with you. I am rather used to it."

"Yes, of course; English it is. Whatever you prefer. As a matter of fact, it's nice to have someone to speak English with for a change, especially someone who understands the language as well as you do."

"Well, thank you. I have studied for many years now. . . . Since I was very young, you see. . . . Look, I . . . I hope I am not intruding. Are you . . . uh, very busy now? You seem, uh. . . . You looked busy when I came in—preoccupied, I mean."

"No, no, not at all. I'm . . . I'm all caught up for a while, as a matter of fact." He managed a little smile, a sincere one in truth, for, even more than yesterday, he was not particularly displeased with the interruption. "How about you? Done with classes for the day?"

"Yes. Well, I was working in the library. I am just preparing for an examination this week."

"Oh? What . . . uh, in what subject?"

"The examination? It will be on Spenser. Have you read him? *The Faerie Queene?*"

"No. I know about Spenser, though, from the history standpoint. . . . Um, Elizabethan England, I mean. I've read a little about Spenser's life. . . . Uh, isn't that hard to read for you, though? Difficult, I mean? He was a contemporary of Shakespeare, wasn't he? Isn't the language pretty complicated?"

"No, not really. I mean, it's *pretty*, but it's not that complicated." She smiled. "I suppose it's a little like what you are doing with your manuscript. One gets accustomed to it after a time. . . . Actually, I very much enjoy reading Spenser. The allegory on so diverse of planes is something like a three-dimensional puzzle, you know? It's quite fascinating."

"Yes, I'm sure it is. I'll have to look it over some time."

"Have you read any of the Hemingway yet? The book I brought you?"

"No, I haven't had a chance. I will, though."

"Yes, you must. It's the book I told you about the day you moved into your room. *For Whom the Bell Tolls*, you know? That's where I got the name 'Roberto'."

"Ah, yes. Well, I hope he's a nice guy, this Roberto. I wouldn't want you to name me after some villain."

"No, no, he's a wonderful man. A hero, in fact, a real hero in the most legitimate sense of the term. . . . He must give up everything for what he feels to be right, even the thing he wants most in the world."

"And what is that?"

"I shan't tell you. You must read the book. But the theme is self-abnegation for the greater good. The title is from . . . do you know where it comes from?"

"No. I should know, though. The Bible?"

"No, not the Bible. It's John Donne. One of his sermons. I have it at home. I'll show it to you if you like."

"I think you could give me a whole course in English literature if I had the time."

"Yes, of course. That is precisely what I'm preparing myself to do. I shall be a *dottoressa* next year, *se Dio vuole*. Like you, Dottor Roberto. . . ." The girl suddenly stopped and put a hand up to her brow. "Oh, I was . . . I mean, I have forgotten to tell you: I found the candles for you. Of beeswax, you know? The ones you asked for? It was too late when we returned home to bring them up last night, but I got a box of them for you. I hope you like the smell of . . . uh, *gel-somino*. I don't know the word in English."

"Uh, 'jasmine', I think."

"Yes, well they are scented strongly of it—jasmine, yes. I hope that is all right. Those were the only ones they had. Of beeswax, I mean."

"Yes, sure. That's very nice of you. How much do I owe you for them?"

"Oh, no. They were only a few *lire*. I have them in my room. I can give them to you later."

"Well, that was very thoughtful of you. . . . Listen, are you hungry? How about having something to eat with me? I haven't had a proper meal all day."

"Oh, well I wouldn't want to impose. . . ."

"Impose! No, don't be silly. I'd appreciate the company."

"Well, if you're sure. . . . All right then. . . . I *am* a little hungry myself."

"OK, come on. Let's go."

"But . . . mustn't you put away your papers?"

"No. No one's going to bother them. Actually, there's not that much of value for someone to disturb anyway. . . . Come on. Let's get you something good to eat—in exchange for the candles."

The city was built in Roman times on three hills—or, more properly, on a steep upland with three flattened peaks. Today, each peak represents a central point of Siena, and each houses one or more important monuments.

On the broad plateau of Siena's northeast promontory rest two imposing structures, the Church of San Domenico and the Medici fortress. The church, a vast though spartan basilica, is best known as the repository of the remains of the illustrious St. Catherine, the most celebrated of the city's female offspring. She it was who urged the errant papacy to return to Rome during its long "captivity" in Avignon from 1307-1370. Her home, perfectly preserved, lies below the church in one of Siena's intervening valleys; her street, untouched by time, looks much the same today as it did when the gentle and literate lady trod upon its paving stones six centuries ago.

The tourist, having seen St. Catherine's house and viewed her relics in the Dominican church of her sepulture, will wander past the municipal stadium farther west to a large fortress that rises imposingly to dominate the hilltop. Massively bastioned and impressively gaited, it was built by the Medicean rulers of Siena in the sixteenth century when Florence held all of Tuscany in subjection. Today it is a quiet park and sparsely-frequented museum.

Exiting the fortress and departing the northeast hill for the center of town, the visitor will descend steeply on the age-worn stones, then ascend again. If he proceeds southeast, he will climb to the Duomo, Siena's incomparably magnificent cathedral, which occupies a second of Siena's three high plateaus. It is an enchanting building, this Duomo, with a facade of gold and polychrome mosaic, an exterior of banded black and white stonework, and, inside, a floor of carved and inlaid marble. The tourist will linger there, no doubt. He could spend a week or more taking in the Duomo's beauty, then touring the adjacent structures: the cathedral museum, the baptistery, the wonderfully frescoed Hospital of Santa Maria della Scala. These four structures alone would be enough to make any town in Europe an attraction—even in Italy, where magnificence is commonplace. But there is much, much more. For, sooner or later, descending the Duomo hill and heading to the southwest, our visitor will climb at last to the third of Siena's peaks, where he will find the Piazza del Campo, the very hub and focus of the city.

This amazing place, the 'Campo', as it is called for short, is arguably the most endearing and magnificent public square in all of Italy—which is to say in all the world. It has a D-shaped layout, semicircular like an ancient theater. So actually it isn't a proper 'square' at all, and doesn't have the feel of one, lacking the spacious openness of a public area in Paris, say, or in Madrid, or Rome. Unlike most European 'plazas', the Campo is decidedly medieval, enclosed, drawn in upon itself like a coliseum, with encircling walls of contiguous structures—gothic palaces abutting one directly to another around the curved part of the 'D', then a grand public building, the Palazzo Pubblico with its huge Mangia tower, on the flat side. The enclosing edifices are tall, four or more stories, with battlemented roofs and projecting towers here and there. Their height and verticality add mightily to the sense of enclosure, as does their contiguity. And since they *are* contiguous, except for a couple of narrow gaps on the eastern side, one gains access to the Campo chiefly through some tunnel-like alleyways, like stadium passages, beneath the ancient buildings themselves.

The whole place, in short, has not just the *shape* of a theater, but the *aura* of one as well. It is an effect enhanced dramatically by the fact that, theater-like, arena-like, the pink brick pavement of the Campo slopes uniformly downward from its upper curved edge to its lower straight one. It seems a perfect site for spectacles, and, indeed, twice each summer, that is precisely what the lovely square becomes.

On those two days, July 2 and August 16, a quarter of a million people gather in the flattened, oblong piazza to attend the *palio*, a bare-backed horse race pitting rival districts of the city, one against the other. For ninety seconds, seventeen riders prod their horses around the circumference of the Campo to the accompaniment of rabid demonstrations from the crowd. Though the outcome is relevant solely to the Sienese, thousands travel through the length and breadth of Italy to attend. For the *palio* is a festival, an event, like *carnaval*, or *mardi-gras*, or the running of the bulls in Pamplona. But both the site and the spectacle are more magnificent than anyone not fortunate enough to have seen them can imagine. The race lasts just a minute and a half, the spectators celebrate and party and commiserate their losses. Then, a week having passed, the Campo is cleared and scrubbed and polished again to its scallop-shell brilliance, the refuse removed, the rough bricks smoothed, and citizens return to stroll again in the Campo's summer sun.

"Where are we going?" Filomena asked.

"Where? Across the Campo," said Robert. "Come on."

"Now? But where?"

"Nowhere in particular. Just to take a walk."

"A walk? Now? But. . . . Well, OK," she said, keeping up with him. "What time must you return to the palazzo?"

"I don't know. Uh . . . no special time, I guess. How about you? Do you have to be somewhere soon?"

"I? No, of course not. I . . . I don't want to intrude, though."

"Intrude?"

"Yes. I felt that sometimes I . . . I was intruding, you know? With what you were doing. Yesterday, for example."

"No, no. Not at all. What gave you that impression? I, uh . . . I enjoy your company. . . . Very much, in fact. . . . I like talking with you."

"Good. That is good. I did not want to. . . ."

"No, don't be silly. Look, did you have enough to eat?"

"Yes, of course."

"Well, you didn't have very much."

"Oh, I *did*. I am quite filled up, I assure you. And you? You ate only that small dish of pasta, the *penne*."

"I guess I didn't have as much of an appetite as I thought. Maybe the heat." He stopped in the very center of the Campo facing the Palazzo Pubblico, looking up at it, with its massive tower outlined in azure sky to their left. Filomena, beside him, wiped her brow and ruffled the front of her blouse which was starting to stick to her skin in the blazing mid-day sun.

"Yes," she said, "the Campo can be very hot this time of day. You see, there are not many people about."

"Well, they're missing a beautiful afternoon, a beautiful scene. This must be the grandest piazza in all of Italy. Or anywhere, really. Anywhere in the world, I'd guess."

"Do you think so? I have not been to very many other places. . . . I mean, outside of Italy. . . . I suppose you have, though."

"Yes. In Europe, anyway. You're not missing too much. Ninety percent of the beauty in the world is in your country. Maybe ninety-nine percent. I'm in love with everything Italian, the people, the art, the history . . . even the food."

"Well I am pleased that you like the people. We do try to be pleasant. And the art I suppose compares well with that of any other place. But the food? I of course enjoy it, but they say it hardly rivals the cuisine of, well, for example, France. It's certainly less sophisticated than French food, at any rate."

"Well, I don't care much about that kind of sophistication. To me, it's more about whether you can eat the same kinds of things every day and not get tired of them. Italian food is never boring—or maybe satiating is a better word, you know?—*saziante*? I really think it's better than French cuisine in that way. When I'm here, there's not too much I miss—as far as the food goes, I mean. But when I was in France, I kept dreaming of the restaurants back home . . . in Chicago, that is."

"Oh? And what kind of restaurants do you have there that are so special? I mean, that you liked well enough to dream of when you were in France?"

"I don't know; different kinds. There are dozens of them. Every variety of food you can imagine."

"Well, I can't imagine much. All I know is what we have here. But if you can tell me some specific dish that you would like to eat, perhaps *Mamma* and I can prepare it for you. You know, something special that you crave . . . so you don't have to dream about Chicago all the time."

"No, no, it's just in France that I do that—all those rich sauces, you know? Here I do pretty well, between L'Agrigento and La Torre. I get along just fine in Italy."

"Yes, La Torre is very good. I hadn't eaten there for a long time. Until today, I mean. That was very good, indeed. Thank you. But . . . is there nothing you would like in particular? I would be honored to prepare it for you. I shall owe you a dinner in exchange for the nice meal you bought for me today. . . . Uh, tell me Roberto, what kind of food would you select if you could have anything you wanted right now?"

He chuckled. "Nothing, really."

"Why do you laugh? Did I say something foolish?"

"No, no. I wasn't laughing at you. I was just thinking of a place in Chicago that I like."

"Yes? And what kind of place were you thinking about? Tell me, or I shall think you have been making fun of me."

He shook his head, smiling. "No, no, don't think that. . . . All right, then—it's crazy I know, but my favorite restaurant in Chicago makes hot dogs. That's what I thought about more than anything else when I took my trips to France. That's what I was smiling about."

"Hot dogs? Those are sausages, aren't they?"

"Yes, have you ever had one? An American hot dog?"

"No, I don't think so. . . . No, I am certain that I haven't."

"Well, they're fabulous. Delicious. They start with a sausage, but it's not like Italian sausage. It's more like the German ones, but made of beef—the Chicago dogs, anyway. They serve them on little buns: like *panino* rolls, but soft, steamed, you know?"

"Yes, I think so."

"Then they put everything on them. The Chicago dogs, at any rate: mustard, pickles, onions, sometimes a tomato slice. It sounds awful, I know, but they're really great. They're addictive, in fact. . . . Anyway, that's the main thing I miss when I'm away, and the first thing I go for when I get home."

"You know, we have a McDonald's here, near Piazza San Domenico. Maybe they can make your hot dog for you."

"No, it's not on their bill of fare. Believe me, I've tried all over—here, Rome, Florence. . . . You know, when I was here six years ago. . . . Look, don't worry. I'll survive well enough on the local cuisine."

"Yes, well, tell me, is there some special Italian food you might like, then? Have you eaten *pappardelle alla lepre*?"

"That's rabbit, right?"

"Yes, it's very good. It is traditional Tuscan cuisine."

"Uh, I don't know. The thought of eating rabbit. . . ."

"Ah, Roberto, do you know what things go into your sausages, your hot dogs?" She laughed.

"Actually, I try not to think about it too much."

"Well, the *pappardelle alla lepre* contains only the *papardelle* pasta and rabbit. And the rabbit part is meat only, no eyeballs or noses. I shall make it for you to try. If you don't like it, you can take me back to La Torre for dinner, OK?"

"All right. I'll close my eyes and pretend it's chicken."

"*Bene, bene.* Good. *Aspetti,* Roberto,"—she used the familiar now quite openly, and had likely lapsed into Italian for the purpose of doing so—"the Campo is very hot. Too hot, really. I should like to. . . . Do you have a little more time to let me take you someplace else?"

"Yeah, sure. Why not? . . . Where would you like to go?"

"There's a place that I want to show you, a place you may not yet have been."

He nodded and let her lead him across the baking Campo, up the steps leading outward onto Via di Citta, then across it onto the Via Pellegrini. There the cobbled street rose steeply upward toward the Duomo.

"We're going to the Duomo? The cathedral?"

"No," she said, "not exactly."

They turned into Piazza San Giovanni, where the ancient baptistery appends itself to the rear of the Duomo like a handle on a teapot, then through the open arches of masonry once intended to be so massive an addition to the already grand cathedral that the augmented structure would have become the then-largest house of religion in the world. When the great Black Plague struck in 1348, all work on the project was canceled. Losing most of her citizenry to the pestilence, then the larger part of her economy to the Florentines, Siena never completely recovered. St. Catherine lived her later years in a declining town.

"So where are we going, then?" Robert asked. They had entered the Piazza del Duomo. To his right rose the great cathedral itself in all its splendor. Up a platform of marble steps, bright and luminous in the afternoon sun, it soared skyward: massive, delicate, and spectacular. Like carved ivory in its luster and intricacy, but sheathed in alternating layers of black and white stone, it had always reminded Robert of an enormous twenty layer torte, made all of icing, stripes of chocolate and vanilla, sliced through its middle, then frozen and polished to a crisp and glassy sheen.

"Come," she said. "This way." She took his arm and led him along the spine of uncompleted masonry, once meant to support the grand new cathedral, to the Museo dell'Opera del Duomo. This, an impressive art gallery, is housed in three of the ultimately-enclosed arches long left as mere skeletal remnants after the Great Plague disaster of 1348.

"Yes, the museum. I've been here before. Back in '93 when I was working on my book."

"I was sure you had seen it, but . . . have you been up to the *loggia*?"

"The *loggia*? Uh, I don't know. I don't think so."

She bought the tickets. "No, no," she replied to his protest. "Now you are my guest. . . . I pay only a few *lire* anyway. As a student."

"So what is this *loggia*?"

"Just be patient, Roberto. I shall show you."

They went upstairs, then through a long chamber to a sort of hidden corridor, along it, then finally up another steep ascent toward an opening where daylight seemed to enter. In a moment, they had stepped out onto a magical place, a roofless platform atop the massive stonework once intended for the frontspiece of the grand new cathedral. They stood at eye level with the very top of the existing cathedral's dome, looking down on the remainder of the structure from a position never envisioned by the original architects when they had planned their splendid master-piece back in the twelfth century. From where he stood, beside the young Miss Dall'Olmo, the Duomo looked, if anything, more torte-like, more delicate, more beautiful, than it had ever looked to him before, a piece of polished ivory, jewel-encrusted, crystalline, set with gold, striped with onyx, and carved by the most ingenious and masterful of craftsmen.

"God! It's . . . it's breathtaking!"

"Good. Good. I am happy that you like it. It is my absolute favorite place in Siena."

"I . . . I don't even know what to say."

"No. This is not a place for conversation. Uh, look, Roberto. Look over this way." She turned him around to face northeast. There, front-lit by the sun in slow declination behind them, lay the city ahead and below, spread out upon its hilltops, with the great Mangia tower of the Palazzo Pubblico reaching skyward above the Campo like a candle on a birthday cake. About it, and about the gaping square, ran a swarm of terra-cotta roofs curling and streaming across the city, along its curvi-linear streets, like cracked earth after a drought of unnumbered brilliant days. Then the terra-cotta ended, with the hillside, giving way to bro-ken vegetation in the plain, rolling below the roof tiles like a verdant sea lapping at a patch of land. And beyond even this, for the afternoon air was translucent as crystal, lay the purple hills of Umbria, thirty miles and more to the west.

"See out there, Roberto? You can see as far as Umbria."

"Umbria. That's . . . Assisi is in Umbria, isn't it, Filomena?"

"Yes, this way." She pointed east, out past the Piazza del Mercato, toward a blue-gray corrugation of the distant land. Above it, slung low in the pastel sky, lay a single cumulus cloud, rising softly from the hills.

"It is Lago Trasimeno. There. Over there below the cloud. Assisi is beyond."

"Lake Trasimene. Hannibal defeated the Romans there."

"Yes. I remember from my history course."

"I must go to Assisi."

"*Ma perché, Roberto?* Why?"

"Colangio went there, to study St. Francis. I must see what he saw. Maybe it will help me understand."

"To understand? Colangio?"

"Yes. This business with St. Francis changed him in some way. I need to find out how."

"Ah, San Francesco. Of course. He was a wonderful man, a miracle worker. And Colangio too. He too was wonderful, brilliant. And you are brilliant too, Roberto. When you travel to Assisi, I shall go along."

~~~~~~~~~~~~~~~~~

REVELATION

SUBJ: Doc's research project
DATE: 6/02/00 10:22:28 PM Eastern Standard Time
FROM: auntwon99@aol.com
REPLY-TO: auntwon99@aol.com
To: Robtmar@attglobal.net

Hi, Doc. Got your message. I figured out the number of permuta-tions and combinations in the letters you got and it comes out to like 10 to the 14th, so you ain't going to work it out by yourself. You right when you say that the decoded incantation thing got to be in the box somewhere, so if you sure it aint in the manuscript, I'd say to look at the box itself. Like a cavity in the wood or maybe one of the inside sur-faces or underneath the box.

You got any idea what it's for yet? If you want, you could send me a copy of the stuff you found already and I could do some research on it here. As you know, the university library has a pretty exhaustive ref-erence collection of medieval and Renaissance sources for me to check out for you. Whatever the thing you found is for, it sure dont sound like Colangio, but remember what you said about them aliens. Maybe it's like a plan for a space ship or something like that—Ha, Ha.

My job start next week. It aint the restaurant thing like I told you before, but something Dr. Rogovin got me at the library on campus (I could do your research shit and get paid for it, in other words—Ha!). I don't know exactly what the job require, but they pay eight dollars per hour which is like some serious financial recompense to me.

OK gotta split, man. I'll keep you highly informed as to what's up here. The Bulls ain't shit without Jordan.

Vale magister a discipolo suo—Ha!—that's Latin shit, man!

Auntwon.

Robert started to type in a response—"Hi, Auntwon, thanks for the.
. . ." 'Suggestion,' he was about to add, but the note had gotten him
thinking. "The box!" he said out loud. The box! Of course, why not?
Maybe some writing scratched on its bottom, or on the under-surface of
the lid—he hadn't even *thought* of looking there. . . . Or . . . or . . . what
about a shred of paper stuffed into a cavity in the wood someplace? Sure!
The sides were thick enough; top and bottom too. Well, on Monday he'd
go over the whole thing in detail with the illuminated magnifier, tap on
the panels to reveal a hollow if there was one. Sure. Jesus! Why hadn't he
thought of that himself? You really had to hand it to that kid!

He looked at his lap-top computer screen: "Hi, Auntwon, thanks for
the. . . ." Oh, hell, he didn't feel much like writing now: he was too excited;
there was too much on his mind. That was the beauty of e-mail, anyway: as
instantaneous or unresponsive as you cared to make it at the time. Flip a
switch, log on, and you've got your best friend in the room with you. Not
in the mood? Forget it; turn him off. No excuses; no hard feelings. Not that
Auntwon Miller would be offended in the least by a less-than-immediate
response: what did the screen say—9:46? That would make it, what? eight
hours earlier in Chicago: quarter to two in the morning? Hell, Robert
thought, he had plenty of time. He'd get back to Auntwon tonight.

He shut down the computer and went to the window, opening the
shutters on another scorching day. There was a little breeze, though, fra-
grant and refreshing—being a few degrees cooler than the city air—that
rose up to Siena from the lowlands beyond its walls. It smelled of drying grass and flowers, scents that were potent enough and sweet enough
to nullify the customary smell of dust and car exhaust filling Siena's
streets most summer days, then, thankfully, diminishing by nightfall.
The town was motionless this Saturday morning. His view of it was,
anyway; facing, as it did, southwest, outward past some residential districts toward the olive groves and vineyards in the valley below.

He turned back to his room. Quarter to ten: lots of time to shave
and dress. What time had she said, anyway? Ten-thirty? Yes, that was it.
The two of them were up and about by now, Filomena and her mother.
You wouldn't know it from the sounds—his room was far enough
removed from the family living quarters to be noise-proof from any-

thing but the street. But the scents: coffee in the morning, olive oil and garlic at night; those seeped indelibly through the walls. The signora must have spent half her waking hours in the kitchen, to estimate from the aromas of things.

The aroma of the moment was coffee, and he drew it in with every fresh breath. All right, he thought, today would be diverting, just seeing Assisi again after all these years. He'd snoop around a little, try to get a feeling for what Colangio had seen. And felt, too. Something had happened to the man, clearly.

Oh, nothing would be obvious. It didn't work that way; just a series of impressions that added up in the end to a feeling for your subject, a sort of comprehension of the way things formerly had been, the way the world once was when someone—Colangio, in this case—inhabited it all those centuries before. That had taken Robert months of effort last time, so today would be merely a beginning and nothing more. But, slowly, inevitably, he'd hew a path through all the layers of obscurity. Sooner or later he'd hit upon a clue, and that single clue would open up a whole new train of other paths to follow: a whole new world, in effect, rather like a one-way window in a time warp. Meanwhile he'd plod along, gathering shards of information, like the unimportant manuscript, the more important diagram. . . . And that missing incantation—if it could just be brought to light!

Ah, that box, that box—it might really hold the answer! Auntwon was a smart little son-of-a-gun to figure things out so fast, thought Robert. Too bad he'd have to wait till Monday now to find out anything for sure.

"Good morning!" said Filomena downstairs, outside her door.

"Good morning," he repeated.

"Would you like some breakfast? Please, come in. *Mamma* can cook you some eggs if you like."

"No. No need. We'll pick up something on the road."

"Ah, Roberto, there is really nothing at all until we reach Assisi. We shall have lunch there if you wish, but you must take something now. . . . Uh, maybe some bread and cheese. And olives. We have everything fresh, I went to the *panateria* today. Early this morning."

"All right, I'll take a piece of bread then. I don't want to disturb your mother."

"Nonsense! She likes nothing more than to prepare food. I think she would feed the rats if we could attract some."

"*Mamma*," she called toward the kitchen, "*possiamo avere un sacchetto con qualche fetta di pane e formaggio? E anche delle olivi, per piacere!*"

"*Si, si, due minuti!*" came the signora's voice, muted, from within. "You can eat it in the car," said Filomena. "Do you like some wine too?"

"No, no. Really, I. . . ." But she turned and vanished through the doorway, then reappeared two minutes later with a little plastic grocery bag in her hand.

"OK, let's go, *andiamo*," she said, heading for the big front door with Robert close behind. "You can have your breakfast on the road."

It was growing hot already by the time they stepped outside. "This way," said the girl, pointing with a motion of her head. She led him half a block down from the house to an alleyway, then down it, in turn, to a small building with a garage door opening into its ground level. This she proceeded to unlock with a key, pulling the awning door upward with a facile motion. Inside was a big, black car, bechromed and elegant, a top-of-the-line Mercedes sedan, looking ten, maybe fifteen years old, but bright and shining as though it had come fresh from the factory a week before.

"It was my father's car. We use it only for trips to Firenze—Florence, you say. And one time to Roma, but I usually take the train to go there."

"It looks brand new."

"Well, *Mamma* takes it out only once per month or so. To Firenze, as I said. For shopping. She drives there and I drive home. It is difficult for her in the dark. . . . OK, let me just pull it out so you can get in."

She maneuvered the vehicle out of the garage into the alley, then turned it, after four or five intricate back-and-forth passes, in the direction of the street. Robert pulled the garage door shut and climbed into the passenger seat.

"It's nice of you to take me, Filomena, and nice of your mother too to let us use the car."

"Oh, no, Roberto, it is *my* car."

"*Yours?*"

"Yes, entirely mine. My father left everything to me. The house and car and everything. *Mamma* didn't mind in the least. She was too dis-traught at the time to take care of even the smallest matter."

"Yes, Caterina told me a little of what happened."

"Did she? Well, that is very old news nowadays. It has been more than ten years now. *Mamma* has quite recovered."

"And you? Have *you* quite recovered?"

Filomena made a funny face, pinching her lips together in a manner that suggested concentration. It could have been the rigors of her driv-ing, though, for they had reached the bottom of Siena's hill near the city walls. It is there that the road in its slow declivity curves gently toward the motorway, and there too that braking trucks and idling taxis slow traffic to an annoying and often hazardous crawl.

"Yes," the girl said, after a moment. "I *have* recovered. . . . Not that I do not think of it. I shall never get the picture out of my mind of Papa in that room with the rope around his neck. No, I shall never forget that. . . . But one must make a choice—either to dwell on the past or to proceed with one's life. I have decided long ago to resign myself to things which cannot be changed, but to do everything within my power to make the few things which I *can* change better."

"That sounds like a very good philosophy."

"No, Roberto, it is not a philosophy at all; it's a way of life. And I would heartily recommend it to you for your use."

They reached Assisi after noon, parked below the church, and climbed the steep streets ascending toward it. The air was hot, dusty, and thick. A bus-load of tourists—Germans, they turned out to be—headed down from the monument, passing them. "*Mittagessen,*" said one, "*Ja, bald,*" another. They were evidently hungry.

"How about you," asked Robert. "Ready for lunch yet?"

"No, not right now. I ate that cheese. But if *you* are. . . ."

"No, no, I can wait. Let's visit the church first."

It wasn't crowded. Lunchtime for the tourist is ideal. They stepped through the entrance and passed into the upper nave, looking at the fres-coes on either side. Running up the walls in multicolored splendor were the magnificent achievements of Giotto, who prefaced the Renaissance by fifty years and gave the world a taste of what it would encounter two generations hence. Colangio would have visited this place, seen these very things: fresco upon fresco, scene upon scene, the life of St. Francis writ large in illustration. But such illustration! Colors of jewel-like brilliance, figures arranged with geometric perfection, faces virtually alive, individualized, expressive of palpable emotion. It was like an illustrated version of the life of St. Francis, but done by a master; drawn, in truth, by one of the great visual artists of all time, painting St. Francis' story the way Picasso might have adorned the works of James Joyce, or Rembrandt the plays of Shakespeare. One could almost feel a sense of holiness in a place like this. Perhaps the great Colangio had felt it, once, like those thousands of pilgrims, traveling by foot halfway across Europe to stand in the place where St. Francis had stood. Poor, half of them, illiterate, most. What did it matter? Look up on the walls and you could read the humble saint's whole incredible story in some of the most glorious imagery on earth.

"It's something, isn't it!" Robert exclaimed.

"Yes. He was a wonderful man," answered the girl.

"You mean Giotto?"

"Giotto? Ah, yes, Giotto, too. He too was wonderful."

"Who else, then?"

"Why . . . San Francesco, of course! Truly blessed by God."

"Oh, yes. I see. You're religious, then."

"Why, yes, of course. And you? Are you not a religious man yourself, Roberto?"

"Well . . . no, I'm really not. I'm . . . I guess I'm a lot like Colangio, a skeptic. Probably that's what attracted me to him in the first place. To his writings I mean. I guess I'm a true historian—a good historian, I hope. I try to look at things dispassionately and understand them on that basis. But I don't accept anything solely on faith."

"Then this place is not really for you, I'm afraid."

"Oh, but it *is*! I can appreciate the beauty of the paintings without accepting the scenes they portray as fact."

"Ah, but the beauty lies in the reality. You know what Keats said about beauty being truth and truth beauty? What do you think he meant by that?"

"I never really understood that poem." He laughed. "How do you interpret it?"

"Well, it's about an urn painting, remember? A grecian urn. Keats says that the artist has preserved the figures he has painted for all eternity."

"Like Giotto here."

"Yes, much like Giotto. . . . But the excellence of his work lies not in the permanence alone, but rather in the reality—the truth."

"And what *is* truth, Filomena? What does that mean to you?"

"I think truth is—I don't know the word in English—when a majority of persons agree about something."

"Consensus?"

"Yes, perhaps. 'Consensus' will do. Well, truth is an overwhelming consensus. Something that a big majority of people think to be true."

"Yes, but majorities have been wrong before, even huge majorities."

"Of course, Roberto, but only about minor things—you know, politics and such. They are not wrong about fundamentals. Such as what is good or beautiful or important to mankind. That is what Keats meant, I think."

"That there's a consensus about truth?"

"Not exactly. What he says to me is that truth is so universal that a consensus must accept it. Sometimes the belief of a great majority may be the surest sign of truth."

"Well, now you're talking faith again, I think. I won't argue the point, but, as for me, I've lived my whole life as a realist—a rationalist. I've got to see some indisputable facts to believe them. As for accepting even the least important concepts because a consensus does—accepting things purely on faith—I'll always be a skeptic. Maybe that's why I'm a professor of history and you're going to be a *professoressa di letteratura*, eh?"

"Yes, I suppose so." She turned to him and looked into his face with her wide, expressive eyes. "But there is hope for you, Roberto. I know you are intelligent enough to appreciate the beauty of the truth when one day you experience it for yourself."

They strolled the streets of Assisi for half an hour, then had lunch in a little *trattoria* near where the car was parked. It had white tablecloths, few other patrons, and the friendliest proprietor imaginable.

"*Siete una bella coppia,*" he said, embarrassing them. They were a handsome couple. He brought them, in recognition of the fact and compliments of the house, two enormous glasses of *vin santo*, a sweet red wine that got Filomena flushed and made her a bit unsteady when she stepped out into Assisi's heat.

"Are you OK?" Robert asked, taking her arm, for she had stumbled on an irregularity in the pavement on their way down to the car.

"Yes, yes, the wine, perhaps. And the heat a little too, I think. . . . I'm quite all right, though."

"Well, we'll head back now. I'll drive; you rest. Take a nap."

"No, Roberto. There is one more thing I want to show you. . . . Have you ever been to Santa Maria degli Angeli?"

"Uh, no, I don't think so. Is that another church?"

"Oh, yes, indeed, a very special one."

"Well, to judge from the place you took me in Siena, it must be worth a stop."

"Yes, I think you'll find it so."

She drove; a matter of a few miles' descent into the valley outside Assisi. Soon they came to an enormous, baroque structure faced with gray-white stone, a church like a hundred of its kind in Rome and a thousand throughout Italy. It was a place in no way exceptional with regard to its facade, and, opening, as it did, on an enormous paved parking lot, no more distinguished in its surroundings, either. Robert recalled the view from the *loggia* in Siena and concluded that there must be some such sweeping panorama awaiting him here, a magnificent vista spreading outward from the rooftop of the building or the summit of its tower. The viewpoint would face a different direction, though: there was nothing in the least appealing about the parking lot.

"This it?" he asked.

"Yes. We must step inside to have a look."

The church was empty. There were three other cars in the huge lot out front, and, when he and the girl entered, they saw only a group of brown-clad Franciscan monks wandering about the cavernous hall. In truth, the interior was nicer than the facade, bearing huge pilastered columns on either side of the nave and a polished marble, diagonally-checkered floor that was bicolored in white and, appropriately, Franciscan brown. Where the nave opened into the transept, daylight swept the floor and columns, entering through a multi-windowed cupola above.

Everything was elegant enough, though rather standard in a grandil-oquent sort of way. What was unusual—singular, in fact—was a small structure in the center of the floor, two-thirds of the way down toward the cupola. It was a little church, reminiscent, from that distance, of a dollhouse. The size, roughly, of a hermit's cottage, it was otherwise pro-totypically churchlike, with its pointed roof, arched portal, and gilded, frescoed facade. Here was a minuscule church-within-a-church. But what a contrast between the two! On the one hand—or, rather, at the periphery of the enormous enclosing space—stood a lofty structure, ele-gant, lavish, but grossly overdone. On the other hand—within the for-mer, and dwarfed by it—sat this diminutive object, this peasant's-cot-tage-of-a-thing, that somehow retained its dignity, its significance, in the process of being utterly overwhelmed. What was one to make of it?

"What *is* that?" he asked.

"Ah, good, you see the reason for our coming here. It is the *Porziuncola*."

"'Little portion'?"

"Yes, I suppose. I don't know why they call it that, though it is quite small. '*Chiesetta*' would be better, perhaps."

"So? What is it?"

"Come, I shall show you."

They walked down the checkered marble floor to the little church-let. A friar stepped out through its door, as though vacating it for them, and they entered, alone now in this absurdly out-of-scale, minuscule place-within-a-place.

It was ancient, infinitely older than the huge basilica surrounding it. It had a single rough-cut stone vault, as crudely fashioned as an old conduit or granary. And it was practically bare as well, the only interi-or decorations being a fine but unobtrusive inlaid floor and a cluster of simple paintings behind the altar. These too were very old and very plain, as though they and the little chapel itself had been placed in posi-tion solely as a foil for the overbearing grandiosity that enclosed them.

"So? What do you think of my little chapel?" asked Filomena with that wry smile of hers again, that wide-eyed, communicative grin. "Have I chosen well a second time, Roberto?"

"Yes, it's wonderful. But what exactly is it?"

"This, Roberto, is San Francesco's church. He was a simple man who had no need of gold and silks and precious stones. He lived for the good of all people—all creatures, really. He was a wonderful man who did only kind deeds in his lifetime. He died here in this little church. Right here. To me, that big church around us is nothing but an envelope to protect this little one. There is a spirit here in this little chapel that is lacking in the big one with all its marble and . . . and. . . . What is a better word for bigness?"

"Uh, 'grandiosity' I think. *Grandezza.*"

"Yes. That's the word: 'grandiosity'. I like that. Grandiosity. This little chapel lacks grandiosity. But it has beauty, poetry. Like the frescoes, like the Grecian urn. Do you understand now what I mean?"

"Yes, maybe I do a little." He answered thus, but without a shred of feeling, for the spirituality she had spoken of was completely lost on him. Oh, it was a charming place all right. But all this verbiage about human saintliness and godly grace was plain old fantasy as far as he was concerned, not all that different from Miss Lipsky's palmistry and horoscopes. Yes, it was all so much hogwash.

But just back then she had said something that had started him thinking. It was . . . it was . . . yes, a moment before she went off on that religious slant. He thought a little, trying to recall, as they walked toward the exit door and then out through it, into the heat, out to the car. What was the thing she had said exactly? The little church and then the big one: like an envelope, a cover. Yes, a cover that has nothing in common with its contents, unless one looks carefully into the matter and then can sense a relationship. What was it that he'd been reminded of? He started the car and followed her directions to the *autostrada*, heading home. What was it he was trying to remember?

Ten miles farther on the road to Siena, a thought surfaced. The cover. The *cover.* *THE COVER!* That folded folio sheet sitting in his drawer at the Dall'Olmos', sitting there neglected with the blank page stowed within. Damn! If he were Colangio planning to store some cryptic fool inscription in acid ink, he'd probably have put it there!

CHAPTER FIFTEEN

≈≈≈≈≈≈≈

INCANTATION

"Doc!"

It was Auntwon; you couldn't miss the voice. Robert looked at the clock on his desk, which read 4:15 p.m. That would be quarter after eight Sunday morning Chicago time. Auntwon was up and about amazingly early today.

"Auntwon! How are you? How are you doing? What time is it there?"

"Uh, it's early. Like eight-somefin'."

"Yeah? So what's up? Everything OK?"

"Yeah, Doc, I'm doin' great, man. Hey, I just got through checkin' out you e-mail. So, look-a here, man, whassup? What's been happenin'? . . . I mean, that other thang, that, like, incantation thang, you found it, huh?"

"What? Oh, yeah. . . . Yeah, it was right in front of me the whole time. . . . In that folio cover—you know, the double sheet that blank page was originally stuffed into when I found it. I think I mentioned that before in an email, didn't I?"

"Yeah, I 'member somefin' 'bout that, I think."

"OK, well that's where it was after all. Last place in the world I would have ever thought to look. . . . You know, after that email you sent me yesterday, I was about ready to tear the whole damn box apart. And I probably would have too, but . . . anyway, it's a long story: I took a little trip to Assisi yesterday, and on the way back it sort of dawned on me to check out that folded sheet, and. . . . Sure enough, I found the damn thing there last night. It's nothing particularly earth-shattering, though; nothing I can really use. . . . So, wow! how'd you get hold of me, Auntwon? Where are you calling from?"

"Oh, Dr. Rogovin gimme you number whey you at in Siena. I'm, like, *workin'*, man. Yeah. Like right now, I mean. Like eight a.m. and shit! It's—you know—that job he went and lined up fo' me at the library? They, like, ha' you work on Sundays too. Like filin' books away and shit. And best of all is you get to play wif the computers all you like and, like, call out on the phone to anyplace you want to call to. . . . Well, maybe they don't ezac'ly know whey you callin' to, but, anyhow, I got some—you know—access to a phone and I figure it be 'bout time to do some direc' voice to voice communication wif you, you dig? See what you doin', like—you know what I'm sayin'? So anyways, OK, lemme ha' the fo'-one-one on what it was ezac'ly that you found. That incantation thang, you know? Man! Aliens, I betchu, like the bof' of us said befo'."

Robert laughed into the phone, shaking his head in a happy medley of pleasure and surprise. Auntwon was a genuine character, all right, unique in all the world! Sure, he'd make a few illicit phone calls through the summer months. Maybe sneak off, too, to some secluded corner of the building and memorize a couple of the volumes he was supposed to be stacking away on shelves. But then, as a kind of justifiable recompense, he'd likely come up with a new and extraordinarily efficient cataloguing system for the librarians that would revolutionize the way they did their work. Yes, Auntwon Miller was special, all right: if he anticipated aliens in Siena, they just might happen to pop up some day.

"No, Auntwon; no sign of aliens yet. I'll keep on the lookout, though, I promise. . . . But, to answer your question seriously, it's—the thing I found, I mean—it's another crazy watermark just like the last one. I looked everywhere for it, as I told you, every damn page of that manuscript. Then last night coming back from Assisi I somehow thought of the folio sheet—actually it was the girl I drove there with who gave me the idea in the first place—kind of unwittingly, I guess. . . . Anyway, to make a long story short, it was right there the whole time, plain as day: the goddamn crazy thing I'd been looking for all week. . . . So finally I find the damn thing and it winds up being hardly worth the effort. It's a kind of incantation, all right, just like the diagram described, but—I emailed you about the stuff in the diagram, didn't I?"

"Yeah, yeah, you to'd me about all that stuff. . . . So what it say?—

that incantation thang, I mean. . . . And what about that girl—you got yo'se'f anovver girl friend awready, Doc? *Man*!"

"No, no, don't get excited. It's just somebody I met. She's honestly no more than a girl who happens to be a friend. . . . Anyway, about the incantation, it really is useless. It's in Latin and in Colangio's writing— the watermark, I mean—but it's every bit as crazy as the diagram—no, no, *crazier*. I mean . . . the language . . . it's like—I don't know—like an invocation to the devil or something, the way it sounds. . . . It's just. . . . I just can't imagine Colangio being involved in this kind of foolishness. It makes the diagram look like a scrabble game in comparison. It's—I don't know—it's really . . . unbelievable!"

"So what it *say*, man? Tell me. Come on, give it up."

"Give it up! Why? . . . Look, it's not worth the twenty cents a minute it'd cost the library for me to read the goddamn thing to you on the phone."

"Come on, Doc! Jus' read it to me, man. Hey, *you* the one who got me interested in all this Colangio bullshit in the first place, man! Come on!"

"Look, honestly, Auntwon, it's really just a bunch of garbage. I can't quite figure out what could have gotten into Colangio's head to make him save this kind of thing. . . . Let alone *use* it!—My God! He might have even tried to *use* the goddamn chart for something! I don't know, it's just. . . . Look, you read my book; and Colangio's writings, too, some of them, didn't you? You've gotta have some idea what I'm talking about. Colangio was a rationalist, for God's sake. A skeptic. He fought this kind of nutty superstition all his life."

"Well, you cain't say *all*, Doc. We don' know nuffin 'bout them last twenty-some years, right? . . . But OK, OK; I know what you sayin'. I read a couple of his thangs, sure. I know whatchu mean. But, OK, like I to'd you: when he drop out like that, you know? When he stop writin' and shit?—that weird enough all by itself."

"Yeah, you were right—this *is* getting pretty weird. I was hoping this . . . this incantation or whatever the hell it is, would help clarify things, but now. . . ."

"So whatchu gon' do?"

"Do?"

"Yeah, to, like, figure thangs out."

214 | STEVEN M. GREENBERG

"I don't know. Just what I've been doing so far, I guess. . . . You know, keep going through the manuscript and hope for another clue that's a little more useful."

"You ain't gon' try it out?"

"Try *what* out?"

"Hey man! The diagram and shit. . . . You know, now that you got the whole thang togevver. Man, you gots to try it out.

"You're joking, right?"

"Yeah, maybe. . . . But, I don't know . . . maybe I'd jus' go ahead an' try it out if I was you."

"You would? Why?"

"Well, you tryin' to find out what happened wif Colangio, right?"

"Yeah?"

"OK, so, lessay somefin' in that diagram had a crazy effect on him."

"Like what, an oyster shell?"

"No, man. Look, you got some ovver shit in there too, ain't that right?"

"Yeah, a beeswax candle, an egg yolk, holy water, and soil from an olive grove. What are they supposed to do, change iron into gold?"

"No, man, but. . . . OK, OK, lessay the—some kinda candle you say it was?"

"Yeah, beeswax. Made of beeswax."

"OK, so lessay the beeswax give off some kinda fumes that combine wif somefin' else. Like the calcium in the oyster shell or the sulfur in the egg yolk. Lessay them fumes did somefin'—maybe made him high or some kinda shit like 'at."

"That's pretty far-fetched, don't you think?"

"Yeah, maybe. But the whole thang seem pretty far-fetched to me. I'd say to go ahead an' give it a try. You got to start someplace, and thass a start."

"Yeah, it's a start all right. And here's another start for you: This thing's useless and crazy, and I don't need to go out and collect a bunch of oyster shells and egg yolks to convince myself of that. But I'd sure like to know how a guy as brilliant as Colangio managed to delude himself to the contrary!"

He set down the phone and sat a minute with his elbow on the desktop thinking . . . then opened the center drawer and took out the transcription he'd made the evening before. A full third of the folio page it consumed, that crazy watermark, line after line, absurdity after absurdity. It wasn't even passable Latin: Not Colangio's polished Augustan prose, but rather something corrupt and medieval; written, most likely, by some half-literate—though enterprising—charlatan a hundred years or more before Colangio's birth. Such was its style and crudity. Perhaps it was a joke. Yes, however unlikely that seemed, its being some kind of pathetic practical joke would account for its existence and content with the greatest degree of plausibility.

"*Magister. . . .*" it began. That's how devotees addressed the devil in those benighted, superstitious days—though maybe it didn't reach that high; maybe it was just some lieutenant-level sub-demon the silly words were seeking to invoke.

". . . *ad nomen tuum devovemus. . . .*" it continued. And on and on from there the fool thing droned; thirty close-spaced lines of exaltation, of conjuration, for some unidentifed master spirit. Then, at last, at the very end, came a request—for whatever purpose, whether a plea for communion with a departed soul or an inquiry about the weather:

> Master, to your name we consecrate our souls, now and at the moment of our deaths [*ad mortis temporum momentum*]. . . . All-powerful Master [*Magister potentissimus*], bring these forces together. Bring the spirit of the brilliant sun [*solis clarissimi*], the silver moon with all its nightly radiance. Bring water from ocean and river, and bring earth and all the products of the land. Then bring these final things, hot fire and ever-present wind [*ventus omnipraesens*] to produce that which is good and needful to your servant, bringing desired things to him for the benefit of more than one, and let none glean evil therefrom. Exalted spirit [*numen laudatus*], I ask that you command these things to be, and in the names of sun and moon, water and earth, fire and wind, make that which is not come to be and that which was once exist again, make from nothing something or let that which is not desired cease to be. Let this be so and I shall dedicate my spirit to your greater glory. What I request, that it may bring contentment to my soul, is____

And thus had he found it the previous evening in the fabric of that blank folded page. Thus had it emerged in translucent characters from beneath the last six ounces of watermark fluid remaining in the second of the plastic bottles, eked out drop-by-drop into the big, black baking pan. Thus had it barely been deciphered—for the fluid had quite run dry at the end, and Robert's throat had all but choked off from the vapors. . . .

But he had found it! Finally! Incredibly! After a long, frantic search and five long centuries of neglect! Here it was: this writing that had been laboriously decoded by the great Colangio himself. Then secretly etched in acid, preserved in a casket, and buried for half a millenium in a wall. Something of vital importance to him, obviously. A prized document direct from the psyche of the greatest of Renaissance thinkers.

And what this incomparable treasure seemed to be saying was this: "Honored Signor Satan, please to send a message from the dear departed, and, by the way, can you read my horoscope this weekend?" Or some such errant nonsense, at any rate. This was the precious inscription that Colangio had passed down through the ages! The invaluable secret Robert had driven himself almost frantic, nearly sleepless, and half-insane these past six days to find!

Well, he had it now; here it was, found; and all it served to do was confirm the fact that his poor Adalberto—the rationalist, the skeptic, the genius—had been utterly deranged in these, his final, unaccounted years. No hint as to why, or how, or even precisely when the derangement had begun. No, those were the questions another book might be written to answer—another big seller, too, if all the facts could be discerned.

Well, Robert surely had his work cut out for him: First he'd have to finish with the text of the manuscript—for there might be clues even there. Then he could try to trace the diagram back to some medieval source. Meanwhile, in the process of doing both, he could take a day or two off to prowl around the area some more. To Assisi again, perhaps, then Perugia. Each had once been St. Francis' home, and thus a place Colangio might have visited at the time of his transformation.

He might check out the demonology angle, too, to see if either of the inscriptions—either the diagram or the associated incantation—had surfaced somewhere else. If one of them had, he could investigate the source, find the cult involved, then try to learn the thing's intended use. Those might all be pathways to a fuller understanding. . . . Sure, what the hell, thought Robert, he'd figured out a sane Colangio once before. Sane or deranged, no reason he shouldn't be able to do the same damn thing yet again.

"Oh, I did not mean to disturb you," said Filomena half an hour later when he opened the door. He was fresh from the shower and wearing a pair of old jeans and a pullover shirt that stuck annoyingly to his undried skin.

"No, no, that's OK. I was just getting dressed to go out. Uh, a friend from the Piccolomini—the archivist, in fact, Caterina's boss. I think she's coming along too. . . . Look, uh, you could join us if you like. . . ."

"No, thank you. *Mamma* and I are going to Firenze again. Is there anything you need? Some more candles, perhaps?"

"No, no. I still have the candles. But thank you for the thought."

He excused himself. The people coming would be there in fifteen minutes. "You're sure?" he asked her. "You're welcome to come along if you like." He said it more as a closure than an invitation, swinging the door to a little, diagonally between them. But the girl wasn't in the least offended, or didn't seem to be.

"No," she answered, "I'll be off then." She smiled and turned, and Robert shut the door, got dressed, and was downstairs and out in front of the Dall'Olmos' place barely ten minutes later.

Fabbri pulled up at quarter-past-two, exactly, to the minute. Caterina was in the front passenger seat—probably with her stop-watch—so Robert squeezed into the back, sitting sideways in the little Fiat to accommodate his legs. They drove out of town, down the sinu-ous road that leads into the valley at the foot of Siena's hill, out to the highway, then north on it toward Florence.

"So where are we off to?" Robert asked. "To Florence—*Firenze?*"

Fabbri's head turned maybe twenty degrees around. "*Una sorpresa,*" he said: a surprise. Half an hour later they pulled off the road in the direction of a hilltop town in the distance, crowned at its summit with a garland of crenellated walls.

"It's Monteriggioni, dottore, have you ever been here?" asked Caterina, shouting over the whoosh and flutter of the highway.

"No. What's here to see?"

"Wait," she said in her determined voice, "you shall find out in a little while."

Five minutes it took for the little Fiat to wind its way around the hillside to its top. They entered through a monumental archway into a picture post card of a place, a thirteenth century fortified town on a steep granite peak: an ancient Sienese outpost against the hostile Florentines. Yet one more of Italy's countless treasures, the town possessed perfectly preserved fortifications that had somehow escaped the ravages of eight chaotic centuries. The stones, the walls, the towers looked new, fresh, as though the ancient fortress were a fortress still; the ancient town still bustling with urban life. And when they parked the car within the ambit of those massive walls, Robert discovered that indeed the place *was* still living: a quaint little piazza appeared around them, composed of nothing but massive masonry, a decrepit church, a couple of tiny shops with souvenirs and foodstuffs, and, finally, a rustic but wonderfully oil- and garlic-scented restaurant they climbed down into just a few short meters from the Fiat's front bumper.

"We have lunch here," said Fabbri. "I pay for every-theen. It is my party. It is my—Caterina, *come si dice 'compleanno'*?"

"'Birthday'. It is Signor Fabbri's birthday, dottore."

"Today? Well, I should treat *you*, then," Robert offered. "Happy birthday!"

"No, no. I pay. I call for the party, so I pay. Besides, you pay the last dinner, so even more I pay thees time."

They got into some bench-like seats by the window. The two men sat opposite Caterina at one of maybe half a dozen tables in the place, all of which were perfectly clear of tableware and—the other five at least—devoid of patrons. It looked as though no one had eaten there in decades; centuries, perhaps. The unpartitioned room had so dependent a ceiling and such rugged stone walls that it gave the impression of having been chiseled wholesale into the living rock of the hilltop; or maybe bored into the fortress walls themselves, so sturdy, dark, and cryptiform did its interior appear.

In a minute or two, a young waitress came over and brought them menus, which had the look and texture of having been printed individually on a mimeograph machine, stained selectively with multi-colored foodstuffs, set in the sun to fade, then finally encased in cracked, wrinkled, and frosted plastic for the customers' visual delectation.

"It's quaint, all right," said Robert. Then, noting the perplexity in Fabbri's face, he translated: "*singolare.*"

"Ah! '*Singolare' vuol dire* 'quaint'. Good, I shall remember."

"Well, signori, despite the way things may appear, the food is very good here," said Caterina. "I actually discovered it some years ago and recommended it to Signor Fabbri for the present occasion."

"Now why doesn't that surprise me?" asked Robert, less sarcastically that the words might have seemed to imply. "Caterina, you're truly amazing!"

"*Ma figurati!* It is my job . . . like arranging your accommodations." She reached across the table to tap the back of Robert's hand. "So, dottore, tell me: is everything satisfactory at the Dall'Olmos'?"

"Yes, indeed. Perfect, really. The girl's been great."

"Excellent," she said. "And how is your work proceeding? All those terribly illegible words!"

"Yes, Dottor Bob," Fabbri interjected, "how is your work on the *manoscritto?*"

"Slow but even progress, Taddeo. Nothing new. . . . Oh, no, that's not entirely true. . . . I found the incantation."

"What is it that you found, if I may ask?" Caterina set her menu down and looked straight into Robert's eyes, unblinking. To his left, with the farthest periphery of his visual sense, he perceived a determined shaking of Fabbri's head, as he began to explain things to the secretary:

"Uh, did Signor Fabbri tell you about the diagram?"

"No, dottore, nothing. I would like to know."

"Well, that page I showed you when you came in my work room the first day—the blank one, remember?" Caterina nodded. "OK, well, it turned out to contain a sort of secret inscription—a kind of watermark."

"A watermark?" she asked. "I'm not really certain. . . ."

"Like in the stamps, you know? A *filigrana*. It must have been made with acid ink, so that it produced a kind of hidden inscription in the paper. Signor Fabbri was the one who figured it out in the first place—from the stamps in his collection I guess. . . . Anyway, there turned out to be two of them, actually—two watermarks, I mean. One's a sort of magic diagram and the other is an incantation that goes along with it. That's the one I discovered last night."

"Where? Where do you find thees?" asked the *Archivista* gravely, still shaking his head.

"It was in the folio cover—the *coperta*."

"Ah, *si, si. La coperta. Ho pensato*."

"*L'ha pensato! Allora perché non me l'ha suggerito?* . . . Why didn't you *say* something if you thought it might be there?" Robert repeated in English, shaking his head in disbelief. He was astonished. He'd spent six agonizing days looking for the damned fool thing, and all the while. . . .

"Why! Why! I tell you before why. It is dangerous!"

"Dangerous! Come on, Taddeo!" said Robert, but he caught himself and stopped at that. The *Archivista* was a kind and decent soul and was only doing what he considered prudent—for whatever silly reasons. For an awkward minute or so, no one spoke. Caterina commenced looking at her menu; whereupon they all did, following her cue. Then finally, after the uncomfortable minute had passed, she set the menu deliberately on the table's surface and gazed up again straight into Robert's eyes.

"All right, dottore, tell me: what are these *filigrane* for, really? What is it that they say?"

Fabbri made neither sound nor gesture to prevent him, so Robert began to explain. There was, he told the secretary, this sort of hexagram of separate circles requiring objects to be placed on them, and then that esoteric incantation was supposed to be read. . . .

"I have seen such theens before," said Fabbri now, suddenly interrupting. "No thees exact kind, you know, but for the same *disegno*."

"Purpose? . . . You have?" asked Robert. "But you told me you hadn't."

"No. No ezackly the same, thees is true. But similar. For the same magic *disegno*—'purpose', you say."

"Where? Where did you see such things—things like this? . . . Where?"

"We have in the achives many ancient theens—for . . . eh, *stregoneria*. Like that. How you say, Caterina—'*stregoneria*'?"

"For witchery, no?"

"Witchcraft," Robert corrected.

"*Si,* 'weetchcraft'; ah, yes, I remember. We say thees before. . . . You must be verr' careful of thees."

"Careful! Look, Taddeo, I've been agonizing about this thing for a week. If you had some knowledge about it—anything at all—you should have said something a week ago."

"Ah, Dottor Bob, I *say* you a week before: such theens can be . . . eh, eh, *pericoloso* . . . eh, dangerful."

"OK, look, look . . . this is crazy. I mean, the watermark is crazy in and of itself, granted. But the way you're reacting to it is even worse. The thing is some kind of sorcerer's diagram, for God's sake! Don't tell me you believe in witchcraft now—in *stregoneria*!... Look, we don't even know what the goddamn thing was supposed to be *used* for— what it was supposed to *do,* you know? How can you say it's danger- ous if you don't even know what it's supposed to accomplish?"

"*Beh,* thees is even more . . . eh, dangerous."

"How? You aren't really saying you believe in the efficacy of such things . . . uh, *che sifatte cosi hanno efficacia*!"

"*Si, ci sono molte cose che non capiamo affatto.*" Lots of things we cannot understand at all, the *Archivista* said.

"*Non capiamo*! Taddeo! Come on! Sure, there are phenomena we don't completely understand, but stuff like this is just plain crazy, don't you think? Come on, Caterina, help me out here, will you?"

"Ah, signori, leave me out of this argument, please! I don't believe in such things either, but if you cannot agree on this matter, why not try it out? See if it works. Then you can decide which of you is right. It can be a kind of experiment." Caterina was smiling slyly, amused by her own wit perhaps or maybe just pleased at having found herself moder- ator of the debate.

"Try it out!" Robert chuckled. "That's exactly what my student told me. Exactly those words: "Try it out," he said. I talked to him maybe forty minutes before you guys picked me up, and he said the exact same thing. God! I think everybody's gone absolutely nuts today. All of you. 'Go ahead and try it out.' Jesus! You're as crazy as the dia- gram, the whole damned lot of you, totally insane."

"So if it's so crazy," Caterina smiled again, "if we're *all* so crazy, then there's no harm in your trying it. Isn't that right? Then you will know absolutely for certain one way or the other."

"Hey, I already *know* for certain!" Robert laughed. "Look, why are we discussing this anyway? What's the point?. . . . All right, Caterina, let's say I *did* want to try it. . . . What would I try it *for*? I don't even know what it's supposed to *do*. The damned thing doesn't say what precisely you're supposed to *do* with it."

"So find out," she answered. "What kind of objects do you need to make the magic work? You said there were objects that needed to be placed on the chart."

"Thees is dangerous," said Fabbri, gravely, shaking his head. "You must be verr' careful with such theens. I should never to remove thees paper from the palazzo. *No, non avrei mai dovuto rimuoverla.*"

"Well, it was nice of you to do it, anyway, Taddeo. It really was, and I appreciate the trouble you took." He patted Fabbri's arm, but the *Archivista* kept his eyes locked firmly on the table.

"What kinds of objects do you need, dottore—to go with your diagram, I mean? Tell me... Just for curiosity, that is," said Caterina again, smiling a little less slyly.

"What kinds? Well, let me see. . . . Beeswax candles and oyster shells, and, well . . . sophisticated things like that. Very profound, as you can see. . . . It seems I have the candles, though. Filomena picked up some for me."

"Good," said Caterina. "Excellent. Then I will order oysters and you will have everything you need."

"Oh no, not quite; there are a few more essential things. Let's see: an egg yolk, for one thing—well, that's pretty simple I guess. And earth—soil, it says—from an olive grove; it's got to be from an olive grove, for some reason. . . . Oh, and holy water . . . ."

"*Ah, L'acqua santa*! That is the most dangerous. Verr' bad. I should never to take. . . ."

"OK, OK. Look, Taddeo, I'm not gonna use it, all right? You don't need to be concerned. I haven't the slightest *intention* of using it. . . . But . . . what makes you say that *acqua santa* makes it more dangerous?"

"*L'acqua santa*, Dottor Bob. . . . When one use holy theens for . . . for weetchery— *eh, stregoneria*. This is verr' bad, verr' dangerous; more dangerous than anytheen other."

"OK. Look, let's just have our meal in peace and forget the witch-craft business for a while. I need a big glass of wine right about now."

They got that, some good, dry *brunello*, and then another bottle, making the room presently feel warm and close, but very pleasant too. The food was rather good, but rather salty as well, rich and salty, so that they had to order yet a third *brunello* to wash it down, and this was over half-consumed when Caterina seized the occasion to ask about the girl.

"Tell me, dottore: Filomena comes to visit you often these days. Do you like her better than you said before?" Caterina had barely touched her wine—maybe a glass and a half—and seemed now to project an aura of intimidating sobriety.

"Filomena? Yes, yes, I like her a lot. She's a wonderful girl. Wonderful." She really was wonderful for a girl so plain, Robert thought, though perhaps it was partly the wine that had made her seem so especially wonderful at the moment. "We're friends, you know? Really good friends, too. It's best that you told me about her father, though. . . . You know, she took me to Assisi yesterday."

"Assisi?"

"Yes, for some . . . uh . . . research on my manuscript—the one I'm working on, that is. We went to a big church there with a little one inside: Santa Maria degli Angeli was the name. You know it?"

"No, I don't think so. That isn't the church of San Francesco, is it? The basilica?"

"Uh, San Francesco? No, not the famous church, no. It's another one, a big church outside Assisi with a little one inside. It's . . . . Uh, I don't know; I lost my train of thought. It's a tiny little church inside a great big one. You've really got to see it sometime."

He looked over at Fabbri, whose eyes were closing and head nod-ding jerkily onto his chest. The *bistecca* on the plate under his droop-ing chin was less than half consumed. Robert made a funny face and pointed toward the *Archivista* with his thumb, whereupon Caterina shook her head and smiled.

"Don't point, dottore. I think you are not very much in better condi-tion than Signor Fabbri now. I shall have to drive you *both* home, I think."

"Yes," said Robert. "That's a very good idea. He's in no condition to operate a vehicle."

"All right, then. Let me just go to the ladies' room and I shall help the two of you out to the car."

Robert paid the bill, Caterina returned from the rest room, and they headed out the door. Fabbri slid limply into the back seat, lying sideways with his gaunt face on the coarse fabric, his long legs bent awkwardly in the cramped space. Caterina walked away, across the piazza somewhere, then came back a few minutes later with her purse in her hands. She got into the driver's seat, set the purse on the floor beneath her legs and started the engine. Halfway back to Siena, the vehicle turned off the highway, stopped along a wooded back-road somewhere, and she got out.

"What are you doing?" Robert asked foggily. Fabbri was purring softly behind him.

"Nothing. Stay there. I'll be right back." *She has to pee*, he thought, which sounded funny in his mind, so he chuckled to himself, then seemed to doze again with the car once more in motion. Caterina woke him after what seemed like an exceedingly short time.

"All right, dottore, you must help me to get Signor Fabbri inside. Can you do that?"

Robert was dazed at first, but the effort revived him remarkably. Some neighbors of the *Archivista* were out front, sitting on lawn chairs or standing about in little clusters chatting. They frowned and shook their heads. "*E ubriaco fradicio!*" said one old woman testily—"He's dead drunk!" The woman, with a thrust of her hand, walked away abruptly, back into the building. But someone came along to help: a young man who managed at last to extricate Fabbri's two enormous feet from the floorboard behind the passenger seat and get him standing.

They hauled the *Archivista* up to his apartment and placed him in his bed, rumpled and flaccid as he was, then left. Robert was annoyingly awake by now, dry and hollow. His tongue felt cottony, and there was a powerful taste in his mouth of salt, garlic, and over-ripe grapes.

"Now I shall get you to your lodgings too," said Caterina. "I think you can make it up the stairs yourself, though. Can you?"

"Sure, I'm perfectly fine. Perfectly fine."

The place looked empty and quiet when she drove him up to within an arm's reach of the door. It was 7:50 now by his watch, just commencing to grow dark.

"Are you certain you can make it upstairs by yourself?" Caterina asked.

"Absolutely. I'm fine, just fine."

"All right, then. Here. Take these." She handed him a little paper sack.

"What is it?"

"Why, your magic things of course!"

"My *what*? . . . *What*?"

"Yes, I got them all for you. An egg yolk and an oyster shell from the restaurant where we ate; and some holy water from the church there—in Monterrigione, I mean; in the piazza. That's what I did before we drove off, remember? It's in the aluminum foil in there: see? I made a little cup for it with foil on top. . . . And there's the soil in there too. I stopped to get it in an olive grove when we were nearly home, when I pulled off the highway back there almost to Siena—remember?. . . . So you can do your experiment now, dottore. If it works to tell the future, try and find out which *contrada* will win the *palio* in July." She laughed. "Go ahead and do your little experiment and let me know tomorrow how it turns out." She waited until he had opened the door, then started off, waving through the little Fiat's window.

The house was still; soundless, the Dall'Olmos not yet back from Florence, he supposed. Between his fingers, the little paper sack felt nearly weightless as he plodded his way up the creaking stairs, breaking the ambient silence. He reached the third level, stepped into his room, and sprawled out on the bed. . . . But he was awake now, fully and unremittingly awake, whether from dissipation of the wine or the physical exigencies of climbing those two endless flights of steps. He propped himself up on an elbow, then rose fully, standing. The little paper bag was on the desktop where he had dropped it. Through the window, the last feeble rays of daylight leached in lazily, growing thinner, fainter with each departing minute.

Robert stepped over to the desk and took his yellow pad from the center drawer. He leafed through to his rendering of the diagram with its hexagram of circles, pulled out the page, then pulled out the overlying one—the copy he had made of the magical incantation that had seemed so patently ridiculous to him just a few hours before.

Well, it *still* was ridiculous—of course it was. . . . But . . . but . . . somehow the idea of a simple experiment—secret and perfectly harmless—seemed suddenly less frivolous to him now, less outrageously absurd. Sure, there was a quantity of alcohol still in his bloodstream. That had left him dazed, though no less awake for all he had consumed. Still, maybe the surfeit of *brunello* had clouded his judgement somewhat, diluted somewhat his inhibitory sense of reason. That might explain the untoward itch of curiosity he'd begun to feel.

But then, too, there were his interlocutors this memorable Sunday afternoon. After all, these were three not unclever people he'd been dealing with: Auntwon without a doubt; Caterina also in her compulsive way; and lastly Fabbri, clearly wise in his knowledge of ancient writings. Hadn't they—all three of them in fact—been perfectly unanimous in their promptings? And adamant too, each of them, in his own peculiar way: "Try it out," one had said; "Do an experiment," another; "It's dangerous," the third—well, after all, that final admonition had been even more of an endorsement than the rest, if you took the time and trouble to read between the lines.

All right, he thought, nodding his head in acceptance, then shrugging: what the hell! It would be absolutely dark in ten minutes, then, in an hour more, the time would be exactly right: one hour past sunset, the diagram had instructed, precisely. He opened the shutters, set the transcribed papers on the bed, lined up the arrow at the diagram's upper margin with the sky at the point of the sun's decline—the diagram had specified that too—fetched the items Caterina had gathered from the little paper bag, then went to the bureau for one of Filomena's beeswax candles. OK, he thought, what the hell. Lets take the damn thing out for a test drive. If a genius like Colangio had found solace, or wisdom, or pleasure in an oyster shell, who was Robert Martin to cast such benefits away?

It was pitch black outside: the sky, the street. The room had darkened too, just a dim lamp going, back behind him on the desk. Two minutes left . . . then a minute-fifty-five. . . . He had a throbbing headache now, dull, hollow, synchronous with his pulse, a product of the wine.

Everything was set in place: the shell, the soil in its wrought aluminum wrapping, the shallow pool of water in its crinkled cup. The egg yolk had a tendency to roll out of its circle, but he pushed a little dimple in the paper to contain it. He set the candle in its designated place closest to the arrow. Then lit it. Then waited. . . . Thirty seconds . . . twenty-five . . . twenty. . . . What did it matter? The time was just approximate anyway. As to the exact moment the sun had set, who could say for sure? Who, with all those buildings in the way? All right, then, ten seconds . . . five. . . . It was full time now, by his watch: just an hour after sunset.

Magister," he read, "*ad nomen tuum devovemus.* . . ." Then on and on chantlike through the crude, medieval Latin text, stopping, finally, at its end. "Specify the wished for thing," it said. What? he thought. What? . . . "What do you feel like, Bobby," came Sheldon's voice into his mind's ear, from that final day they'd spent together. "Anything, anything."

"OK," he'd answered, "a hot dog."

"A hot dog," he said aloud, which sounded rather silly following the Latin verbiage. But the whole thing was silly anyway, wasn't it? Sure. The whole thing was as silly as a big-time wrestling match to a dedicated scholar. Nevertheless, he read it through once more, as the diagram specifically instructed. Twice, it said. Fine, fine; twice, then. He finished with the second reading, coming again to the underlined space, the "wished for thing." "A hot dog," he repeated, for want of a profounder thought or the faintest expectation that his most trivial request might conceivably be granted, then blew the exhaled air from his lungs. Straight across the hexagram of circles it went, in the direction of the arrow, extinguishing the candle's flame.

Some minutes passed, and . . . nothing happened. Just as he'd thought. No, *known*. He'd *known* the whole thing was foolish, as well as he'd ever known anything in his life. His system of belief was founded on it. A rational universe was requisite to man's stability of mind, and magic diagrams accorded poorly with that. So it was good that nothing had happened. And yet. . . .

There was a pleasant breeze now, scented of hay and verdant vegetation. A truly splendid evening for a walk, and he decided to take one, going softly down the steps past the Dall'Olmos' living quarters, so as not to disturb them. They were home now. He heard the radio or television crackling mutedly with speech and music. And there was water running, too, somewhere inside, within their ground-floor walls.

He closed the monumental coffered door, not locking it, for he would not be out too long, then strolled down the Via di Pantaneto toward the Campo. There were lights on there, the *Mangia* tower floodlit, casting a spectral brilliance on the crenelated rooves around the piazza. Two of the restaurants were open yet. A few groups of diners sat beneath their awnings and the ubiquitous advertisements there for *Cinzano* and *Pellegrino*. Robert took a seat at an isolated table and ordered a *cappucino*, then another. Caffeinated drinks never seemed to bother him at night, even a double *cappucino*. He drank them leisurely, paid the waiter, tipping generously, went out to the warmly lit declivity of brick-clad pavement, and walked the circuit of the Campo, once, twice, then headed back toward his commodious room.

These last few days he had thought about Cassie less often: once an hour or twice, but then he'd put her from his mind, forcibly, determinedly. This evening that was harder to do. Maybe the caffeine, after all; or maybe the vacuousness that he felt inside, the loneliness, the disappointment he had begun to sense within him now that his work had turned so fallow, so utterly meaningless. Here he was, entering the mind, not of a genius, but of a demented soul: sick, deluded, or senile. Where was the joy in that? Where was the delight he'd hoped to regain in his once-beloved studies? Wherever might he find a tenth the ecstasy he had once known in his Cassandra's arms?

He locked the outside door behind him and climbed slowly to his room. He was still wide awake, though it was nearly eleven now. The caffeine maybe; one *cappucino* would have been enough. Oh well, perhaps a bath would help to soothe his body and thus potentially anesthetize his mind.

He filled the tub and soaked for twenty minutes or so, then dried himself off and read: a chapter on France from the *Cambridge Modern History*, Volume I: Charles VIII, that strange, malformed sovereign who had once invaded Italy with his quixotic legions, then limped home, victorious in retreat, but not a whit the better off. Colangio had lived through those days; Robert knew their events practically by rote. Each page in the *Cambridge* had been underlined and circled, read by him a dozen times or more. Still he found them fresh, informative.

Twenty minutes more he read. It was nearly midnight now. Perhaps he'd better try and get some sleep. He pushed himself up, went into the bathroom, and brushed his teeth, looking at his image in the mirror. Yes, he looked all right. Cassie had loved him once. Perhaps, somehow, some day, he would find another such love again. It had happened once, so who could say nevermore? He was young enough, attractive enough. He rinsed his face, used the toilet. . . . Then he heard something: a knock on the door, it sounded like, but soft, hesitant. He wasn't absolutely sure.

"Yes?" he said, not very loudly either, not entirely convinced of having heard anything for certain after all.

"Roberto?" came a muffled voice. Filomena's voice, again.

"Yes? Filomena? Just a minute. Let me just put something on." He slipped on his jeans and a tee shirt, then went to the door. She was standing just outside it with something in her hands: a sort of casserole dish, it appeared to be.

"I heard you running the water, so I thought I would see if you were still up. *Mamma* and I made a surprise for you, from our trip to Firenze. Here."

She handed him a covered plate, and when he had asked her in, put her in the desk chair by his bed, then seated himself on the mattress facing her, he opened the plate's ceramic lid, finding there two pungently aromatic hot dogs on little buns, made Chicago-style, with mustard and pickles and tomato slices, pretty much the way he had always ordered them at home.

CHAPTER SIXTEEN

~~~~~~~~~~

REVELATION

SUBJ: The test you asked for
DATE: 5/19/00 8:36:28 AM, central European time
FROM: Robtmar@attglobal.net
REPLY-TO: Robtmar@attglobal.net
TO: auntwon99@aol.com

Hi, Auntwon,
I tried it out last night per your request and something peculiar really
did happen. Probably just coincidence, but strange. Worth rechecking,
which I am going to do today. Or tonight, rather. Will let you know.

Doc.

It would be a long day, tedious. Sitting there, waiting, trying to keep
occupied. . . . He'd head to the Piccolomini, put in his eight interminable
hours, get through another dozen pages—maybe more if he could keep
his focus—finding nothing much of interest. Again. Just passing time till
evening, till sunset, finally, and then that one last hour more when the
time would be appropriate to try the damn fool thing again.

He went downstairs at twenty-to-nine, ten minutes earlier than usual,
and knocked on the Dall'Olmos' door. There were some questions in his
mind, some clarifications he wanted made if that were possible: Like
when had the women planned that splendid midnight snack for him? And
why? Whose idea had the whole thing been? It *had* to be coincidence, just
had to, he assured himself. Otherwise. . . . The signora opened her first-
floor door, looking crumpled and sanguine and remarkably blasé.

"*Ah, buon giorno, Signora Dall'Olmo.*" He smiled at her; and she smiled back, with all the customary warmth and benevolence she had shown him from the very first. She was a genial soul if ever there was one, this little lady. And the girl was just as nice, just as agreeable, but . . . but. . . . "*Mi scusi, signora,*" he finally managed to get out, "*ma. . . .*" He shifted his weight over to the opposite foot, scratched his head and stammered on: Could he . . . might he . . . might he ask a question or two of her?

Ma certamente!" she responded, just as sweetly as always, nodding. "*Certamente, dottore!*" Would he care to come in? Have a cup of coffee? Tea?. . . . No, he answered. He'd have to be at work soon. . . . The signora shrugged. "*Va bene,*" she said—OK—then smiled again, wryly, and raised her eyebrows: Had he liked his little surprise, she asked—his "*piccola sorpresa?*"

"*Si, si, ma ovviamente*! *Ma. . . .*" but . . . he had something he would like to ask about that. He was curious: when exactly had they . . . uh . . . conceived their wonderful *sorpresa* for him? How long had the two of them been planning it exactly?

"*Ah, vediamo un po'* . . . . *Forse tre giorni. . . .*" she said: three days or four, she wasn't absolutely sure. Filomena had come home one day—Friday, she thought it was—and told her: "'*Vorrebbe una salsiccia americana' ha detto.*" "He'd like a hot dog—his favorite dish." So they'd planned the drive to Florence, arranging it for yesterday. Then last night when they'd heard him return, heard his footsteps on the stairs around eleven, heard the water running in his bath, Filomena had become impatient. "*Le fabbrichiamo. . . .*" Let's make them now, she'd said, right there, right then. "*Adesso, adesso!*" She couldn't wait a single day longer to give him his surprise. No, not a single hour more!

"*Se ne vuole piu. . . .*" said the signora. If he wanted more, well, they had a whole pack of *salsiccie americane* they could cook up on demand. Little buns too, *panini.* . . . She had a dozen sitting in the freezer. All he had to do was say the word.

"*Grazie, signora.*" He thanked her profusely. Sincerely too. She'd been more than kind, and Filomena, he enthused, was a dear, sweet child. A good friend, in fact, already, though he'd known her just a matter of days. The signora grinned even more widely at that and shook his hand: "*Se ne vuole piu. . . .*" If he wanted more, she repeated, he need only ask. "*Grazie tante,*" Robert told her, departing, waving from the open door. He headed for the Piccolomini.

Well, that was a whole lot better; mere coincidence, after all. What had he been thinking? Still, it *had* been an unsettling event, something any skeptical person might find a little disconcerting at best. One could hardly discount it. No, the silly thing deserved another try, if only to put one's inevitable doubts to rest. Tonight, perhaps, he considered; then decided with an involuntary bob of the head: yes indeed, he'd give it one more try again tonight.

Robert reached the top of the palace staircase and headed toward his work room. There was no sign of life in the corridor, but it was early yet, just a minute or two after opening. He snapped on the lights, got his wooden box down and over to the desk, pulled out the manuscript, then started pondering. . . . OK, he thought, let's say he *did* go ahead and try the thing again. What should he ask for *this* time? Not another hot dog, of course; no, nothing so frivolous as that—even if the mere question, the very concept itself, was—well—flawed in the extreme. But, nonetheless, whatever request he might formulate this evening should be something definitive, something unequivocal, something that could yield no alternate interpretation whatever. . . . Not that he believed for a minute that. . . . No, of course not, but still. . . .

He went through a list of options in his head—delicacies, gemstones, artifacts—then came to one specific item that seemed pre-eminently suitable: that little blue stamp. Yes, that would do just fine! Ideally, in fact! And Fabbri would be delighted to no end, if . . . well, if it worked, of course . . . ! He laughed to himself and shook his head—if, by some unfathomable happenstance, the damned thing really did work!

All right, then; Robert looked at his watch, calculating: just twelve hours from now and he'd know. He set to work on the insipid manuscript, starting with the place he'd left off Friday—up to page thirty-seven now—then kept hard at it, putting the inconceivable thoughts aside, finishing four more nonsensical pages by lunchtime. Caterina stepped through the door at twelve-fifteen.

"Well, dottore, *buon giorno*! Did you try your little experiment last night?" she asked, smiling sarcastically.

"Yes, Caterina, as a matter of fact I did. . . . And I owe you a word of thanks for getting all those things together for me, the shell and soil and. . . ."

"Yes, of course. The holy water too. I'm thankful that no one saw me take it from the basin. . . . In any case, you are most welcome. . . . But you must tell me: did anything occur? Have you discovered anything amazing? Did you manage to communicate with the dead?"

"No," laughed Robert, "nothing quite that dramatic! Actually I'm not absolutely a hundred percent sure what *did* happen, Caterina. Maybe nothing so remarkable after all. . . . I think maybe I had a little too much wine to drink yesterday."

"Well, yes, dottore, I believe you did, as a matter of fact. Signor Fabbri too seems just a bit beneath the weather today. . . . But . . . well, tell me: did your experiment at least reveal who will win the *palio* in July? That would be of great benefit to me to find out—in exchange for all of my efforts on your behalf, you know?" She chuckled a little, openly, having some obvious fun at his expense.

"No, Caterina, I'm sorry. The *palio*'s still up in the air. . . . All I got from your benevolent labor was a couple of hot dogs, but they tasted pretty good after all that veal and pasta I've been eating these past few weeks."

"*Hot dogs*, dottore?" Caterina's eyes narrowed into frank suspicion; her smile vanished.

"Yes, exactly. It's quite an involved story. . . . But anyway, I had two nice Chicago-style hot dogs delivered fresh and warm to my room a little after midnight. But . . . look, never mind. . . . Maybe I'll give the diagram another try in a day or two and find out about your *palio* for you if I can. I'll be sure and let you know."

Caterina smiled again. "Yes, do that, please. . . . Oh, by the way, may . . . uh, might I pick up something for lunch for you? I don't think I can find any more hot dogs anywhere around here, though."

"No. That's perfectly all right. I'm going to take a break soon, so I'll stop and get something myself. I've got a little errand to run anyway. . . . But. . . . Look, I'll see what I can find out on that *palio* thing for you, OK?"

She nodded, said good-bye, and left; and he took off his cotton gloves, closed up the legal pad, and headed out the Piccolomini's front doorway a few minutes afterward. It was lunchtime now and he was getting annoyingly impatient, and a little hungry too. Besides, he had things to do, things to get ready for this evening's ceremony. He'd take a little break from the dreadful manuscript; stop off where he had to; make his purchases; grab a sandwich in the Campo; finish up at the Piccolomini by closing time; have a leisurely dinner in one of the *trattorie* downtown; and be back to his room with enough time remaining before sunset to set up the chart properly.

No more vague coincidences. No, this evening he was going to get out his crazy diagram, fire the damn thing up, then run it pedal down, flat out flaming, and see if it would fly.

The Filatelia Crespi was calm and quiet, a refuge from the mid-day turmoil of the street. There was a single customer at the counter of the little place, a fiftyish man in a frayed blue suit, leafing through some sales books full of stamps. Robert watched as he selected an item here and there for his collection. He had a check-list beside him, to his right on the cluttered counter top, which he referred to constantly, ticking off various entries as he took the little shards of paper from a loose-leaf binder open beneath his chin. Signor Crespi, a short, plump man with a full mustache, stood over the man magisterially, nodding, pointing, recording prices, making the odd comment. Neither showed the least awareness of Robert's presence. Both, rather, seemed entirely engrossed in the task at hand, scrutinizing the tiny specimens, assigning to several of them an appreciative new home.

It was like adoption from an orphanage: deliberate, intense, and bittersweet. Three minutes passed or four of the two men's rapt absorption; then at last Signor Crespi deigned to look up. There was a clear sign of recognition in his face: that watermark fluid Robert had purchased two weeks before. Aha! said the proprietor's gaze; a cash customer. He arched his back, raised his chin, narrowed his eyes, and, at long last, spoke.

"*Si, signore? Posso aiutarLa?*"

"*Si. Grazie. Vorrei. . . . Uh . . . mi bisogna. . . .*" He needed a bottle of watermark fluid, Robert explained; another one. Well, repeat orders weren't entirely unwelcome, it seemed. Signor Crespi nodded, turned about in military fashion, and fetched the appropriate bottle from a shelf.

"*Vuole qualche altra cosa, signore?*"

Uh, why yes, as a matter of fact; there *was* something else: Did . . . did the signore happen to have a copy of that parcel post stamp? The . . . uh . . . the rare one?

"*Raro?*"

Si, si, the *pacchi postale* with the watermark of a winged wheel, *filigrana ruota alata*, the—what had Fabbri called it?—the *mille lire pacchi postale*?

"*Il pacchi postale di mille lire? Con ruota alata?*" Signor Crespi shook his head gravely. "*Ah, no, sfortunatamente. Cose come questo. . . .*" such things as the *mille lire*, he apologized, came to market only at auction these days. And even then . . . even *then* ...not very often. "*E molto raro, e. . . .*" —and for a little shop like this in a backwater town like Siena, well. . . .

"*Ebbene. . . .*" Well, then, how about the cheap one? The, uh... the one with the more ordinary watermark? What was it again? Little five-point stars? "*Filigrana stelle?*"

"*Ma Certamente!*" said Crespi, smiling at last. That one, naturally, was always in stock. He reached around again, fetched a thick, ringed binder from a middle shelf, set it on the counter, opened it to a stock-page near its end, and tweezered from one of the slotted spaces a small blue strip of paper perforated vertically through its middle. "*Pacchi postale di mille lire, filigrana stelle,*" he announced officially. "*Eccolo.*"

Might he have two of them? Robert asked.

"*Due, signore?*"

"*Si, si, due. Per favore.*"

Crespi shrugged, raised his eyebrows, and plucked another stamp from his book. "*Eccoli, signore: due. Va bene? Desidera qualce altra cosa?*"

"*No. Solo questi, grazie.*"

"*Prego, signore. Beh, quello ammonta a. . . .*" He fingered his calculator for a moment. "*Ah, bene—novemilaottocentocinquanta lire.*"

Five dollars and change, fluid included. Robert nodded and handed him the cash. "*Grazie, signore. Ma. . . .*" But, he asked Signor Crespi sheepishly: *Scusi*, but . . . was the signore absolutely certain that the *filigrana* was correct? "*Filigrana stelle, no?*"

"Hmmph!" sneered the customer at the counter over his shoulder. "Hah!" ejaculated Crespi.

"*Ma signore, ha paura di comprare...?*" Was the purchaser afraid of being sold two stamps valued at three million lire each for a buck apiece? Was the *filigrana* correct!! Indeed!... Don't worry, Crespi reassured him: "*Non si preoocupi!*" Yes, of course; they were *filigrana stelle*. Naturally they were! What else on earth could they be?

Robert smiled apologetically at the two philatelists. OK, sure; he understood. He shook Crespi's hand, nodded to the other customer, took the little paper sack from the stamp-strewn counter, and headed out the door.

"*Pazzi americani!*," said a muffled voice inside as the door closed behind him—crazy Americans!

"*No,*" came the marginally louder answer, "*Non sempre sono pazzi, ma hanno troppi soldi.*" Not always crazy, but they're too damned rich!

There was a knock on the door, very faint. Filomena probably— again! He blew out the match. . . . Yes, the candle was going, flickering with a thin, transparent flame. It looked secure enough propped up where it stood; therefore quite safe to leave unattended for a moment alight the way it was.

"Just a minute," he called out toward the door jamb. . . . "Filomena?"

"*Si*, Roberto. May I come in?"

Great! What an awful time she'd picked! Maybe another hot dog, he considered. But the girl undoubtedly meant well. And he'd made that solemn resolution to be nice to her. He got up and went the door, opening it just a matter of inches inward.

"Look, Filomena . . . uh, I'm a little busy right now. Can you come back later?"

"Later? Yes, of course. What time would be best for you?"

"Uh, let's see. Give me . . . give me an hour. Say ten o'clock or a little after, OK?"

"Yes, OK. Ten will be fine. Are you hungry?"

"No, no. Look, I'll take you out later for some coffee and dessert,

OK? But first I've got something I have to do just now. Just give me an hour, all right?"

"Yes, certainly." She tilted her head and looked past him into the room. "Is that the...? Oh, Roberto, you have lit your candle! I can smell it. But . . . but . . . is it on the bed? That will not be safe, Roberto. Will it? You should. . . ."

"No, no, it's perfectly all right. It's on the chair there. I'm watching it. It's just for a kind of experiment anyway, you know? I'll put it out in a couple of minutes. . . . Look, uh, Filomena . . . I'll see you in an hour, OK? . . . Ten, on the dot, all right?"

He closed the door, locked it this time, and went back to his diagram. Outside the open window, it was pitch dark now, a full hour after sunset: just about time.

"*Magister,*" he began, rolling the egg yolk back into the depression he had poked into the page . . . *ad nominem tuum devovemus.* . . ." He ran through the remainder of the verbiage methodically, just as he had done the day before. Then, coming to the blank space at the long paragraph's end, he read out a string of words from the small slip of paper in his hand. An hour earlier, he had put them into passable Latin—just to be sure: *Mutandum essere.* . . . May the stars etched in the substance of the blue bit of paper be changed into an appropriately-sized winged wheel—*ad rotam alatam in magnitudine aequo.*"

It was an amazingly simple request: that a tiny cluster of five-point stars, visible only when immersed in the proper fluid, be transformed into something minutely different: a crude flattened circle with a scruffy little wing. That was the particular "wished-for thing" tonight. A small thing, too, almost inconsequential. A matter, really, of some all-but-invisible images rearranging themselves. It was an alteration not one person in a thousand might detect if it *did* transpire. So subtle indeed. . . . Yet how momentous!

For if such a thing could be brought about in so miraculous a manner. . . . Why, then, the whole world—the very universe itself and all within it—would be transformed forever. Every aspect and recess of reality would mutate wholesale with those little stars. For there were no such things to be found in the *Cambridge Modern History*; nor in a thousand books on physics; nor taught in any classroom by Robert's clever colleagues at the university. No such anomalies *anywhere*, documented and proven to the world's satisfaction. Legends, yes; myths, indeed. Tales, perhaps—unverified. But actual observations of documented fact: of magical transformations, spontaneous metamorphoses, combinations of words perturbing matter? No, there were none such recorded, by any verifiably accurate observer, ever, anywhere.

He took a deep breath, hearing the heartbeat in his ears, feeling his palms moisten, his fingertips grow cold. . . . Not that he accepted the *premise* of it: No, not one bit! Those hot dogs had been a strange coincidence, nothing more than that. Scientists did experiments more often than not to see them fail, to demonstrate the absurdity of the errant theories they were based upon. Well, *this* experiment was bound to fail utterly; for its theoretical basis was nil. Robert shook his head in disbelief, laughed to himself at his own credulity, then blew out the air from the hollow of his lungs, straight across the diagram—whoosh!—extinguishing the candle. . . .

Nothing happened. He felt no different; nor did the room; nor the temperate breeze from the window. Almost ashamedly now, he put everything away, like a teen-age boy with some smutty magazine. The papers went back in the desk's center drawer, the shell and soil and candles in the dresser. On the desktop beside his computer sat the little bag from the Filatelia Crespi with its bottle of watermark fluid and those two blue stamps inside. How long might such a transformation take? Assuming it would work, of course. . . . *Assuming*! My God! How far he'd come in this past extraordinary day! But, still, there *was* a possibility. After all, those hot dogs, when he had specifically asked for them; and just a little later too. . . .

Very strange. Yes, well, it would be much better—yes, much, much better—if nothing whatever transpired this time. Then those two delicious hot dogs would be the coincidence they *had* to be, and the whole experience would stay a mere misunderstanding. The world as he had known it all his life would remain just the same, just as empirically comprehensible. There would be no negation of every belief, no questioning of every concept, a rational man would find ample and sufficient as a basis for his life.

Robert nodded to himself in tacit agreement. Yes. Certainly. Better if those little stars were right there where they belonged. He stood up, went to the desk, took his black pan from the bottom drawer, set it on the desktop, dropped the two stamps into it face down, and dribbled onto their tiny gummed surfaces several droplets of fluid.

A distinct cluster of stars appeared on each. So! Good! Nothing! Nothing at all! Whew! That was a relief. Truly . . . though there was, mixed with it, he felt himself admit, the tiniest feeling of regret.

For what if such things *could* come to be: transformations, miracles, possibilities yet unimagined—what a magical place this world would be to live in! Incomprehensible, true; illogical, manifestly—but full of exorbitant wonder! Mankind had dreamed thus since the beginning of its history, maybe since the beginning of intelligent thought itself, inventing ornate systems of belief to glorify the mysteries of what men had hoped and prayed and dreamed might come true, but had never really turned out to be . . . at least from all available evidence and observation. Like Auntwon and his aliens! Well, even he himself—even the renowned Robert Martin, professor and acclaimed historian—had now succumbed to the very charm of it. And all because of a hot dog! He'd think less fatuously the next time!

Filomena knocked again at 10:05. They went out for some wine and pastries, sitting at the very table in the Campo he'd sat at the night before, drinking his *cappucino*. There was a bit of wind stirring this late evening, wafting the dust from the Campo's pavement, swirling it around in a little dance that caught the light thrown from some footlights upward onto the ancient buildings—a spectral image commensurate with his thoughts.

This lovely square had seen so much of everything: glory, wealth, plague, famine; French soldiers and Flemings; Germans with their Augsburg armor; Spaniards up from Naples; Medicean rulers and Napoleonic deputies; then Piedmontese kings and Mussolini; and finally contemporary peace under a Republic of men as wise and benevolent and foolish and corrupt as all the rest of them had been through twenty centuries and more.

"It's a wonderful place, your Siena," Robert told the girl. He felt comfortable, at ease. The world was still stable, familiar. Those two hot dogs had been nothing but a strange coincidence. Filomena had asked him the other day—"What's your favorite dish?"—and he had told her: hot dogs, Chicago style, with pickles and mustard and relish. A clear description, too; detailed. He'd made a point of saying how he'd always missed such things while traveling. Yes, and that was only Friday last. It would still be vivid in both of their minds. So what if the subject had surfaced again last night? All right, maybe at the very same moment for each of them, but what of that? What was so peculiar in her cooking him something special she knew he would like? What was so bizarre about that?

He must have been staring at the girl a little too strangely or a little too long, for she looked back at him in a quizzical way, knotting her brows askew, so that one slanted slightly above the level of the other. The wind had caught her hair, blowing it sideways off her forehead. The shifting, dust-strewn light reflected from the ancient buildings' facades gave Filomena's face the aspect of a magical sprite in some medieval fantasy play.

"*My* Siena!" she said. "Why do you call it mine?"

"Oh, it *is* yours. You're a native Sienese, aren't you? Well, Sienese citizens own the town as much as anyone can."

"Maybe. Well, I suppose it is a pleasant place to be, though I have had little with which to compare it."

"'Little to compare it to,' we say in America. You'll have to learn our American way of speaking if you want to teach English. English means American English practically everywhere these days."

"Yes, I know. I can talk both ways, but the *English* English seems more proper to my ear. But I'll try to talk like 'youse Chicago folks' if you prefer, Roberto. Whatever you like. . . ."

"I asked your mother about the hot dogs this morning."

"Yes, she told me that you spoke with her."

"There's a—this is a little hard to explain—there's. . . . I have a kind of crazy diagram I found while I was doing my research. A sort of magic diagram, you know? It was in Colangio's papers, of all places."

"A magic thing? But you don't *believe* in such concepts, do you? In magic?"

"No, of course not, but. . . . A funny thing happened last night. I . . .

well, for some reason, I tried to use the thing, and it specifies that some- thing be asked for. "The wished-for thing," it says. Well, I didn't know what sort of thing that meant, so I kind of asked . . . uh . . . for a hot dog."

"A *hot dog*! That is the thing you would most want in the whole wide world? A hot dog?"

He laughed. "Well, no. I mean . . . I didn't have any idea that some- thing like that might actually work, so I just sort of named *some*thing, sort of at random, you know? And a hot dog came out."

"And when I brought the hot dogs upstairs to you, you thought it was a magic act of some kind! How cute you can be sometimes, Roberto! And how charming!"

"So you did have it planned before? Before I did my . . . uh . . . lit- tle ceremony?"

"Last night?"

"Yes, last night. An hour after sunset, it says. . . . About nine o'clock, I think."

"Well of *course* I planned it before that! What did you think? Three days ago I planned to do it, when you told me about your favorite food, remember? That is why we went to Firenze yesterday."

"OK, good. I really thought I was going crazy there for a while! I feel a lot better now."

"You feel better from the wine, Roberto, and I do too. . . . But, the magic thing—is that what you were doing earlier with the candle?"

"Yes."

"And what happened? What did you wish for this time?"

"Oh, this was just an experiment, trying to change one kind of pat- tern into another. And it wasn't for my sake, anyway, but for a friend."

"Well? And did it work?"

"No."

"You tested it to see?"

"Yes. Nothing happened."

"Well, that *is* better. It is better for people not to have control over such things. Normal people, I mean, like you and me."

"Yes, I thought about that too, and I agree with you completely, but . . . you talk as if you believe in such things yourself; magic diagrams, I mean, and . . . well, you know. . . ."

"Yes, of course I do. I *do* believe that such things can occur. . . . But only when they are done with the aid of God. Or very holy men—like your San Francesco, for example. Saints like him were able to work miracles; I am convinced of that."

"Well, I won't debate you about it. I've always been a skeptic, though, as I told you. I believe only what I can see or hear or what reason assures me is true. Nothing more."

"Yet you were experimenting with the magic thing again tonight, no?"

Robert nodded reluctantly and shrugged.

"All right, Roberto, tell me: what would you have wished for next? Tomorrow, I mean, or the next day, if your magic thing had worked this time. What would you most want to have in your life?"

"What would I want?" He shrugged. "Oh, nothing really. I might have said I'd like my life back the way it was a year ago, or two years. It would be wonderful to be back there, then, and have time frozen at that point, forever. But I wouldn't really want it if it got done by some artifice, you know? The real beauty of it was the . . . I don't know, I guess the spontaneity of it, the naturalness, the feeling that everything was right and perfect. . . . I guess it's hard really to explain."

"You were so very happy then?"

"Yes. Yes, I was happy. So happy I can't even tell you. It was the best my life has ever been. The best I ever thought my life could be."

"And . . . what was she like, this woman who made you so happy?"

"How did you know...?"

"Ah, I can tell it. I can see it in your face. So tell me, what kind of person was she?"

"Look, I don't want to talk about it. I'm sorry, it's just. . . . I can't now, you know?"

"Yes, I understand. Please forgive me for bringing it up. I . . . I just knew that there was something. . . ."

"Something?"

"Yes, something in your mind. Below the surface, I mean. You have been very kind to me, very considerate, but I know that there is something missing in our friendship. I thought that it was something like this."

"Listen, Filomena, I like you very much, but. . . ."

"No, no. You need not explain. I understand the situation very well. I have one question, though: you have been very kind to me. Unusually so. Tell me, why is that the case?"

"Why? I think you're a wonderful girl, smart, interesting, good-hearted. . . ."

"And there is nothing else? Is it at all because of what Caterina told you about my family? About my life?"

"Well, maybe in part, but that. . . ."

"No, Roberto. If you heard about it and then became more sympathetic. . . . Look, I don't want your pity. Any more than you would want that artificial happiness you alluded to; can you understand? Pity is a thing I could not take from you. . . . But . . . I suppose Caterina has told you everything about my father? The reason for his suicide?"

"Yes."

"Well, you know, that was a long time ago. Ten years already. You need not feel sorry for me now. Then, yes, perhaps; but not now. Now, if anything, it has made me better, stronger. He . . . he was a wonderful man, my father, a brilliant man, kind, and handsome. We were very close. . . ."

"Filomena. . . ."

"No, allow me please to finish. I wish to explain it all to you right now. . . . When he died, when I saw him there like that, hanging from that rope the way he was when I came into the room, I was shocked at first—anyone would be shocked, of course—but then, after some days, I started to look at everything in a different way—a different 'light', as you Americans say. I thought: here was a great man who had every reason to live, throwing away his life like the poorest beggar. He lacked the courage to confront his problems—to face the world—and fix everything so that it was right again. You understand?"

Robert nodded again.

"Well, I decided right then and there that I would never be so weak or so foolish. If there is something that I want or something that I want to be different, I just go ahead and get it or make it different. You will never find me despondent like that. If I cannot understand a certain book like Spencer or Chaucer, for example, I just keep working at it until I do. If I lose one friend, I go out and find another. . . . No,

Roberto, you need never feel sorry for me. My life is good now because I have *made* it good. If yours is not as happy as it used to be, if you cannot have what you had before, perhaps you ought to reconsider whether that is really what you want right now."

"All right, Filomena. Look, we're friends now, whatever the reason. You're like a little sister to me. I wouldn't hurt you for the world. So . . . anyway . . . if having a kind of big brother in residence is the kind of thing that you can live with, whatever I've done that might have hurt your feelings, don't give up on our friendship. I really *do* care for you."

"Good, then, Roberto. Having a big brother like you would be very nice, and, remember what I said before: I never give up on *anything*."

It was after eleven when he got back to his room. He read for a while, but couldn't really concentrate. So much had happened in the last twenty-four hours. Yes, he thought, just a day, but what a day!

He got up and went to the computer, clicking it on and logging onto the internet. There was a message from Auntwon, of course. "Doc," it said, "what the hell's goin on?" Well, he had left the kid hanging, after all. What had he told him? "Something happened; I'll let you know." That was this morning, with the tallow of the hot dogs still flowing in his veins.

He typed in a reply: something brief, concise: "False alarm. Garbage—as I said before. Regards to Annamae."

The place was quiet, Signora Dall'Olmo likely in bed, Filomena reading or half-asleep herself. He wasn't really tired yet. It was strange: he'd almost hoped the crazy thing would work. Sure, it would have distorted his world view—or rather shown that his view of the world had *always* been distorted, but was now confronted with a new, less comprehensible, actuality. Inconvenient, yes, but not without its charm. He went into the bathroom and brushed his teeth, then came back out and sat down at the desk. It was twelve-thirty now. He ought to try and get some sleep.

He started up, then sat down again, reflexly. Yes, inconvenient, but not without its charm. Those tiny little stars: what if they *had* changed? How would he have reacted? He scarcely could imagine. And suddenly he felt the compulsion to look at them again, those little persistent stars that anchored him to reality, to the world as he had always known it, to the world as it *must* be, would *always* be. Constant stars, they were, fixed and immutable as the firmament above, incompatible with change.

He opened the packet and dropped the two little shards of gummed paper, blue on their obverse sides, into the big, black pan, then dribbled a bit of fluid on their shiny back surfaces, one drop at a time, mindful of the vapors. Tiny stars materialized on one, clustered, five-point figures, unmistakable. But on the other suddenly appeared . . . an oblong wheel, distinctly seen, with a funny little cupid's wing at its top.

It was twelve-forty-five that Tuesday early morning, and Robert Martin's world would never again feel remotely the same.

CHAPTER SEVENTEEN

EXTRACTION

"Dottor Bob! I look for you thees morning."

"What, Taddeo? Oh, I slept in. Well, not really slept—I didn't really sleep very well—but, anyway, I just got here—just now, I mean. . . . Here." He lifted the little paper bag to waist level. "I've got something for you."

"Ah, Dottor Bob, I am sorry for the other day. . . ."

"The other day? Oh, your birthday—*compleanno.* . . . Never mind; it doesn't matter. Look. . . . Uh, here. I got you this." Robert set the bag on Fabbri's desk and slid it over toward him, but the *Archivista* seemed to take no notice.

"Yes. . . ." Fabbri looked a little shamefaced. "...*Si,* but . . . but Silvio from downstairs tell me that you must take me up the stairs, you and Caterina. I cannot remember, but. . . ."

"Yeah, uh. . . . Look, never mind. *Non importa.* . . . I got something for you. In the bag there." Robert pointed to the desktop where the little paper sack reposed, entirely ignored. "Go ahead and open it."

Finally Fabbri did, taking out, first, the nearly full plastic bottle of watermark fluid, and then, from the very bottom of the bag, the translucent packet with its little blue stamps inside.

"What. . . . Ah, *pacchi postali. Grazie,* Dottor Bob. I have already these. I show you. . . . But I can use for—*eh, come si dice 'duplicati'? Ma grazie.* It is verr' nice from you, verr' nice."

"You got the *mille lire* one, then? The rare one?"

"*Beh,* no, of course, no the rare one; but thees one, with *filigrana stelle,* weeth the stars, like I show you. Thees I have already. No the espensive one, you know. But thees, *si*, the ordinary one, yes, I have, of course."

"Well, don't you have to check the watermark to know if it's ordinary? I mean, how do you know they aren't the rare ones? With the little wheel, I mean."

Fabbri laughed. "No, Dottor Bob, I have check so many ones before thees. Everybody check. All the rare ones... eh, eh . . . somebody already discover long time before."

"Well, go ahead and check these. Can you?"

"*Si*, later, if you like. When I weel be at home."

"No, now. Please. Can't you just check them now?"

"Now? But. . . ." The *Archivista* looked up at him for a moment with his head tilted, lips pursed, then finally nodded, first side to side, then vertically, his expression and demeanor the very manifestation of skepticism overcome by affability. "OK, sure." He nodded more vigorously, then shrugged and smiled. "Sure, I do it, if you like. First I must find a tray. . . . A *portacenere*, maybe—*come si dice*?"

"An ashtray?"

"*Si*, 'ashtray'. I shall remember. That can maybe do OK. A black one, maybe, if I can find. . . . OK. Wait, I weel check."

Fabbri got up, stepped around his desk, and went out of the room, then returned a few minutes later with a dark blue ashtray in his hand. He sat back down behind his desk, took the two stamps from the packet, dropped them printed side down into the tray, and drizzled a bit of watermark fluid onto their gummed surfaces. Robert kept his eyes fixed on the *Archivista*'s face. Within a second or two of applying the fluid, Fabbri's expression turned from one of self-satisfied bemusement to what is generally considered the archetypal picture of shock. For a full minute or maybe a minute and a half afterward, he didn't speak, but rather stared fixedly into the blue ceramic tray, shifting it a little sideways, tilting it over toward the light. Then suddenly he cupped his hands around the rim, protectively, looked up at Robert, eyes wide, mouth agape, and all but shouted in an agitated voice:

"*Ma . . . ma . . . non e possibile*! *A trovato . . . ma dove? Dove. . . .? Ma quanto costa? E impossibile*! *Ma dove*, Dottor Bob? Where have you find thees? How much it costed!?"

"Look, I just *found* it, OK? I bought two stamps, and one of them turned out to be the rare one, I guess. It looks like it, anyway. It has the little wheel, doesn't it? I was pretty sure it did."

"*Impossibile*! *E impossibile*! You cannot find! You cannot!"

"Well I did. But, whatever, it's all yours. . . . If you want it, that is; I'd like you to have it, if you like."

"If I *like*! Of *course* I like, but . . . but I cannot take. . . . OK, OK, maybe I can pay you for it. I pay over some months, OK? Two or three months, OK?"

"No, no. Look, it didn't cost me anything, you understand? I don't want anything for it. I got it to give to you, that's all. Put it in your book and enjoy it. I owe you that much anyway for helping me out with the manuscript. You know, if you hadn't smuggled out that page for me. . . ."

"Ah, dottore, this was notheen. But such a theen so valuable. . . . I cannot take. I know what you must pay for . . . for. . . ."

"No, look, don't worry, Taddeo. Have fun with your stamp—if that's what you do with them. Just enjoy it and don't worry about the cost or anything else. It isn't stolen, after all. I can assure you of that."

Fabbri got up and walked around the desk to where Robert was standing. He put out his hand, took Robert's smaller hand in his larger one, leaned down, and grasped Robert's right arm with his big left hand in the very same manner Auntwon had done it eight weeks before. Auntwon's hands were smaller, true, and the boy had reached up, not down, for his height was so much less than Fabbri's. But the gesture was just the same. Identical. How odd, thought Robert; how peculiarly unreal this whole thing felt. Yet, at the same time, how familiar! It was incredible how far he had come since that awful morning of Cassie's departure and that set of keys thrust strangely into his hand. Then, not ten minutes afterward, had come the unexpected dialogue with Auntwon, and the gentle hand upon his arm, just as it was now with Taddeo Fabbri. It had seemed a lifetime, just those two interminable months that had passed since then. How very strange! How inexplicable the whole universe had grown, the very concept of reality!

He glanced up at Fabbri, and Fabbri looked down, his eyes moist, the pressure of his two hands as familiar and unremitting as a mother's embrace:

"Ah, Dottor Bob, thees is the most nicest theen anyone have ever done for me. . . . I . . . I. . . . *Non so le parole.* . . ."

"*Mi ha fatto piacere di farlo*, Taddeo." He'd been happy to do it. "Look, I'm going to be away for a few days, uh . . . out of town, you know? I just wanted to make sure you got this first. . . ."

"Out of town? But where?"

"Oh, different places. I've got some research to do. I've rented a car. . . . Look, I'll be back in a week or so. . . . I'll see you then."

"*Ma* . . . but . . . where do you go?"

"Well, first of all to Florence, to the library at the university. Then probably Arezzo. When Colangio died, he left everything he owned in the world to a monastery there. I need to find out why."

He stopped once along the way, at an autostrada restaurant, filling his belly with some pasta and chicken, for he had quite forgotten to eat these past sixteen hours. Eight minutes, ten, it took to throw the supper down and buy a map of Tuscany, then into the rented Ford once more and back out on the road. He couldn't rest, couldn't halt his movement long, for inactivity meant thought, and thought was the one particular torment of his life just now. Constant thought, agonizing thought, gnawing at him throughout last night and then this morning too like some noisome toothache. It was all confusion; the world, the universe was. And the more he considered it, the more intractably confusing the world and universe became.

He wasn't crazy; no, Fabbri had seen that little winged wheel of a watermark too. It had changed itself, or been changed in some unfathomable way. Robert had seen the transformation with his own two eyes: a spontaneous alteration of matter from one thing to a wholly different other. He had seen it. *Seen* it! He hadn't been sleeping, dreaming—or if he had, the dream itself had turned preternaturally detailed and consistent. So? What else did that leave? Truth? Reality? But what kind of truth, what kind of reality would that constitute? A thing deranged and unfamiliar, unlike any sort of world-view he had accepted as valid throughout his life.

Better not to think of that just now. Such thoughts led circularly nowhere, like some optical illusion that had quashed all sense of space and time, a helix winding simultaneously up and down, a pattern now projecting, now recessed. The more one gazed at such conundrums, the less defined they grew. Like vague, unanswerable questions—the meaning of life, the origin of matter, the nature of existence—crass imponderables whose mere consideration bred perplexity. Whatever was the point? Might one presume to fathom the unfathomable?

No, all of it was better left unthought about for now. Yet there were aspects of this business that one might find amenable to thought. The riddle of Colangio's life, for instance, a mystery that was suddenly rendered clear, like some jigsaw puzzle with its missing pieces slipping into place. That queer incantation and its wondrous power—never mind how or why—at once illuminated everything: Colangio's sudden fortune, his enormous palace, the twenty years of perfect silence—the silence in particular, for, after all, what would be the benefit in laboring over tiresome, esoteric research when one's whole frame of reference, one's whole world view lies deracinate, root and branch? All of Adalberto's studying, writing, analyzing—popes, kings, philosophers, scientists—what would be their significance in an incomprehensible universe? Besides, Colangio, the quondam scholar, would now possess the treasure of the ages: every need fulfilled at will, any wished-for item practically synthesized to suit each passing fancy.

Like the marriage. It too now fit the picture as snugly as a custom frame, making perfect sense. Here was Ginevra, a woman Adalberto had coveted, loved passionately in his youth, then lost—first, to some scion of the landed nobility, then, finally, to the all-consuming church. Suddenly, miraculously, with the mere recitation of a chant, the mere snuffing of a candle, he could win her at last, forever, without impediment, without delay. The woman of his fondest dreams delivered gratis, willing, on a platinum platter. . . .

Then had come the palace, the luxuries, the wealth. Yes indeed, all the pieces of the puzzle suddenly fit, thought Robert, as he followed the stream of traffic northbound toward Florence: Colangio had come upon the incantation and the diagram, discovered them back in 1503, in the midst of some recondite research—for old Cardinal Antonelli, no doubt. Why, Robert himself had done the very same thing, right down to trying the fool thing out. Just like Colangio, probably—just as skeptically, just as tentatively. That was it! Right there you had your whole explanation for everything, plain as day!... Well, but for the underlying premise, of course, which was best not considered in detail just yet. That would take a bit of time for ferment and digestion. But anyway, the great enigma of Colangio's life had been convincingly explained, his opaque years rendered limpid. What an amazing new book the whole affair would generate!... If any reader—if, indeed, the very author himself!—could be brought to accept the fantastic phenomenon that lay at its core.

There was some traffic and construction starting north of Poggibonsi, so it was nearly three p.m. by the time he made it to the university library in Florence. The building was open until nine, giving him six full hours to work; and he spent the whole of them at a little desk, researching, making copies. Not a great deal there of use, but the little that he found was helpful: a few ancient texts, some obscure church transcripts.

His key words were 'Franciscan' and 'mysticism'. Everything seemed to center on the Bogomils or Cathari, a group of thirteenth century schismatics who had believed in a kind of dualism: good versus evil, God versus the Devil. Mystics, practitioners of the occult, necromancers, they had been condemned, suppressed, and finally eradicated, but not before a number of their brethren had joined with the Franciscan movement. Those Cathar friars, too, had been weeded out over time, but had not grown extinct until two full centuries had passed. Culled by attrition, they survived in ever-diminishing numbers until the 1400s. The last of their recorded kind, one Fra Simeon Melanitzes, had been indicted by the Inquisition in 1447. His trial and condemnation took place in the religious house where he had lived, worked, and studied. Which was no other than the Franciscan monastery in Arezzo, the very place Colangio had specified as his sole beneficiary: the recipient of his whole estate, every picture, every florin, every chest and book and paper he had accumulated through a lifetime of scholarly work and magical acquisition. If it was just a pure coincidence, it was a purely extraordinary one.

So Robert's guess had been correct: Arezzo was his requisite next stop. He collected his notes and photocopies at the library's closing time, ate a tasteless plate of pasta along the highway, slept restlessly at a roadside motel, climbed back into the car at daybreak, and made it to Arezzo by ten.

The monastery lay six miles from the town on a two-lane road that led back toward Siena. It was decidedly not a tourist stop. Though ancient and indubitably historic, no artistic treasures adorned its exterior walls. Nor was the edifice itself distinguished in the slightest way— old crudely-baked brick, unstuccoed, fashioned into a large, plain basilica-type church with residential wings and a cloister off to one side. The whole complex looked untended, decrepit, with sickly-looking ivy winding up the basilica's wall and a dull chartreuse moss inked into the mortar of the adjunct wing. Robert parked in front, found the main entry to the church itself bolted and chained, so walked around the monastery's wing to a side door. Finding that unlocked and untended, he raised a latch, swung the door in, and entered.

He stepped into the middle of a long, dark corridor, leading both to right and left, but the light from the right was a little more intense, so he turned that way. There was a sort of business office through the first door on the left-hand side, but it was vacant. He passed it and walked on down the corridor, hearing voices, finally, as he approached its end. Following the sounds, he came at last to a larger room on the right. This was an eating area, from the look of its painted wooden tables and bargain-basement chairs arrayed about them. Barracks-style, spartan, it looked like the messroom of a Salvation Army kitchen awaiting indigent clientele. Halfway across the room, seated at a table with coffee mugs before them on the long, bare surface, sat three brown-clad Franciscans, tonsured, clean-shaven young men who spoke indecipherable Italian in their low, commingled voices. In a second or two, one of the men, seated facing the entrance, stopped and looked up; then the others turned around, silent but for the rasping of their chairs' legs on the floor tiles, and stared inquiringly in Robert's direction.

"*Mi scusi, signori, ho bisogno delle informazioni.*" He needed some information, he explained.

"*Prego*," said the man facing the door—the one who had seen him first—and beckoned him over with a kind of self-directed, sidewise wave. All three men, now facing outward, smiled and nodded in a most obliging way. "*In quale maniera. . . .*" How could they be of assistance? the first man asked.

"*Sto scrivendo. . . .*" He was researching a book, he explained, telling them, too, about the University of Chicago, a name that often opened up some tightly locked doors. Yes, yes, they said, practically in unison: "*Si, si, eccola!*" Well then, he must meet with Fra Tomacelli. . . . Yes, Tomacelli was the perfect man to talk to.

One of the men, who had originally been seated with his back to the entry, but who had by now turned his plastic chair a full semicircle around, got up and headed out the door. "*Lo faccio venire*," he said: he'd go and fetch him.

It took just a minute or two. This fourth friar, Tomacelli, was short and slender, ascetic-looking, with a dark complexion and hollow cheeks. He entered the room with a thin-lipped smile.

"I understand you're from Chicago," said the friar in completely unaccented American English.

"Yeah. . . . Uh, yes! I wasn't expecting to hear English spoken here. . . . Um, Chicago, right. I'm with the University now; but I was born there too—in Evanston." Robert put out his hand and Tomacelli took it solemnly with three cool fingers

"Yes. I as well. From Highland Park. My family lives there," he said.

"Well, what in the world brings you here?" asked Robert. "I mean, to Arezzo, for God's sake. . . . Oh, sorry, I didn't mean. . . ."

"No, no, that's perfectly all right. We're actually quite a liberal lot nowadays. . . . So, anyway, my fellow Chicagoan . . . welcome to our modest abode. How may I assist you?"

"Well, actually, I'm doing some research. . . ." Robert explained enough to get admitted to the place: his name, position, interest in the Renaissance, sabbatical duties. . . . Did they have a library? Some old volumes that might have been around for a few hundred years? Things that Rome or Florence or the Germans hadn't pirated away for what was euphemistically called safekeeping over these last enlightened cen-

turies? Might one at least see the room an early sixteenth century schol-
·ar would have worked in if he'd come to do a little research here?

"You mean someone like Colangio?" Tomacelli asked.

Robert's eyebrows arched, though he strove manfully to keep their
elevation contained. "Why, yes, how in the world did you guess that?"

"You said 'Martin', right? Robert Martin? I read your book."

"You did!"

"Sure. Every person here has read it—in translation, anyway.
Colangio is something of a local hero to us. I mean, with all the prop-
erty he left to the monastery—although you'd hardly know it to look
around the place today. . . . But you know better than I about his will.
You wrote the book, after all. . . . You mean you've never been here
before?"

"No. I guess I somehow missed it. In retrospect, it was kind of a
foolish oversight."

"Ah, perhaps so. Colangio must have spent a good deal of time here
in the last few weeks before he . . . well gave up writing and so on. . . .
But I'm afraid I'm delaying you. Come, let me take you to our modest
little library. That's certainly the place where our Great Colangio would
have worked when he did his research here."

Tomacelli took him back down the corridor he had traversed earlier, past the door he had entered, down to the long corridor's end, then
right. There was another very long passage, leading ultimately to a large
room near the junction of the residential wing with the church. This
was the monastery's library, replete with stacks of modern books, cloth-
bound and paperback, a few single desks, more garage-sale plastic
chairs, and, against the far wall, a large glass case filled with what
looked like very old manuscript volumes, but in manifestly abysmal
condition. Their bindings were either skeletal or missing entirely, and
there were several sheaves of unbound, yellowed papers lying flat
between the disintegrating books that stood, tentatively, upright.

"That's the oldest material over there in the case. Practically all of
what we had originally was burned in the fires."

"Fires?"

"Yes, there were two of them, as I understand. One I believe around
1750 and the other sometime during the war."

"The last war?"

"Yes, the Germans. You can readily imagine. There's not a great deal left now. Just the material in that case.."

"I see. So look, uh . . . Fra Toma—"

"No, no, it's perfectly permissible to call me by my prename. Anthony. Call me Brother Anthony."

"OK, Brother Anthony—you haven't told me how you got here."

"Oh. Certainly. . . . I went to Bonaventure. Are you familiar with it?"

"Sure. That's a Franciscan university, right?"

"Correct. In upstate New York. And afterward I joined the Order. One is permitted to pick one's assignment in certain cases. And I suppose I was rather a successful student, so. . . . Well, at any rate, here I am. I do many of the theological studies for the monastery now, and, if all goes well. . . . Well, hopefully, one day I'll be in Rome. Rather like Colangio himself, I imagine, although I hardly aspire to direct the Vatican as he did. And then, too, I certainly intend to continue with my research indefinitely rather than retiring from society at Colangio's early age of forty-three. . . . Why in heaven's name did he do that, do you suppose? Your book seems to have left the question unanswered."

"Yes, I know. As a matter of fact, I'm working on that very problem right now."

"Ah, I see. Well, good, then. Whatever we brethren can do to help solve the mystery. . . . Anyway, to the task at hand. Would you like to have a look at the older material still remaining from Colangio's time? It isn't particularly exciting, I'm afraid. In fact, it's rather abstruse, actually, and there's probably nothing much of interest. . . . But, at any rate. . . . Have you ever heard of the Bogomils?"

"Man, wheyyou been, man?" asked Auntwon. It was six p.m., so probably eleven in the morning Chicago time. Robert had paged him at the library, something he could have hardly been expecting, thus he had seemed a little nonplused to begin with. And then the sound of Robert's voice. . . .

"Dr. Rogovin and me been tryin' to get aholt-a you for like a week-ten days, man! Wheyyou been?"

"I . . . I had to go out of town to do some research."

"Man, fo' a whole week!?"

"Yeah. Well, I took some time off to think a little too. I went up to Lake Como for a few days. Just to get my head . . . you know, my thoughts together."

"OK, OK. So, evvythang cool now, right? I mean, you OK and evvythang?"

"Yeah, I guess. . . . Look, I'm gonna need you to do a favor for me."

"Yeah, sure, doc. Whatever."

"OK, well, I've gotta tell you something first, something kind of crazy. . . ."

"Crazy? Whatchu mean crazy?"

"I mean *really* crazy. Something basically impossible to believe."

"Hey, man! . . . OK, go ahead, I'm listenin'"

"Well, you know that incantation that I found? The diagram and stuff? The stuff I talked to you about?"

"Yeah, sure. Last you told me somefin' happened but it was prob'bly just a co-inci-dence."

"Yeah, well it wasn't. It works."

"Works? What works? Works doin' what?"

"Well, I'm not completely sure about the full extent of it, but. . . . Somehow I managed to change something into something else."

"You *what*?" asked Auntwon. "Whadju say?"

Robert explained as briefly as he could about the watermarks on the stamps, how he had observed the little angular stars on both, and then the appearance—no; no, *revelation*—of that curvilinear winged wheel. "OK, I know how weird it sounds, but *you're* the one who told me it might be weird—you know, all that stuff you said about Colangio's life being stranger than aliens and everything. . . . And . . . and—what was it, quantum theory?"

"Yeah, OK, but, like, this *is* weird, man—whatchu said, Doc. . . . I mean, you *sure* the thang, like, *changed*? Maybe you—you know—got them two thangs mixed up, like—you said they was stamps, huh?"

"Yeah, two little Italian stamps."

"OK, so maybe, like, the one on the left floated over to the right while it was in that fluid, you know what I'm sayin'? Like shifted over a little, you know?"

"No. Look, Auntwon, it wasn't set up that way. I mean, I'd have to show you. . . . Anyway, like I said, I've gotta ask you to do me a favor. I e-mailed you a list of books and articles I need you to photocopy for me. I did an Internet search, and . . . anyway, the problem is, there's nothing much here. I mean in the university libraries in either Siena or Florence. I spent a couple of days going through them. So I thought . . . maybe you could do a search there for me on your link-up at the library. . . . I mean in addition to the list of things I emailed you."

"Yeah, well, sure, Doc. Sure. I offered to befo', remember? Jus' tell me whatchu wamme to research ezackly?"

"What? Well, there's some stuff on the Bogomils—you ever hear of them?"

"I don' know. I maybe heard the name someplace or ovver I guess."

"Well, they were dualists, like the Manicheans, you know? They believed in an eternal conflict between God and the Devil, good and evil. They were also called 'Cathars' and in southern France 'Albigensians'. . . ."

"OK, yeah, I read all about the Albigensians."

"All right. Good. Well the Bogomils were the same group. Some of their members joined the Franciscans and started a kind of internal movement within the order. . . . I'm pretty sure that's where the damn thing came from."

"What? . . . Whey *what* came from?"

"What I've been talking about—the diagram and incantation, like I told you."

"OK, yeah, right. So whatchu need?"

"Well, there's a Ph.D. thesis on the Bogomil Franciscans by a guy named Kenneth Parker from Michigan. I need that—a reprint, you know? And some other stuff—it's all on the list I emailed you, OK? I need that stuff and . . . and anything else you can find on the subject. . . . Look, you know how to do a cross-search: Bogomils, Cathari, dualism, Franciscan mystics . . . that kind of thing—you know how to word it as well as I do. I'll . . . I'll be happy to pay you for your time. . . ."

"Aw, c'mon, Doc!"

"OK, OK, I . . . look, how about if I arrange the trip to Italy for you. Yeah, that's it! You do some research for me today—tonight—and

I'll . . . you can bring the stuff over to me in a day or two. Bring it to Italy. . . . Oh, damn! I forgot. You don't have a passport, do you?"

"A passport? Yeah, I got one. I got it las' year, jus' in case Auntie win the lottery. Man, even if she don't I'm gon' get the cash to go to Europe summer a'ter next fo' sure."

"So you've got a current passport? That's great! Great! There's no reason you can't come right away then, right?"

"Ho'd on, man; you sayin' you want me to fly right over there jus' like that? I already to'd you Auntie ain' gon' let me take no money f'om nobody. . . ."

"So? What about the lottery then? What if she *does* happen to win it? She said she'd send you then, didn't she? I was thinking about that a little last night. . . . Sure, why not?"

"Yeah. Yeah, OK. If she win the lottery: OK I fly over. Thass a deal."

"Good. Maybe Thursday or Friday then. You fly to Florence through Frankfort. If you let me know the flight time, I can pick you up at the airport."

"What the fu. . . . I mean, whatchu talkin' 'bout, man?"

"The lottery. I'd say there's a good chance she'll win it. I mean, I don't know for sure. I don't know the range of this thing."

"The *range*! Man, you ain't still talkin' 'bout that. . . ."

"Yeah. Yeah, I am. I'm not sure how far it goes, though—the range, you know? Maybe it only works for local events; I'm really not sure. I mean, I haven't tried it yet outside Siena. Look, we'll see tonight. If it works, though, I expect you here this week with a lot of stuff for me. Reprints and stuff."

"Wait a minute, Doc, wait a minute! You sayin' you gonna make Auntie win the lottery?"

"Sure. I'll try, anyway. I think I just may be able to. We'll find out tonight, one way or the other. It must be around midnight or so that it happens. Midnight here, I mean. So later this afternoon for you. Maybe five or six p.m. What time is it there now?"

"Now? Eleven somepin'."

"OK, so maybe about five then."

"C'mon, Doc. . . ."

"Look, it may not work that far away. I'm not a hundred percent sure. But if it does, you should hear something around five."

"Around five. . . . Auntie gonna win the lottery around five. . . ."

"I don't know. Maybe. We'll see."

"OK, Doc, sure. Hey you gon' be they fo' a while? In you room?"

"I guess so."

"OK, look, I call you back."

"Bobby?" It was Sheldon.

"Shelly! Can I get back to you? I'm expecting a call."

"What call? Auntwon? Is that the call you're waiting for, or did you call somebody else too? Look, where the hell have you been? Rochelle and I were worried sick."

"Yeah, sorry. I had to go to Arezzo. . . . And then I went to Como for a couple of days."

"Jesus! OK, look, what the hell's going on there? Auntwon said. . . ."

"Auntwon? Did he call you?"

"Yeah. I mean, look, he's here—here in my office, I mean. Just what the hell is going on over there?"

"What did he tell you?"

"Crazy stuff."

"All right, all right. Look, I know it sounds. . . . What did he tell you exactly?"

"He told me about your magic diagram. What the fuck's going on there, Bobby?"

"Nothing. Look, forget it. How can I explain it to you? Something crazy happened. . . ."

"Are you feeling OK? Um, has anything been bothering you?"

"Come on, Shelly; I think it's crazy too. But something happened. Look, you know me. I'm the last person in the world who would go for some metaphysical bullshit like this unless. . . ."

"Unless what?"

"Unless something verifiable happened."

"And what was that?"

"It's hard to explain. Do you know what a watermark is?"

"Yeah. Like the thing you found. You told me about it, remember?"

"OK, right. Well, I changed one watermark into another. I saw it happen. There's no explanation for it otherwise. Look, I couldn't believe it either until I saw it for myself. I *saw* it, I'm telling you!"

"So why would you want to change a watermark anyway? What the hell does *that* do?"

"It's a long story."

"Hey, it's my nickel, man."

"All right, there's a guy here, where I'm working. The archivist. He collects stamps—you know, Italian stamps. Anyway, I changed the watermark on a cheap stamp to turn it into a rare one that he wanted for his collection."

"So *he* put you up to it, huh? This archivist guy?"

"No. Hey, look, he doesn't even know what happened. I didn't tell him how I got the stamp."

"OK, that's good. Don't tell anybody else. . . . Hey, why don't you fly back home for a week or two? Maybe you need a break. Bring the thing—the diagram—and you can show me. We can test it."

"OK, Shelly, OK. Look, I'm not one of your patients now. Give me a break here. . . . Put Auntwon on, will you?"

"All right, just a minute. . . . Here," Sheldon muttered beside the receiver, "he wants to talk to you. . . . *Jesus Christ almighty!*"

"Auntwon," said Robert, "look up the stuff I asked you to. I'll try to book you a flight out later this week."

CHAPTER EIGHTEEN

~~~~~~~~~~

STUPEFACTION

"HOLY SHIT, DOC!" IT WAS AUNTWON. ROBERT LOOKED AT THE CLOCK: twenty minutes past midnight. *Must have worked*, he thought. *Right on time, too.* The room smelled of jasmine, candlewax, and sulfur: that dried-up egg yolk starting to decay. He'd have to get a fresh one tomorrow.

"Well? What happened? I guess it must have worked."

"God DAMN!"

"Ten thousand? That's the number I specified. . . . I figured Annamae could use the extra cash."

"Damn! Yeah. God *damn*!"

"OK, good. I wasn't sure about the range—how far the thing could reach, I mean. So. . . . OK, you don't think I'm crazy now, I guess. . . . It's pretty amazing, isn't it? Could you ever imagine...?"

"Yeah. Yeah. God DAMN. I got to *see this* shit!"

"All right. Good. You're coming, then. . . . Did you find that stuff I asked you for?"

"Well, to tell you the truf. . . ."

"You thought it was bullshit, didn't you? That I was crazy or something."

"Yeah. I mean, I ordered that thesis you axed me fo' and printed out some articles, but. . . ."

"OK, well, you've still got a day or two before you leave. Try and get anything you can for me in the meantime, will you?"

"Yeah, Doc, sure. I'll work on it all day tomorrow."

"Did you check the flights?"

"No, man. I mean, I just found out about . . . *you* know."

"OK. Look, I'll call and get a ticket for you. I'll put it on my credit card. Maybe for Thursday. Annamae can pay me back for it later if she wants to, after she collects her money. I'll e-mail you with the departure time. . . . I'll have them hold the ticket for you at the check-in counter of whatever airline I find. Probably either American or Alitalia, but I'll let you know for sure."

"OK, Doc. Look, man, thanks—I mean, if you, like, made this all happen somehow. . . . Fo' me and Auntie, I mean. . . . I guess you did, though, huh?"

"Hey, it didn't take a whole lot of effort on my part. But, you know, I'm glad you're finally getting to go . . . to come here, I mean. I know it's been something you've wanted for a long time. And . . . and I'll be really glad to see you, too, Auntwon. Maybe you can help me to understand some of this crazy business. With all of your physics background and everything, you know?"

"Well, I'll try, Doc, but . . . God DAMN!"

He was the last one off the plane, seated, no doubt, in the very last row. Robert was afraid the kid had missed his connection in Frankfurt until he saw him, coming through the door into the terminal with two Alitalia flight attendants immediately in his wake.

"Hey, doc, man how you *doin'*?" Auntwon put out his hand, then dropped it and gave him a hug, burying his head in Robert's chest, then jerking back to arm's length and grasping Robert's arm high up near the shoulder in his customary fashion. "Man, iss good to see you, man."

"And great to see you, too, Auntwon—hey, I want you to meet a friend of mine. This is Filomena Dall'Olmo. Filomena, meet Auntwon —Auntwon Miller."

Auntwon turned and put his hand out. "*Un pia-ce-re, signori-na*," he said, not unaccented but not badly spoken either—spoken, that is, in the sort of patois one learns from a phrase book with phonetic subtext. Something he'd assimilated on the plane, no doubt.

"*Ah, parla italiano! Bravo!*" answered Filomena, taking his hand and giving it a firm shake.

"You learned some Italian!" Robert patted Auntwon's shoulder, then let his hand rest, squeezing the bony shoulder affectionately. It was good to have Auntwon there with him, comforting: a familiar, benevolent face, and more besides: a sort of anchor to what had once been unquestionable reality.

"Yes. I, like . . . I mean, I studied a little on the plane. Overnight. I been . . . that is, I've been up for . . . I guess about twenty-four hours."

"All right, come on. You can take a nap in the car."

They collected his things at baggage: a medium-sized suitcase, beige and tattered, that must have been a long-time possession of Annamae's, and a cardboard carton full of the books and reprints Robert had asked for.

"Thass yo' stuff in there, in the carton. Do the lady know about it?" Auntwon asked Robert after Filomena had gone out to fetch the car.

"No. Not much, anyway. I told her just a little before I realized the damn thing worked."

"You gonna tell her?"

"No. No reason to now. I mean, it's better kept private, don't you think?"

"Yeah. Yeah, I'd say so. . . . So . . . she a special friend? Like a girlfriend, I mean?"

"What? No. My God! She's the one I told you about before, the landlady's daughter—you know, the one I went to Assisi with. Anyway, she insisted on coming along to pick you up. Well, it's her car, of course. . . . But we've . . . I guess we've become pretty good friends. She has a kind of crush on me. Nothing serious, though. I mean, she's just a kid, really. And even if she weren't—you know, if she were more my age— she's nothing like my type at all."

"Yeah, I guess she kind of plain, like. Average, I mean. . . . Fo' a white lady."

"Yeah, I guess so. . . . So anyway, is everything OK with you? Annamae and the family OK?"

"Yeah, she cool wit' evvything. Man, she was happy wit' that money, I tell you that!"

"You didn't say anything about...?"

"Man, you think I'm *crazy*? On'y one I to'd is Dr. Rogovin. . . . And I had to say som'pin to him. He know too much awready."

"Like what? What exactly did you tell him?"

"Well, that you wasn't nuts or nuffin'. Like that magic thang ain't all bullshit, you know?"

"And what'd he say?"

"Oh, he kinda looked at me funny, so I started explainin' to him 'bout quantum theory and stuff—you know, that Heisenberg principle and the spontaneous generation of particles in empty space-time, and after a couple-a minutes of that, he kinda like walked away and left me alone."

Signora Dall'Olmo made up a bed for the kid in a room down the hall from her own. Auntwon hadn't eaten, so she dug out some bread, cheese, and chicken, and the four of them sat snacking in the kitchen until, a little after eight, Auntwon collapsed for the night. Robert saw him to his room, thanked the signora, then dragged the carton of books and papers fresh from Chicago upstairs. Setting it on the bed, he tore its top flaps open and spread the contents on the twin blankets, sorting by date and subject: here Bogomil, there Cathari, across from it Albigensian; then Franciscan mystics to the left, inquisitional testimony to the right. Before he'd gotten very far, Filomena gave her habitual little tapping at the door.

"Roberto," she called through the wood, knocking gently with a knuckle.

"Yes, Filomena. It's unlocked. Come on in."

She stepped into the room and over the bedside. "Oh, you are busy. I'm sorry."

"No, no. Just the papers and things Auntwon brought for me."

"Are they private? Should I leave?"

"No, not at all. It's just . . . research stuff. I'm . . . you know, trying to figure out that diagram and incantation I told you about. Trying to figure out the provenance of it—where it came from. Here, sit down, have a look." He offered her a place on the opposite side of the bed, with the multiple stacks of papers spread out between them. The girl plopped down sideways, then swung one knee up onto the blanket and turned her body to face him in three-quarter profile.

"Ah, yes, your little diagram," she chuckled, "the thing that made me cook your hot dogs, no? . . . But it didn't work when you tried it the second time, did it? You told me that the night before you ran away."

"I didn't run away. I had some other research to do. . . . But that's right, when I talked to you last week, I told you about it not working the second time I tried it. That's exactly right."

"And have you used it again since then?"

Robert smiled. "Just to win the lottery."

"Well? And did you win?"

"Me? No, not a *centesimo*."

"Ah, how unfortunate! Still, if you would like more hot dogs, just light another candle, read your incantation for me, and I will be sure to see that you get some."

"Yes, well, maybe in a day or two. . . . By the way, it was very nice of your mother to put Auntwon up for the night. I'll get a room for him at the hotel tomorrow."

"The hotel?"

"Yes, the Garibaldi, where I stayed."

"No, that is not at all necessary. He can remain here."

"Here? In your place? But he's in your living area; I mean, right next to your room, isn't he? Right down the hallway?"

"Yes? So?"

"Well, what about your privacy? I mean, how many bathrooms do you have?"

"There are two on our floor. This is a big house. Certain of the rooms we never even enter."

"You mean like . . . ?"

"Yes, that room in particular. I never go in there. Or in Papa's bathroom either. Auntwon may use that one. It is quite clean; we have a domestic come in and scrub the whole house from bottom to top every month or two. Even the rooms we never use."

"Well, it's very nice of you to offer, but I think. . . ."

"No, no. It will be only for a matter of weeks, I suppose. *Mamma* would like him to stay as well. She told me so. She can help teach him Italian."

"Well, I don't know. We'll talk about it tomorrow, OK?"

"All right. He seems very nice."

"Auntwon? Yes, he's great. Brilliant, too, though you wouldn't always know it to talk to him. He talks like . . . have you ever listened to rap music? The lyrics, I mean?"

"Yes, a bit. He *does* talk like that a little, I suppose."

"Yeah, sometimes *I* even have trouble with a phrase or two of his. But he's amazingly bright. Really outstanding. He's the most promising student I've had in my whole career."

"Really! Well, of course, he must be special if you have asked him to do this research for you. . . . So, what is it that he has brought you in the box? May I look at it, or is it some type of deep, dark secret?"

"No, no, it's. . . . Sure, have a look. . . . Have you heard of the Bogomils? Or the Cathari? They're pretty much the same."

"No, I'm not familiar with either of those names."

"Well I guess that's understandable; they're relatively obscure. . . . They were thirteenth century heretics who believed in a duality of good and evil, God and the Devil, in other words, you understand? They seem to have worshipped both. That diagram I mentioned—I've got it pretty well traced back to them."

"Oh! And did they like hot dogs too?"

"Very funny! *Very* funny! I'm only telling you because you asked. . . . I don't make fun of Chaucer, you know."

"I don't think you could. He was a great genius, like your Colangio. . . . But . . . what does this tell you about him, about Colangio, all these papers on the Bogos. . . .?"

"The Bogomils. . . . Well, for instance, whether he was into satanism or some such practices; what books or sects might have influenced him. That sort of thing."

"All right. Well, let me help you with it, if I may. What can I do?"

"To help? Uh, OK, you can go through this stack to see if there's anything that looks like the chart Colangio used."

"Well, I don't know at all what that is like."

"You don't?—oh, that's right. Well, it's just a ring of circles."

"So? May I see it? I know you have it in the room someplace."

"Uh . . . the diagram? It's, uh. . . ."

"No, no; I understand. You needn't show it to me if you don't want to."

"No, hey, don't be silly. Why *wouldn't* I want you to see it? . . . Here, wait a minute; I'll get it for you." Robert went to the desk, took out his copy of the diagram, and brought it back over to the bed.

"Here. This is a copy I made. It's basically a hexagram—you know, six-sided, but the points are circles. There are some instructions inside the figure—here—to tell how it's used. And the writing in the circles names the objects you're supposed to put inside each one."

"Like the candles I got for you in Firenze? The *cera d'api*?"

"Yes, exactly. Here." He pointed at the topmost circle. "That's where it goes—the candle, see?"

"Ah, yes, I see. '*Una candela di cera d'api*,' it says, no? And this one here—what is it '*Acqua santa*'?"

"Yes, holy water."

"You know, Roberto. . . ."

"What?"

"It seems to me difficult to believe that you actually tried to use such a thing. I mean, with your—what do you call it: skepticism?—it just doesn't seem at all like you."

"No. No, I guess not. Actually, it was kind of a joke at first. Or a dare, maybe."

"And who was it that dared you?"

"Caterina. She got some of the objects for me. Most of them, in fact."

"Yes?"

"All but the candles."

"Yes, that's right, I got you those."

"You did, indeed."

"And the hot dogs!"

"Yes." He laughed. "That was really nice. It was a very nice surprise."

"I'm glad. And I can imagine your surprise after the. . . ."

"After I used the incantation. Yes. I'm not quite sure you *can* imagine that! No, I'm not really sure *anyone* can. . . ."

"Well, are you very sorry that your magic diagram didn't work when you tried it for the second time?"

"Sorry?" He paused for a few seconds, shaking his head. "It's hard for me to answer you, Filomena. I don't think I'm sorry about anything, really. I mean, I'm not exactly sure *how* I feel just now."

"Oh? About what?"

"Uh. . . . Nothing. Nothing. Don't pay any attention to anything I say right now. I . . . I guess I'm tired; and maybe excited too, having Auntwon here and all. . . . All right, come on, let's have a look at those papers. You know what to look for now, don't you?"

"Yes, I think so. Six circles, like your drawing."

Robert leafed through a stack of computer print-outs and photocopies, Filomena through another. There were some books too, originals and reprints; and a spiral-bound reproduction of the Ph.D. thesis Robert had asked for, still in the Federal Express packet Auntwon had received it in. The boy had done his research tirelessly and well.

They found histories of the Bogomils and Cathari, interrogations of heretical Franciscans. There were specimens of necromantic charts: pentagrams and sectored circles, stars and multi-sided figures, that really *looked* metaphysical—strange things, they were, with strange illustrations: crescent moons, zodiacal signs, pictures of cats and worms and toads. And arcane verbiage too: none of your eggs and oyster shells, but blood of reptiles, serpent skin, bat wings, beetle dung, mare's urine, human hair. Nothing at all, however, remotely resembling the diagram he had found so oddly watermarked in that peculiar page of Colangio's papers.

"You won't find anything like your diagram here," said Filomena after half an hour of concentrated labor. "These are all. . . . I don't know the word: *demoniaco*."

"'Demonic' I think. Or 'demoniacal'."

"Yes. That's right: demoniacal. Your diagram is not like that."

"Why? Why do you say that?"

"Well, for one thing, the holy water. That is not a demoniacal thing."

"No? Caterina's boss says it is—that it makes the whole process even more powerful and more satanic."

"Well, he is wrong. No, the diagram you have is nothing like these others."

"So what is it, then? What in the world do you think it is?"

"Ah, that I do not know, but you will not find anything like it in these papers."

They went to breakfast at the Hotel Garibaldi. Auntwon, after twelve long hours in his bed at the Dall'Olmos', would be hungry.

"How do you feel?" Robert asked, after Auntwon had cleaned his second fully laden plate—had cleaned it, moreover, with the aid of three or four *panini* swept voraciously across its surface, of every molecule of foodstuff formerly present—and had finally leaned back from the table to rub his belly and catch his breath.

"OK, OK, not too bad, Doc. That was good, man—Doc. . . . I was hungry!"

"You sleep OK?"

"Yeah, till like around three. Then I was kinda in and out, you know?"

"Sure, the jet lag. I've been through it plenty of times myself. . . . So? Tell me. What do you think?"

"About . . . like yo' thang, you mean?"

"Yeah, the whole God damned thing. Have you got any—you know—ideas? Suggestions?"

"No, man, I don' know. . . . How would I know, Doc?"

"Well, I figured you being a science major and all. . . . I thought maybe you might come up with some kind of explanation—well, not really an explanation exactly: theory, I guess I meant; theory. . . . Look, you're the one who told me Colangio's life might turn out to be so strange. What did you mean by that? And what about all that particle physics stuff you talked about? Quantum theory, remember? Hey, you're the one who. . . ."

"Yeah, OK, OK. Well I cain't figure how that, uh . . . how any kind of physics, like—you know... *apply*. . . . OK, OK, lemme work on it a little. Maybe I come up wit' somepin' at least to, like, do some testin'. I gotta think it out fo' a while, though. Gimme a hour or two, OK?"

"Sure, It's not like there's a rush or anything."

"Naw, man, we got time. I'ma be here a week."

"A week!"

"Yeah, 'bout a week, then I gotta go check out, like, Rome and Florence and shit. A week gon' be enough. We don't figure somepin' out in a week, we ain' never gonna figure nuffin' out at all, you know what I'm sayin'?."

"Yeah, I'd say the latter; it doesn't sound like a soluble problem."

"Maybe, man, maybe. . . . So tell me: whatchu find out 'bout them Bogomils?"

"OK. Well, they were dualists. . . ."

"Yeah, yeah, I know all 'at shit, man. I mean, I read all 'at stuff I got fo' you f'om the library. What I'm axin' you is whadjou find out in Arezzo?"

"Oh yeah, I never told you that, did I?"

Auntwon shook his head.

"Well, they had a whole case of Renaissance era papers—some earlier ones too. It took me three full days to get through them. . . . There was a friar from Chicago, of all places, who helped me. . . . Anyway, the biography of St. Francis I was working on—you know, Colangio's manuscript?"

Auntwon nodded.

"Well, it's an exact copy of a work by this guy named Simeon Melanitzes. . . ."

"The dude got busted by the Inquisition."

"Yeah, you read about him too, eh?"

"Yeah, I read it all, man. All 'at stuff in the box. I awready to'd you that."

"OK, well I found a fragment of the biography in different hand-writing—Melanitzes', I guess—and, even more important, I found part of the incantation too, like six or seven lines of it with numbers and figures on the page, just like in the manuscript. That was in Colangio's hand for sure; so probably a kind of work sheet or something."

"Man! The same incantation thang you used?!"

"Exactly. Word for word; maybe about a third of it."

"So whey you find it at? Same place?"

"Yeah, in with the stuff they had in Arezzo—I mean, it was only a fragment. . . . On the back of a page—a torn page, too, you know? Half of it was missing."

"So thass it, then, man. That gotta be whey it come f'om, fo' sure, right?"

"Yeah, I think it's safe to conclude that. Colangio must have figured out the incantation was hidden in the biography of St. Francis by Melanitzes, and then. . . ."

"Yeah, yeah, then he decoded it and found out it worked. How you think he come up wit' that?"

"You mean the code and everything? Hey, I doubt we're ever gonna get an answer to that question."

"OK, but we know about his life now—them last twenty years, I mean. You know, that palace and shit. . . ."

"Yep. And his wife and the money—everything. . . . You were right, after all."

"Me? 'Bout what, Doc?"

"How weird it all turned out to be."

"Yeah, I had a feelin'. Nuffin' like this, though."

"No, neither of us could have imagined anything like this." Robert drank the last of his coffee, took the hard boiled egg from his plate, wrapped it in a napkin, and slipped it into the pocket of his jacket. "OK, you ready? You have enough to eat?"

"Yeah, yeah, plenty, man. . . . So whatchu gon' do wit that egg? You savin' it up fo' later? That all you takin', man? That one little bitty egg?"

"Yeah. . . . Uh, no. . . . I mean, it's not to eat. I don't usually eat much of anything in the morning. This is . . . it's just something we're going to need later. I'll show you tonight."

"You mean fo' the . . . ?"

"Yeah."

"A egg?"

"I'll show you later. Come on."

So Robert took him for a walk around the city; first to the Campo: inside the Palazzo Pubblico, with its thirteenth century frescoes, then out into the hot June sun and over to the Mangia Tower, which the kid felt an irresistible urge to climb.

"You comin' up, Doc?"

He declined. "Wave to me from the top when you get there. I'll watch for you."

Auntwon disappeared into an arched doorway, then reappeared twelve minutes later at the top of the monument, minutely visible, flailing both arms scissorlike, signalling. Then, eight minutes more having passed, he was back at Robert's side, breathing hard and wet with perspiration.

"That was fast."

"Yeah, c'mon, man; I gotta go see that cathedral, that big white thang wif the dome, you know? Iss *somefin'*, man. I got, like, a real good look at it from up top. Iss, like, krunk, man. C'mon. Over that way."

"OK, OK, Auntwon, take it easy. I know where it is, for God's sake. We'll get there. What's your hurry?"

"Me! Hey, *you* the one who so impatient about yo' thang, ain'tchu?"

"Yeah? So? What's that got to do with the cathedral?"

"Well, I figured out what we gotta do to check the thang out. You know, like, test it. On'y . . . on'y I got to see that cathedral place firs', befo' we get to workin' on it."

"You figured it out? How? When? Up on the tower there?"

Auntwon shrugged.

"Come on, you couldn't have been up at the top for more than a minute or two. What the hell did you see up there that made you figure everything out so fast? The cathedral? What?"

"No, man, nuffin' up there. . . . I ditten see nuffin' but the view. But climbin' up them steps. . . . I mean, iss, like, a *l-o-n-g* way up and I ditten have nuffin' else to think about fo' maybe five, ten minutes, you know? Nuffin' but them big steps and catchin' my breaf. . . . So I come up wif a pretty good plan on my way up."

CHAPTER NINETEEN

VOLITION

"OK, FIRS' YOU GOT TO, LIKE, SHOW ME HOW YOU SET IT UP," SAID
Auntwon. They were seated on the far side of the bed, with the diagram spread flat on a chair seat by the window. "That whatchu use the
egg fo', right?"

"Yeah, the six things go in the circles—all but the air, which is just
an exhaled breath. Here, I'll demonstrate." Robert put everything in
place: the oyster shell, the little cup of holy water, the foil-wrapped soil,
the beeswax candle, unlit as yet; then, last of all, the egg yolk, divested
now of white and shell.

"That it?"

"Yep, that's all. Then you line up the arrow with the setting sun. . . .
See? Like this. . . ." He shifted the paper a few degrees in the direction
of some horizontal shafts of light entering the window. "... then you read
the incantation twice and blow out the candle . . . across here, like this."
Robert blew a stream of air out audibly, directly in line with the arrow
and incident sunlight. "You're supposed to read the incantation twice
through, and name the thing you want each time, just at the end, then
blow. That's it. That's all there is to it."

"OK, I got it. Ain't much to that, man. How long we got—a hour
after sunset, right?"

"Yeah, so maybe an hour and ten minutes from now. I don't know
how exact that is, though. I just kind of waited till the sun seemed to set,
then read the thing about an hour afterward. It might have been a couple minutes off one way or the other, but it seemed to work all right."

"Yeah, thass fo' sure, man. Th' other day, anyways."

"Well, you'll see what I mean tonight. . . . So what's your secret plan? How do you suggest we test it?"

"OK, what we gon' do is just check it out and see how, like, specific it is, you know what I'm sayin'?"

"The *time* you mean? I already told you. . . ."

"Yeah, OK. I know you say the time could be off a little bit maybe, but we gon' check out th' other stuff too. You know, like figure out the margin of error? Thass what we'd do if we was testin' it in a lab, say. Like a physics experiment, you know? I thought all about it goin' up that Mangia Tower place."

"So what exactly does that tell us? I don't. . . ."

"OK, OK, look: that tell us, like, the operative thang, you know? Like the part that do the work."

"Yeah, I know what 'operative' means."

"Yeah, OK, Doc, sorry. Most t' time I'm talkin' to dudes who *don'* know what operative mean, you know what I'm sayin'? I, like, got a tendency to forget sometimes. You know, I talk to you like my buddies, like my family, I mean."

"Yeah, you explained all that to me. . . . The frightening thing is, your speech is starting to sound normal to me: I'll be talking that way myself pretty soon. . . . OK, well, anyway . . . what do you want to do? What is it exactly that we're supposed to test?"

"Well, like, evvythang, man—eventually. We got to test it all, I mean, but, like, one thang at a time, you know what I'm sayin'? . . . Like, firs' we change the diagram—all that stuff there, I mean—you know—like the egg and shit: misplace it a little, rearrange it, one thang o' 'nother, OK? Then, like, a'ter that, you try and mess wif the incantation some. You know; like skip a word or somefin'. . . . Stuff like 'at."

"Yeah. . . . *Yeah*! OK! I see what you mean: maybe certain parts of the ritual are unnecessary, like the oyster shell or soil or whatever."

"Yeah, Doc. Thass it. You gettin' it. Like maybe all's you need's the incantation and the other shit don't do nuffin'. Or either the candle do the work, or the egg yolk, you know? You got to break it down to the essential part, you dig? The operative part. Then you got to research that one thang. Break it down, man, break it down."

"Yeah. . . . That's terrific, Auntwon! That's great!... So . . . so what do you want to start with first? What part do we leave out tonight?"

"Tonight, Doc? Naw, man, not tonight. . . . Tonight I got to see this damn thang *work*."

And it did, of course. That night, Friday night, or Saturday morning, the sixteenth or seventeenth of June, at just twelve midnight—twelve o'clock precisely, for they watched it happen. And though the clock on Robert's nightstand read 12:02 when it began, he discovered just the next morning when the nine o'clock church bells rang that his errant little clock was precisely two minutes fast. So twelve midnight on the dot it was, when a glass of Siena's water fresh from the tap somehow transformed itself into wine. Nor was it any generic sort of wine at all, but a particular variety specified by Auntwon: the sweet, full-bodied—though much maligned—*MD 20/20*. No costly *brunello* or *pinot noir*, no, but a more pedestrian beverage eminently familiar to the boy, tasted by him on more than one occasion as a child, courtesy of his cousin Tyrone, who had preferred it to all its competitors and had dispensed a drop or two for the underage Auntwon, at periodic intervals, to taste.

They watched the metamorphosis take place, Auntwon Miller and Robert Martin, silently, motionlessly—the one completely awed, the other by now a little jaded. They watched the liquid ripen, with such subtlety and haste that it seemed to them, if anyone had asked them, that nothing really had occurred until the whole transformation was complete. If anyone had been around to ask, each would have said that it took five minutes or ten. Yet when the liquid had fully darkened to a rich claret hue, darkened to its end-point and ceased to darken more, the little clock read 12:03, as if the element of time itself had been transformed—gelled, congealed, and frozen—along with the transmuted wine.

"*Ho-ly* shit, man! Didju see that?" Auntwon got up from the bed, went over to the glass, and sniffed at its contents.

"That what you asked for?" Robert asked. "Go ahead and taste it. It's all right. . . . I mean, I didn't get sick from the hot dogs or anything."

"*Ho-ly* shit!"

"Well?"

"Yeah. Yeah. Thass the stuff awright. *Fu-u-uck* me! . . . Oh, sorry, Doc, sorry, man. I jus'. . . ."

"Yeah, sure, that's OK. I think I said the same thing when I saw the watermark change. . . . All right, now let's try and understand it."

And they did try, proceeding systematically with Auntwon's plan. For six days they followed it with the utmost care, from Saturday till Thursday. On the first night they left out a line of the incantation; on the second, they placed the egg yolk a fraction of an inch outside its circle; on the third, they skewed the chart so that its arrow was a little off axis from the sun at its point of decline. On Tuesday they read the incantation only once; on Wednesday they omitted just a single word of text. Then, finally, on Thursday evening, Robert merely substituted the Italian word *maestro* for the Latin *magister*. Result: for six days running nothing happened. Nothing: no wine, no watermarks; even a simple triple coin-toss on the final evening could not be predetermined.

"Well?"

"It come up tails, Doc."

"Damn! So it's that specific! I mean . . . what in the world do you make of it?"

"Hey, we know it work if you do it right."

"Yeah, we *do* know that. Not a whole lot more, though."

"No, man, nuffin' more."

Nothing to be sure. Auntwon was absolutely right about that. They knew two things only: that the chart was magic indeed, and that its instructions must be carried out, literally, to the letter. It was as though just that specific arrangement of objects, just that particular combination of words had somehow tapped into a fundamental principle of nature, into some undreamt-of defect in the fabric of the universe.

"Well, there's got to be an explanation."

"Yeah? Well I don't know of none."

"Nothing you can think of?"

"C'mon, Doc, this shit ain't in the books."

"Well, what about that quantum theory stuff? Or string theory? . . . Should we ask somebody?"

"Ax somebody! They lock you up or either take it to use in the pentagon or some shit like 'at. *Ax* somebody! You kiddin' me, Doc, or what?"

"No. I don't know. . . . So . . . what do you suggest now?"

"Suggest?"

"Yeah. Can you think of anything else to do? Any other tests to run? *Something?*"

"*Man.* . . . Hey look, Doc, you got the keys to the kingdom here, you know what I'm sayin'? Hey, you got to go widdit. You know, get whatchu want—get evvythang you want. . . . Man, if I had somefin' like this, I'd. . . ." Auntwon fell silent, looking contemplative.

"OK, what? . . . What would you do with it?"

"I don' know. Maybe nuffin'. I got mostly what I want, and the rest I can get. You know, I got the resta my life, man."

"Yeah, but there must be *something* you really want. Look, let's do it. Let's get you something special that you'd really like to have or want to happen."

"Naw, man. Look, you use it. Look-a-here, nobody know how long the thang gon' work, right? Maybe it jus' last fo' a while, you know? Maybe iss, like, dependent on the time-a year or the orbit of the earph and shit, you know what I'm sayin'? Maybe it work on'y evvy five centuries or like that. We don' know."

"Yeah, we don't know anything at *all*, it seems."

"I guess so, but expecially 'bout *this*. . . . You know, Doc, Colangio ditten live fo'ever."

"No, that's true. There must be a finite limit as to what it can do."

"Or either a time limit maybe. . . . I mean, his wife died befo' him too, ditten she? He cooten save her, right?"

"I guess. . . . She died suddenly, though, so maybe he couldn't get to the diagram in time."

"Or maybe the power jus' run out."

"Yeah, could be that too I suppose."

"OK, so fo'get all 'at ovver shit, man. I say go get whatchu want. . . . Look, Doc, you got to think about it. What the thang you really want most in the whole world? More 'n anythang else?"

"I don't know . . . world peace."

"Sh-e-e-y-a-t, man! Come on!"

"All right. . . . I don't know. I mean, I'm like you: I'm pretty happy the way I am. I don't need a lot more money or anything."

"Well, you a whole lot better now, but you sure ditten seem so cool back eight, nine weeks ago. . . . OK, Doc, look-a-here: tell me somefin': what was the happiest you ever been in yo' life?"

"The happiest? . . . I don't know."

"Yes you *do* know, man. You do too know."

"OK, well, the past five years were the best. . . . The past five years up until that day at school when you talked to me the first time, remember?"

"Sure, man, sure. . . . So it was wif' you lady, right? The one come see you that day."

"Yeah, I guess."

"You guess?"

"No. You know what I'm saying. . . . That was the best part of my life—by far the best. Yeah, sure; no comparison. The best years of my life, the best moments, were with her."

"Why? What made evvythang so good?"

"You don't understand it, do you?"

Auntwon shook his head.

"You've never been in love, then."

"Yeah. I mean, I been wif' some girls. You know. . . ."

"No, that's not what I mean at all. . . . I don't know. . . . I didn't understand it at your age either. I . . . I can't explain it really. Maybe you'll meet somebody special and understand all of it yourself some day."

"Damn! I hope not, Doc. Not a'ter all 'at bullshit you been th'ough. But, look-a-here, if you was so happy wif' yo lady, then why donchu jus' use the thang an' get her back? How hard could somepin' like that be?"

"No, Auntwon, it wouldn't feel the same. Part of it—how can I explain this to you?—OK, a lot of what I felt, the *joy* that I felt, was in knowing that she loved me the way I loved her. You understand? It was that kind of common thing we felt for each other—the intimacy—that was so good. I could never get that again: not by making her come back to me by some artifice; by some magic formula. . . . No, that part of my life is over. So there's nothing much I really want. I mean . . . even another successful book wouldn't be worth anything unless I did it on my own—you know, not by some artificial contrivance."

"Yeah, that part I can certainly relate to. I wooten want that fo' myself neither. . . . But yo' lady—man, you oughta at least get even wif' her, you know?"

"You mean hurt her? Hurt her somehow? No. No, I could never do that; not after what she . . . after what we meant to each other. . . . I could never hurt her in any way."

"Well you gotta get her back then. Thass it. Thass it, man."

"No, I already told you. . . ."

"No, thass bullshit, Doc—'scuse me, but thass jus' plain old bullshit. Look-a-here, what all this incantation stuff show you?"

"What did it show me?"

"Yeah, yeah, whatchu learn f'om it?"

"I don't know. . . . You tell me."

"Well, fo' instance—OK?—What ezackly do you know about reality?"

"Reality? . . . Yeah, I think I see where you're going with this. OK, it *did* change my view of that—of the world."

"How?"

"Well, it, uh . . . it showed how little I know, *we* know—everybody, I mean—about things—about reality, I guess you'd say."

"OK, good. So what do it tell you about all this ovver shit? I mean the book you planned on writin' and the . . . the fact that yo' lady love you a li'l bit more or a li'l bit less? What do it tell you?"

"I guess that nothing's what it seems. . . . That nothing we know or do is really all that important; nothing we *think* we know, I mean."

"Good, Doc. You gettin' it now. So whatchu got here to prevent you from gettin' evvything you need to make you happy? Shit, I say you got to go fo' it."

"Is that enough?" Robert asked.

"Enough! Man thass two thousand bucks!"

"Yeah, well, Rome's expensive. And Florence too. I don't know what a room is gonna run."

"OK, but they got hostels and shit, man. This much gonna last me till August at least."

"You're coming back, though, right?"

"Yeah, sure, maybe in a couple-a weeks."

"OK, if you need anything, just call me, all right?"

"Yeah, yeah, I'ma be fine. . . . I pay you back when I get back home, OK?"

"Right! Like sending contributions to the vault at Fort Knox!"

Auntwon laughed. But he was sad to go; you could see it in his eyes. Still, the trip was his idea. And the best thing for him, too, at the moment.

They drove him to the station in the Dall'Olmos' car, Robert in the back seat with the kid, Filomena and her mother up front.

"*Ciao, Antonio*," said the signora on the platform, hugging him like an only son gone off to war. "*Ci vediamo fra poco.*" We'll see each other soon.

"*Si, si, signora. Arrivederci.*" He'd miss her a lot, Auntwon added in halting Italian—with Filomena's help. His eyes were wet, so he wiped them on his shirt sleeve. Filomena hugged him, then Robert did too, and the kid climbed onto the train with his beat-up little case in his hand and that tattered orange jacket tied around his waist.

They stood there as the train began to move, then waved to the face behind the window of his car until the car itself was out of sight. When she turned around, the signora had tears streaming down her cheeks.

"I shall miss him, Roberto," said Filomena when they got into the Mercedes.

"Yes, I think we all will."

"*Mamma* needs another person to take care of."

"She needs another student, you mean. He learned a lot of Italian in a week."

"Yes, he is amazing. I understand what you meant about him. . . . Well, did he help you in your research? I hardly saw you all last week."

"Yes, that's right. We were busy. . . . *I* was especially."

"Doing what? Your research? . . . Have you traced your magic diagram to its source?"

"No, not yet. . . . I mean not beyond the Bogomils. I made it through that whole carton of articles without finding a thing."

"See? I told you. The diagram you have is not at all demoniacal. . . . You tried it again, didn't you?"

"What?"

"The magic thing. You know."

"Why do you say that?"

"Well, the jasmine. From the candle. . . . I could smell it."

"Oh, well, yes, we were sort of . . . of . . . acting the thing out, you know? I had to demonstrate for Auntwon."

"Yes, it seems that you showed him many times."

"I did. A few."

"And did it work those times?"

"No. Nothing happened at all."

"I should have known. I felt no urge to cook a hot dog for you all week long."

Robert laughed. "No, no. We just did it as a test. . . . Like a fire alarm, you know?"

"Ah, yes. A drill—isn't that what you say? Well do me a favor, then, Roberto: Ask your magic thing again for a hot dog tonight. And not just as a drill this time, please. *Mamma* needs another person to cook for just now."

They served him supper in their dining room, a large paneled chamber with a walnut table twelve feet long. Filomena lit some candles—plain ones of ordinary wax—and opened a bottle of sweet white wine, which went poorly with the hot dogs. Otherwise the food was superb—his favorite meal, after all. And authentic! Chicago dogs, soft little buns with poppy seeds, pickles, relish, mustard. God knew where they found the stuff! Oh, Florence, of course; but maybe real Vienna wieners brought in special for some homesick American soldiers at a nearby base.

"Were they as tasty as the ones you order in Chicago?" asked the girl while her mother cleared the table.

"Pretty close."

"Perhaps we should have made them while Auntwon was here."

"No, I think he preferred your mother's pasta. My taste in food is rather unique."

"Well, we have more whenever you like. You needn't waste your magic diagram in asking."

"No, I won't. I . . . I'll have to find some other use for it."

"Like the lottery?"

"Sure. Why not. If it worked on that I'd be a millionaire."

"Well, not in *lire*. A million *lire* won't go very far."

"No, I'll get an American lottery ticket. A million dollars is—what—two billion *lire*?"

"Almost. If your magic worked you could have all that."

"There'd be no limit, would there?"

"No, no limit at all, that's right. Think, Roberto, if the magic really worked, you could have your life back the way it was when you were so happy. With that woman you told me about."

"I didn't really tell you all that much, did I?"

"You told me quite enough."

"Maybe I did at that. . . . Listen, Filomena, let me ask you something —just hypothetically, I mean: If you had a magic diagram like that— one that worked, that is—and you could do whatever you wanted with it—anything at all. . . . Would you do that kind of thing? Take yourself back in time like that? What I mean is: would you, well, for example, bring your father back? Negate what happened to him? Give him a second chance to do things differently?"

"What a question, Roberto! But you are quite serious, aren't you? You want a serious answer." She thought a while, sitting beside him at the table, sipping her cup of tea. The signora had gone into the kitchen. Robert heard her working, clattering dishes, splashing water in the sink.

"You cannot erase the past, Roberto," said the girl, starting up abruptly after a silent minute of thought. "People themselves do not change. If I could bring my father back, it would make me happy for a while, but he would live the same life again, commit the same errors, endure the same torments. He would be the same person he always was with the same terrible demons. I would be subjecting him to the same kind of unhappiness that brought about his death in the first place. But this time I would be conscious of it, guilty of it myself in a way. It would be a tragedy for both of us, greater and more intolerable than the one we both lived through before. . . . So, no, Roberto, I would not use the magic thing for that."

Filomena paused, then looked up at him and smiled. "I would use it to get you a more delicious hot dog."

꧁꧂

CHAPTER TWENTY

DECISION

SIENA'S SUMMERS ARE HOT AND DRY. SUCH PRECIPITATION AS COMES THEN to central Tuscany is scanty and infrequent. Thus the storm that swept in on Saturday, the twenty-fourth of June, was as singular as it was unexpected. Leaden clouds presaged it at sunrise, strong winds trumpeted its imminent arrival at ten, and by noon, the town was slick with rain, thick sheets of it, clattering on the barrel tiles and siphoning down the cobbled streets like sand through an hourglass.

It was no day to be outdoors. Nor had Robert any cause to leave his room. What was needed now was a decision, and this dismal day was optimal for that. From nine when he awoke until Filomena tapped on the door at noon, he pondered. He thought of Cassie, of the incantation, of the reasonable things that Auntwon had said. Then, finally, he remembered his conversation with Filomena the evening before, if only to discount it. "The keys to the kingdom," Auntwon had told him. Well, why not? Everything he had ever found beautiful in his life returned to him again. Forever. Without impediment. Without end. Artificial, to be sure. . . . But wasn't the whole world artificial now? Wasn't the whole of supposed reality?

Filomena's inconspicuous tapping came, not unexpectedly, just at noon. And it was welcome indeed to Robert, for an entire morning of uninterrupted thought had been mental anguish enough.

"Yes, Filomena, just a minute," he called out. He unlocked the door and ushered her in. "That's quite a storm we're having," he remarked.

"Yes. You cannot possibly go out with the weather so bad. *Mamma* is preparing lunch for the three of us."

"That's very nice of her, but I hope she doesn't feel obligated."

"Well of course she doesn't. But you must come down promptly at one-thirty. It is something very special."

"Not the rabbit, I hope."

"No, no. Not rabbit. It is a veal dish, but very good. A big meal for the big storm, all right?"

"Sure, fine. Sit down a minute."

"Of course, I would be happy to."

Filomena took the desk chair, Robert the mattress, the two of them facing each other in exactly the same positions they had assumed on that very first day they'd met, having hauled his heavy luggage up the steps. So many things had changed since then, thought Robert, his life, his philosophic certitude; his very universe, in truth.

"So . . . how is your mother getting along without Auntwon."

"Sadder a little, Roberto. She misses him a lot. Even after his being here just a week. I think the company was good for her."

"Yes, I think so too. You know, I was sad to see him leave, myself. He and I have gotten pretty close these past few months."

"Yes, he seems to like you very much. . . . But he is coming back, no?"

"He plans to. In three or four weeks, I think."

"Good, then. . . . *Mamma* will be pleased. . . . By the way, Roberto, I'm curious: You didn't do your experiment last night, did you?"

"With the diagram? No. No I didn't."

"Why not?"

"Well because . . . I had no reason to."

"You have finished with the experiments, then?"

"Well, no. . . . But Auntwon and I were—you know—kind of doing them together."

"And you cannot do them alone? . . . Perhaps I can assist you."

"Yes. Yes, perhaps you can. We'll have to *both* make a wish with it sometime."

"And what shall we ask for, Roberto? What else would you want? Beside the hot dogs."

"You mean supposing that it worked, right?"

"Yes, let us suppose that for the moment."

"We talked about that a little last night."

"Yes, but you asked me what *I* would do if I had a magic thing like yours. With my father, that is. Now I'm asking you what *you* would do with it—assuming that it worked, of course."

"Well, I'm really not sure *what* I'd do. I've been thinking a lot about that."

"Yes, it occurred to me you might have been."

"You seem to know a lot about me, Filomena, don't you?"

"Yes, we are *simpatici*, Roberto, don't you realize that? . . . Or maybe you don't yet."

"Look, Filomena. . . ."

"Yes, Roberto, I know that you think of me as a little sister. . . . But we are closer than that. . . . We are very much closer than that."

"No, Filomena, we can *never* be closer. You must understand that now. We can *never* be closer. Or maybe never be closer in the way you'd like—or *think* you'd like."

"Because of that woman?"

"Yes. . . . Well . . . I don't know. I had something unique with her. I don't know if I can ever get that back. I doubt that I ever can."

"Oh, you can. Of course you can."

"I sincerely doubt it."

"And was she—is she—a *nice* woman? A *kind* woman?"

"She was to me . . . at times."

"I see." Filomena paused a moment, thinking. "You and she were *simpatici*?"

"Yes. That we were. . . . For sure. . . . For sure."

"Then that's it, Roberto. You must get her back. You must, if only to cleanse yourself of her spirit. . . . You must call her."

"Call her?"

"Yes. Call her. Telephone her. Do it right now. This instant."

"No, no. I'd need to think a little. . . ."

"About what? You know what you want, don't you? Get it. Go after it."

"I don't know. . . ."

"You don't? Well I do. I know. I cannot understand a person not fighting for what he wants. Fighting and fighting with every weapon he can find. Giving in to hopelessness is a concept that is utterly foreign to me. Come downstairs at one-thirty, Doctor Martin, and we shall have your meal ready. My advice would be for you to call your lady friend."

But it was Shelly that he called first.

"Bobby?" Sheldon asked, "what's going on?"

"Nothing much. I'm by myself now. Auntwon left yesterday."

"He left? For where?"

"He's doing a little tour of Italy. He'll be back here in a few weeks."

"He . . . he said you were OK. That what you were saying wasn't as crazy as it seemed."

"Yeah, I guess I managed to convince him of that."

"So what is it—that thing you've got?"

"I don't know. A kind of magic formula, I guess. It's a sort of . . . a sort of mystical ceremony that makes things happen; gets things that you want. . . . But the damn thing works. It really works."

"That's what the kid said."

"I've gotta decide what to do."

"What to do? Well, what are our options here?"

"They seem pretty much unlimited."

"Look, Bobby, notwithstanding as smart as you and Auntwon are, and your general credibility . . . this stuff is still pretty hard for me to swallow right now. Let's talk in general terms, OK? You want my advice, right? I assume that's why you called."

"Don't be angry with me, Shelly. I'm having a tough enough time as it is."

"No, no, Bobby, I'm not angry. . . . Look . . . it's just that . . . well, it's hard to even know what to say. . . ."

"Yeah, I know that. But I really need your input now. I've got to make a tough decision, and I don't know which way to go with it."

"Yeah, I can guess. Cassie, right? You think the thing might get her back."

"I'm pretty sure it will. I mean . . . it seems to have worked that way for Colangio. He wound up marrying a woman he'd loved since adolescence. . . . Plucked her right out of a nunnery. And it all happened around the time he found the . . . the thing."

"So what's your problem? That's what you want, isn't it? Your girl friend?"

"I'm not sure. It might not be. Things might not be the same."

"Why?"

"I don't know—the artificiality of it, I guess. It's like. . . ."

"Like masturbating?"

"Well, that wasn't exactly what I was going to say, but maybe it is in a way. . . . Maybe it's too much like fantasy."

"So what? People fantasize all the time. Look, if this one woman is the only person in the world who can satisfy you, then do whatever it'll take to make yourself happy. Hey, I hate the bitch, you know? But I'd rather see you happy with her than miserable without her. I say go for it. Shit, maybe you can do something with your magic formula to straighten her little skinny ass out at the same time. Like a lobotomy—yeah, that would serve her right. Lobotomize the bitch. . . . So, anyway, what did Auntwon say? He's your chief consultant, isn't he?"

"He said pretty much the same thing as you—except for the lobotomy part, that is."

"That's 'cause he doesn't know her like I do. . . . So? What the hell's your problem? You got unanimous yes votes from your two consulting analysts. Crank up your crazy formula and turn little Miss Fullerton into a sex slave. I think I'd pay to see that shit myself."

By nightfall the storm had passed. The air was thick and warm, saturate with humidity. Robert sat on the edge of the mattress before the open window, dressed in tee shirt and shorts, the diagram spread flat on the wooden chair seat, just as it had been placed by him and Auntwon two evenings before. To the west were broken clouds now, no longer obscuring the descent of the sun, and he lined up the arrow unerringly. He had an hour or so to wait, sixty-odd minutes more to think, but his mind was quite made up. Cassie's life, as his own had ten days earlier, was just about to change.

The hour passed interminably, like syrup through a drain. But nine-fifty-five arrived at last and found everything fully prepared: the holy water—a fresh supply fetched just two hours earlier from San Spirito on the Via dei Pispini; the soil—in the same little aluminum foil cuplet Caterina had borrowed from the restaurant in Monterrigioni; the oyster shell and egg yolk and beeswax candle, alit now but soon to be extinguished.

Robert read his long transcription of the chant: "*Magister*. . . ." he began, then the rest of it, thirty full lines, not dropping a word this time, nor substituting an Italian for a Latin ending. All of the objects, too, were placed precisely on their designated spots, the arrow set unerringly toward the sunset; for a positive result was wanted, desperately. When he came to the "desired thing" Robert asked, simply, that Cassandra Fullerton of Winnetka, Illinois, born December 16, 1968, be made to love Robert Martin, now residing in Siena, Italy, in exactly the same manner and to exactly the same extent as the said Robert Martin had loved the said Cassandra Fullerton during the five years preceding. No more, no less, he would have added, but for fear of running too long in his speech and letting the allotted time elapse. He read the whole passage twice, named the 'wished-for' thing twice too, as required by the ceremony's rules, then blew his expired breath across the chart, as he had done so many times before now, in drill and in earnest, putting out the candle's flame.

Then he waited.

The days were longer now, just two days past the summer solstice. So the time till midnight would be brief: two hours or less to go from when he stowed his magic gear away. Yet it passed interminably. The whole afternoon had been like that—the abject agony of lingering anticipation. He went to read, but that was simply futile, as useless as a grieving widow's tears. So he sat silent by the open window, staring out into the darkness, waiting . . . waiting.

Midnight came in uninterrupted silence . . . then twelve-fifteen, the time passing like a paralytic snail, interminably . . . interminably. . . .

Nothing happened. He grew anxious, then restless, then wild, pacing the room as he had paced the condo on the day of Cassie's departure. The outside air was warm, thick, oppressive. He was sweating briskly, yet his hands were icy cold, his mouth a piece of chalk. He went into the bathroom for some water from the tap, then drank just a sip before it choked him. The magic hadn't work this time. Its power had run out; its time expired. Or maybe everything—the hot dogs, the winged wheel, the lottery, the diagram itself and all perceptible existence around it had been nothing but a phantom all the while. . . .

So one o'clock arrived and went, then one-thirty. Still, no sound came to break the silence. The room felt barren, insular, still. The wait had never been so long before: those hot dogs, the watermark, Auntwon's favorite wine—all had come at midnight or just minutes after. But now . . . an hour and a half past twelve and there'd been nothing, no effect at all. The crazy incantation—whatever the hell it was, however the hell it worked—had failed for once; yes, it had failed him utterly this time. Pathetically, too . . . the one and only longing he had felt in his life, the only wish he'd ever wanted answered for himself— that sole request and nothing more. . . . Yes, once he'd finally made up his mind, once he'd let his heart be opened wide again. . . .

But then he shook his head, shaking off the useless self-pity. What good did *that* do? Nothing—less than nothing. And anyway, maybe this one-time failure wasn't a fatal flaw, wasn't permanent. What if—sure— what if it turned out to be a simple error he had made? Maybe he'd skipped a word; lined the arrow up wrong; placed an object a fraction of an inch off-center. That's what he'd done with Auntwon the past week, and look what had happened—nothing! OK, so maybe by accident. . . .

Well, at any rate, he was no worse off than the day before. All but for his hopes, that is, his fondest expectations. Yet even the fondest of expectations could be recovered from in time. And there was always tomorrow, when he could try the thing again. . . . Ah, but if it only could have happened! . . . If he could have only heard her voice once again, seen her! . . . For once he had made up his mind at last, it seemed so hard. . . .

And just then—*just* then—at 1:43 in the saddest of all possible mornings . . . the phone rang.

"Robert? Is that you?"

"Yes...?"

"It's me . . . Cassandra. . . . Look, can I talk to you a minute? Don't hang up on me, Robert, please."

"No. I won't. Of course I won't."

"Listen, Robert . . . I know you're angry . . . I know you must be angry with me. . . ."

"No, not so much now, Cassie. . . . I mean . . . Cassandra."

"No, call me Cassie if you like. It's OK. You used to."

"Yes, but you said. . . ."

"I know—I always thought it was a little girl's name. But it's all right, though. I don't mind anymore."

"Are you. . . . I mean, is everything OK?"

"Yes, I'm fine—I feel all right, I mean. . . . Look . . . I miss you."

"Yes, well I've missed you too for weeks now. Months. It was almost intolerable at first, but now I'm starting to get a little better."

"So then you . . . you don't feel the same way as before?"

"Are you asking me if I still love you?"

"Yes. Yes, I am. I am."

"Hey, I never gave you the slightest cause to doubt my love, did I? . . . Look, all right, all right, never mind. . . . Yes, Cassie. Of course I still love you. Otherwise I never would have. . . ."

"What? Never would have *what*?"

"Nothing. I mean . . . I don't know. . . . I never would have . . . stayed on the phone, I guess. . . . Look, let's not talk about me right now. How do *you* feel? Do *you* love *me*?"

". . . Yes!" She was sobbing now, sounding woeful on the phone. "I need to see you, baby. I . . . I need to talk to you."

"Well, you know where I am, don't you?"

"Yes, of course. I had to call that friend of yours to get the number there. That guy Sheldon. He wasn't very nice to me. He's never been, you know?"

"Yeah, I know. He gets moody sometimes. . . . So what do you want to do?"

"I've got to come there."

"To Italy?"

"Yes. . . . Yes."

"OK. When?"

"Now. Whenever I can get a flight out. Maybe tomorrow or the next day."

"Do you need some money?"

"No, no, I'm fine. I've got more than enough."

"So what did you tell your pizza guy. Did you say anything?"

"Yes. We had a terrible fight. I left. I'm at my friend's place now. You spoke to her, I guess—Lenore? . . . Barris?"

"Yeah. So when did all this happen?"

"I don't know. It's been coming for a while. And then this evening—or tonight I guess it was—suddenly I just looked at him and knew that it was over. Just like that." She started sobbing again, so that she couldn't seem to speak for a while.

"Are you sure you're OK? He didn't hurt you or anything, did he?"

"No . . . no." She spoke between sniffles. "I . . . Robert, I . . . I love you, baby . . . I love you so much, I . . . I can't wait to . . . to see you. . . . Please don't . . . don't hate me. . . . Please . . . please!"

"I tried to hate you Cassie, but I couldn't. There's never been anyone else in my life but you. Never . . . never. You should have known that from the first, and never doubted it for an instant. You should always have known . . . always. . . . All right, look, the flight goes out Chicago to Frankfurt, then comes in to Florence, OK? On either American or Alitalia."

"Yeah. Yeah, OK. American or Alitalia. I'll write it down."

"All right, call me with your arrival time. I'll be at the airport waiting."

CHAPTER TWENTY-ONE

RECONCILIATION

HE WAS DREAMING OF HER—SOME BLISSFUL CONSTRUCT OF THE TWO OF them together on their sofa in the condo—when Cassie called back at seven. "Oh," she said, "I'm sorry, baby; were you sleeping?"—"No, no, just dozing," he answered, "it's all right."

She'd made her travel plans, she told him, working on the Internet until two in the morning Chicago time to get things done; a pair of Alitalia flights getting her in to Florence at one-fifteen p.m., Tuesday, June 27. "That's the first flight out I could arrange, darling. I can't wait to see you," she cooed. "Yes. Yes. Me too," he answered. He was half-asleep, though nonetheless elated, and so slipped back promptly into a postscript to the same delicious dream.

Then up at ten for good, shaved and dressed and out the door by 10:35, walking on a cloud, out into a street abandoned at that hour by Saturday night revelers and Sunday morning worshippers. He bumped into Filomena half a block down from the house.

"Good morning, Roberto."

"Ah, Filomena, hello! You're missing church today."

"Yes, *Mamma* is not feeling well. . . . So I went out to do some shopping." She held up a plastic bag with the heel of a bread loaf protruding from its neck. "And you? Where are you off to so early on a Sunday?"

"Oh, I've got some errands to do. I've got to rent a car and then reserve another room back at the hotel. . . . And do some shopping myself as well, but I guess nothing much'll be open today."

"No, not on Sunday. . . . But another room? Is . . . is Auntwon coming back, then? . . . But, well, he can stay with us, no?"

"No, it's not for Auntwon; it's for me—for *us*. . . . I'm getting some company."

"Company? But who...?"

"A lady friend."

"A lady? But. . . . Oh, I *see*—the woman you told me about, eh? The one who made you so happy."

"Yes, that's right."

"So you *did* call her, then, just as I told you to do."

"Yes, I guess I did—in a manner of speaking."

"I see. . . . And she will be coming here? To Siena?"

"Yes. Tuesday afternoon. Day after tomorrow."

"Ah, so soon!... Well good, good. . . . Yes, I am really happy for you, Roberto. It was truly the thing that you most wished for. . . . Yes, it is better after all that I convinced you to call her. I am really glad for you. Really."

"Well, I'll be moving out, of course. You'll tell your mother?"

"Yes, all right. I can take care of that. Certainly. . . . So then . . . you will return to a hotel now?"

"For a while—a week or so. Then we're off on a drive around Italy. Cassie's never been here. I want to show her Florence and Rome and Venice. . . ."

"I see. . . . Yes, that will be very nice for her. Well, Roberto, this is quite a surprise! But . . . yes, it is indeed for the best. Perhaps now you will be really happy again, the way you said you were before. . . . All right, let me just drop off these things and I shall go with you—to make your arrangements, I mean. You will need some help, I'm afraid."

"Help? Why do you say I'll need help?"

"Why! Don't you know what next week is? We spoke of it at supper yesterday, remember?"

"What?—Oh, that *palio* business, right?"

"Yes, of course, the *palio*. Look at all the banners in the streets! Haven't you noticed them?" Filomena pointed to a red and yellow flag of her *contrada*, the *Leocorno*, hanging from the facade of a building beside her. Oh, he had seen them, all right, the dappled Unicorn flag here and all the myriad others scattered throughout Siena, strewn like multi-colored blossoms above and along the ancient city streets. You couldn't really miss such garish things as these, unless you were half drunk or nearly blind. And even then, even if some putative drunk or blind man had made it past the bright, ubiquitous flags in dazed oblivion, he would soon enough have run into the barricades. Those, a whole monumental ellipse of them, were going up around the Campo to enclose the climactic horse race the Sienese plan a year in advance, run to its three-lap conclusion, then start the next year's planning for all over again.

They'd talked about it yesterday at luncheon, Signora Dall'Olmo going on and on about the race next week and their *contrada* and how fine it would be to beat the hated *Nicchio* and *Giraffa* districts' horses. He had heard her declaim about it; he had seen the banners and barricades; he knew very well the date the race was due to be run—July 2, a Sunday, a week precisely from today. He knew there would be festivities, too. For the *palio* is to Siena a sort of mardigras and Super Bowl and Kentucky Derby all rolled into one. He knew, finally, that tourists flocked to the city from far and wide to watch it, and that for the Sienese themselves the *palio* was a grand obsession, bordering on madness. . . . Yes, Robert knew everything essential about the race. But somehow, with so much weighing on his mind these past two weeks— the incantation and its amazing efficacy—well, the ramifications of all this *palio* nonsense had quite completely escaped him.

"So?" he asked, in understandable perplexity, "why do you say I'll need your help?"

"Why!—Roberto!—Because all the rooms within a hundred kilometers of Siena have been booked *months* ago—*years* perhaps!"

"They *have*?"

"Well, of *course* they have. *Mamma* can get two million *lire* a week for your room during *palio* if she chooses to rent it for that time alone. Siena will be a crazy place next week—how do you say it? A 'mad place'?."

"Uh, 'madhouse', we say. 'Madhouse'. . . . God, I hadn't even *thought* of that. It never even *occurred* to me. . . . So what do I do now? What do you suggest I do?"

"Well, let me just drop off these things at the house and we can get the car and drive around a bit to look. Maybe there will be a cancellation somewhere."

And so they did, starting with the Garibaldi, then going on to every other fashionable and rather less fashionable venue within and without the city walls. They tried some places on the highway, too, and in surrounding towns as far off as Grosseto. . . . But there was nothing, absolutely nothing, as Filomena had forecast: not a vacant lodging, not a bedroom, not an empty *cot*, anywhere within forty kilometers of metropolitan Siena.

And as for a car, well, every vehicle, from the nicest, biggest Opel down to the tiniest, most economical Fiat, was prereserved for the next entire week. When Robert inquired at the local Avis rental counter in the train station, the clerk laughed in his face. By four p.m., he was in a veritable frenzy.

"So what do I do now? What the hell am I supposed to do now?!"

"All right—look, it isn't so disastrous after all. You still have a room to stay in, at any rate."

"Yes, but. . . . You don't know Cassie. She won't stay there for long."

"No, I realize it isn't as nice as the hotel. . . ."

"Look, Filomena, I'm not saying it isn't nice. It's only that. . . ."

"Yes, I understand. But think a little, Roberto: it will be only temporary anyway. You can leave within a few days. Just explain to your friend about the *palio*. It's something she'll enjoy—the spectacle of it at least. It's really something incredible to see. Have you ever attended one?"

"No. I, uh . . . I came just after it was over—when I was here before. Six years ago, I mean."

"Well, this time you will see something truly amazing, I assure you. People come from all over the world to witness it. Last year I met a nice couple from the United States—from Pennsylvania, in fact—a Dr. Arthurs and his beautiful wife who studies art history. They came to see the art works of Siena and stayed in our home an extra week to watch the race. They loved it. It's really wonderful. Everything will begin on Thursday when the horses are assigned. Then there are parades and festivities up until the race on Sunday. It's like a carnival. Your lady friend will be fascinated, I can promise you that."

"I don't know. It takes a lot to fascinate her."

"Well, this will do it, I promise you. And I'm sure she'll understand how difficult it would have been for you to make any alternate arrangements at such late notice. She will be fine in our house for a few days, just fine—I shall see to it personally; and then you can rent your car and travel wherever you care to go."

"Yes, I suppose that makes some sense. I can take a taxi on Tuesday to pick her up in Florence. Then we can rent a car the Monday after *palio* and head out on our tour."

"That's right; you can leave immediately afterward. But a taxi will be terribly expensive. It's completely out of the question. No, Roberto, on Tuesday I shall drive you to the airport myself."

"Well?" asked Shelly on the phone at nine that night—it was two in the afternoon Chicago time—"She's really coming, eh?"

"Yeah. She called you, I heard."

"Sure did. Always a pleasure hearing that chirpy little voice of hers. . . . She sounded pretty humble, though. Different. . . . Look, let me ask you something, Bobby: this . . . this crazy thing you used—it's. . . . I'm not exactly sure what's supposed to have happened here."

"Nor I, Shelly. Nor I."

"All right, but . . . well, there's got to be some rational explanation for it, doesn't there? I mean, maybe somebody else was in on it. You know, some other person who could have called her for you, facilitated things. . . . How about Auntwon?"

"No. Look . . . the thing really works. It really does work."

"There's no chance it might have been just coincidence? You know, that she just happened to think of you at the same time you were thinking of her?"

"No, no, believe me: something strange is happening—*has* happened. Look, Auntwon saw it too. He was sitting right here in the room with me."

"And what exactly was it that he saw? What happened—I mean with Auntwon there?"

"It's hard to describe over the phone. Things change. . . . People change too—as you've seen."

"You mean Cassandra?"

"Yeah, sure. Who else?"

"Oh, I don't know. I wouldn't be too damn certain of the kind of change you'd like to see in her—not with your girlfriend anyway. Look, what exactly did you tell the thing to do?"

"I asked it to make her love me."

"That's it?"

"Yeah, that's the only thing I really wanted. . . . The *only* thing."

"Well, maybe you should have asked for the lobotomy too—for her I mean. . . . Look, for what it's worth, I'd guess your—whatever it is— worked on the love part. She sounded pretty obsessed with finding you when she called here last night. Almost frantic, in fact. But she's still the same awful person she always was, Bobby. Be careful."

"Careful? I don't know you mean."

"Come on! You know *exactly* what I mean. Exactly. She's a sadistic little bitch, your girlfriend. I don't think the greatest love in the world is gonna change that."

"You haven't seen her with me, Shelly. She can be wonderful."

"Wonderful, eh? Well, just be careful. You've got ten thousand bucks in your account and I'm not gonna transfer another goddamn penny into it until you get home. Just be careful, Bobby. I hope you haven't wished for something even your best friend can't protect you from."

Filomena was sweet as usual but taciturn, wrapped in thought all the way to Florence. They got to the airport a full hour early at his vehement insistence, then sat at a little table with some *pasticcini* and coffee till the plane came in at one-fifteen, right on time.

Filomena took a seat in a departure lounge chair, while Robert stood waiting as close to the arriving passengers as the moderate crowd would permit. When the exit door swung open and the first passenger stepped through, his heart rose to his throat. Ten people came out, twenty. . . .

Then he saw her: the elegant form, the faultless face, just as he had visualized her in his mind so many hundreds of times before. And her extraordinary beauty drawing nearer, a beauty at once both simple and exquisite on this petulant-sweet, girl-woman, with her incomparable little pout and jet black eyes. In all his life he had never seen any other woman so perfect, any other woman so mesmerizing. Whatever she had done, whatever it was that had separated them meant nothing to him now—now that she was here, beheld, experienced. Everything so recently painful had vanished utterly. For she would be with him again, irrevocably, from this moment forth, forever.

She inched a little closer, slowed by the deplaning passengers, not able to see him at first for the close-packed crowd of greeters at the gate. But finally, half a dozen steps away, she glanced up into his eyes and broke into a frightened little smile. She looked exhausted, anguished . . . but beautiful . . . so beautiful that it made his mouth water, his heart race.

"Robert!" she said, nothing more, then rushed up and buried her face in his shirt, wetting it through with her tears. Around him the universe swam, then vanished. And there was nothing beyond him but Cassie . . . Cassie . . . as he melded with her, became one with her. The scent of her hair and skin, the feel of her body in his arms, the whisper of her breath, filled him with something indescribable, something he had feared he'd lost forever. . . . Ah yes, he remembered: those chemicals they'd told him about—some kind of epinephrine, and the other one . . . oxy-something. . . . Ah, what did it matter! Whatever the names, the feelings they evoked were delicious, overpowering. . . .

"God, Cassie!" he whispered, "how I've missed you! I've missed you so much! So much!..."

She stroked the back of his neck, up and down, up and down, her hand tremulous, insistent. "I know, I know," she said. "I'll never hurt you again, baby. I'll never hurt you. Ever. . . ."

"OK; it's OK. Let's not even think about any of that stuff right now."

"No, you're right. It's all behind us. I love you, Robert; I really do. I never realized how much until just the other day."

"All right, look, none of that matters now. It doesn't matter what happened or when. Don't think about anything but the present. And the future. We'll be happy from now on, Cassie—Cassandra—I promise you that."

"It's OK to call me Cassie, baby: I told you that the other day. Really, I don't mind at all."

"All right, then, Cassie. Cassie." He kissed her on the brow. "I do love you, baby. I always have. More than you could ever know. . . . And we'll be happy together; I'll *make* you happy. I'll give you everything you could ever want."

"I just want *you*, Robert. Just you. Don't you know that? I mean, I . . . I had everything I thought I wanted and I left it for you. Don't you understand that?"

"I guess so. I guess I do. . . ."

"You're still angry, aren't you? . . . It's all right; I don't blame you."

"No, I'm really not. Not anymore, I mean. Maybe I was at first, but that's all over with. All I care about is that you're back. That's all that's important to me right now. Nothing else."

"Well, I've got a lot of things to explain, I know. God, some of it I can't even understand myself. I mean, how could I have *done* what I did to you? How *could* I have? And how could it have taken me so long to realize what was really important in my life? . . . You know, Robert, it's amazing how it all came to me in an instant like that. . . . It was like . . . like I was asleep and suddenly woke up. . . . I don't know. . . . It sounds really crazy, I guess. It's hard for me even to explain."

"All right, never mind; we'll talk about it another time. . . . Look . . . uh, look. . . ." He backed a little bit away from her, still holding her by the shoulders. "I want you to meet someone." He waved to Filomena and the girl got up and stepped over beside them.

"Cassie, this is Filomena Dall'Olmo; Filomena, Cassie—Cassandra Fullerton. . . . Filomena and her mother own the house I've been staying in."

Cassie put her hand out, but rigidly, icily, casting off her newfound amiability like a threadbare coat.

"Filomena, is it?" she asked.

"Yes, ma'am."

"Oh, you don't have to call me 'ma'am'. I'm not all that much older than you are."

"No. I know. That is . . . I just meant to be respectful, Miss Fullerton."

"Of course you did. . . . But . . . why don't you just call me Cassandra, OK? Let's be friends" She gave Filomena that radiant, billion-dollar smile.

"Yes, OK. . . . Cassandra, then," said the girl, smiling back but with dentition of considerably less worth.

"And you're from around here, are you? From Italy?"

"Yes, ma—I mean, Cassandra. . . . From Siena."

"Really! And you hardly have an accent. It's amazing."

"Yes, well, I am a student of English literature, so I've been speaking English for many years now. I expect to teach eventually."

"To teach! Great! I hope things are better for teachers here than they are in the States. Half of the Ph.D.'s in English there are driving cabs or waiting tables. But I'll bet that you're so clever you'll get a position of some kind eventually."

The girl drove them home in her shiny Mercedes, Cassie beside her in the front seat. Robert, meanwhile, dozed in the back, not having slept a wink the night before in restless anticipation. Just outside of Siena, he awoke groggily to hear the two women speaking.

". . . .and where is that?" Cassie asked.

"It's west of Siena. About a three-hour drive."

"So far? Well, wasn't it nice of you to take him all that way!"

"Oh, I enjoyed it. Roberto is. . . ."

"*Roberto?*"

"Yes, that's what I call him. It's the Italian version of his name."

"Yes, dear, I would have been quite capable of figuring that out all by myself."

"All right. I'm sorry if I. . . ."

"No. Never mind. . . . So what exactly did you do there, the two of you?"

"In Assisi? Not anything exciting. He just wanted to visit the town and the basilica."

"Why?"

"Well, but for his research, of course."

"And what research might that be?"

"On Colangio—you know: the manuscript."

"Oh, not more of that old Colangio stuff again! I thought he'd mined that subject dry ages ago!"

"No, those new papers they found—he must have told you about them. . . . I find it quite fascinating, actually."

"Yes, it sounds as if you do. . . . Maybe you'd like to be his next research assistant—He loves to have sweet young research assistants around."

"I don't understand. . . ."

"No? Don't you? . . . I think maybe you do."

They had reached the exit for Siena, and Filomena turned off, then started up the rugged hillside toward the town. There were distractions now, the dramatic aspect of a Tuscan fortress-city, its monumental walls. The women fell silent, Filomena probably attentive to the traffic, Cassandra, perhaps, to the strange and lovely sights she was seeing for the first time.

The narrow, populous streets of the city slid by, and Robert awoke again to find the car coming to a stop outside the Dall'Olmos' front door. He shook off his stupor, grabbed Cassie's two cases from the trunk, and started in with them, while Filomena, with a nod, set off for the garage.

The bags were infinitely lighter than Cassie's standard gear, so it was effortless for Robert to get them upstairs. Cassandra, following on his heels, wheeled on him in fury the instant they stepped into his room.

"Did you sleep with her?"

"What?"

"That girl. Did you screw her?"

"Filomena? No, of *course* not. How can you even *ask* me that?"

"How?—I saw the way she looked at you; the way she talked to you—that's how!"

"No—come on Cassie! She's just friendly like that. Candid, sort of."

"Friendly? *How* friendly?"

"Like a sister, all right? Nothing more than that. Nothing."

"You swear it?"

"Yes, of course I do. She's been a friend, that's all. . . . Look, what's gotten into you? Come here." She stepped over dutifully to where he was standing by the bed and he kissed her properly, at last, open-mouthed, the way they hadn't been able to kiss at the airport. She clung to him, strangely tactile, rubbing against his chest, his belly, kissing his neck.

"Can we go to bed now?" she asked, running her hand along his pant leg. "I know you want to."

"Oh, God. . . . Not yet, though, not yet. They'll be knocking on the door in a minute—Filomena will: she'll be up to see if we need anything. Look, we've got the whole night ahead of us, baby—I can hardly wait, either. . . . I guess you can tell, though, huh?"

She smiled and looked up at him, eyes narrowed, lips apart, sweeping his face with those black-brown eyes of hers, locking him in. "I miss the feel of you inside me," she said, then reddened and looked away like some adolescent schoolgirl sensing passion for the first time. "God, look what you're doing to me, Robert! I can't believe I said that! God!"

Five minutes later, still entwined in her arms, her breath still warm in his nostrils, he heard Filomena's inevitable tapping on the door. He pulled himself away, straightened his inseam, set Cassie reluctantly on the bed, and ushered the girl in.

"*Mamma* is preparing something for the two of you to eat. Cassandra, you must be rather hungry after the long flight."

"Yes, dear, thank you; that's very nice. I suppose I *could* eat something."

"Well in half an hour, please, come down and we shall feed you both."

"Thanks, Filomena," he told the girl. "Cassie's probably exhausted, so we'll get a little supper in her and get her into bed."

The meal began well enough: ravioli and a delicious pork dish that Robert had never tasted before. Cassie seemed famished. She ate more ravenously than he had seen her eat in years. But when she had finished with her meat and pasta and had emptied the second glass of wine that Filomena poured out for her, the look in her eyes began to change. She became by degrees less cordial; then, moments afterward and by less subtle degrees, her manner turned noticeably cold and distant. Wine coupled with fatigue often affected her that way, so Robert failed to realize the meaning of her mood swing in time.

"Can I help you with the dishes, dear?" she asked Filomena after finishing yet a third glass of wine. Her voice was as sweet as usual, but there was a subtle hint of rancor submerged in it.

"No, no, you are our guest."

"But I'd *like* to. *Please*. It'll give us womenfolk a chance to talk."

"To talk? But . . . well, all right then, if you wish." The girl got up, picked up her plate and her mother's, then reached for Robert's: "Have you finished, Roberto? Would you like some more wine?"

"Yes, *Row-bear-tow*," echoed Cassie, mocking the name, "drink up. You're gonna need it tonight!"

He smiled her ridicule away and answered the girl. "No thanks. . . . Uh, look, Filomena . . . maybe Cassie and I had better head upstairs. She's had a really long day. . . ."

"Don't be silly, Robert! I'm fine, just fine! I'm wide awake now." Cassie pushed herself up now too, grabbed the dinnerware in front of her, and followed Filomena into the kitchen. That left him and Signora Dall'Olmo alone at the table.

"*Che bella ragazza!*" said the nice little lady, remarking Cassie's beauty.

He thanked her for the compliment, then, more effusively, for the meal. It had been unnecessary, unexpected, but was no less welcome for its spontaneity; she had been an exemplary host to take the time and trouble to prepare so excellent a supper for them on such short notice.

"*Ma si figuri!*" she answered: Don't mention it! His lovely lady seemed very nice, very elegant. It had been an honor to meet her, as it had been quite as well to have him in their home these past few weeks. . . . "*A proposito*," she said—by the way: Had he heard yet from "Antonio"? She meant Auntwon, of course. No, not yet, he answered, *non ancora*, the kid—*il ragazzo*—should be leaving Florence for Rome any time soon. He'd most likely phone when he arrived.

They chatted amiably on for five minutes more, exchanging vague pleasantries while water splashed in the kitchen sink a doorway away and dishes clattered on the kitchen counter. Then, jarringly—so jarringly that the signora nearly popped straight out of her chair—a dish shattered on the kitchen floor, its clash of demise unmuffled by the masonry between. Just seconds later Filomena burst through the door, her eyes glistening with tears. She rushed past the dinner table, then out the exit door to the hall. Through the open doorway, Robert heard her footsteps on the stairs, ascending hurriedly to the residential rooms above.

Cassie stepped from the kitchen maybe ten seconds later, a calculated smile upon her face.

"What happened?" Robert demanded, rising from his seat. She shrugged.

"*Cosa succede*? echoed the signora, repeating his question in the present tense. She was standing now too. She turned a little to her right to face Cassie, then a little to her left to face Robert, then a little farther leftward toward the open door. Finally she set off slowly toward the doorway, passed through it, and followed her daughter's footsteps up the stairs.

"Cassie, for God's sake! What the hell happened in there?" He reached for her arm and grasped it tight, turning her to face him frontally.

"Nothing, darling. She dropped a plate; that's all."

"Dropped a plate! Come on! Did you see her? The girl was crying!"

"So? Maybe they cry in Italy when they drop plates."

"Yeah? You think so?" He shook her angrily, still holding her by the upper arm. "Come on! What the hell did you say to her? You must have said something. . . ."

"Said something? Like what?"

"I don't know what, Cassie! That's why I asked you. Now what the hell's going on? What the hell happened in there?"

"Nothing, Robert. Nothing. Really."

"No? Nothing? You come with me right now. We'll discuss it when we get upstairs."

He pulled her to the staircase then let her go, running up the steps two at a time, leaving her half a flight behind—notwithstanding those forty-minute sessions of hers on the stair climber. And when he had reached his room, and she had slunk in behind him, visibly subdued, he turned to her and in a voice a little out of breath but manfully controlled asked:

"All right, Cassie, now what did you say to her? You need to tell me. NOW."

"Nothing, Robert. Really. . . . I . . . all I did was ask her. . . ." She stopped in mid-sentence and wrenched her head down and away from his gaze.

"Ask her what? What was it that you asked her?"

"About you."

"What *about* me? What specifically did you ask her about me?"

She kept her head everted and said nothing.

"*What*, Cassie? What exactly did you ask her? I want to know NOW!"

"I . . . I asked her why she was hanging around you so much. Chasing you, you know?"

"You *what*!... How could you do that, huh? I told you, didn't I? I explained it all to you. . . ."

"Come on, Robert, I'm not blind; I'm not stupid. I know the girl likes you. Don't tell me she doesn't. Don't try to lie to me. I can tell she does. I can tell."

"Jesus, Cassie! So what if she does? What if she *did* have a schoolgirl crush on me? She's just a kid, for God's sake, like a little sister, that's all."

"To *you*, maybe. She's like a little sister to *you*. She's got other ideas. Don't try to tell me that she doesn't."

"I don't know. Look, I never touched her, all right? I never so much as touched her. . . . You know, I've got to get used to this. You've never been jealous of me before. Not in all those years we were together."

"I'm *not* jealous. I'm *not*! It's her! It's *her*! She's. . . ." She turned her back and started to cry, to sob, covering her face with her hands. He reached out to her, touched her shoulder and she turned back around and fell shuddering against his chest.

"I love you so much, Robert." Her words were muffled by the pressure of her cheek against his shirt. He felt the moisture of her tears clear through to his skin, warm and sticky-wet. "I . . . I never realized how much until these past few days." she continued, muttering nasally between sobs. "Don't you . . . understand that? . . . I don't know, Robert. . . . I just don't . . . I just don't know what's come over me. I . . . I feel powerless. . . . I. . . . It's different from anything I've ever felt before. . . . I don't . . . have any control over . . . anything. . . . I just. . . . I don't have the least control. . . ."

Her words and tears and flagrant misery erased his anger. "OK, look, look," he said, tracing the curve of her wet and aesthetically perfect cheek with a finger, "I understand. . . . I'm sorry. Look, Cassie, I never meant for any of this to hurt you. . . ."

"So you *did* sleep with her, then! You *did*!"

"No. I didn't. I swear to you."

"Then what did you mean about hurting me? How could you have hurt me if you didn't sleep with her? Hey, *I'm* the one who's supposed to have hurt *you*, remember? *I'm* the one."

"Yes, I know. I know. . . . All right, look, I swear I never touched the girl. I never even thought of it, OK? . . . Come on: we've talked long enough, haven't we? We're alone now. We're finally alone." He sat down on the bed and put out his hand, drawing her to him. "I've dreamt for the last three months about being with you again, baby. Let's not talk anymore, OK?"

"No," she said, "you're right, you're right. I'm sorry." She leaned into him, her lips on his neck, her left hand on his thigh, trembling, kneeding. Then the hand moved up to his collar and undid each button of his shirt in sequence, top to bottom, slowly but insistently. She spread the fabric open, put her lips to the center of his chest, licked him with her tongue, then ran the tongue in a straight line up to his throat.

"Come on, darling," she said, "come on. I can't wait a minute more. I want you inside me." She crawled around him, stretched out flat on the bed and began to undo her blouse.

"All right," he answered. "Let me just go to the bathroom for a minute, OK?"

"Yeah, OK . . . but hurry."

He used the toilet, rinsed his mouth, brushed his teeth in haste. She was a different woman this evening, radically different from the calculating lover she had been these five years past. Since they had met, the preface to their coupling had followed an invariable pattern: she would fold away her clothes, bathe thoroughly, brush her teeth, floss them, cleanse her body so completely that not a trace of human scent could be discovered clinging to it anywhere. She smelled then solely of *Quelques Fleurs* and balsam shampoo and bath gelee and—if there happened to be a glass of it on the nightstand beside her—from time to time of fruity *pinot noir*.

His own ablutions would of necessity be the same. It was required of him that he, too, brush, floss, pare his nails, then scrub his skin as aseptically clean as a surgeon's hands before he made the slightest move to touch her. The room would have to be pitch black, the blinds and windows shut. And, finally, unfailingly, a bath towel, fluffed and freshly laundered, would be carefully arranged beneath her buttocks, lest an errant drop of fluid trickle down to soil the bed-clothes beneath.

But not, as it seemed, tonight!

No. Amazingly—*Amazingly!*—this one extraordinary evening, no precoital preparations of any kind had been demanded or performed. Here, then, was Cassie, fresh from an exhausting day of travel running on to ten full hours in the air. Her clothes had gone unchanged and now lay strewn haphazardly beside the bed. The natural chemistry of her body remained unaltered; her teeth unflossed, her mouth no doubt fresh enough, but certainly unsanitized.

And no demands had been made of him either—no preparatory shower, no antiseptic spray. "Make love to me," she seemed to be saying for the first time in their lives together. "Here. Now. Without hindrance or delay. Make love to me, as I will do to you; the hazards of contagion be damned."

He stepped back into the bedroom, aroused by the thought of her, the unaltered female scent, the natural spontaneity of their passion. There was a lamp on, illuminating her body sideways on the right-hand conjoined bed. The covers had been thrust aside onto the fellow mattress, the under-sheet exposed. And he could see her perfect form foreshortened, her black hair splashed upon the pillow, then the thick fur triangle down below her belly, like some fervid little creature lying silent on her lap.

"Come on, baby, come on," she murmured, raising one knee, bringing her cleft into view, and he moved toward her, unashamedly erect. The room was warm, despite the open window, for the evening was sultry. He snapped off the light and slid in beside her, kissing her wetly, tasting the pork and capers and smelling now a hint of perspiration, which he had never before sensed upon her body—never before in all those five indelible years they'd been together. It excited him uncontrollably.

He moved down and kissed her immaculate breast, then beneath it, touching her now beneath the wet fur of her pelvis. . . .

"Oh, God," she said, "Oh *God*!" and clasped his neck tightly. . . .

But then, suddenly, her hand relaxed. He felt her body loosen too and fall minutely away. She cleared her throat, slipped her fingers down to his shoulder, pushed him gently up and off of her, slid a little to the side, then spoke:

"Darling. . . ." she murmured, whispering as softly as the inconspicuous wind itself, fluttering in gently at the window:

". . . Robert darling . . . I'm afraid you've forgotten our towel."

~~~~~~~~~

SOLUTION

THE NEXT FEW DAYS WERE LIKE A HONEYMOON, AND CASSIE . . . WELL, Cassie was like the dream he had always had of her, like the woman he had always wanted her to be: Beautiful—which she had never ceased to be to him—but sweet too, and affectionate. And, on top of it all— on top of everything else—demonstrably and excruciatingly in love.

They strolled around the city like a pair of star-struck teens, hand-in-hand or arms about each others' waists. She would stop and kiss him on the street, hungrily, lingeringly, to the tittering of women passers-by. She would touch his thigh at table during lunch or dinner. Then, back in their room, she could hardly get enough of him, always with the towel beneath her, perhaps; but with a frenzied intensity that was stridently different from all those other times they'd been together in the past.

He took her to the Duomo, to the Medici fortress, around the Campo, up the Mangia tower. They ate at *La Torre* and *L'Agrigento*, sipped cappuccino at outdoor cafes across from the Palazzo Pubblico. They read to each other, bathed each other, stared into each others' eyes at twilight. On Thursday he found her a proper salon—Caterina provided the directions—then sat looking on in rapt admiration while she had her hair styled, her nails done, an hour-long facial in a separate room. Amazingly, she didn't complain too much. Oh, the stylist was a little antiquated, the manicure short of Chicago standards, the facialist clumsy and provincial. . . .

But she was content, subdued. A look from him—a single frown or word of admonition—would serve to quash any pettiness she might begin to show. She seemed dependent, domesticated. Of course he kept her to himself—exclusively to himself—for she could quickly turn vicious with other females around. Like Filomena, for notable example, whom they saw only now and then on leaving in the morning or returning in the afternoon. Just a 'hello' or '*buon giorno*' or '*buona sera*' was all the conversation that the three of them exchanged. The girl herself must have scented Cassandra's latent fury, and known enough to stay a room or two away.

Three memorable days that lasted, from Tuesday morning right up to early Friday. Then, that Friday morning early, a little after nine, Filomena climbed the long, protesting staircase and tapped on Robert's door in her habitual little way.

"Roberto? Cassandra? Are you in there?"

"Yes, come on in, Filomena. The door's unlocked."

She looked neat as a teenage schoolgirl in her pleated skirt and short-sleeved blouse. There were a couple of portentous-looking volumes in her hand, thick trade paperbacks of the exegetical and literary type, announcing her imminent departure for class. "Ah, good morning," she said. "I . . . I wanted to tell you: Auntwon called last evening."

"He called *you*?"

"Yes. It seems that the two of you were not in your room at the time."

"No? . . . Oh, that's right. We took a little stroll after supper."

"Who is she talking about, Robert?" Cassie asked. "Is that the student you told me about? The, uh . . . uh . . . *you* know."

"Yeah. Auntwon Miller—the kid who was here visiting me. . . . So what did he say, Filomena? Does he need anything?"

"No. He's leaving Florence and traveling to Rome."

"When?"

"Tomorrow."

"OK, good. Did he say he'd call back?"

"Well, actually . . . I talked him into stopping here on his way south."

"You did!"

"Yes . . . to see the *palio*, you know? I told him all about it."

"That's great!... That's great, Cassie; you'll get to meet him."

She shrugged and raised her eyebrows.

"So when? . . . When is he due in?"

"Tomorrow about noon. *Mamma* is making up his room right now."

"Terrific! She doesn't mind?"

"*Mamma*? With her 'Antonio'?"

"No, I guess not." He smiled. "Well, thank her for me, will you?"

"Yes, of course. . . . Listen, Roberto . . . I have a friend who has a house in the Campo, and I have been thinking. . . . You plan to attend the *palio*, no? The horse race?"

"Sure, as long as we've got to stay in Siena anyway. And we can't leave till Monday morning when there's a car available, so. . . . ." He shrugged.

"Well, I was thinking that . . . perhaps you would like to watch the *palio* from my friend's home. The crowds are really horrid in the square and if you don't go hours early it's hard to see a thing. . . . But I could— if you would like me to—arrange for all of us to watch the race from an excellent vantage point. There is a big room on the third floor of my friend's house that we have used in previous years. Besides, you and Cassandra will be leaving soon, and we can have a kind of farewell party for you there if you agree. Auntwon will be back by then, and I can ask Caterina and Signor Fabbri to come as well. . . . And anyone else you can think of if you'll just let me know."

"Caterina? Who's Caterina?" asked Cassie, warily.

"*You* know. . . . Fabbri's secretary—she gave us directions to that beauty shop, remember? You met her over at the Piccolomini a couple of days ago."

"Oh, yes, that older woman; that's right. OK."

"So it's all right to arrange things then?" asked Filomena. "Is it all right with you, Cassandra?"

"Yes, why not? I don't care. We'll be leaving soon after that, won't we, Robert?"

"Yes, of course; the next day. I just have to pick up the car Monday morning."

"Fine, then." Cassie answered the girl without a glance in her direction. "It's fine with me. I wasn't planning on standing around for hours in a crowd anyway."

"Excellent!" said Filomena. "I'll arrange things today then. Signor Fabbri will be at the Piccolomini this afternoon, Roberto?"

"Sure, far as I know."

"OK then, I'll stop there after lunch to invite him. . . . Oh, Roberto. . . ."

"Yes?"

"I shall ask *Mamma* to prepare something special for our guests on Sunday. . . . Would you like to have your favorite dish once more?"

The four of them got to the train station at quarter to twelve. It was crowded: no one departing on this day before *palio*, but thirty or more Sienese there to meet arriving passengers. Maybe fifteen people got off, Auntwon dead last, stepping down onto the platform expectantly, with his threadbare orange jacket tied about his waist and Annamae's battered little suitcase in his hand. Cassie was cordial, though cool, on being introduced. Auntwon, on the other hand, was at his sanguine and articulate best.

"It's a pleasure to meet you, ma'am," he said. "It's real nice that you got a chance to come over to Italy and visit the Doc here."

They rode together in the back seat, Auntwon, Robert, and Cassie. Just a ten minute ride from the station to the Dall'Olmos' place, but the kid had filled them in on every particular of his trip thus far by the time they reached the house.

"So where did you stay?" prompted Robert.

"OK, there's, like, this. . . . I mean, there's—that is, I found a kind of hostel. I met a lot of people there, too, from all over the world. And I seen . . . I mean I *saw* everything there was to see in Florence. . . . Man! That San Marco—you know, with the Fra Angelico paintings...?"

"You're from Chicago, is that right?" Cassie asked.

"Yes, ma'am, right near downtown, a little bit south of the loop."

"Ah, yes. Not a very nice area, I'd imagine."

"No, well I don't have . . . uh, anything to compare it with. There's some rough places around there, though, that's for sure."

"And you were in one of Robert's classes, I understand?"

"Yes, ma'am, the Renaissance history course."

"Tell me: did you know a girl named Lipsky from the class?"

"Uh, yes, ma'am. Sandra. Sandra Lipsky. She sat in front of me."

"What's she like?"

"Like, ma'am?"

"Yes, what does she look like? Is she pretty?"

"Damn! I mean . . . I don't know. It's hard for me to judge. I guess she looks OK for a. . . ."

"For a what? What were you going to say?"

"Uh, nothing. I forget. I musta lost my train of thought. I guess she looks OK for . . . for . . . one of the ladies from the University of Chicago. The school ain't . . . uh, *isn't* exactly celebrated for, like, feminine pulchritude, you know what I'm . . . uh, what I mean?"

They pulled up to the house a minute later. Auntwon dropped off his suitcase, Filomena stowed the car in the garage, and the five of them walked over to the Campo to watch the preparations for the following day's events.

It hardly seemed the same historic place it had been a week before. Barricades and stands had been erected around the circuit of the piazza; sidewalk cafes had been retracted into buildings; circumjacent awnings had been furled; and there was now, beside all that, "*terra in piazza*," a thick layer of clayey earth laid down like an unpaved country road along the course the race would be run. Twenty-eight hours to go, and the entire Campo—the whole city of Siena in fact—had been converted into nothing but a makeshift racecourse in a fancy setting.

The earthen track itself was a hotbed of activity. Jockeys milled about inspecting some of the horses; grooms attended others, brushing them, sponging them down, leading them around the track. Then beside and between the animals and their human accompanists were men of pageantry. Clad in Renaissance costumes echoing the colors and patterns of their individual district banners, they marched, pranced, and tossed multicolored flags, rehearsing for their famous display of standards prior to the next day's race. Meanwhile, outside the flattened oval track, over against the buildings, stood captains of *contrade* in coalescing groups arranging their districts' alliances and conspiracies.

Filomena explained it all to them: the curious participants, their functions, the hazards of the race. Now and then she would turn and ask her mother something: a detail of the *palio*'s history or a bit of gossip about a rider—then translate the answer into English for Cassie and Auntwon. They strolled about the Campo for an hour or so, then Robert took them all to *La Torre* for lunch. Cassie, thankfully, was hungry, ate with remarkable gusto, and thus spoke not a syllable during the meal.

"Hey, Doc," said Auntwon when he had finished his dessert, "come on with me. I want to climb up that tower again."

"What, *now*? After we just ate?"

"Yeah, we'll go up slow."

"I don't know, Auntwon. . . ."

"Come on, man, I'm only in town for a day."

Robert shrugged. "You want to join us?" he asked Cassie, who declined as he'd been certain she would. He walked with Auntwon along the periphery of the earthen track until they had reached a point a hundred yards or so beyond the restaurant. Then the kid abruptly opened up:

"Hey, Doc, I was tryin' to getchu away f'om her to, like, rap witchu some in private, you know?"

"Yeah, I kind of thought that's what you were up to."

"OK, man, so whass been happenin'? You used the thang, right? On yo' lady friend back there?"

"Yep. Just as you prescribed. It worked amazingly well, as you can see."

"Yeah." Auntwon shook his head and smiled. "Thass cool, man. . . . She don't know nuffin' yet, though, right?"

"Are you *kidding*?"

"Yeah, thass cool, man, thass cool. Don' tell her nuffin' neither, OK? . . . So, anyways: thangs been workin' out OK witchu? I mean, the lady cool wif evvythang?"

"Well . . . yes and no. I mean, she's OK when we're alone together. But she's . . . well . . . almost intolerable with other women around. . . . Like Filomena, for example—I was a little bit afraid of leaving them together in the restaurant back there."

"Yeah, I know whatchu mean. She was lookin' like crossedways at Filomena. I figured somefin' gotta be up."

"It's crazy, Auntwon. She's like a devil when she gets into that jealous mode of hers. She gets absolutely paranoid, you know?"

"You sure ditten ax fo' nuffin like 'at, huh?"

"Hardly. It's strictly a side-effect. . . . I just asked the damned thing to make her love me—to make her feel about *me* exactly the same way I felt about *her* back at the beginning. And I guess she does. . . . I guess she finally does."

"Well you know what they say, man: 'be careful what you wish fo'.' . . . But you cool widdit all, ain'tchu? I mean, it, like, workin' out satisfactorily fo' you, right?"

"Yeah. In general it is—only. . . ."

"On'y what?"

"I don't know, I guess the artificiality of everything still bothers me. . . . And besides . . . I feel a little guilty about changing her into . . . well, into what she's become. It isn't *her* exactly. Sometimes—I don't know—sometimes she seems really miserable. Unhappy I mean, you know?"

"Yeah, jus' like you a coupla months ago."

"I guess so. Love can be wonderful, but it can also be devastating. It's hard to make someone you really care for get that sad."

"Man, I woult'n feel too guilty aboutcho girlfriend a'ter what she done to you. No, I say you got to go wif the flow, Doc, go wif the flow. . . . So, I gotta ax you somep'm else, man—you ain't got ta answer me if you don' want to."

"No, that's OK. What is it?"

"I jus' been wonderin'—so, look-a-here, you still love the lady like you did befo'?"

"Yeah. . . . Yeah, that'll never change—not now, for sure, the way she is with me. . . . But . . . well, I'm just coming to realize she's not quite as nice a person as I once thought she was."

"Shit, man, you thought she was *nice*? Man, you *really* fucked up!—Sorry, Doc, but thass the honest truf."

"Well, Auntwon, it might seem like that to you, but—I don't know—she was nice to *me*. At first, anyway. And then she changed so gradually, so subtly . . . I guess I really never noticed the change. . . . But she really *can* get mean—almost sadistic, I think, at times. Once you come to accept that, it makes everything a whole lot harder."

"So why don'tchu jus' use that thang on her again? You know, kinda like transform her nature? I bet that'd work."

"Yeah, I thought of doing just that, and I might actually have to in the end. But it's got to be some time in the unforseeable future—you know, after we've moved into more spacious quarters. Right now I can hardly get away from her long enough to brush my *teeth* in peace, let alone do all the stuff I'd have to do to use that incantation again. . . . And if she ever caught wind of the fact that I'd found something like that, and then figured out what I might have *used* it for. . . . God, I can't even *imagine* what she'd do!"

Their steps had brought them finally to the Palazzo Pubblico, which they entered to find an endless line of people waiting to tour the place, and then a second line, not a whole lot shorter, queuing up to climb the tower. Robert started toward the ticket booth, but Auntwon grabbed him by the shirtsleeve and held him back.

"Whatchu *doin'*, Doc?"

"I've got to get the tickets."

"Hey, man, you don' actually wanna climb this thang for real, do you?"

"Me? No, not in the least; I thought *you* did."

"Shee-yit, man, no. . . . Naw. I jus' wannit to rap witchu fo' while, like I said. . . . OK, look-a-here: less jus' set here fo' a little bit, then get on back and ax yo' girlfriend if she seen us wavin' at her f'om the top."

There were thousands in the streets, revelers and lookers-on. Through the open window came a babble of inseparable voices, talking, laughing, cheering; male and female, drunk and sober, old and young. Then, high above the chattering cacophony, a distant trumpet blared. "Ta-ta-TA," it went, "ta-ta-TA. . . ." until the patter of the crowd subsumed its strident melody again. Robert, beckoned by the chaos, stepped to the window, stuck his head through, then pulled back inside and swung the shutters inward, muffling a portion of the din.

"Whew! It's an oven out there," he muttered, mostly to himself; then, in the direction of the bathroom, called out in a louder voice: "Hey, baby, you about ready?"

"Almost, darling. You really want to go to this horse race thing?"

"Yeah, sure. I mean . . . they're having a party for us, you know?"

She snapped the bathroom light off and stepped through the doorway, looking radiant as ever. "Oh, that party!" she said, with a wave of her hand. "Who cares? Who cares about those people anyway? It's not like we're ever gonna see them again."

"Well, I'm sure I'll be seeing lots of Auntwon at least. After we get back home, I mean. . . . Hey, you look great! Where'd you get that blouse?"

"Oh, someplace in Winnetka. . . . Uh, listen, Robert . . . . by the way . . . I just can't understand why you're spending so much time with that kid."

"Auntwon you mean?"

"Uh-huh."

"You've got to get to know him better, talk to him a while. . . . He's brilliant."

"Well you sure wouldn't know it to look at him. . . . Did you see that jacket he had on? . . . But . . . Robert?"

"Yes, baby?'

"You wouldn't . . . you wouldn't have him over to our place, though, would you?"

"What place?"

"Our condo, of course."

"In Lincoln Park? Oh, that's right. I never told you, did I? I never even thought of it till now. . . . It's sold."

"*Sold*! What do you mean, 'sold'?"

"Well, *sold*. I sold it."

"You sold it! But . . . but what about our things? All our stuff there?"

"Sold."

"The Phaidon sofa? The antiques?"

"Yep. Sold. Everything. . . . Hey, don't worry, we can get plenty more."

"With what?"

"We'll have lots of money coming in. More than ever before. Plenty more."

"Really?"

"Yep. That's the last thing you'll ever have to worry about. . . . Look, Cass, we've gotta go."

"OK, darling, OK. . . . So . . . where did you get all the money from?"

"Oh, no place special—just a deal I've been working on. Another thing related to Colangio. We're really in the chips."

"Really? . . . So . . . so when did you find out about this sudden windfall?"

"Oh, not too long ago. Just the last few weeks."

"God, if I'd only known. . . ."

"What? *What* if you'd known?"

"Oh, nothing. . . . I love you, Robert."

"Yes, Cassie, I know you do. And I love you too . . . which you know perfectly well—which you've *always* known, I imagine. . . . Look, it's our last night in Siena, baby. Try and be as sweet as a little angel tonight."

The Campo was filled to capacity when they arrived, maybe a hundred thousand people on foot in the central D-shaped infield, then several thousand more arrayed on bleacher seats in the peripheral rim. Between the spectators, seated and standing, lay the earthen race track, a gray-beige swath of inchoate activity enclosed by barricades on either side. Atop its surface, along the ambit of its course, was strung a pageant straight from the Renaissance.

There, clothed in gorgeous silk habiliment, stood dozens of standard-bearers, horsemen and trumpeters. The former, set off two-by-two abreast, held enormous banners of richly colored fabric precisely matching their costumes. Their twinned flags, bearing the heraldic designs of the various *contrade*, shone like silken butterflies in the transverse sunlight, while beneath the flags, beside them, the equally resplendent riders and grooms primed their animals for the evening's main event. It was an extraordinary display.

Robert led Cassie along a tenuous passage in the crowd to the house of Filomena's friend. This was a five story structure built in Siena's heyday, 1300 or thereabouts. A municipal ordinance of the time imposed uniformity on the Campo's circumferential ring of palaces, and this edifice conformed rigidly to it, with its mandated brick facade and triple-mullioned windows facing out on the Campo's declivitous slope. The entry door of the house was standing open, and the two of them passed through it into a darkened Gothic corridor, then up an interminable stone staircase, following the sounds of first indistinct, then randomly familiar voices that grew more familiar and more distinct with every upward step. When they reached the third floor landing, Robert spotted Auntwon standing in a doorway and led Cassie by the arm in the kid's direction.

"Hey, Doc! . . . Doc's here, Filomena. . . . *Sono venuti, Signora Dall'Olmo!*"

Everyone was there: Filomena and her mother, of course, but Caterina too, and Taddeo Fabbri. And then there were the folks who owned the place and a number of their friends and relatives as well. Still, the room was scarcely crowded, cavernous as it was, vast and high-ceilinged. Auntwon steered them in and, in a second or two, fifteen friendly faces turned around to say hello.

"The race will start in about an hour," Filomena explained, having stepped across the chamber to where they stood. "Come with me. I want to introduce you to the DiSalvis."

They were pleasant people, those DiSalvis, and Cassie was on her best behavior too—when they arrived, at any rate. So everything got off to a splendid start. Cassie flashed her luminous smile at Fabbri, who, on his part, bowed down like an Elizabethan courtier to shake her hand. She smiled at Caterina too, and thanked her for the "perfectly adequate" salon she had recommended to them. Signora Dall'Olmo, back against the far wall of the room, had cooked up the proverbial storm, so there was food aplenty, two buffet tables groaning with it: three varieties of pasta, four kinds of sauce, a veal dish, a chicken dish, the dreaded rabbit concoction, and a beef rollatini that smelled invitingly of garlic and a medley of herbs.

Then in a separate covered plate, which the signora passed to Robert after the introductions were complete, he found three prototypically Chicago-esque hot dogs impeccably adorned with just the condiments he generally dressed them with at home. Cassie, clinging to his arm, was incredulous.

"What in the world is *that*?" she asked him.

"Hot dogs. Just like the ones in Chicago."

"What are you going to *do* with them?"

"Well, eat them, of course—a couple of them, anyway."

"*Hot dogs?*"

"Sure."

"You *like* them?"

"Cassie, I go out twice a week for hot dogs—Sheldon and I, mostly to Portillo's. I've been eating them either there or at Flukey's at least twice a week ever since I was a kid. . . . It's my absolute favorite food."

"You never told *me* that."

"You never asked. And anyway, why *should* I have told you? Would you have ever gone with me to a place like that for dinner?"

"To a hot dog stand?"

"Well, Portillo's has other things too, like pizza and stuff. And ribs."

"Really! And you'd actually want to go there for dinner?"

"Sure would, if I had somebody to go with."

She shrugged, filled her plate with alternate selections, and wandered off to a sofa to consume them. He shouldn't have left her alone.

"Hey, Doc," said Auntwon, coming to the table for another helping of linguine, "evvythang OK?"

"Yeah, fine so far."

"You gotcho dogs I see, huh?"

"Sure do. You want one?"

"Sh-ee—yat! You kiddin'? Wif aw-dis good stuff?" The kid laughed and shook his head. Past Auntwon's shoulder, twenty feet away, sat Cassie on the sofa, entirely alone. As Auntwon turned away to ladle out some sauce, Robert glanced above the kid's bent head to see Filomena step over to the sofa, lean down, hand Cassie a glass of wine, then, regrettably, take a seat beside her. He should have gone over. He thought of it, in passing, but then decided, in one of those pivotal moments that can transform a human life forever, that there was no urgent need. After all, he reasoned, Cassie had been on her best behavior—charming, in fact, to everyone in the room thus far. It was to be their final evening in Siena. And Filomena was clearly trying to be nice. Nothing much could happen for the worse now; nothing could turn sour . . . could it?

"So you're off to Rome tonight?" he asked Auntwon, back in front of him again with a heaping plate.

"Yeah, Doc, there's, like, this nine p.m. train that get in to Rome at twelve. Filomena gonna drive me to the station."

"You need some more money?"

"You jivin', man? I ditten spend but two hundred bucks so far." Auntwon twirled his fork in the mound of pasta and stuck four prongs-full in his mouth.

"You can afford a decent room, you know. You don't have to stay in hostels." Robert bit another divit off his hot dog and glanced back over toward the sofa. There the dialogue seemed bland and amicable. Cassie had pivoted to face the girl, knees abutting, plate atop her lap. She was speaking calmly, looking perfectly pleasant, perfectly benign. True, her wine glass was empty now, but what of that? Just one glass? Hell, that was generally an upper for her: she seemed just fine at the moment, anyway. And Filomena looked OK too—from the back, at any rate. The girl sat quiet, passive, listening, nodding from time to time in agreement or agreeability. . . . Nothing but a nice, friendly, female little chat before a sufficiency of hours and kilometers would separate these two immiscible women forever. . . . Yes, he would have nothing at all to worry about tonight; in confidence of which, Robert turned his body maybe twenty degrees counterclockwise from the sofa to give Auntwon his undivided attention.

"So whatchu think?" asked the boy, between swallows.

"About what?"

"Man, that *palio* thang. Like I jus' axed you, man!"

"Oh, sorry. I guess I didn't hear you. . . . What about it?"

"I axed you if you thought it was worf my while to come back here to see it."

Robert swallowed the last little bite of his first hot. "The palio? Sure, sure—I mean, I haven't been to one before, myself . . . but I hear it gets pretty wild. About half of the *contrade*—nine of them, I guess—enter horses in the race. The jockeys ride them bareback three times around the Campo. Then whichever horse finishes first, that *contrada* wins a special banner. That's what's called a *palio*—the banner, I mean. That's where they get the name from. People come from all over Italy to see it."

"Yeah, thass what Filomena said. She said it don't take but, like, a coupla minutes from start to finish. . . . Man, there be like a million dudes out there, you know? . . ."

"Yeah, more like. . . ." He reached down toward his plate, ready for the second Chicago dog, ready, more pertinently, to give his comfortable assessment of probably a hundred-odd thousand revellers in the square. . . .

But just then, *just* then, almost imperceptibly, he sensed a sudden movement with the utmost periphery of his sight. Over by the couch, it was. Yes, *there*, to his left. And he turned reflexly towards it to see Filomena rise abruptly from her seat and step away. She came toward him, pallid, tremulous, visibly distraught. And when she neared him, then passed two yards to his right, he noticed that her eyes and cheeks were glistening. He turned to see her footsteps slow, then finally come to a halt near the door he had entered with Cassandra thirty minutes before, as far away from Cassie and the sofa as a diagonal of the chamber would permit.

"Oh, shit! Here we go again." He set the second hot dog back down. "Hold on, Auntwon. Stay here, OK? Here, take my plate."

"What . . . ?"

"Just wait here, OK? Take this."

When he reached the girl, she was facing away, out toward the open window, her head declined so that the nape of her neck emerged palely through the hair swept to either side. He put his hand atop her shoulder and turned her a little toward him, still with her face downcast. But he lifted her chin with a finger to see her eyes and cheek bones saturate with tears. He touched one side of her face with his other hand, drying it a little, finding it temperate and slick.

"What's the matter? What happened over there?"

"Nothing, Roberto. It's . . . it's nothing. Just let me be for a little while."

"Did she say something again? Tell me what she said to you."

"Nothing. Really." She shook her head. "It's all right."

"*What did she say?*"

"I told you Roberto." The girl tried to turn away, but he coaxed her chin back toward him with his finger. "It's nothing," she muttered. "They are only words."

"Only words, are they? Stay here. You stay right here! I'll be back." He left her by the window and walked back across the room to where Cassie was sitting, still cross-legged on the couch, lounging there in flagrant placidity. But her upper foot was jerking a little, up and down, up and down arrhythmically; just a matter of a few inches, but enough to evince a degree of agitation in her mind.

"What did you say to her?" he asked, leaning down to within six inches of her left ear to get the words out quietly but forcefully.

"To *whom*, darling?"

"*To whom*? TO WHOM?" This a little louder, though growled more than spoken. "Listen, you'd. . . . All right. . . ." He strove manfully toward restraint, and achieved it with moderate success after a second or two. "All right, listen to me carefully: I want an answer from you now. NOW! What did you say?"

"Why? What did she tell you? Did she come crying to you like a little child? Like some whining little child?"

"No. No, she didn't. Now tell me what you said. . . . RIGHT NOW!"

"All right, sit down, Robert. Please. Don't make a fuss." He took a deep breath, stepped across her legs and sat, crosswise, facing her, clenching his fists in unspent fury.

"Tell me what you said, Cassie."

"All right, all right. Calm down. . . . I just. . . . I just told her the truth. She's been acting like a whore and I told her so—like a nickel-dime whore the way she's been chasing you around. Look, that's what she is, you know, a little foreign whore. She'd stick her ten cent ass in your face if you'd let her."

"Oh, for Christ's sake, Cassie! I've had enough of this! I don't want to hear another word from you like that, do you hear me? And no more goddamn wine, either. Give me that glass." She passed it over obediently, visibly abashed. "Now sit here, *stay* here! And don't say another word to anyone, do you hear me?"

"Yes, all right, I'm sorry. . . . I don't know what gets into me. . . . I. . . . It's like I have this strange obsession with you now. . . . I've never been like this before, Robert. . . . God! I . . . I think I'm losing my mind sometimes!" She started tearing, then sobbing almost imperceptibly. "Honest to God, I . . . I feel like I'm . . . like I'm just totally losing my mind!"

"Oh, shit! Shit!... All right, look . . . just sit here quiet for a few minutes, OK? Can you do that?"

She nodded twice, mechanically, then put her hands up to her face, covering it, her shoulders shuddering in sobs, though in perfect silence.

"OK? Did you hear me?"

"Yes," she answered through her fingers, sniffling. "I will. . . . I'm. . . . I'm so sorry. . . . It's because. . . . It's only because . . . I . . . I love you . . . so much.. . . . That's the only reason . . . that's the only reason why. . . . I'm so sorry. . . ."

"All right, all right. Look, just sit here quietly, OK? Can you do that? I'll . . . I'll come and get you in a minute, all right?"

He went back across the room to Filomena. Caterina was with her now, holding a knotted piece of tissue to the girl's face.

"What did she say?" Caterina asked him.

"Something inexcusable as usual. I think I calmed her down, though."

"You calmed *her* down? *Her*? Your lady friend, you mean? . . . And what about Filomena here? Who's supposed to calm *Filomena* down? Are you capable of doing that too?"

"I hope so. . . . If you let me, I'll try."

"Well, yes, I'll let you; I'll certainly let you. And while you do, I'm going to have a little talk with your lady friend over there. She needs to know just what she's been doing to this girl."

"I wouldn't . . . ," he started to admonish, but Caterina was gone by then, off in the direction of the sofa where Cassie sat alone, staring down in silence at her crossed legs, or at the sofa, or the floor. Robert left both woman to their imminent conflict, turned his eyes on Filomena, and put his hand again upon her shoulder.

"Are you OK?"

"Yes, Roberto. I'm all right... I'm quite strong . . . as I've told you before. Angry words are not all that important in the scheme of things." Her eyes were brimful again, notwithstanding Caterina's recent effort with the tissue.

"I don't know why she gets like that—well, maybe I do; she thinks that we. . . ."

"Yes, yes, I understand. I understand fully. Her words leave little to the imagination. . . . But she is right, though, in a way. Not about my nature;

I am far from what she accuses me of. But with you, though; with you. . . .
I *would* take you from her if I could. . . . I *would*, Roberto, if you liked me
more. . . . I've never said that before to anyone; I've never *felt* that way—
this way—before. The way you feel about her, I suppose. . . ." She grasped
his arm with both her hands. "Don't be angry with me for saying so,
Roberto. I never told her that. I wouldn't have. Not ever."

"Yes, I know. I know you wouldn't. It's all right. . . . Look, Filomena,
I'm sorry. I'm truly sorry." He put his other arm around her shoulders and
held her to him. She started sobbing softly, too, silently, like Cassie. The
two of them! he thought. One here within his arms, the other thirty feet
behind him. . . . *Be very careful what you wish for*, someone had said; then
Auntwon had reminded him of it, presciently, just the afternoon before.

"Look, she's just jealous—you know how women get. And she and
I were apart for such a long time. I don't think she meant anything personal by it really—or not as personal as it probably came out. None of
this is really about you. . . . It's not about you at all."

"Yes. . . . Yes, Roberto, I understand." The girl pushed back away
from him hesitantly, a little more composed now, and looked up into
his face. "I don't blame her, really. I'm not angry; honestly I'm not."

"Well that's very generous of you, but she had no right. . . ."

"No, it's OK. Really. . . . I'm fine, but . . . but listen, Roberto . . . I
. . . I won't see you again after tomorrow, will I?"

"Sure you will. We'll be back. I paid your mother for the room
through August. . . . We'll be back before then. And Auntwon can stay
in my room if he gets here before we do."

"All right. . . . Yes, all right. That will be good." She wiped her eyes
with Caterina's knot of tissue and gave him a pallid smile.

Just then he felt a touch, and then an arm slipped around his, assertive,
familiar. He turned to see, and . . . beside him was Cassie! Yes, Cassie here
with her arm in his, facing Filomena, with a strange, imponderable look
upon her face. Cassie! And he'd just got through telling her . . . !

"Is this a secret conversation, or may I join in?" she asked in that cloy-
ing voice she was wont to summon from time to time. Her manner was
thoroughly placid now, though the mottled mascara about her eyes, visible
in ninety-degree profile, gave her impeccable face a strangely garbled look.

"If you're civil, sure; we can all talk reasonably," Robert answered

her. "But if you'd really like to say something, you might start by offering Filomena here an apology."

"Yes. Yes, I'd very much like to do that. . . . I'm afraid I've hurt
your feelings—haven't I, young lady?"

"No, it's all right. I think I understand."

"You do? You understand how I felt? How I feel?"

"Yes, I think so," said the girl. "But there was really nothing. . . ."

"Yes, I know: nothing between the two of you—so Robert has
explained. . . . Anyway, your friend over there. . . ." She pointed to
Caterina, looking on expectantly from the sofa she herself had just now
vacated. "Your friend—Caterina is it?" Filomena nodded. "Yes, well
Caterina made me promise to come over and apologize for what I'd
said to you before. She told me I should be kinder to you, more understanding. . . . Because of your little problem, I guess—you know, with
your father and all. She figured that her telling me all that historical
business would make me more compassionate. And I can see her point.
That must have been a terrible thing you went through—especially as
young as you were at the time."

"Well, yes, it was back then. But I've recovered ages ago. . . . It's
kind of you to be sympathetic, though. I'm sorry that I. . . ."

"No, no, don't be sorry. If I'd felt sympathy because of that, I
would have never spoken harshly in the first place."

"But I don't understand. . . ."

"No? Let me explain it to you then: Your friend assumed I hadn't
known that little story about your father."

"Well, you hadn't, really, had you? How could you have known?"

"Why, well, Robert told me, of course! We've been laughing about
you and your suicidal father all week!"

"What the hell . . . ! What the hell are you saying!" he shouted, grabbing her by the arm, but Cassie continued, opaque to his protestation. She
spat out the words, vomited them, smiling throughout as though her speech
contained nothing but the blandest and most innocuous of pleasantries:

"Yes, we've been laughing all week at your pathetic little tale—that
hanging daddy of yours and his poor orphaned daughter. Tell me: did you
just study English to trap some rich American man, or were you . . . ?"

"CASSIE!" he hollered and jerked her sideways by the arm, throwing her off balance for a moment so that she staggered backwards on her spike-heeled shoes. But there was no stopping her now, no stopping that mouth of hers with whatever mere physical force a mortal might apply. She recommenced the moment she had regained her footing. Freeing her arm from Robert's hand with a determined pull, she stepped sideways just beyond his reach, and leaned down into Filomena's face, spewing out the words now, her lips frothing at the angles as she spoke:

"You're PATHETIC, you little BITCH! . . . PATHETIC! . . . No *WONDER* your father killed himself. He killed himself to get away from YOU!"

Robert grabbed her violently by the shoulder, spun her around to face him, and slapped her hard, forehand, across the mouth—THWACK!—finally stanching the flow of venom. But it was too late. The words had found their mark, irretrievably. The girl had dropped down to her knees, crossed arms clutching at her belly: "*No, Roberto, non e vero,*" she whimpered—it can't be true! "You couldn't have," she sniffled out, between sobs, in fractured fragments of Italian. "*No, Roberto, no, no. . . .*"

"She's lying, Filomena. I never said. . . ." he began to explain, to deny. But the girl, retracted catatonically into herself, was oblivious by now to any explanation he might have offered. Cassie reached out toward her, as though to grab at Filomena's hair, but Robert caught the hand and wrenched it back violently. "My God, Cassie!" he hollered, "what's *wrong* with you? What the hell's *wrong* with you?!"

Everyone had turned by now to face the three of them, twenty-odd frontal bodies, rigid and silent, splayed out in a concave arc to his back and right. Then the rigidity exploded into movement: three people rushed forward. First came the signora, frienziedly, clutching up the skirt of her apron in a hand. Then came two more, Auntwon and Caterina in the signora's wake. The other guests moved too—the DiSalvis, Fabbri, and the rest. They slithered away, inching toward the far end of the room, like dancers in slow motion. There they coalesced in silent little groups, as far removed from Cassandra as the chamber would allow. The lot of them strove to look casual, or occupied, or just plain unconcerned. But there was panic in the place, and anger, and inconsolable sorrow. One could sense it, and the sensation was overpowering.

He jerked again on Cassie's arm, turning her another ninety degrees or so away from Filomena, then dragging her across the room to its lone vacant corner laterally opposite the girl. Behind him, Filomena knelt immobile, quivering with sobs; the signora knelt beside her, gathering the girl's face onto her breast, cradling her head as some grieving woman might cradle the head of a mortally stricken child.

"Are you fucking *CRAZY*?!" he hissed, once far enough away to be inaudible to the others, spraying an aerosol of spittle into Cassandra's face in his fulminating fury. "How could you *SAY* that to her, huh? How can you have that kind of fucking *CRUELTY* in you?!"

"What? What? I told you, Robert. I explained it all to you. . . ."

"Explained! SHIT! How could you *tell* her that!? How could you even think *up* something that fucking cruel?"

"I. . . ."

"How? HOW?!" He shook her roughly, one hand on either shoulder, and she began to shudder again and weep.

"Oh, God, I'm sorry, Robert. I . . . I just saw you standing there with her. You had your arm around her. . . . You know, I just went nuts again. I don't know what's happening to me, honest to God I don't. I'm losing control. I don't . . . I don't know what I'm gonna do. You've got to help me." She started sobbing again, uncontrollably, clinging to him, dropping her head toward his chest, though he held her off, pushing her shoulders back and away.

"Please, Robert, please don't hate me. . . . Please! I love you. . . . It's all because I love you so much. Can't you understand that?"

"No, Cassie, no! I *can't* understand. What you said makes me *sick*. It . . . it just makes me sick, that's all. . . ."

"OK, OK—Oh God!... Look, let me apologize then. I'll go over . . . I'll go over and talk to her."

"Talk to her! *Talk* to her! Haven't you said enough already? Look, you stay the hell away from her, you understand? You stay the fuck away!"

"Oh, God, I'm so sorry. . . . I'm not myself, Robert. I've never been this way before. I . . . I just don't know what's going on, I swear it. I'm. . . . You've got to help me! Please, please!"

"*Help* you? *Help* you?" He pushed her farther back still, to arm's length, and stared at her downcast face. The mottled mascara had been entirely displaced now, forming a pair of quail egg ovals around her eyes. From her nose ran a thick stream of mucus, snaking sinuously down that perfect pouted lip to her chin. He had never seen her like this. Never. Not in all their five years together had she wept so, nor lost so flagrantly her impeccable control.

He shook his head. "*Shit*!" he said aloud, then whispered it again to himself: "Shit!" What had he done? What awful thing had he done!? Was this what he had wanted? *This*? His perfect Cassandra reduced to the pathetic spectacle in front of him? And for what? For what? Love? Was *this* his brand of love? He had loved her—or some imagined concept of her—all his lifetime, it seemed. And it had finally reduced itself to this! to this pathetic sight! What had he been thinking of? What deluded folly had he wrought? . . .

"Look, Cassie," he stammered, after an interminable minute of speechlessness and sobs. "Look, I'm sorry. . . ."

"Sorry?" she sniffled. "I'm sorry too. I'm . . . I'm . . . please don't hate me, Robert. There's something wrong with me. There's something really wrong."

"Yes, I know. I understand. All right, listen. . . . Maybe I can help. . . ."

"You . . . you can? You can . . . help me?" She choked out the words, speaking them to the floor.

"Yes, maybe. I think so. . . . I think I might be able to."

"How? Oh, God! Tell me how." She turned her eyes up toward his face and he released her arms, finally letting her settle in closer, her head against his chest.

"Look, I'm not a hundred percent sure it'll work, but—I don't know—there might be a way. Anyhow, don't worry about it right now. Just give me a little time, OK? We'll see."

"I can't stay here any more, Robert. I can't stay in this place."

"No. No, I realize that."

"Take me away somewhere."

"Yes. I will."

"I can't stay in their house tonight. I just can't."

"No. No, I don't think either of us can. Not now."

Just then there was movement again, off to his left. Robert turned his head a little to see—and it was the signora, who must have stepped unheard across the room and was standing now, grim-faced, at his elbow. "*Cosa ha detto?*" she asked—What had Cassandra said?

"*E malata*," he told her—She's sick.

"*Si, si, l'ho pensato.*" She'd thought as much.

"*Dobbiamo. . . .*" They'd have to leave tonight, he explained.—"*Si, si,*" that was best, the little lady answered.—They'd take the train, go to Florence, he said; then he'd be back in a day or two to get their things.—"*Va bene:*" fine, all right; the signora nodded. "*Bene, bene.*" Wait. She held up a finger. "*Aspetta.*"

She stepped away across the room and came back a moment later carrying her purse, then reached into it and took out a set of keys, holding them out toward him just as Cassie had done with a different set of keys so many weeks before.

"*Eccole,*" she said. Here. Take them. Take the car.— No, no, he couldn't, he answered.— "*Si, si, sta bene,*" she told him. It's all right. Go ahead and take it. You can bring it back in a day or two, if you like. Or not. It really didn't matter. . . . Just take the woman away. Take her as far away from here, as far away from Filomena, as he could. Now; right now. "*Le supplico, dottore. Le supplico.*" She was begging him. He was a good man—he and Auntwon both—like her own two sons, she said, two sons she might have suckled at her very breast. "*Le supplico, dottore. . . .*" Just take the woman away, take her anywhere. To Florence or Assisi in the big Mercedes. Or to Rome, even. Bring the car back whenever he liked. Or not. It didn't really matter to her at all.

He took the keys thus proffered, and the signora set off again toward her daughter. Beyond the open windows, the sea of humanity down in the Campo had come to life, a hundred thousand commingled voices rising in a crescendic roar. Their welcome clamor erased the deafening silence within the room; erased, as well, the diminutive murmur of Filomena's sobs. The girl knelt on the stone floor entirely inert, her mother beside her once again, hovering protectively.

Robert took Cassie by the arm and led her from the room, turning back for an instant at the threshold to nod good-bye to Auntwon. The boy stood now at the signora's side, both of them close above Filomena, the signora's hand on the girl's right shoulder, Auntwon's on her left. The kid looked up solemnly and shook his head.

CHAPTER TWENTY-THREE

RESOLUTION

THE ROAD DOWN TO THE AUTOSTRADA WAS EMPTY. NO ONE, IT APPEARED, ever drove to or from Siena on the evening of a *palio*. He had packed a little overnight case, leaving Cassie out in the street while he'd gone up to their room. Then he'd pulled the big Mercedes out and loaded her in it, teary-eyed and clinging as she was. Avoiding the Campo, he had snaked his way along through the back-streets of the city, and finally made it down Siena's precipitous hill and out securely beyond its cyclopean walls.

Once on the quiet conduit of highway, he let himself sink into the monotony of the road. Cassie lay against his shoulder, asleep perhaps or feigning sleep. She had stopped sobbing now, and was breathing softly, regularly, but was otherwise silent, speechless. "Help me," she had begged him. "I'm not myself at all." And she wasn't; there was no denying that. What she had become—maybe what she'd always been, in truth—was insufferable: a burden to him, a torment to herself. And who'd been more to blame for that than he? Yes, he and he alone had brought this terrible curse upon her—had *infected* her with it, in a way. He'd been the cause of her disease, and he alone must find a cure. Thankfully, the specific remedy was close at hand.

Yes, he thought, as he steered toward Florence on the quiet Autostrada: that incomprehensible incantation had worked its inexplicable miracles before—had worked a little too well, if anything. And it would no doubt work again. Of course, no reason for it not to.

All right, then, since its use seemed appropriate—seemed unavoidable, in truth—he'd need some time alone to get things done: an hour or two around sunset, back in Siena. . . . Tomorrow, perhaps. . . . Yes, why not? After all, he'd have to pick up the rental car anyway. He could switch vehicles in the afternoon, hang around the Dall'Olmos place till sunset and. . . . Yes, that would work just fine. He'd be back in Florence by midnight, maybe even earlier—right in time to see her change! "Make her kind," he would ask the incomprehensible chart to do, or "considerate", or "benevolent". That should do the trick. And if it didn't? If his chosen verbiage didn't sedate her a little, or make her a little more compliant, or give him some reasonable peace of mind once more . . . well then, he'd just rephrase his request the evening after and run the crazy thing again.

They made it to Florence a little after eight, parked at the train station, then walked arm-in-arm to a tourist booth, where a morbidly friendly woman found a bargain room for them a couple of blocks away.

"It won't be luxurious," he told Cassie on the way there.

"That's all right," she answered, still clinging to his arm. "I don't care."

He left his credit card and passport at registration, as such places usually required, and carried their little hand case up to the room. It wasn't nearly as bad as he'd imagined: the furniture was a little worn and dated, the bathroom smelled of antiseptic, the lighting was dim, but the room itself was spacious, comfortable, and quaint in a European sort of way. He got into the shower, she followed him next into a long, hot bath, and they lounged on the bed for an hour or so afterwards holding hands and talking.

"Are you still angry with me?" she asked him, looking as genuinely disconsolate as a scolded child.

"No, no, not anymore. It's not your fault."

"It's not? Why do you say that?"

"Why? . . . I don't know. . . . Look, it's been a shock to the both of us, these past couple of months."

"Yes, that's true. . . . I can't believe you aren't more angry about the other thing."

"What other thing?"

"You know . . . my leaving. . . . And the way I treated you."

"No, no, forget all that. I'm not angry now about anything. I . . . I just wanted us to be happy, both of us. That's all I ever wanted in the first place."

"All you really *wanted*?"

"Yeah. You know—all I *want*."

"Well, anyway, I apologize for the way I've been acting lately. It's just. . . ."

"No, that's all right. Never mind. We don't need to talk about it right now."

"I just can't understand what happens to me, though. I just get crazy. . . . I mean . . . I totally lose control. . . . You know, Robert, it scares me; it really does."

"I know, I know. Look, everything's gonna be fine. I promise."

"That's what you said before. . . . You told me you could help me, remember?"

"Yes. I think I can."

"How?"

"How? . . . I don't know. I'm not a hundred percent sure. There's . . . there's somebody I've got to talk to. Back in Siena. . . . Look, I'll stop there tomorrow when I bring the car back and pick up the rental."

"Who? Who do you have to talk to? A psychiatrist, you mean? Do you think . . . ?"

"No, no, it's nothing like that. Don't worry. It's just a kind of . . . um, adviser, I guess. There's something I've gotta do. . . . Look, I'll drive back sometime in the afternoon, drop off the Mercedes, get the rental car, and be back around . . . well, before bedtime."

"Before *bedtime*! Like *when*?"

"Maybe eleven, twelve."

"Twelve *midnight*? That late?"

"Yeah. Maybe a little before then. . . . There's just some stuff I've got to do—you know, before we leave on our trip. . . . Look, I have a feeling you're gonna feel a whole lot better by tomorrow night. . . . I'd bet money that you will."

"What are you *talking* about? How can you *say* that?"

"Just trust me, OK? I'm gonna try and fix things. Just relax and trust me."

"How can I trust you if you don't tell me anything? . . . Come on, Robert, what's going on? Tell me."

"*Nothing*'s going on, Cassie; nothing, OK? I've just got some stuff to do in Siena tomorrow, that's all. Just leave it at that."

338 | STEVEN M. GREENBERG

"You're not going back to see that little bitch, are you? Are you going back to see her? . . . Sure. Sure! I should have known!"

"No, come on, Cassie! It's not that at all. It has nothing to do with her. . . . Look, she's been nothing but a friend to me, just the landlady's daughter, for God's sake! I don't know . . . this behavior of yours is. . . ."

"*What*, Robert? *What* is it?"

"I don't know. Never mind. Just forget it. . . ."

"Oh, God, I'm sorry, baby. . . . I'm so sorry!"

"OK. . . . Shit!. . . . All right, look, c'mere, OK?"

He drew her to him and took her in his arms. The feel of her body was as hypnotic as it had always been to him. It had always been thus with Cassandra, ever since the moment they had met: one look at her, one touch, and he was mesmerized, defenseless. . . .

But *why*? Why this specific woman among all the thousands of others he had known, seen, passed on the street, spoken with, lectured to? Sheldon had tried to explain it to him, but, hell, Shelly probably hadn't quite grasped the thing himself. How could he have? Had Shelly ever loved this way before? Had anyone? What was there about this one single woman among all the innumerable others in the world? It was an enigma as deep and unfathomable as all those other mysteries he'd encountered these past few months. It was, like all the rest, immune to understanding. Like an infinite universe, like existence itself, love and lust and working incantations were simply incomprehensible. One just had to accept them with a childish sense of wonder and muddle on with the task at hand.

"Listen to me, baby," he whispered to her, nuzzling her perfect hair, "there's never been anyone but you. There never *could* be."

"You promise me? You swear it?"

"Yes, of course I do."

"You won't see her tomorrow?"

"Filomena? I have no intention of seeing her. She's nothing to me. Honest to God. Absolutely nothing."

"OK, then. . . . But, Robert...?"

"Yes, baby."

"Do you really think you can help me get better?"

"Yes, I'm pretty sure I can."

"Maybe just by being nice to me—you know, by reassuring me like this. . . . I only get crazy that way because I love you so much."

"Yes, I know you do, baby. I know it. . . . Look, I've got an idea: how about if I run out for a few minutes and get us some wine. I bet that would relax you."

"All right, Robert. Sure. Sure, that would be nice."

"Pinot?"

"Yeah, sure, great! That would be wonderful if you could find some."

"I bet I can. Florence is a big city. . . . OK, let me just throw on some clothes and I'll be back before you know it."

"Shelly?"

"Hey, Bobby! Is that you?"

"Yeah, I was hoping I'd catch you in. What time is it there, around three?"

"Yeah, two-thirty-something. I was just watching the game. Where are you?"

"In Florence. Cassie and I drove up today. . . . Tonight, I mean."

"So how are things working out? She any better? Uh, *different*, I mean."

"Uh, no, not exactly. That's the thing I wanted to talk to you about. . . . Listen, she's, uh . . . she's been almost impossible to deal with."

"Hey, same old Cassandra. . . . You should have done the lobotomy—I tried to tell you that."

"OK, OK, anyway . . . look, maybe that's not such a crazy idea."

"*Meaning?*"

"Well, meaning that anything seems to be possible. . . . Even something as crazy as that."

"Look, Bobby, I know you think this magic thing's for real, and even Auntwon. . . ."

"It *is* for real, Shel. Honest to God it is. I don't know how or why, but the damn thing actually does work. I mean, it does some amazing things, things there's no other explanation for. I don't understand the principle behind it, but. . . ."

"So what do you want to do with it now, turn her into a sweetheart?

. . . Hey, if it can work that kind of miracle, I'll become a believer myself."

"I'm just wondering about the ethics of . . . well, of actually doing something like that to someone. You know, like changing a person's nature. . . ."

"I think it's more than *that* you're worried about."

"You do? Like what?"

"*You* know what."

"No, honest to God, Shelly, I don't."

"No? Well, let me put it into words for you. I'd bet you're worried—consciously or unconsciously—that maybe you love Cassandra not *despite* her nature but *because* of it. . . . I'd bet you're worried—even though you might not be fully conscious of it or maybe you haven't quite admitted it to yourself—that any reconfiguring of the love equation might make it come out wrong. You follow what I'm saying?"

"Yeah, I guess so. You mean that maybe part of the attraction is the—I don't know—the negative qualities of her character that help to make her who she is. That I love the meanness in her, in other words. . . . I suppose I might have been a little bit concerned about that myself—unconsciously at least."

"Well, I'm not sure what to tell you, Bobby, but. . . . Look, where is she now? She isn't there with you, is she?"

"No. Hell, no, she's up in the room. In the hotel. I ran out to get us some wine and came over to the train station to call you."

"All right, let me think for a minute. . . ."

"Sure. . . . You guys been OK?"

"Yeah, fine, fine. Rochelle says hello."

"Tell her hi from me, too."

"Yeah. . . . OK. . . . Listen . . . let me ask you something."

"Sure."

"Do you get excited when you have a fight with her?"

"A fight?"

"Yeah, when you and Cassandra get into an argument with each other. Does that excite you?"

"You mean make me angry?"

"No, not angry. I mean sexually. Does arguing with her excite you sexually? Does it turn you on?"

"Shit, no! It depresses me. I get turned on when she's nice to me and—you know—warm, affectionate. . . ."

"Well, it doesn't sound like you get off that much on her cruelty, then. . . . Hell, I'd say it's reasonably safe to lobotomize the bitch. God, I hope to hell it works!"

They climbed under the covers at ten, half a bottle of pinot inside each of them. The wine made Cassie passionate, but had quite the opposite effect on Robert. He excused himself to get some sleep.

"Are you too tired, darling?" she asked him.

"Yeah, kind of. But tomorrow morning I'll be wide awake. Tomorrow morning for sure, first thing."

"You promise?" she murmured, holding him to her for a minute or two, until she finally turned lazily away and seemed to fall asleep.

There was a glow of light from the window's edge, slipping in around the curtain. For twenty minutes or so he lay awake, his back against Cassie's, rehearsing his plans for their immediate future one last time. It was pretty much decided now: With Shelly's educated blessing, he'd use the incantation again tomorrow night. The performance would take till almost ten; then he'd get on the road and be back in the room here maybe an hour and a half afterward. By eleven-thirty he'd be sitting on the bed with Cassie, sipping some fresh *pinot noir*. Then thirty minutes later—thirty minutes by the clock—she'd suddenly become quite another person: nicer, gentler, sweet as a little lamb to everyone. Everyone—including Filomena. . . . Yes, the girl deserved at least that much, kind and considerate as she'd always been to him. And as for Cassie.. . . . Well, she'd be happy too, in a certain sense. And in a general sense as well. He'd see to that. . . .

But somehow—oddly—he found it hard to fix his mind on Cassie's happiness. Somehow—likely from some toxic brew of compassion and guilt—Filomena kept intruding on his thoughts: the malicious way she had been treated, her indomitable strength, her stoic sorrow. Yes, the least he could do, the very *least*, was to make Cassie apologize, reign her in demonstrably, *tame* her like a broken steed, thoroughly, observably. That would give the girl a bit of consolation. Sweet and kindly as she'd been, she deserved at least that much. . . .

And on those final thoughts he slept. It was a fitful sleep, though, oddly deranged, as though something long suppressed had started stirring deep inside him. He tossed and turned in semi-stupor, until the same persistent glow of window-light awakened him. . . . Or maybe not in fact the light at all. Maybe, rather, it was the peculiar way he felt, the strange uneasiness of it. . . .

Whatever, whether the errant light or the queasy feeling, he woke now fully. It must be nearly dawn, he reckoned, having slept with such satiety. But when he stepped into the bathroom, shut the door, snapped on the light, and looked at the watch he had left lying by the sink, he found the time to be unaccountably early—only minutes after midnight. He clicked off the light, crept back over to the bed, sat down as gently as possible upon the bottom corner of the mattress, and glanced around at Cassie behind him.

A lunar glow from the window played across her recumbent form—the onyx hair, the trim shoulders, the girlish hips. These were, as ever, incontestably lovely, incontestably the very archetype of hair and hip and shoulder that had been fixed within his mind's eye forever as ideals of feminine perfection.

But somehow now Cassie looked . . . what? Well . . . *different* to him. *Altered* in some strange way. Perhaps the wrenching angst of last evening, seeing the way she'd abused the girl. Yes, that must have affected him more deeply than he'd thought, for he couldn't quite eject it from his mind. The way she'd acted: not just cruel, no, but actually *sadistic*, in a way. She'd been a little like that with him too, not so very long ago, and with everyone else she'd encountered, to varying degree and occasion.

Yes, Cassandra had that propensity; there was no denying it. One could hardly pretend it wasn't there. After all, he himself had tasted her venom, had seen it in full use, had just last night been sickened by that vision. Yes, *sickened*. My God! those things she had told Filomena! Things about him, too—as though he ever could have talked that way about the girl behind her back. . . . And the poor kid had believed it too, or half-believed it anyway. How could he have *permitted* that? How could he have left her sobbing there, without a single word of explanation? What sort of man had he been? Weak? Yes. Complicit? No doubt. My God, he thought, that poor defenseless girl! How could he have watched her suffer and done nothing to help? She was good, kind, loyal—the very opposite of the woman lying here. . . .

And she was pretty too, Filomena was. Not classically beautiful, no, but lovely in her own peculiar way. How had he not quite perceived that till now? But he'd been so obsessed with his Cassandra that it had all but blinded him to the nature and virtues of everyone and everything else. . . .

He heard a sound, a nasally aspirated breath, and then the rustle of bedclothes. . . . And suddenly Cassandra, half-awake behind him, spoke:

"Robert? What are you doing up? Get back in bed."

"You *hurt* that girl, Cassie," he heard himself say. "Couldn't you see how you hurt her? You *lied* to her. About me."

"What? . . . What are you talking about?"

"You know what I mean: The girl, Filomena. You *hurt* her. For no reason at all."

"Did I? Well, so what? She hurt me too, the way she kept chasing after you. Whatever I did, she more than had it coming. I told you that before, Robert. Now get back into bed. She'd stick that little ass of hers in your face if you'd let her."

"She never would have said those things to *you*, those terrible things."

"So? She's weak. That's all. She's a weakling. You and she would have made some pair!"

"Why, because I'm weak, too?"

"No, darling, no. . . . I didn't mean that at all. Look, Robert, you're *not* weak. I never said you were.. . . . Now stop all this foolishness and get back into bed."

He snapped on the bedside lamp.

"What are you doing, Robert? I'm trying to sleep!"

"I don't understand how you could have treated her like that, Cassie. I mean, that stuff you said. Telling her that we laughed about her father—it was despicable . . . *sickening.*"

"She deserved it, I told you. She deserved every word I said."

"No, Cassie, *nobody* deserves that. Especially not her. She's a decent person, a kind person. It makes me *sick* to think about the things you said to her."

"Well we can't change that now, can we?"

"No? Maybe we can. . . . Maybe *I* can."

"You? How? What are you talking about?"

"I've got to make it right, Cassie. I've got to go to her and make it right."

"What? WHAT? You're not going there! You promised me you wouldn't! You promised!"

"I'm sorry. Really. . . . But I've got to. It's something I've just got to do." He stood up and began getting dressed.

"What are you *doing?*" she asked, sitting up now, her palms on the bedsheet. "Are you *crazy?*"

"No, that I'm definitely not. Not any more. . . . Look, I'll . . . I'll leave you everything I've got with me—all the cash in my wallet. There's almost a thousand dollars here. And my Visa card's downstairs. I'll leave it too. You can use it to get a ticket home. Just give them the numbers when you make your reservation."

"What? What are you *talking* about? Robert, what the hell are you *talking* about?"

"I've got to go to her, Cassie. I'm sorry. I'm truly sorry."

"Robert, for God's sake. . . . Look, all right, I'll apologize, OK? I'll call her tomorrow morning. Will that make you happy?"

"No. No, that won't make me happy at all. . . . Listen, there's the cash on the dresser, and I'll leave my credit card at the front desk." He opened the door and stepped out into the hallway, then turned back. "I'll ship your stuff back to Chicago in a day or two, OK? Shelly can get it to you later."

"Robert! Wait! What are you doing? I don't understand. . . . *Robert!*"

He closed the door and fifteen minutes later was on the highway to Siena.

There was a light on in his room. He could see it faintly through the open shutters, three floors up. It was the desk lamp, no doubt, feebly as it seemed to illuminate the ceiling. Maybe in his haste to throw their things together he had forgotten to snap it off.

The rest of the house was inky black, Filomena and her mother certainly asleep by now—after all, at half past two. . . . He parked the Mercedes in the street and let himself in through the downstairs door.

The place was stone silent. . . . Too bad, he thought. He had wanted to speak with the girl tonight—now, this early morning—to tell her. . . .

To tell her what? What had he been thinking? Just a few short hours ago he'd been obsessed with his beloved Cassandra, but now . . . now. . . .

He paused at the door to the Dall'Olmos' second story quarters. No, the place was shut up tight, all right, dead still. . . . He might knock, awaken them—but then what? What could he possibly say? And how would she respond? *How?*—after he'd left her like that, with Cassie's bitter words echoing in her ear. Sadistic words, too, with him tied in as a chief accomplice. . . .

He shook his head and started up the second flight of steps, the staircase groaning as always beneath his weight. From half-way up the landing he could see some light appear from within the door jamb—not just *below* the door, but from its *side* as well. That was odd—perplexing, in fact: he might have left the *lamp* on, but he hadn't left the *door* open; of that he was absolutely sure. Yet here it stood maybe an inch or two ajar, letting the lamp light seep into the hallway. He reached the landing, pushed on the unresisting wood, and swung the door in. . . .

And she was *there*.

THERE!

Filomena!—seated in the desk chair with the lamp aglow behind her, sitting in precisely the same place and with the same insouciant posture as on the very day they'd met, when they'd dragged his two huge cases up together. There was a pervasive scent within the room, something eminently familiar, though he failed to distinguish it as jasmine right at first.

"I have been waiting for you, Roberto. I was hoping you would come," said the girl in a quiet voice, deliberate and haunting.

"You were waiting? For me?" He stared down at her, at her frontal silhouette, back-lit by the lamp atop the desk. She looked different somehow, altered. . . .

Lovely! Yes, unspeakably lovely! How could he not have sensed her loveliness before? Oh, it wasn't a classic beauty, no. But rather the kind of fragile beauty that can flash from ordinary to exquisite in a second. How could he not have noticed that before? How had such obliviousness been possible? For her face and figure were precisely what he had always dreamed of in a woman—every curve and feature absolutely flawless and sublime. He stared at her for a long moment that felt like all eternity, finding himself at once bedazzled by her beauty, enraptured by his love.

"God, Filomena. . . ."

"Yes, Roberto, come to me, *mio caro.*"

And he did, obediently, longingly, dropping on his knees at her feet, his arms about her waist, his head declined upon her lap.

"I love you, Roberto. I always have." She stroked his hair; he smoothed his cheek against her thigh.

"And I love you too, Filomena," he murmured. "More than I ever thought possible. I never really realized how much in love a person could be until tonight."

"Yes, *caro*, I know."

He lifted his head from her lap and looked up into her face, wide-eyed, breathless. "How could you know? How could you possibly know? I've only known it myself for . . . for just. . . ."

"Ah, since midnight, no? Was it then that you realized you loved me, Roberto?"

"Midnight? I'm not sure. . . . But . . . maybe *so* . . . maybe it *was* just around midnight. But. . . ."

"I made it happen, Roberto. Please don't be angry with me. . . . We caused it, I and Auntwon. He showed me how. . . . But don't be angry, Roberto. Please, please. . . . She was wrong for you, *caro*, cruel and selfish. She did not deserve you. She never has."

"But I don't understand. . . ."

"Your magic things, Roberto. Auntwon and I. . . ."

"You. . . . You used the. . . ."

"Yes, the two of us did it. We used your magic things—I and Auntwon used them."

"But, but . . . how did you know...?"

"Auntwon showed me. He showed me everything. She was wrong for you, *caro*, entirely wrong. But I . . . I shall love you for the rest of my life. Better than she could have ever done. A great deal better."

"And I'll love you, too, Filomena. Always. I know I will. I feel it in my heart. I'll make you happy too. And rich."

"Ah, the riches we shan't need."

"But we can have them. . . . I can give you everything."

"We *have* everything, Roberto. Love alone is everything."

"Yes, but I want to buy you things, too. I want to buy you everything you've ever dreamed of. . . ."

"Well, buy me one of those electric grills to make your hot dogs for you, then. And take me on a visit to America to meet your family. We can certainly afford that. Riches we shan't have or need, Roberto. Your magic things are gone."

"Gone?"

"Yes, such things are not for mortal men to use. . . . Except in extraordinary situations."

"Did Auntwon take them, then?"

"No, Roberto. We burned them. All of them. Everything in your drawer, the copies and the originals. The candle flame consumed them all. What is done now can never be undone. Never. We shall love each other as long as we both shall live."

"Will we?"

"Yes, of that I am certain. Auntwon assured me that the magic works. And now I *see* that it does, too. . . . You are not angry with me then? For tricking you?"

"Angry, Filomena? I love you. I think I've loved you all my life. . . . It wasn't the incantation at *all* that did it. No, no, it was in me all along. It was in my heart from the very first. I've loved you since the moment I was born, before I ever found that crazy incantation. It was *your* form that I thought I saw in Cassie. It's always been you. You alone, only you, and for the rest of my life I'll never love another."

"Good, Roberto. Excellent. That is precisely what I asked the magic thing to do."

Cantico del Sole
BY FRANCESCO D'ASSISI

Altissimu, omnipotente, bon Signore,
tu so', le laude, la gloria e l'honore et onne benedictione.
Ad te solo, Altissimo, se konfano;
et nulle homo ène dignu te mentovare.

Laudato sie, mi' Signore, cum tucte le tue creature,
spetialmente messor lo frate sole,
lo qual'è iorno, et allumini noi per lui.
Et ellu è bellu e radiante cum grande splendore:
da te, Altissimo, porta significatione.

Laudato si', mi' Signore, per sora luna e le stelle:
in celu l'ài formate clarite et pretiose et belle.

Laudato si', mi' Signore, per frate vento
et per aere e nubilo et sereno et onne tempo
per lo quale a le tue creature dai sustentamento.

Laudato si, mi' Signore per sor'acqua,
la quale è multo utile et humile et pretiosa et casta

Laudato si, mi' Signore, per frate focu,
per lo quale ennallimini la nocte:
ed ello è bello et iocundo et robustoso et forte.

Laudato si, mi' Signore, per sora nostra matre terra,
la quale ne sustenta et governa,
et produce diversi fructi con coloriti flori et herba.

Laudato si, mi' Signore, per quelli ke perdonando per lo tuo amore,
et sostengo infirmitate et tribulatione.

Beati quelli ke 'l sosteranno in pace,
ka da te, Altissimo, sirano incoronati.

Laudato si', mi Signore, per sora nostra morte corporale,
da la quale nullu homo vivente pò skappare:
guai a'cquelle ke morrano ne le peccata mortali;
beati quelli ke trovarà ne le tue sanctissime voluntati,
ka la morte secunda no'l farrà male.

Laudate e benedicete mi' Signore et rengratiate
e serviateli cum grande humilitate.

Canticle of the Sun
BY FRANCIS OF ASSISI
Translated from the Italian by Fr. Anthony Tomacelli of Arezzo, Italy

Oh, highest, most omnipotent Great Lord
To Thee be the praise, the glory, and the honor of every benediction.
To Thee alone, Greatest Lord, belong these things;
And no man has worth enough to speak Thy name.

Praise to Thee, my Lord, with all Thy creatures,
Especially the noble Brother Sun,
Who brightens each day, and illuminates us thereby.
And who is beautiful and radiant with his grand splendor:
And who brings tidings of Thee, Greatest Lord.

Praise to Thee, my Lord, for Sisters Moon and Stars:
In heaven hast Thou made them, bright, precious, and beautiful.

Praise to Thee, my Lord, for Brother Wind
And for skies both clear and cloudy, and other days
By which Thou givest sustenance to Thy creatures.

Praise to Thee, my Lord, for Sister Water,
So humble and useful and precious and chaste.

Praise to Thee, my Lord, for Brother Fire,
By which the night is lit:
And who is handsome and happy and robust and strong.

Praise to Thee, my Lord, for our Sister Mother Earth,
Who raises and sustains us,
And yields the various fruits and vegetables and colored flowers.

Praise to Thee, my Lord, for those who forgive their brethren for Thy love,
And undergo disease and tribulation.

Praise to those whom Thou sustainest in peace,
For by Thee, Greatest Lord, shall thay be crowned.

Praise to Thee, my Lord, for our Sister Bodily Death,
Whom no man living may escape:
Woe to them who die in mortal sin,
Blessed be those who do Thy holiest will,
For final death shall bring to them no harm.

All praise and bless my Lord, and give thanks
And service to Him with great humility.